AN F EYE
O
AN R EYE

MARK SCHORR

AN EYE
F
O
R
AN EYE

A THOMAS · DUNNE BOOK

ST. MARTIN'S PRESS NEW YORK

This is a work of fiction, and any resemblance to actual persons or events is unintended and purely coincidental.

BOOK DESIGN BY JUDITH STAGNITTO.

Library of Congress Cataloging-in-Publication Data

Schorr, Mark.
        An eye for an eye / Mark Schorr.
                p.   cm.
        "A Thomas Dunne book."
        ISBN 0-312-03335-4
        I. Title.
        PS3537.C598E9 1989
        813'.54—dc20

                                                        89-10370
                                                        CIP

First Edition

10 9 8 7 6 5 4 3 2 1

TO DAVID

ACKNOWLEDGMENTS

Thanks to retired LAPD detective supervisor Steve Hodel and David Keene, M.D., for their comments and suggestions on the manuscript. Additional thanks to the men in D-Platoon, LAPD's SWAT Unit. 41-54 forever.

Any inaccuracies or distortions which have crept into the story are the fault of the author.

PART ONE

PART ONE

1 "Scared?" Bob Odin asked, his fingers cinching the straps on his bulletproof, multipocketed tactical vest.

"Nah," Frank Fleming, Jr., answered, too quickly. Fleming, a few feet behind Odin, was still tying up his high-topped black paratrooper boots.

They both wore dark blue jump suits and dark blue caps with SWAT in white letters across the front. After dressing, they removed tear-gas grenades, rope, folding grappling hooks, and extra ammo from the back of a dark green Plymouth.

The unmarked, multiantennaed car was parked on a fire road in the Hollywood Hills, overlooking the shake and orange tile roofs of Del Rio Place. There were a half dozen houses on the cul-de-sac shoved into the side of the hills.

The two cops geared up silently. Odin was a lean, muscular forty-year-old. Fleming, the youngest member of SWAT, was a Norman Rockwell kid in his midtwenties, the newest member of the elite group, a "SWAT pup" with eight months in the unit.

It was a little after six A.M., the sun not yet up, night chill still in the air. Fleming shivered.

"Nothing wrong with being a bit scared," Odin said. "Adrenaline gives you an edge."

"I'm just cold, that's all," Fleming said. "I can't believe *you're* ever scared."

"Before we go in my heart's bouncing off the side of the tac vest. Once we're inside it quiets down and I cruise on autopilot." He clipped a couple of tear-gas grenades onto rings attached to his vest.

"How long did it take to get like that?"

Odin shrugged. "A few years, Junior. Better get set."

As Fleming did, Odin reviewed his equipment. Browning .45 automatic and two spare ammo clips, K-bar knife, Kel flashlight, Motorola walkie-talkie, first-aid kit, pry bar, gas mask. A total of more than twenty-five pounds of gear.

Junior finished and Odin checked him over. As he patted pouches and verified that straps were in place, he said, "Tell me about the house."

"We've been over this already."

Odin frowned and Junior hastily began his recitation. "Three bedrooms, two thousand square feet. Conventional ranch style layout. Gary Mokley the only known resident. Used to be a writer. Now no visible means of support. Doper, has an Uzi. No guard dog, bars on windows, or alarms. Did I pass?"

"Entry?"

"Me, you, and Baby Huey hit the door. Birdman and Dagger do a rear window."

Odin took a Heckler and Koch 9-mm submachine gun from the trunk and handed it to Fleming. Junior snapped a thirty-round clip in. Odin removed his own Remington auto shotgun and worked the action. A 12-gauge shell clunked into the chamber.

"I appreciate your pulling for me," Junior said. "I mean, this is really important to me."

There was a sound in the bushes. Both men aimed their guns, but Odin's finger wasn't white on the trigger.

Eustas "Huey" Nichols, the lieutenant in charge of the SWAT squads, came out of the undergrowth.

"You gonna frag me or what?" Nichols, dressed the same as Odin and Fleming, was a six-foot-four-inch powerhouse with nineteen years in the department.

"Sorry, sir," Fleming said.

"Junior, go hook up with Birdman and Dagger," Nichols said. "They've got an OP about twenty yards down the ridge."

Fleming nodded. Nichols and Odin watched wordlessly as he trotted toward the observation post.

"I've forgotten how much fun it is getting up at the crack of dawn," Nichols said, barely stifling a yawn.

"Hard night last night?" Odin asked.

"Hard enough. She's a cocktail waitress over in Hollenbeck. A weight lifter. Tits as hard as cantaloupes. When she wrapped her legs around me, I thought I'd never get loose."

"Well, thank you muchly for joining us."

"I miss the fun and games since I became a full-time paper pusher." Nichols sighed. "What about Junior?"

"A bit skittish."

"He shouldn't be team leader."

"He's just a little green. This should be an easy one. It's good to let him do it," Odin said. "He needs to build his confidence. How'd you like to be the son of Brass Balls Fleming?"

"How would an ofay like that explain having a son as black and beautiful as myself?"

"He could tell everyone he fucked his wife up the ass."

"You got a foul mouth, white meat. If I didn't need your skinny white ass on the team, I'd kick it down the hill."

"You're ugly enough but you ain't tough enough."

They glared, then grinned at each other. It was a ritual as necessary to the psyching up process as football players smashing each other on the shoulder pads.

Nichols and Odin synchronized their watches.

"I'd feel better if you were leading," Nichols said.

"But you're not ordering it?"

Nichols shook his head.

"Then I'm gonna let Junior lead," Odin said. "The kid's heart is in the right place."

Nichols frowned and depressed the switch on his walkie-talkie. "Bagels, this is Bravo, do you copy?"

"Roger, Bravo," answered Bagels, the narcotics sergeant who waited with another narc in an unmarked car just down the hill. Bagels was a meticulous cop whose paperwork always held up in court. The fact that despite his unthreatening appearance—slight potbelly, thinning hair, soft features—he was also a tough street cop was an added bonus.

"We're about to start the party," Nichols said.

"I'll bring the appetizer," Bagels responded, and they heard the engine on the car starting up. Bagels and the other narcs would follow the SWAT cops and do field tests on any drugs recovered. They also had gathered intelligence on Mokley and briefed the SWAT cops beforehand.

Bagel's backup drummed his fingers on the dashboard of their Plymouth. He checked the safety on his 9-mm Beretta. Bagels didn't bother checking his. With SWAT handling the entry, there was little chance the narcotics cops would need their own guns. That was why SWAT was called in. Some of the old-timers missed kicking in doors, but most preferred leaving it to the Special Weapons and Tactics team.

Whenever there was a risk of an armed encounter, a fortified residence, a dangerous suspect, SWAT was called up to make the entry and arrest. This morning, the Bravo squad had a no-knock search warrant for the residence of Gary Mokley, as well as a warrant for his arrest on suspicion of possession of amphetamines with intent to distribute.

Gary Mokley had been arrested several times and had a history of skipping out to avoid prosecution. He had boasted to an informant that the next time he was cornered, he was "taking a bunch of pigs with him." The narcotics informant believed that

Mokley was "a bullshitter from way back," but there was no point in taking chances. The informant had seen paraphernalia for manufacturing amphetamines as well as an Uzi in Mokley's house.

The sun was rising, the dew glistening on the sage and scrub brush. Tiny droplets of water caught the orange light and glowed. The light created hard shadows from the jagged agaves and cacti that dotted the hillside.

The five cops moving down the slope towards the building didn't notice the natural beauty. Their eyes were on the building and its immediate environs. Any sign of activity could mean danger. Or it could be an innocent jogger. They would have to react in milliseconds, make a decision that would mean life or death. They fanned out, approaching the building from different angles, able to see movement from any side and to cover their fellow team members.

They had been through it many times before. Even Junior Fleming, with the least runs under his belt, had been on nearly twenty-five call-ups. Odin had the most, well over two hundred, with Nichols a close second.

The other two men in the SWAT team, Walter Finch and Peter Daggett, had about one hundred and fifty each. They were both taciturn, blond, ex-Marines who had been buddies in Vietnam, and ever since. They both had wispy mustaches, drove matching black Honda 1000-cc motorcycles, and had married petite brunettes who were as similar in looks as were Finch and Daggett. The two cops were nicknamed Birdman and Dagger, and jointly called the Bobbsey Twins.

"What the fuck—"

Fleming stumbled and fell, arms waving, cursing. There was the sound of a struggle. Daggett and Birdman dropped instantly, guns ready for a possible ambush. Nichols and Odin advanced to aid Junior.

They found him rolling in the grass, scuffling with a scruffy man.

Odin lifted the man up by his hair, spun him around and knocked him out with one punch. The SWAT sergeant clicked handcuffs on the man. Nichols helped a dazed Junior to his feet.

"What happened?" Junior mumbled.

The homeless man had been half buried in a foxhole, with trash bags, empty bottles, and assorted debris to keep him company.

There was a thin trickle of blood on Junior's temple. "He hit me?" Junior asked.

"That's what it looks like. You probably scared the piss out of him." Nichols wrinkled his nose at the acrid urine stench from the derelict. Huey relaxed his grip and Junior sagged. Nichols lifted him upright as if he was weightless.

Odin was studying the foxhole. "Look at this."

The foxhole was perfectly dug, sloped to allow drainage, with a grenade and water sump at the bottom, dirt step, and raised earthen parapet.

"Haven't seen one like this since Nam," Odin said.

The neatness of the hole contrasted with everything else about the derelict. He was white, but it was hard to tell under all the dirt and stubble. Lice were visible in his hair and his clothes were torn in as many places as they were whole.

"Dumb fucker. Bet he's a vet," Nichols said. "What do you want to do?" Junior's out of commission."

"I'm not," Junior said, pulling away. He wobbled. "I'm fine. I just sprained my ankle is all."

Odin looked in Junior's eyes. The pupils were both the same size. There was no bleeding from his ears or mouth. The blood on his forehead came from a superficial cut.

"I think he's okay."

"I have to lead," Junior said. "I can do it."

"I'll take over," Odin volunteered.

"No!" Junior said.

Nichols called Bagels on the walkie-talkie. "Send one of your boys over to assist Junior. He captured a desperado on the hill here and was injured."

"I can spare him," Bagels said.

"Let's go," Nichols said to Odin.

"No! I have to do it," Junior said.

"Shhhhh," Odin hissed. "There'll be another call-up."

Junior limped a few paces and fell as the cops moved off. "Wait! Don't do it. It's not fair. It's my turn."

But the lieutenant and sergeant were already gone.

Junior got up, took a few more steps forward, and passed out.

Odin, Dagger, and Birdman made their way from shrub to shrub while Nichols hustled around to the rear of the house. The windows had heavy bars set into the stucco and thick curtains on the inside. Clearly the occupant valued his privacy.

Finch took a piece of gum he was chewing and stuck it over the peephole in Mokley's door. Daggett unslung the folding battering ram, a four-inch-thick telescoping aluminum cylinder with lead encased in a rubber head. The battering ram weighed thirty pounds. Daggett handled it effortlessly. He flipped the pins that locked the ram solid and attached the straps that allowed him to swing it to pick up momentum.

Odin trained his auto shotgun on the door. The gun had a cut-down stock to allow easier swing in narrow spaces.

Finch stuck a contact listening device to the door. He made a sideways gesture with his hand, signaling no noise from inside.

Finch inspected the door frame, and with a knuckle against his palm, indicated that he felt the door could be knocked in with the battering ram. The cops had small explosive charges they could have used, or they could have attacked the wall next to the door. Dealers buttressed their doors, not realizing how vulnerable the adjacent plaster was.

Pointing with his right index finger, Odin indicated where Daggett and Finch should position themselves. It was hardly necessary. The trio had tackled numerous doors before.

Finch faced the door, his H and K submachine gun level at his waist. Daggett was next to him, ready with the battering ram. His own long weapon, a carbine, remained slung over his shoulder. He had to have complete confidence in Finch and Odin's ability to cover him.

Odin was next to the door. After Daggett crashed it, Odin would throw himself into the room, onto the floor, his shotgun ready to neutralize any threat.

Daggett braced himself, primed to swing the battering ram. Finch braced himself, ready to open fire. Odin checked his watch. He clicked the walkie-talkie button three times.

Nichols, at the rear of the house, clicked back. He was ready. It was less than two minutes since the team had come down from the hill.

Odin gave a thumbs-up to Finch and Daggett. Daggett pulled back the ram. Odin signaled for him to hold off and tried the doorknob. It turned. He grinned.

The door caught on a chain lock. Daggett wouldn't need to throw all his weight into the ram. A little tap would rip the chain right out of the wall.

Odin braced himself just to the side of the door and signaled Daggett.

The battering ram hit the door and it flew open.

At the rear of the house, Nichols pulled his carbine back, ready to slam the butt into the side window.

The plan was for the entry team to hit the front door. As the occupant of the apartment ran to challenge them, Nichols would break the window, drawing his attention. Mokley would be pinned between the two groups, mind foggy from sleep.

Before Nichols could hit the pane, it came out to meet him.

There was a flash of light nanoseconds before the blast. The explosion knocked him to the ground, blowing his carbine out of his hands.

Even before he consciously knew what had happened, he was up and bulldozing his way through the neglected shrubbery to the front of the house.

Dense smoke billowed out of the door and flowed up over the edge of the tile roof. Nichols held his .45 at the ready as he ran as fast as he could in his dazed state.

There was a cavernous black hole where the front door had been.

Body parts were strewn on the porch. The Bobbsey Twins had taken the full force of the blast. No way to tell which part belonged to whom.

Odin's body was sprawled on the front walk. Nichols knelt over him. The sergeant's standing off to the side had shielded him from some of the force of the blast. But not enough.

His bullet-proof vest had protected his torso but his face and hands were burned. Nichols felt at his carotid artery.

He found a pulse. He shouted into the lapel mike from his walkie-talkie.

"Officer needs help! Officer down on Del Rio Place." His voice was raw from the smoke.

He had repeated it three times before he realized his walkie-talkie had been broken by the explosion.

Bagels and another narcotics cop raced up hall.

"Shit!" Bagels said.

Bagels's backup man looked at the blood on the wall, smelled the burnt flesh, and promptly threw up.

"Bob's alive," Nichols said. "Need your radio."

Bagels took his walkie-talkie out. "Officer needs help. Explosion. Nineteen Fourteen Del Rio. Need an ambulance. Code Three."

Nichols couldn't hear what was said because of the ringing in his ears.

There was a second explosion, which knocked the three standing cops to their knees. The normally powerful Nichols needed Bagels's help to move Odin from the stairs to curbside.

"Are you okay?" Bagels asked the SWAT lieutenant.

"What?"

"Are you okay?" Bagels shouted, moving his lips slowly.

"I'm fine," Nichols said, and he passed out.

2 Nurse Jan Golden raced down the corridor pushing the crash cart before her. Code Blue in room 315. That would be Mr. Johansen. Eighty-eight years old. Comatose. Already had two strokes. What was the point?

How could she think like that? What had changed the idealistic twenty-three-year-old summa cum laude nursing school graduate into a cynical thirty-six-year-old assistant charge nurse?

There wasn't time to wonder. She rounded the corner, shoes squeaking, wheels creaking on the worn floor of Queen of Mercy Hospital. It had a reputation as being the best medical center in the San Fernando Valley. If it was the best, she shuddered to think what went on at the worst.

The rest of the Code Blue team would meet her in the room.

Then the paging system operator announced, "Code Blue in Room Three-oh-nine."

Two acute emergencies simultaneously. It had happened only a couple of times in Golden's experience. She had brought up the subject once at a staff meeting and the administrators said they would take it under consideration. That had been nearly a year ago. There was no contingency plan.

Golden wheeled the cart through the door of room 315. Johansen lay on the bed, color rapidly fading to match the sheets. The green-glowing monitor indicated ventricular fibrillation—his heart was beating so wildly it was doing no good.

Two other RNs hurried in. Kathy and Susie. Both had less than six months experience. Kathy got the Ambu bag and placed the mouthpiece on Johansen's face. The ventilating bag looked like a giant perfume atomizer.

Susie was slowly unbuttoning his pajama top. Golden nudged her aside and ripped open the top.

"Get out the jelly," Golden ordered as she turned on the defibrillating machine and lifted the paddles. The machine quickly charged up.

For a healthy person, four minutes without oxygen meant brain damage. For someone in Johansen's state . . .

Susie stood frozen. "Jelly?"

"Electrode jelly. On the cart."

Where was the rest of the team? Probably in 309.

Susie seemed to be moving painfully slow, nervous about handling the crash-cart gear. "No jelly," Susie said, after pawing through the cart.

Golden grabbed the jelly right off the top. She smeared it on the panels. Just the right amount to aid in conduction. Too much, and she'd burn the patient.

Kathy squeezed the bag, forcing air into Johansen, but at an irregular rate. No time to correct her. Golden had to concentrate on the defibrillator.

She adjusted the machine for two hundred joules, the low end of the scale for an adult. She slapped the paddles down on his chest, one to the right of the upper sternum, the other to the left of the left nipple. Golden leaned on them enough to ensure good contact, yet not so much that they would slip.

"Is the oxygen valve closed?" Golden asked.

Susie nodded.

"Double-check it."

Susie did, and nodded again.

"Stand clear," Golden ordered, making sure the floor underneath her was dry.

Susie and Kathy stepped back and Golden discharged the paddles. Johansen spasmed, nearly jumping out of the bed.

The monitor showed his heart was still fibrillating. Golden adjusted the machine to two hundred fifty joules.

"Stand back." It was unnecessary to say it. The two young nurses watched from the far side of the room. Golden zapped him again. The waves on the monitor changed. The beats slowed to an acceptable 150.

The doctor—an officious man with a silly, thin mustache—breezed into the room. He glanced at the EKG as Golden removed the paddles.

"Well, that seems to be okay. Let's get a lidocaine bolus going, sodium bicarb in the IV, and oxygen." He smiled at Golden. "Nice job."

"Where have you been?" Golden snapped. Before he could answer, she turned on her heel and marched out of the room.

Golden sat in Mary Tallero's office, eyeing the box of chocolates on her desk. Tallero, the unit coordinator and Golden's supervisor, was talking on the phone with another hospital administrator about an upcoming fundraiser.

"I still think it's crummy to call ex-patients and try and hustle them for a donation," Tallero said.

She made a couple of "uh-huhing" sounds as the person on the other end made points. Tallero was a middle-aged Filipino divorcée, with two kids, an old-fashioned hairdo, and a body sagging under the pressure of gravity and life. She was a stern but loving mother to the nurses.

"You do what you have to," she said. "Let them try and put the screws on me. Gotta go."

She hung up and stared at Golden.

"May I?" Golden asked, pointing to the chocolate.

"Better you than me, honey," Tallero said. "Though you're getting a bit of a pouch yourself."

Golden pinched at her abdomen, and found Tallero was right. She put down the chocolate. Too many hastily grabbed doughnut lunches. "Why'd you call me in?"

"Doctor LaRoche came to me complaining about you," Tallero said.

"Who's he?"

"The doctor you yelled at after the Code Blue on Johansen," Tallero said. "Claims you humiliated him in front of a couple of nurses."

"That low-life weasel. Did he tell you that he was nowhere to be found?"

"He said he was busy on another ward. Do you know for a fact that he wasn't?"

"I know him. He was either sleeping somewhere or trying to put the make on an X-ray technician."

"You shouldn't have yelled at him," Tallero said. "He was actually working. Looking in on a patient. You know the starlet who was in a car accident? She's been getting great attention on that hairline thigh fracture from the male staff. He thought someone else was providing backup for the Code team."

"And when we had two Code Blues, I'm standing there with no one to help me but two dinks who don't know electrode jelly from peanut butter and jelly."

"No one can anticipate two simultaneous Code Blues."

"I did. I told the procedures committee we needed to establish a policy. At Cedars Sinai—"

"Let's not talk about Cedars, okay? When we have their money, we'll have their procedures."

"So this roach filed a complaint?"

"He wanted to. But during the course of it, he commented that it must be because you were either 'on the rag' or 'just needed a good fuck.' I made it clear I would include that verbatim." Tallero worked a cigarette into a holder and lit the tobacco. She inhaled deeply. "I pointed out to him that the new chief of staff is a woman and would appreciate his perspective. He mumbled and grumbled, and withheld his complaint."

"Thanks."

"I called up your file to check how things are going," Tallero said.

"You could've asked me."

"I could've. But sometimes it's important to see how others see us. You know what I found?"

Golden reached over, took a chocolate, and defiantly popped it into her mouth. "No."

"A half dozen negative evaluations. None involving complaints from patients. In fact, you've got a bunch of letters of commendation. Staff, however, is a different story. Rude, abusive, confrontational. And those are your friends talking."

"I don't suffer fools lightly."

"Do you really think barking at a doctor does any good? Or chewing out a nurse so severely she leaves crying?"

"That was only after she overmedicated a patient so badly we had to rush him over to ICU. How can anyone give diuretics to a dehydrated patient?"

"If you're looking for perfection, you're in the wrong business."

"I'll settle for mere competence," Golden snapped.

Tallero reached across the desk and took Golden's hand. "What can we do to make things better? Would you like to transfer again?"

"I've worked the ER, ob/gyn, psych. It's all the same."

"Have you considered changing tracks? Maybe you could rise higher in the administration, steal my job."

"I'd see even more incompetence."

"Thanks."

"I didn't mean that as an insult."

"But your tone makes it sound that way. See. And I'm your friend."

There were a few moments of silence. Tallero puffed on her cigarette.

"You know, the other night I was listening to the radio and that song 'Is That All There Is?' came on," Golden said, gazing at a poster for Club Med on Tallero's wall. "I started to sniffle. For no reason."

"That's why I got out of nursing into administration. Burnout is an occupational hazard, my dear."

"Medicine has changed," Golden said. "Expensive electronic hardware, used solely because it's there and they have to recover costs. More and more terminally ill in the wards, with easy procedures done on an outpatient basis. But patient loads haven't changed." A wisp of hair fell across her forehead and she brushed it back. Her brown hair was increasingly streaked with gray. Cut short to follow hospital regulations, it framed a pretty, high-cheekboned face. Her eyes were dark brown and locked on people with a challenging intensity. "Everyone I see is either a teenager who rode a motorcycle without a helmet or an elderly person with everything going wrong."

"Yeah, it's terrible," Tallero said. "Those sick people should go elsewhere."

"You know what I mean."

Tallero's phone buzzed. "Yes?" she asked on picking it up. "I'll call him back in a couple minutes." She hung up. "Why don't you float for a while? ICU needs help. Stat."

"What's going on?"

"A bomb killed two cops, wounded three others. One of the survivors is the son of a police honcho. Another is a hero cop."

"You know how I feel about cops."

"Yes, Miss Kneejerk Liberal. The next time you're about to get mugged, holler for your ACLU lawyer."

"You better get to your call," Golden said, standing.

"Jan, this is for your own good. As an administrator, it's for the hospital's good."

"It's an order for me to go to ICU?"

"A request. They need you there."

3 Outside the ICU, TV camera crews jockeyed for position. Newspaper reporters buttonholed anyone wearing white and tried to get information. Orderlies wheeling patients on gurneys had to struggle through the crowd.

Golden elbowed to the center of the maelstrom, where Assistant Chief Frederick Fleming held court. She recognized his Central Casting perfect face—strong jaw, black hair graying at the temples, deepset but twinkling blue eyes.

There were three assistant chiefs, but as the head of the largest bailiwick, operations, Fleming was first among equals. He was expected to become police chief, and from there, who knows? She had seen him numerous times on the TV news, spouting the credo of law and order.

"My own son was a victim of this tragic violence," Fleming was saying. "Now one of our best men lies on the other side of this door, in critical condition. Why? Because simple sisters care more about the rights of murderers than they do about the rights of you and me to be safe in our homes."

Golden finally reached the door and the orderly guarding it let her in.

The unit had a good feel to it. Gleaming, pale blue walls. Just the right amount of antiseptic smell. The tinkle of glass being handled carefully. The various beeps and hums of life-monitoring and life-saving equipment.

The nurses moved about crisply, efficiently. Golden recognized a few of her more competent colleagues. She strode to the nurses' station and flipped through the charts.

"Hey, Jan, good to see you."

She looked up. It was a young intern she had dated briefly. They had been smart enough to recognize early on it wouldn't work and had parted amicably. They had even gone to see a few films together, once their relationship was clarified. His name was Peter and he was going to be a urologist. He had curly hair and a boyishly good natured bedside manner. He gave the impression that one day he would be very rich.

She looked up from the reports, gave him the best smile she could muster, and then returned her attention to them.

"Hi, Peter. Sorry but I'm really busy right now."

"You always are. You have one of the bomb victims?" he asked, then without waiting for an answer, said, "I had one of the other cops."

"I just got here. I'm floating."

"I know the feeling."

She looked up. "What's the story with the bomb victims?"

"They pulled me down to ER to give a quick hand. High priority. One cop was checked for a concussion but he doesn't have anything aspirin can't cure. Got off without even a burn mark. We had to baby him, his daddy's the assistant chief making all the noise outside. He's a golfing buddy of Charleston Murray. As in the Charleston Murray Wing of this illustrious institution."

"He still shouldn't be allowed to disrupt us like this."

"You should know the five-hundred-pound gorilla rule by now. By the way, nice job on LaRoche. He was bitching about you in the doctor's lounge. You want to know what he said?"

"That what I needed was a good fuck and he was just the one to give it to me."

"Pretty close. I was tempted to tell him better men than him had tried."

"What about the other injured?"

"A big *shvartze* named Nichols. Not too bad. He'll probably be discharged in a couple of hours. Temporary hearing loss. Superficial lacerations."

There was a sudden increase in noise as the orderly guarding the door was swarmed by reporters. The orderly regained control and the door was pulled shut.

"Who's in the ICU?"

"Robert Odin. He's got third-degree burns, internal hemorrhaging. They've given him more blood than Dracula takes down in a month. I'd say he's got a fifty-fifty chance of making it."

"Odin? Is he, well by now he'd be about forty? Brown hair, good shape, cleancut type?"

"Hard to say. His face took a lot of abuse. He's definitely in good shape. Keene says that's about the only thing keeping him alive. You know Odin?"

"I think so. There was an incident in the ER, when—"

The door swung open again and Fleming stuck his head in.

"Excuse me, nurse, I must have a word with you," he said.

Peter had disappeared. He obviously had no desire to complicate his career by getting involved in the matter.

Golden picked up the phone and punched the line for security. "I need a half dozen officers here. Stat."

She hung up and walked towards the door. The crowd in the hall had grown, bulging at the seams of the hallway.

"Out of the way, out of the way," a nurse was shouting, trying to shepherd a patient on a gurney through the door.

The reporters blocking the gurney tried to obey but there was nowhere to go.

"Sweetheart, can you just tell us how Bob is doing?" Fleming asked Golden.

"He's in critical condition."

"Can you tell us more?" Fleming was acting like he was a reporter, all but holding a mike under her nose.

"Yes. I can tell you something."

TV lights switched on. Reporters held their pens poised above the paper. Fleming sidled in closer, to be sure to be next to Golden when it was televised.

"You are jeopardizing the life of Mr. Odin and the other

patients in this unit. By forcing the door open, you're endangering the sterile field. By blocking the corridor, you're costing medical personnel valuable time. You, in the back, smoking, you're risking setting off the oxygen we use."

The crowd was silent. But no one moved, fearful that the competition would stay and get an exclusive.

The elevator door opened. Six potbellied but muscular uniformed hospital guards waddled out.

"I'm giving you one minute to clear the area, then the officers will begin escorting you out," Golden said. "Any equipment broken or injuries suffered in the process is your own fault."

The guards formed a solid line, sucking in their collective guts, drawing their nightsticks and holding them in front with both hands. The crowd began dissolving.

"Little lady, you've got what we call command presence," Fleming said, smile in place. "You did a bang-up job."

"Were you responsible for bringing that mob up here?"

"They just tagged along. I wanted to see how Bob was doing."

"Aren't you on duty? Shouldn't you be back at headquarters administering or something?"

Fleming's smile nearly slipped. "Don't get tart tongued, sweetheart. Serving to booster department morale by being seen is a vital part of my duties. Not that I have to justify myself to you."

"Do you ever justify yourself to yourself?"

"Wait a minute. I know you. You're the one who filed the complaint with the commission against Odin. After that incident in the emergency room three, no four years ago. Right?"

"Correct."

"You're taking care of him?"

"He's under my supervision."

"You're sure you can do a good job?"

"Mr. Fleming, I'm not like you and your officers. I believe every human being has the right to be treated as such. If you'll excuse me, I have work to do."

4   There was blackness, the most complete blackness Odin
    had ever experienced. And a loud humming, like a giant
generator about to rip loose from its moorings.

Then he saw a vibrant blue light in the distance and walked
towards it. Each step was an effort but the light pulled him. As
he got nearer, the light grew brighter and brighter, the noise
louder and louder, until he was dizzy from the battering his
senses were taking. Still, he moved towards it, anything to escape the total blackness.

He neared the portal, the window through which the light
and noise were coming. He had grown used to the light and
sound. He almost craved it. A few feet more and he'd be over
the line. Each step was agony.

He had been hurt before. During the Vietnam war he'd
served in the SEALs, the Navy version of the Green Berets.
He'd been wounded in Vietnam, a victim of a VC late-night
mortar attack. As a rookie cop, he'd been stabbed while breaking up a domestic dispute between a couple of newlyweds.

But those were just painful experiences. This was as if his
whole body had been pounded with a sledgehammer. Somehow
he knew if he went over to the source of light and noise, the
agony would be gone. Instantly.

Then he realized what crossing that barrier meant. He
stopped. The light and noise kept pulling at him, Sirens luring
Odysseus and his men to the rocks. He fought against the force
but felt too weak.

He was almost at the line.

"No!" he shouted with a gut-wrenching yell, but the sound
from the other side drowned out his voice. He could hear voices
now, faintly, from the other side. "No!" he screamed again.

Then there was total blackness. Earthly sounds. Voices, beeps, bells, squeaks. Glass tinkling, moans. All barely audible through the ringing noise. He tried to categorize the sounds, what did they mean?

Hospital.

"He's coming around," a woman said. "Get the doctor."

Odin realized he was the one moaning. He tried opening his eyes. Still blackness.

"The others?" Odin croaked, his throat burned from the blast.

"Two other officers have already been discharged from the hospital," the woman said. Her voice sounded familiar, and it wasn't a pleasant memory.

"Finch? Daggett?"

"I don't know," she said.

"Mokley?"

"I can't understand what you're saying. Please rest."

"They get Mokley?"

"I don't know," she said. He heard her moving away. "Yes, doctor. Vital signs stabilized a few minutes ago. He just came around."

"Take it easy," a soothing male voice said. "I'm Doctor Keene. Relax. You're going to have plenty of time here, plenty of time to ask questions." Keene's voice was soothing, confident.

"Pain is bad," Odin said.

"I know," Keene answered. "We can't give you anything for it yet. Anything that kills the pain is going to depress your central nervous system. It'll kill the pain and you as well."

Half of Odin's face felt like it had been burned. On the other half, he felt nothing. He tried twitching his eye on that side. No sensation. Still there was the blackness.

"We've got heavy gauze bandages over your eyes," Keen said, as if reading Odin's mind. "Just take it easy. Let your body do its job. Don't stress it unnecessarily. Rest is the best medicine."

The sounds grew softer until he was alone again.

Assistant Chief Fred Fleming, in dark suit and looking very dashing, deftly worked the crowd in the New Otani ballroom. The two dozen tables were packed with Southern California movers and shakers.

One table belonged to the newspaper dynasty that had done more to shape Southern California than any other family. They had killed mass transit, speculated in real estate, stolen the water from the Owens Valley, and become respectable. Half of them were already too drunk to see straight.

They had been Fleming's entry into the power structure. As a young watch commander, he had picked up one of their sons on a drunk driving charge. Instead of arresting the young man, he had driven him to the family's Beverly Hills mansion. The family had been properly appreciative. He had cemented his ties to them by having an affair with one of the women.

Fleming was bright, did well on the police department tests, and didn't hesitate to use his contacts. He was a hard-nosed street cop who had earned a number of medals for bravery. He was nicknamed Brass Balls after disarming a gun-toting bank robber, his only weapon his fists. Fleming rose quickly.

After thirteen years on the job, he was made captain, the youngest so promoted in LAPD history. After two more years, he was captain of central division and, always charming with the press, came out as a hero after cleaning up a minis-candal involving corrupt cops making deals to let bookmakers off.

Fleming made the transition smoothly from the viciousness in the street to the vicious maneuvering in police headquarters. He was promoted to assistant chief in charge of administration after three years at headquarters. Two years after that, he became the operations chief. He no longer saw himself as a career cop. He knew he was cut out for better things.

Now he reached the table where the political powers held

informal caucus. A key fundraiser was telling an off-color joke about two Polish nuns and an Irish priest. Fleming breezed over just in time to join the laughter.

"How's our favorite supercop doing?" a pollster asked.

"Keeping the streets safe for democracy," Fleming quipped, and everyone chuckled.

"Any leads on that dope dealer who blew up your SWAT team?" asked a deputy mayor.

"We'll find him," Fleming said.

"I'm sure you will," the deputy mayor's wife said.

Fleming made some more chitchat and moved on. Please let Mokley be found dead, or never at all, he thought.

The assistant chief stopped at the Hollywood table, filled with flashy men accompanied by women half their age. A studio exec complained about a problem a producer was having getting a permit to film on Los Angeles streets. Fleming vowed to look into it. He repeated the joke he had heard about the nuns and the priest and got a big laugh.

"You ever leave the cops and robbers racket, you oughta take up comedy," said a producer whose last film had cost forty million dollars and made back barely one-quarter of that.

Fleming grinned and continued his rounds as dutifully as a cop walking his beat. He spotted a couple of call girls he knew on the arms of wealthy older men. He gave the girls a wink and made a mental note to check on them. They often picked up interesting pillow talk and the hint of an embarrassing arrest could make them open up. Figuratively and literally.

His own wife was dutifully sitting at their table, talking with the other ranking civil servants and their spouses. They had been married twenty-seven years and she knew her place. She would slyly let slip anecdotes about her husband that only added to his credibility. How they hadn't had a weekend together in so long, he was too busy working. How much he cared about his job. What a wonderful person he thought the mayor was. How sad it was that the police chief had a drinking problem and his daughter was a Communist.

The Chief had not been invited to the dinner. He was on the outs with the power structure. Fleming had been as responsible for that alienation as the Chief had been. The Chief was a basically decent man with a knack for putting his foot in his mouth.

Fleming chatted briefly with the folks at the aerospace table—he had been an Air Force pilot during the Korean War and could make believable small talk about avionics—and finally reached the table he was heading for.

Unions had never gained the stronghold in Los Angeles that they had in cities back east. But they still were a force to be reckoned with. Local Teamster boss Nicholas Provenzano was the main man at the table. He was nearly as dapper as Fleming. He looked not at all like his father, the union thug and legbreaker who had risen to the top and passed the reins on to Nicky.

Fleming working his way around the table, patting the men on the back, bussing the women on the cheek. He acknowledged the complaint of a bakery union official that the police had been rough in breaking up a strike.

"This isn't the days of the Wobblies," the woman said, unamused. "Your department shouldn't act as union goons."

"Well, from what I understand, a few of your people started throwing things," Fleming responded. "I'll look into it, check on whether excessive force was used."

She grunted and resumed sipping her coffee.

"Nicky, I hear there's been some problem with double-parked trucks blocking traffic in the garment district," Fleming said. "I'd like to talk with you a moment. Privately, if you don't mind."

It was the first Provenzano had heard about any such problem. He nearly said so. But he was smooth enough to play along.

"Yeah, I been meaning to talk with you about that,"

Provenzano said, pushing his chair away from the table. "Excuse me."

The two men strolled to a quiet part of the ballroom. They spoke low, so no one could hear.

"You want to talk about double-parked trucks?" Provenzano asked skeptically.

"Have you been following the Mokley case."

"I read the papers." His voice was harsher, his tones more New Jersey. He had changed roles from sophisticated labor leader to one more in keeping with his family heritage.

"What would it cost me to make sure that Mokley isn't found alive?" Fleming asked.

"You don't need me for that," Provenzano said. "Your boys in blue do a good job taking care of cop killers."

"I want to be sure."

"I'll see what I can do."

"What do you want in return?"

"Just your friendship. Like in the past."

Fleming sauntered back towards the table, feeling better. He began mentally reviewing the speech he would make. He was to accept an award for outstanding service to the city. He looked towards the back of the room. The TV cameras were there. Good.

As Nicky Provenzano listened to the speeches, he wondered why Fleming had come to him. Pro had had a couple of dealings with Mokley. Nothing he'd seen in Mokley made him suspect that the jerk would be playing with toys that went boom. What was it about Mokley that made Fleming want him out of the picture before the cops could get to him?

It would be interesting to know. It could help him in future dealings with Fleming. The cop was clearly going places. It wouldn't hurt to have a little dirt on the future chief of police.

There was talk that Fleming could go even higher. Governor. Senator.

Provenzano leaned back in his seat and lit a cigar.

"Honey, you know I hate when you smoke those things," his wife said.

He leaned in close and whispered in her ear. "Shut the fuck up or I'll shove a lit one up your ass."

He leaned back contentedly and puffed away.

"You were out for close to three days," Huey Nichols was saying. "They said if you were in a coma longer than that, good chance you weren't coming back. I told them you were too mean and ugly to die."

"How about you?"

"I won't be able to hear my Julio Iglesias records so good, but the hearing loss should be temporary."

"I heard on the radio a report that said three cops were injured and two killed. Who's the third?"

"Junior." Nichols lowered his voice to a whisper. "Brass Balls put it out that Junior was with us at the house. The narco guy took the collar from the dirtbag on the hill."

"Why?"

"You think Brass Balls's ambitions got anything to do with making his kid out an injured hero?" Nichols asked cynically.

"How is Junior?"

"He ain't taking it well. Mopes around. He did everything but throw a temper tantrum to get the truth out. But he don't have the guts to stand up to his old man."

"Few people do. The door booby-trapped?"

"You got it. Bomb Squad said either the guy who did it was damn clever or damn lucky. It wasn't much more than a firecracker, a few shotgun shells worth of powder. But it set off the chemicals Mokley had."

"Meth precursors?"

"Right. The flammable shit they use to make meth-amphetamine. Clever cocksucker, ain't he?"

"The lowlife on the hill. That foxhole was real slick. Did he . . ." Odin weakened and his words trailed off.

"Stay cool, white boy," Nichols said, gently patting Odin's shoulder with a big hand. "It's been checked out. Clean, just one of the walking wounded. He was a combat vet but his brains are fried. About all he does now is play with dirt. He's got no connection with Mokley."

"He see anything unusual around the house?"

"Yeah. John Kennedy and Elvis selling dope to Marilyn Monroe."

Odin sighed. "What about Mokley?"

"No sign. Every guy on the job is looking for him."

"I hope they don't find him."

"What?"

"I want him."

"When you get out of here, you ain't gonna be on the job anymore. You know that."

"I know that."

"So it won't be your business going after Mokley. You got to leave that to the PD."

"Sure."

Odin heard Doctor Keene's voice. "I'm afraid you'll have to go now. There's only five minutes' visiting time allowed here."

Nichols got up and squeezed Odin's hand. It was funny how much the physical contact meant to Odin. He had never been a demonstrative type, but he longed for a hug almost as much as he longed for the morphine they'd begun giving him.

"It's time for me to inspect your face," Keene said. "All your other systems are go. You're making remarkable progress."

"When do I get out."

"It's a bit early for that."

As the doctor unraveled the bandages that swathed Odin's face, the injured cop asked, "You know, I heard a woman's voice when I was first coming around. It sounded real familiar. Would you know who that was?"

"Let's see, I'd guess it was either O'dell, Murphy, or Golden."

"Jan Martha Golden?"

"That's right."

"Great," Odin said sarcastically.

"Did I hurt you?"

"No. She's a bitch. Probably rubbed salt in my wounds."

"No, we only do that in old wounds," the doctor said. He switched to a serious tone. "I'd like to take credit for your doing so well, but I can't really. It's thanks to your own body, for one. And the nurses, for another. They've done a superb job getting you through the crisis."

"That's their job."

"True, but you can change a dressing, and you can change a dressing," he said. The second time, he emphasized the word change. "I can tell from the chart the kind of attention that's been paid to you. It's not just because you're a high-publicity case. You've gotten the best care."

"You setting me up for a bigger bill?"

The air felt good on Odin's face. But still there was darkness.

Odin sensed, rather than saw, the doctor moving something right in front of his face. "I still don't see anything," Odin said, fighting to control the quiver in his voice. "What's it mean?"

"Hmm."

Odin felt the doctor's fingers gently touching his face. Burned skin crumpled. "It wouldn't hurt to have an ophthalmologist pay you a visit. A plastic surgeon too."

"What's it all mean?" Odin said, grabbing Keene's sleeve. He had assumed that the darkness was due to the bandage. He refused to believe it could be anything else.

"It's too soon to say. There's been some damage to your eyes. My snap diagnosis isn't worth much. You just relax and keep getting better."

The next day they transferred him out of ICU. He got a private room on the seventh floor. Almost immediately, the phone began to ring. The press had gotten his number. He spoke to a few reporters, giving glib, tough-guy quotes to those he knew. But he tired of it quickly and took the phone off the hook.

The ophthalmologist visited. Saying little, she carefully poked and prodded and shone a bright light that felt warm against his face.

Then the plastic surgeon arrived. The two doctors both examined him and made grunts and inaudible comments to each other.

"I'm not a fucking piece of meat!" Odin yelled. "What does it all mean? Will I see or won't I?"

"We must consult with your doctor," the ophthalmologist said, and she and the plastic surgeon walked out.

Odin had been denying it, believing that any moment his vision would come back, he'd jump out of bed and be as good as new. The realization hit him as hard as the blast. There was a chance he was going to be blind for life. He lay in bed, hyperventilating.

Maybe it wouldn't be so bad, being blind. He could learn to live with it.

No, he couldn't. He couldn't live tap, tap, tapping around with a cane.

It wasn't fair. All he wanted was one thing. To get Mokley. Then he'd give up his eyes. He had to get Mokley.

His fists were clenched in white knuckled anger. He hadn't felt as helpless and hopeless since he was a kid, when he'd hear his father beating his mother during fits of drunken rage.

The TV was playing. The news was on, broadcasting the dual funeral for Finch and Daggett. As in life, they did everything together. He heard the helicopters overhead in the missing-man formation, heard the guns being fired in the final salute, heard the wail of taps.

He could imagine the side-by-side flag-draped coffins, the long procession of black and whites and motorcycles with lights flashing and no siren. There'd be officers from all over the state, maybe even from neighboring states. Crying widows and cops in dark glasses so no one could see their teary eyes. Odin had been to more than a dozen and the images remained. At each funeral there lurked the selfish thought, there but for the grace of God go I.

Two minutes on the TV news. Then they were gone. Move on to the the latest warehouse fire.

Odin supposed it could be worse. He could be dead. But was that worse?

5   Trips to the bathroom were an adventure. Once he left the door half opened and walked into the hard edge. It had started his wound bleeding. But at least after a week of bed rest, doctors had reduced the dosage of painkillers and removed all but one IV.

"Hey, how you doing?" Nichols asked, coming in toward the end of visiting hours.

"I'm alive," Odin said. "For what that's worth."

"I got something gonna make you enjoy living," Nichols said.

Odin heard the big man walk out of the room, then hisses and whispers in the hall.

There was a softer tread, and the door shut.

"Hi Bobby."

A woman. Heavy sweet perfume overlaying a cigarette smell. Bobbin' Robin.

She was a police groupie, a blue belle at "choir practice," the after-hours stag parties to let off steam. Odin had only been to a couple. He found the heavy drinking and frenzied sexuality did nothing to relax him. In fact, it made him more wired being around so many guys on the edge.

"Too bad what happened," he heard her say, as she pulled back the sheets. Her hands lifted the hospital gown. He felt her long nails raking down his abdomen, her breath on his thigh.

He could envision her face—pretty, but with as much makeup as a Kabuki dancer. She had curly blond hair and a figure like a bowling pin.

She made soft purring noises that translated into vibrations. Her hands toyed with his testicles, gently kneading. Then she took him into her mouth. But there was no response. She worked on him for five minutes.

"Am I doing something wrong?" she finally asked.

"It's nothing. Must be the medicine."

"Yeah, happens all the time," she said.

He folded his arms across his chest.

"Don't worry about me telling anyone or nothing," she said. "I can keep a secret. You'd be amazed how many fellas got the same problem." She gave him a peck on the cheek. "I appreciate what you did for my brother. He's still off junk, you know."

"Great." Robin's brother had been a heroin addict. Odin had smacked him around and threatened to do much worse if he didn't go into a substance-abuse program. The threats had apparently worked. But Odin didn't feel like talking about past successes. He wanted to be alone. His first bout with impotence had cut a lot deeper than he'd admit to Robin.

She was still talking, prattling about the peccadillos of various cops she'd met. ". . . over in Devonshire, he could only get it up if I wore my hair in pigtails and talked in a squeaky voice," she was saying.

"Maybe you ought to go," Odin said.

"If that's what you want. Or I could try again."

Her hand wrapped around him and pumped gently. Nothing.

*   *   *

Nichols stood outside the room with Fleming Junior. Both men had had a few beers before coming out on their mission of mercy. The two cops were grinning at each other when Kathy, one of the nurses, came over on her way to Odin's room.

"He's busy right now," Nichols said, blocking the door.

"I have to take his vital signs," she said.

"I'm sure they're fine," Nichols said.

Junior suppressed a chuckle. Kathy gave him a questioning look and stepped forward. Her face was a few inches from Nichols's chest.

"It's my job."

"The job's being done," Huey said.

Junior was nearly bursting from the giggles.

"His, sister, yeah, his sister's in with him," Junior volunteered.

"I thought it was his cousin," Nichols said.

"She's both. They got a tangled history," Junior said.

The cops snickered.

"Get out of the way," Kathy said.

"You're beautiful when you're mad," Nichols said. "Has anyone ever told you that?"

She stepped back, not sure how to react.

"I mean it," Nichols said. "Your brown eyes flash like a summer storm."

Kathy studied Nichols, not sure if she wanted to fall for the line. The big cop was good looking, but she'd known too many lotharios in blue.

The door to the room opened. Robin backed out, saying, "You're the best, Bobby."

Nichols and Junior exchanged a wink as Robin flounced away. Kathy gave Nichols a dirty look and stepped into Odin's room. She slammed the door behind her.

The two cops exploded in laughter.

Odin barely slept that night. The next morning, he got up slowly. Hands outstretched in front of him, he felt his way around. He rapped his shin on a chair and cursed. Stumbling, staggering, he made his way to the window. He could tell where the window was by the warmth of the sun coming in. Brightness and light meant nothing to him.

He felt around the window frame. Sealed. No way he could get it open.

"What are you doing?"

That voice. It was Jan Golden.

"Nothing."

"Why are you out to bed?"

"I wanted to look out the window," he said sarcastically.

Then her arm was around him and she was forcefully guiding him back to bed. It felt good to lie down.

"I know what you were planning," she said.

"Yeah, what?"

"I'm putting a suicide watch on you."

"Thanks, tons."

"You want restraints."

"You'd like that, wouldn't you? You'd like to see me helpless."

"It's for your own good."

"Why should you care what's good for me? I'm the big bad cop, remember?"

"Do you remember that? Or are you too busy feeling sorry for yourself."

"Buzz off."

He heard her writing on his chart. "You want to know how to spell that?" he asked.

"I bear no grudge."

"I can't say the same."

"Whatever."

Odin sat up. "If I want to kill myself, that's my business."

"Not on my shift, it isn't."

Odin began laughing. Loudly, hysterically.

"What's so funny?" she asked.

"I used the same line. On a jumper. Told him he could kill himself, but not in my division. It got him down." The laughs died and just as suddenly he was crying.

Then her arms were around him. He pushed her away. He wanted to be alone. Throughout his childhood, his time in Vietnam, and his years in the department, he hadn't cried. Suffering, pain, death. No tears. Now they flowed uncontrollably, and she was there to witness it.

She hugged him again. Her strong embrace was reassuring, an invitation to let himself go. He allowed her to hold him.

"It's okay, it's going to be okay," she said.

He tried to stop but couldn't. "I can't see. I can't see."

Golden squeezed him tighter. He was as frail as the oldest geriatric or the sickest child.

The change from the way she remembered first meeting him was shocking:

The wounded suspect had been lying on a gurney at the emergency room. Two bullet holes, neither life threatening. The ER staff had stopped the bleeding and was waiting for the trauma specialist to take another look at him. Saturday night, and the usual chaotic scene. A few auto accidents, a coronary, a couple of drunks who cut each other up in the bar.

Odin had bullied his way in.

"What did you do with the girl?" Odin had growled at the suspect. He had grabbed the suspect's hand and twisted it. Right in the emergency room. She had tried to stop it, and Odin had broken two of the man's fingers before several orderlies had been able to restrain him.

Later, after she had filed the complaint, she learned that the victim was a child molester. A girl had disappeared and he was the prime suspect.

That didn't justify Odin's torturing the helpless man, she had believed.

Now it was Odin who was helpless. She repeated soothing words and felt his sobs slowly subside.

"It's not as bad as you think," she said. "It never is. I know someone, he works with handicapped—" Odin stiffened at the word. "With people with disabilities. Teaches them self-defense. It's wonderful to watch. I'll be happy to refer you to him."

He pulled away as he heard Doctor Keene's footsteps.

She felt flustered about the hug and was glad when the doctor asked her to leave.

"How's my patient today?" Keene asked.

"I been better," Odin said, quickly composing himself.

"We have to talk. You have a decision to make."

"Whether to get a cane or a Seeing Eye dog?"

"Those are possibilities."

"What else?"

"I told you there was the possibility of surgery. I've reviewed the results with the other doctors. One of your eyes is permanently damaged. There's nothing modern medicine can do to repair it, I'm afraid. Surgery might help the other."

"So. Let's get going."

"Let me explain. Your cornea is scarred and we will have to do a transplant. The retina is detached and you have glaucoma. Elevated intraocular pressure. Internal hemorhhaging. Fluid is leaking from the vitreous humor. We must operate immediately if we're going to save that eye."

"I haven't got anything better to do."

"But you're barely in stable condition. It's a lengthy procedure and to put you under at all is life threatening."

"I've had my life threatened before."

Keene reviewed the lengthy ophthalmological surgery consent form. The possibility of complications ranging from crossed eyes to dangerous infections was outlined. "I want you to think about it."

"Don't waste time, doc," Odin said. "Tell them to sharpen their scalpels. I'm ready."

Jan Golden came in and prepped him, trimming away the scorched hair that remained, cleansing the area, removing dead tissue. She offered him Valium to calm him.

"I don't need it now. I guess I bottomed out that last time you saw me. I wanted to say thanks."

"It was nothing."

"It was a lot."

"It's my job."

"I'm not some wimp who walks around with his heart on his sleeve. I appreciate it."

"Well, I'm glad. Really."

"I'd like to ask two more favors of you."

She paused in her ministrations. "What?"

"There's a way, isn't there, if, I don't want to be brought around if the doctors screw up. You know, like if I'm a vegetable."

"Yes. It's called 'no code.'"

"Put me down for a no code."

"Talk with the doctor about it. If you're sure."

"I'm sure."

"What's the second request?"

"If I come out of this in one piece, I'd like to take you to dinner. You pick the joint."

She hesitated, searching for an answer. "I don't date patients. It's not good for you. Or me. Sorry."

"I won't be a patient then."

"I'm sorry, I just don't do it."

"C'mon. I need something to live for."

"You've got plenty to live for."

He reached out and took her hand. "Please?"

She turned away from him and tidied up the room, putting

the blood-pressure cuff back on its wall clamp and straightening
the tubes on the volumetric IV infuser.

"Pretty please?"

"Okay," she said, turning to face him.

He lay back down. "All right. Lock and load."

"What's that mean?"

"I'm ready."

6 Through the window to the surgical theater, Eustas Nichols watched as the team worked on Robert Odin. Nichols
could see shiny instruments being passed between scrub-clothed
figures, technicians monitoring consoles, the surgeon peering
down into an eyepiece. Most of the activity was around a six-foot-
high machine with two eyepieces and lots of switches.

He had been brought up a devout Baptist, and though he
hadn't been to church in better than a decade, he found himself
silently praying. Memories of his mother, who put all her faith
in God, and Vietnam, where he learned the truth of the saying
there are no atheists in foxholes, flooded back.

He blamed himself for Bob's injury. Nichols was not the
usual fifth man in the patrol. Perhaps if Wingate—who had
been out sick—had been on the team, it wouldn't have happened. Or if there hadn't been all the confusion with Fleming
Junior. Or if Nichols himself had been the one to take the door.

He wanted to go in and hover over the surgeon's shoulder.
Make sure the surgeon was doing the right thing. Not that he'd
know anyway.

He heard footsteps behind him and spun.

"How is he?" Fleming Junior asked.

"Wish I knew."

"I'm sorry," Junior said.

"What's done is done."

"It's my fault this happened," Junior said.

"You ain't the only one blaming himself."

There was a flurry of activity inside. Clearly trouble. The anesthesiologist hurriedly adjusted knobs. A red light blinked on his console.

"What's going on?" Nichols growled.

"Can we do anything?" Junior asked.

They were silent for a few minutes, until the activity calmed down. The blinking light went off. The anesthesiologist nodded to the surgeon, who resumed his work.

"Oh please, let him be all right, please," Junior mumbled. Nichols saw the young man's lip quivering.

Huey threw his arm over Junior's shoulder and they leaned against each other.

Jan Golden saw the big black lieutenant with his arm over the smaller, uniformed white cop. She hesitated about approaching. But she had specifically taken time off her shift to see how Odin was doing.

She had met the lieutenant at the administrative hearing over Odin's mistreatment of her patient. The lieutenant—Nichols, that was his name—had glared at her almost as hatefully as Odin did.

She braced herself and strode over. The SWAT lieutenant frowned. She stood at the window, silently watching.

"Miss, is there any way of finding out how it's going?" Junior asked.

"You can't really tell anything until it's over," she said. She peered in, eyes roaming from EKG and the other monitors to the postures and faces of the OR personnel. "I'd guess all is going well." She shouldn't be guessing like that. Somehow she wanted to hear it being said.

"What exactly are they doing?" Fleming asked.

"Microsurgery," Golden said. "The surgeon is looking through a microscope that enlarges everything fifty times. The buttons he's pushing control a laser."

"I remember that from *Goldfinger*," Junior said. "They really do use those things nowadays? On an eye?"

"Yes. It's excellent for cutting, cauterizing, or what is similar to spot welding tissue. One of Mr. Odin's problems is a detached retina, which can be easily reattached with a few bursts from the laser," Golden said.

"I shouldn't say easily," she added. "But much more easily and efficiently. Other switches allow the surgeon to control needles, sewing sutures one-fourth as thick as a human hair."

"Wow!" Junior said.

"He can't use his own hands 'cause they can't work precise enough," Nichols said. "Right?"

"Exactly. He has hydraulic controls. It requires as fine a touch as old-fashioned surgery. It meant a great deal of relearning for surgeons. Besides all the controls we can see, there's also foot pedals."

Golden felt more comfortable in a professional mode. She had never worked on a microsurgery team, but had read articles in medical publications, and attended several grand rounds lectures on the subject.

"That's a lid speculum he's using to clamp the eye open," Golden said, like a sportscaster giving a play by play. "That pen-sized instrument he's probing the perimeter with is a scleral indentor." She continued to explain to the cops, making the operation sound as routine as possible.

"What's the success rate?" Nichols asked when she slowed.

"Very high. The surgeon is top notch. Your assistant chief pulled a lot of strings to get him. He's based in Texas."

"My dad didn't even tell me," Junior said.

"Brass Balls wouldn't want word getting out that he had a heart," Nichols said.

*   *   *

For two days, Odin had to lie on his back in bed with his head pinned, absolutely unmoving, by two sandbags. A tiny air bubble had deliberately been injected into his eye to press against the upper surface and hold tissue in place. He was allowed no visitors. Even opening his mouth to talk could cause the delicate surgery to set improperly.

He lay in the darkness—heavy bandages over his eyes again. Three times a day his dressing was changed. At one point, he thought he heard Jan Golden's footsteps, but he couldn't even call out to see if he was right. He convinced himself he was, and he didn't feel so alone.

At times he felt like tearing off the bandages, jumping up. He never thought just lying in one place could be such agony. He grew accustomed to the hospital noises, and tried to pinpoint each one. The nurse with the heavy tread. The cart that needed oiling. The groaner in the room next door. And the smells—effluvium, carbolic acid, fresh linen.

They had taken him off painkillers before the operation and he suffered from a few dull aches. He focused on them, turning them over and over in his mind, sensing his body as he never had before.

Someone set a radio on the nightstand and classical music played softly. He mentally orchestrated his pain. The twinges of sharp agony were the high pitched sounds, the dull aches like the bass. Various throbs and soreness wove in and out, a melody of suffering.

He heard the doctor's footsteps, smelled his characteristic antiseptic scent. "Well, it's that time," Doctor Keene said cheerfully. "Let me shut the blinds."

Bob traced the doctor's footsteps in his imagination. Keene returned and began unraveling the bandages.

"Keep your eyes closed," the doctor said. "They're going to be very sensitive to light at first."

"Hopefully."

"Hopefully."

Then the bandages were off. Odin sensed light against his eyelids. Joyously, he opened his eyes. The pain hit him like a thumb ground into the eye.

"Easy now. Easy," Keene said.

Slowly, his eyes grew acclimated. He opened them.

"Things will be blurry at first."

They were. But when the room snapped into focus, it was the most beautiful thing Odin had seen.

Keene looked into his eyes, held up fingers and had Odin say how many there were. Then he had Odin cover his left eye and do the same.

"How many?"

"Two."

"Very good. Now cover your right eye."

Blackness.

"Shit!"

"The eye just wasn't salvageable."

"In the land of the blind, the one-eyed man is king, doc," Odin said. "Thanks."

"I'm glad you're taking it so well. I'll give you a run down on monocular vision. I think you'll be surprised at how quickly you adjust to it."

"Yeah, yeah," said Odin, still enjoying just staring at the room, letting his good eye rove from object to object.

"Maneuvers like pouring a drink or shaking hands will seem difficult at first," Keene said. "But by doing things like shaking your head slightly from side to side, you'll be able to simulate binocular vision. You know how a range finder works?"

"By a sort of triangulation."

"Exactly. The eyes work the same way. There's retinal disparity, the difference between the images on the two retinas. Then there's convergence, the amount the eye adjusts to merge the images, which is important for seeing up to twenty-five feet, and accommodation, which is the amount needed to focus at about six feet. Do you follow me?"

"Sure, sure," Odin said, not really listening. He held his hand up and looked at it.

"You probably won't have many problems at any distance," Keene was saying. "It's the close-up work that will take getting used to. Like threading a needle."

"I can live without sewing," Odin said. "What about shooting?"

"Well, you probably only used one eye to shoot anyway. Try sighting down an imaginary gun."

Odin did. Everything was blurry.

"Shit! I used my right eye."

"You can relearn. Not that it's that necessary. You won't be a police officer any more. You'll be retired with a full pension, I understand."

"I still have to shoot."

"Target shooting?"

"You might say that."

"You better rest for now. A counselor will come by to describe the service organizations available. A few more days and we'll boot you out of here."

"Thanks, doc. For everything."

Keene nodded and walked out.

Odin lay back and shut his eyes. He'd rest for a few hours, then check himself out. The longer he lay in bed, the colder Mokley's trail got.

Target shooting. Odin smiled. He envisioned Mokley's face on a police silhouette target. Boom. Boom. Boom. His shots blasted out the paper heart.

PART TWO

7 As Vic Polanski rode the elevator to Nicky Provenzano's penthouse office, he wondered what was up. Something obviously too important to discuss at the union office. Polanski's title was organizer. He did about three hours union work every week.

Polanski had worn his best eight-hundred-dollar suit. It was impossible for him to get anything off the rack, even at tall men's shops. Polanski was six feet, three inches, and close to three hundred pounds. Very little of his bulk was fat.

He had always been big. Twelve pounds at birth. Six foot by the end of junior high school on Chicago's south side. His size had been a curse. Though his IQ had initially tested out at over 125, he was always treated as a big, dumb Polack. Soon he came to accept the role.

In high school, he'd broken a kid's jaw during a school-yard disagreement over whether the Cubs would ever win a pennant. The kid's father was a police captain. Vic had been arrested and worked over by the father and his buddies. He still had several scars from that beating. The scars only added to his brutish image. Polanski had taken the beating with stoic resignation. Word of the incident reached "Mad Dog" DeLeo, an underboss in "Momo" Giancana's crime family. Polanski was given a job as a collector. By age twenty he was making more than his father—a cattle herder—did after twenty-five years in the stockyards.

He had no compunctions about breaking bones for his bosses. If you ain't gonna pay, you better not play. Mad Dog, later Sonny Bones, and now Nicky Pro, had all been very good to him. They treated him with dignity, recognized his abilities, and respected the fact that he wasn't just another dumb muscleman.

Polanski adjusted his tie, studying his reflection in the smoked mirror finish of the elevator. He liked wearing fine clothes. It made him feel less like a goon.

"So you want me to bird-dog this Mokley punk?" Polanski asked. "No problem."

"One other thing, Vic," Pro said leaning back in his chair. He put his feet up on the cluttered desk. Pro had several legitimate companies, as well as the union business. There was little to link him to various loan-sharking, book-making, and extortion rackets. A few coded entries in his computer were all he needed. That, and a swarm of lawyers who kept his paperwork in their office safes.

"You ever meet Joe Terranova?" Provenzano asked.

Polanski frowned. "Yeah."

"I want you to work with him on this."

"I never needed a partner in the past."

Provenzano leaned forward and spoke softly. "You just turned thirty-eight, right?"

"Right. I appreciated your present. My wife put the painting in a place of honor."

"I'll have to come by and see it some time."

Polanski nodded. He'd better have notice. That would give him a chance to get the horrible thing out of the garage. Polanski's wife—who had graduated college, he would point out proudly—had pronounced it a piece of "nouveau riche tasteless crapola."

"You don't want to have to retire so young, correct?" Without waiting for an answer, Provenzano continued. "You could be a good influence on Joey. He's too quick with his hands."

"I thought he was still in the joint."

"He just got out a month ago. Maybe some of your polish will rub off on him. His heart's in the right place."

Joe Terranova's a jerk, Polanski thought, but he didn't say it. He'd met Terranova a couple of times. An arrogant creep who liked to pick fights. "Okay," Polanski said reluctantly.

"I knew you'd see it right," Pro said, standing up and shaking Provenzano's hand. "There's a guy works over in the garment center. He was one of the last to see Mokley before he split. He also owes me two gees. Get some info, or the bucks. *Cappeesh?*"

"Sure."

"Here's the address," Provenzano said, handing the big man a slip of paper.

Polanski committed it to memory, then shredded the paper. Pro appreciated his caution.

"Where's Terranova?" Polanski asked.

Pro went over to the wall and tugged at a recessed panel. A door opened to a service corridor. Joe Terranova was leaning against the cinder-block wall. He was dressed in a close-cut suit, his black hair brushed back.

A hidden passageway in a skyscraper. Typical guinea intrigue, Polanski thought. His contempt for the Machiavellian antics of his bosses had never been expressed. Which was why he was a respected enforcer instead of fish food.

Joe Terranova strutted in. He wanted to make a good impression with Nicky Provenzano. He also knew he had been kept waiting in a hallway for fifteen minutes.

Terranova sat on the leather couch and leaned back. Casual

and confident. He glanced over at Polanski and gave him a nod and a grunt. The big dumb Polack nodded back.

Polanski kept the sneer off his face. Terranova looked like a second-rate Vegas lounge act. All style and no substance. It was hard to believe the creep had three clean hits under his belt. And two more rumored.

Terranova, a troublemaker from his earliest childhood, had been reared in foster homes. He had learned early on that the way to survive was to hit first. It didn't take great ability to win most street fights. Smack a guy in the head and while he's dazed, finish him off. It didn't take a marksman to be a hit man, just a willingness to pull the trigger.

His ten-page rap sheet never showed any arrests for hits. All his encounters with the law stemmed from random incidents of violence, like the time he took a baseball bat to the car of someone who cut him off in traffic. Several of his offenses involved sex crimes. The court-appointed psychiatrist said Terranova blamed his mother for abandoning him.

Twenty-two out of Terranova's thirty-five years had been spent in the custody of one government agency or another.

Polanski drove and Terranova talked on the ride downtown. Terranova boasted about chicks he had boffed, screwed, fucked, did, balled, reamed, rammed, played hide-the-salami with, shtupped, slammed, diddled, pronged.

Polanski worried about traffic, and if there was some ulterior motive for his being paired with Terranova. Perhaps Pro had decided to have Polanski killed. It was a perfect setup. But there was no reason to have him killed, Vic decided. He hadn't stolen money, snitched, or had sex with Provenzano's wife. Of course he wasn't a Sicilian, so they might whack him for any imagined reason. But he knew he was enough of an asset to Provenzano that the union leader would think twice before ordering a hit.

Terranova figured that the Polack was really dumb. He just

grunted along at Terranova's best stories. Maybe the big goon was a fag. Ever since he'd been assaulted in prison, Terranova had been an ardent fag hater. He'd shanked two of the cons who'd trapped him in the shower room. After that, no one had bothered him. He'd gotten two years added on his sentence but gained respect. And he got lucky. His actions had impressed a shylock in Nicky Pro's crew who was doing time in a neighboring cell block.

"Let me do the talking," Terranova commanded as they approached the door to Tomorrow's Fashions.

Polanski nodded. Let the creep hang himself. I'll be damned if I'll stop him.

Tomorrow's Fashions was located on the top floor of a five-story building on San Pedro Street. The building had a shabby exterior but the inside had been gutted and completely redone like a turn-of-the-century office building. Oak-veneered wainscotting, smoked glass panels set in hollow-core doors, pseudoantique tile. The refurbishing would wear down within a few years but for now it looked great.

Terranova breezed in. A classy blond receptionist glanced up and offered a meaningless smile. "May I help you?"

"Where's Willie?" Terranova asked.

"He's tied up at the moment," she said. "May I tell him who's calling?"

"I'll surprise him," Terranova said. He moved towards the door at the back end of the office.

"You can't go in there," she said.

She hurried around the desk and stood in front of Terranova. He grinned, grabbed her, and shoved her away. Polanski caught her before she fell. He lifted the receptionist effortlessly and sat her back in her chair.

"We just need to talk to Willie," he said. "If you do anything stupid, like call the cops, someone will get hurt." He picked up a picture of two children from her desk. "Cute kids. They yours?"

She nodded without thinking.

He took the picture and put it in his pocket. "No one gets hurt."

Terranova was already through the door, into Willie's office. Willie was working at a drafting table. When the door had first opened, he'd scrambled to cover up his designs for the following season. Willie was a short man with broad shoulders, who obviously spent considerable time at the gym. "Who are you?" he demanded shrilly.

"I ask the fucking questions, shithead," Terranova said. He grabbed Willie by the lapels of his oversize silk designer jacket. "Where's Gary Mokley?"

"Who?"

Terranova backhanded him.

"Once again. Mokley."

Polanski never would have started off an interrogation like that. A few simple questions. Usually his size and a scowl was enough to get most people to open up. He watched with interest to see if Terranova was effective.

"I haven't seen him in a while. I heard he was out of the city."

"Not good enough, faggot," Terranova said. "Where is he?"

"I don't know. Honest."

Polanski believed him. He was about to say something, when Joe took out a switchblade knife and clicked it open. "How'd you like your own dick in your mouth?"

As he lowered the blade towards Willie's groin, the designer yelled and slapped Terranova. Thousands of reps on the Nautilus machine paid off. The blow sent Joe staggering back.

Polanski closed in, but Willie sprinted out the door, past his receptionist, and into the work area. Vic and Joe were hard on his heels.

The work area was a twenty-by-thirty foot room, filled with

sewing machines, cutting machines, and Filipino, Chinese, and Mexican women working them. At first the women thought it was a raid from Immigration. Then they saw their boss was being chased by two goons.

Willie gave them off holidays, never demanded sexual favors, and paid them a few cents an hour better than minimum wage. Good years, he even gave small Christmas bonuses. He was considered a prince among men compared to most garment center bosses.

As Willie sprinted towards the back, a seamstress rose, waving her big scissors and shouting at Vic and Joe in Tagalog. Another rose and began a tirade in Spanish. A third joined in with Chinese.

When Vic and Joe pursued Willie down an aisle, a hefty Mexican woman blocked their way. Joe shoved her. The yelling got angrier. Two dozen women with large scissors advanced on the enforcers.

Joe drew his gun. Vic grabbed it out of his hand.

"Let's go," Polanski said.

"He ain't getting away from me so easy."

"Let's go," Polanski said.

"That fuck ain't getting away from me so easy."

"Let's go," Polanski repeated.

"I'll burn the place down, and every chink-spic cunt in it."

Polanski grabbed Joe, spun him around, and dragged him out fuming.

The stocky Hispanic orderly effortlessly eased Odin into the wheelchair. The ex-cop wanted to walk but the aide insisted it was hospital policy. Odin was too weak to argue.

Odin wore regular clothing, loose-fitting since he had lost several pounds. He had a light bandage on the side of his face and a black patch over his left eye.

"You that cop, right?" the orderly asked as he wheeled Odin down the hall.

"Yeah."

"Man, life's a fucking bitch, ain't it?"

"Yeah."

Odin was thrilled to be leaving. There had been times when he thought he'd spend the rest of his life in the hospital bed. The thought of revenge nourished him.

Now he was on his way to the outside world. But he felt so weak. Part of it, he knew, was the painkillers. The drugs didn't really kill the pain, just made him indifferent to it.

They reached the elevator. The door opened and Assistant Chief Fleming, in full uniform, got out.

"I was just coming to get you," Fleming said.

"That's okay. You've done a helluva lot already. I wanted to thank you."

"I have my driver downstairs," Fleming said, patting his shoulder. "I'll give you a lift to your place."

The assistant chief nudged the orderly out of the way without saying a word. Fleming nearly toppled the wheelchair as he rolled it into the elevator.

"I appreciate all you've done," Odin said. He felt awkward. He had never been a fan of the assistant chief, and now he clearly owed him.

"Think nothing of it," Fleming said. He winked. "We take care of our own, right? Which reminds me, what do you plan on doing?"

"Finding Mokley."

"That's police business."

"It's my business."

"Bobby, I advise you not to push this. I know a lot of people in the private sector. I can set you up in a nice job. You'll make more than you did as a cop."

"After I find Mokley."

"Let the department handle that. I spoke to your doctor. He said you shouldn't do anything more strenuous than watch TV for a couple of weeks. I give you my word, we'll get Mokley."

A doctor got into the elevator and did a mild double take at seeing the distinguished-looking assistant chief in uniform, pushing the wheelchair.

"I was planning on saying good-bye to this nurse," Odin said.

"I'm on a tight schedule," Fleming said. "You'll have to give her a call. You'll have plenty of time."

Odin was about to protest when the door opened and the TV lights shone in his face.

"Bob, what do you have to say?" a TV reporter asked. "How're you doing?" There was a rush of questions.

"Now, now, Bob's not up to a hallway press conference," Fleming said smoothly.

"C'mon Bob, we need a sound bite."

"I'm feeling better. Not yet ready for the Olympics."

"Chief, what about the suspect?" a reporter asked.

"We're working as hard as we can," he said. "We have several promising leads. That's all, I have to get Bob home. He needs his beauty sleep."

There were a few more questions shouted at them as Fleming wheeled Odin to the car. The driver helped him into the gleaming Pontiac.

"I wonder how they knew exactly when I was leaving?" Odin asked.

Fleming chuckled. "I meant what I said, Bob. Give me a call when you want to go job hunting. And don't go after Mokley."

"With all due respect sir, I can't promise that." Odin felt bad defying the assistant chief. He was used to obeying his superiors. The thought that he was no longer part of a rigidly structured organization flashed through his mind, but he couldn't really comprehend it.

Odin watched the streets roll by as the driver took them towards his apartment. The wounded ex-cop felt like someone just let out of prison.

At the apartment, the good-byes were brief.

As his driver helped Odin up the stairs, Fleming tried to review overdue personnel reports. But he couldn't concentrate. He was nearly as obsessed with Mokley as Odin.

8 It felt good to be home. Hell, it felt great. At least as great as it could feel after three weeks in the hospital. Odin's apartment reflected his Spartan lifestyle. The bare minimum of furnishings, with the living room dominated by a rowing machine. The furniture was from Sears. The only decoration on the wall was a laminated newspaper photo of him guiding a hostage out while tear gas billowed around them. He'd won a medal of valor, the department's highest honor, for that action. The photographer had won a Los Angeles Press Club award for the photo. The hostage had had a nervous breakdown shortly after the rescue.

The medal of valor, along with a few others he had picked up in Vietnam, including a Purple Heart, a Distinguished Service Cross, and a Navy Star, were in a cigar box in his night table.

He walked to the kitchen, reached for the refrigerator handle, and missed it by an inch. He got it the third time. Odin gulped down a beer, then cleaned out the foul-smelling refrigerator. Green, blue, and orange fungus spots had already grown on the little food he kept there.

Walking to the couch, he rapped his shin on the coffee table, cursed, and kicked the table. It fell over. A glass he'd left on top of it shattered. He kicked the fallen table again, hurting his foot. The ex-cop cursed some more.

He flopped onto the couch and looked around the apartment. Not much to see. Odin leaned back on the sofa and sighed.

Fifteen minutes later, he woke up. He forced himself to do push-ups. After fifteen, he collapsed on the floor. Nose pressed to the carpet, which sorely needed vacuuming. He cursed some more.

Before the incident, he had been able to knock out a hundred

Marine-style push-ups, clapping between each one, without working up much of a sweat. He could run three miles, on uneven terrain, in eighteen minutes. Now, walking up the stairs to his second-floor apartment had been an odyssey. He had mis-stepped several times. If Fleming's driver hadn't been helping him, he probably would have fallen down the stairs from clumsiness and fatigue.

He rolled over and did fifty sit-ups. He was panting when he stopped. He lay back on the floor and stared up at the sprayed ceiling. He noticed a water stain he had never seen before, although he had lived in the apartment for more than three years. Ever since he and his ex-wife had split up. An amicable parting, if divorces can ever be called that.

After her hairstyling salon had failed she had decided she wanted a child. He didn't. He didn't want to make himself vulnerable by having a child to worry about. What he saw every day had convinced him not to bring anyone else into the world. Irreconcilable differences.

After they split up, he hadn't dated much. A few one-night stands. A couple of relationships that looked promising but failed. It came down to that he didn't mind being alone. At least not enough to get married again.

He thought about what had happened with Bobbin' Robin. That was a first. Was it a freak incident, or a sign of things to come? In how many ways had he been hurt?

He fished the jar of painkillers from his pocket and tossed it toward the trash can. He missed by a foot. He got up and slammed them inside the can. He wouldn't need the pills. He could live with the pain, use it as a prod to keep himself going.

The apartment smelled sour. Stuffy. He vacuumed, did a wash, and microwaved a TV dinner. As he did the simple chores, his mind kept seeing Mokley. What was the dope dealer doing at that moment?

His efforts exhausted him. He dozed off while watching the ten o'clock news. He was asleep before the one-minute segment showing him being wheeled down the corridor by Assistant Chief Fleming. The reporter described Odin as being in good spirits.

"You look like shit," former LAPD sergeant Dave Palermo said to Odin.

"Thanks for the kind words," Odin responded.

Palermo had retired after getting injured in a shoot-out with a bank robber. He had opened a shooting range off Sunset Boulevard not far from the police academy. It was favored by officers who wanted to make sure they could pass the biannual LAPD accuracy qualifications tests.

Odin had been a champion shooter and spent many hours popping off rounds. There was a genuine rapport and respect between the two ex-cops.

Midday and there was no one else in the range. A fifteen-position facility, with stark gray cinder-block walls. Palermo got him a stack of targets.

"I know how it is when you leave the job," Palermo said in his raspy voice as he handed him protective shooting glasses and ear covers.

Odin put them on and moved into position on the line. He clipped a target onto the wire and sent it out about ten feet. Most real shoot-outs were much closer and in much lower light conditions than most ranges provided.

Odin switched to the police combat stance and fired off all fourteen shots in his Asp. It was a customized Smith and Wesson 9-mm parabellum that had been cut down and fine-tuned by Armament Systems and Procedures, Inc. The gun was smaller, easier to handle, and had a more sensitive trigger than it had when it had left the S & W factory. The weapon felt great in his hands, a pound and a half of finely machined metal with custom wood grips.

He reeled the target in. Two in the head, three in the chest, eleven off the target. He did it again, and again, and again. The concentration and tension of holding his arm still was draining. He leaned against the shelf at the front of the booth.

Palermo came behind him and tapped his shoulder. Odin jumped.

"You okay?" Palermo said.

"Just taking a break." He pulled the target in. All were in the upper chest, a little high.

Palermo eyed the target. "You're breaking your wrist up," the range owner said, mimicking a masturbating motion.

"They're tightly grouped," Odin said defensively.

"You can do better," Palermo said.

Odin fired another clip, taking Palermo's advice. Dead center, the way cops were taught. Forget about shooting the gun out of the hand or head shots. Go for the biggest body mass and hope for the best.

"Can you dim the light a bit?" Odin asked.

Palermo did. Odin squinted. Damn. He could barely make out the target. He fired instinctively, emptying the clip, then pulled the target in.

Half were in the shoulder, the rest just missing it. They were nicely grouped but wouldn't have stopped an assailant.

He put a fresh clip in the 9 mm and did it again.

After he had been there for more than an hour, the range began to fill. Odin was exhausted. His gun hand shook. But at least he felt he could hit a target. Most of the time.

"You didn't try any distance shooting," Palermo said, as Odin returned the goggles and ear protectors.

"I'm afraid of what I'd find out," Odin said.

"I'm open late Sundays. Not too much business. It gets kind of lonely here."

"I'll take you up on that. Thanks. What do I owe?" He reached for his wallet.

"Your money ain't good here. Us former protectors and servers got to stick together."

* * *

Odin felt drawn to the nearby Police Academy, in Elysian Park, about ten minutes from downtown LA. On the hilly streets, baton-toting recruits in blue shorts and white shirts ran chanting under the watchful eyes of instructors. The palms provided little shade. On mats under the hot sun, recruits practiced hand-to-hand combat. In classrooms, several named after Jack Webb, a major contributor to the LAPD, they learned the law. After six months they were supposed to be ready for the mean streets.

The ex-cop wandered the grounds of the academy, listening to the crack of pistol shots on the range, the cadence chanting of recruits, the bellowing of instructors. It was almost like a military base and he'd always felt at home there. Even though he hadn't formally retired, now it was different. He was an outsider.

He headed back toward the parking lot. He wanted to slip away without encountering anyone he knew. SWAT had citywide jurisdiction and he had been involved in sieges in every division. He knew cops from all over the city. He didn't feel like talking to anyone.

"What are you doing here?" He recognized the nasal voice. Werner Greene, a motorcycle cop who had applied for Metro the same time as Odin. Odin had been accepted, Greene rejected. Odin never did find out why. But the burly cop, who had been almost a friend, turned nasty.

"Just getting some air," Odin said.

"I heard what happened. Too bad," Greene said.

"Yeah."

"Finch and Daggett buying it, you winding up a cripple," Greene said. "I'm surprised a whiz-bang like you walked into a booby trap like that."

"We all have our off days," Odin said. "I bet sometimes you don't even make your quota of tickets."

"Yeah, too bad," Greene said, and strutted away.

"He's such an asshole," a man said.

Odin turned. Coming out of the academy restaurant were two young cops. Odin recognized them from the Hollywood division but couldn't recall their names. That division covered the area where Mokley had lived.

The cops saw that Odin didn't recall their names and introduced themselves. Haft was a gangly Okie with a big Adam's apple. Herrera was a stocky Mexican who managed to look exceedingly dapper in his uniform.

They made small talk for a couple of minutes. Haft told a story about how Greene had been assigned to lead a funeral procession and wound up getting in a fistfight with a drunken grave digger. The two men had slugged it out in an open grave. It had been raining and they looked like a couple of female mudwrestlers by the time they were pulled apart.

Odin waited until a lull and asked, "What can you tell me about Mokley? You ever have any calls out to his place or know anyone who did?"

"It came up at roll call," Herrera said. "Mokley used to hang with a half dozen scumbags at this place over in Van Nuys. The cops there rousted them a couple of times, but no word on Mokley."

"Do you remember the address?"

"Maybe we shouldn't be telling you this," Haft said. "Why do you want to know?"

"Just curious. Anything else about Mokley?"

"A couple years ago, we had a call of a domestic dispute out there," Herrera said. Haft gave him a dirty look, but Herrera kept on talking. "His wife. Now his ex-wife."

"Was he arrested?"

"He was the victim. She was slapping him around."

"We better get going," Haft said.

"She still around?" Odin asked.

"Moved to Venice a couple years ago," Herrera said.

"C'mon," Haft said. He had already walked a few feet away. "Any address?"

Herrera shrugged. "I'll see."

As he and his partner walked away, Odin heard Haft saying, "He ain't on the job any more. We'll get in trouble."

"What if it happened to you?"

Haft's reply was lost as the two men got into their black and white.

Odin drove back to his apartment and sagged into the couch. He dozed off. It was amazing how much sleep he needed. He felt tired all the time. Not the kind of healthy tired he used to get after a few hours in the gym. But a kind of postflu sleepiness, an overall weakness and malaise that could become depression if he lowered his guard.

9 "This is Lieutenant Dawson in the Chief's office," Odin bellowed into the mouthpiece of the pay telephone. "Who am I talking to?"

"PAA Banks, sir."

Odin was pleased. A police administrative aide would be easier to bulldoze than a cop. He was glad it was still the lunch hour.

"Right. What's going on with the Mokley case?"

"That's over in North Hollywood division, sir. I can give you the number."

"I don't need the number, young man. I know full well where the incident occurred. What did you say your name was?"

"Banks."

"And your first name?"

"Michael."

"Okay, Banks. I understand that the suspect in that case has a few known associates in your division. And that action has been taken to interview them. I want names and addresses. Right now!"

"Yes sir," Banks said crisply. "I'll go check the file. I'll call you right back."

"No time for that. I'll hang on. Get cracking."

A couple of minutes passed. The operator came on and demanded money. Odin quickly dumped coins into the slot, seconds before Banks got back on.

"Sir, I have an address but no names."

"What's the address?"

"Two-five-six-five Friar Street."

"I'll see what I can do with that. Good work, Banks."

"Thank you, sir."

Odin walked back to his car. He got behind the wheel, checked that his gun was loaded, and drove off.

It was a typical Southern California garden apartment complex. From the outside, it looked like a second-rate motel. It had a name, "The Imperial Chateau," and the developer had spent a few hundred dollars on suitable decor—a crenelated fringe on the front roof and a two-foot-high metal figure of a knight in armor. The knight was tarnished and had a busted lance.

There was a three-foot-high brick wall enclosing a small, decaying garden. The only things that seemed to be thriving in the garden were discarded beer cans and wine bottles. On the brick wall were graffitied a half dozen names—Killer, Disco, Pepita, Mad Dog, Homicide, Wings.

Through an archway, and a broken metal security gate, Odin could see four men in their midtwenties lounging around. They were seated by the side of the small pool that was at the center of the courtyard. Can't live in Southern California if you don't have a pool. Only this one held scummy green water and looked fit only for breeding mosquitos and algae.

Odin parked his car up the block from the building, in front of a deserted park, and walked back to the gate. It was rusting on its hinges and made an Addams family squeak when he pushed it open. The four toughs stopped talking and looked up. They resumed their conversation but kept wary eyes on Odin as he casually gazed around the interior.

There was garbage strewn in stairways—an abandoned dishwasher here, a pile of chicken bones there—and more graffiti, as well as peeling paint and cracks in the concrete. Fully half the windows were boarded up. There was the smell of urine, spilled beer, and the unidentifiable microbes thriving in the pool.

A tough with greasy black hair in a pompadour was talking about a cock fight he had been at the night before. Another switched on a big ghetto blaster. Salsa music echoed off the walls of the compound. Pompadour continued his tale.

Odin walked up the three short steps to the pool area. He stumbled on the last step. The toughs laughed.

As he approached, they pretended not to see him.

"I'm looking for Gary Mokley," Odin said.

"I say the fight was fixed, man, and the next thing these dudes is throwing me out the door," Pompadour was saying.

A stocky man missing a few teeth in the front of his mouth turned on Odin. "You're lost, *maricon*." He looked like a bar fighter, with squinty eyes buried in a scarred face. He'd be the one to watch in a scuffle, Odin decided.

Radio was skinny, all nervous gestures. The fourth man was the kind of doe-eyed baby face who would either run from a slap or be a psychopath.

"You interrupted my story," Pompadour said. "Get the fuck outta here." He stepped up to Odin and shoved him.

Odin was not used to that sort of response. He realized what an unthreatening figure he was. Pale, ten pounds under his fighting weight, his eye bandaged.

"Where's Mokley?" he repeated, trying to keep a command presence in his tone.

"You don't hear so good, do you?" Pompadour started bobbing up and down to the music. "What happened to your eye? Someone poke it out with his dick?"

"I'm gonna ask you one more time, where's Mokley?"

"The pigs been around asking about him already," Radio said. "We told them nothing. We ain't even gonna tell you that."

The bar fighter had uncoiled himself from the lounge chair he'd been sitting in. He was casually drifting behind Odin. The blasting music made it impossible to hear his movements. Odin had to shift position to keep him in sight.

Part of Odin's injury was a loss of twenty-five degrees on his field of vision. He was lucky that he had a small nose. The larger the nose, the more lost, up to about forty degrees out of the normal 180-degree field. He kept making small movements with his head to take in a full field. They looked like a mild nervous tic.

"Who the fuck are you man?" Baby Face demanded.

"I know him. I seen him on TV," Radio said proudly. "He's the cop that got blowed up over at Gary's place."

"Yeah. Yeah," Pompadour said. "Man, that's a bogus deal. Totally bogus."

"Why?" Odin asked.

"You fucking know," Bar Fighter said.

"If I knew, I wouldn't be asking."

"Fucking frame up," Bar Fighter said. "Get outta here, piggy."

"He ain't a pig anymore," Pompadour said. He reached to flick Odin's patch. Odin stepped back.

"You lose your eye, you can't be no cop," Pompadour said. "You can only be a cop if you lose your mind."

The toughs laughed.

"He still smells like a pig to me," Pompadour said.

"Oink, oink," Baby Face said.

"Oink, oink," Bar Fighter said.

Radio made grunting and rooting noises.

"Oink, oink, oink," Pompadour said. "What's your name little piggy?"

Odin saw Bar Fighter's nostrils flare, and Pompadour reached for Odin's lapel.

The ex-cop stepped aside from Pompadour's reach and grabbed his arm. He moved in closer, simultaneously drawing his automatic. He shoved the gun in Pompadour's ear.

"Hey, cool it, cool it," Radio said.

"You fucking cool it," Odin growled. "Where's Mokley?"

"Don't know," Pompadour said. "We ain't seen him in weeks."

"Where would he go to lay low?"

The only sound was the music. Odin ground the gun in deeper. His arm was wrapped tightly around Pompadour's throat.

"Maybe Venice, his old lady lives there," Pompadour said.

"Where?"

"Above an ice cream store. On Washington. Near the beach."

"What business did you do with Mokley?"

"Nothing. Just friends."

Odin jerked his arm tighter on Pompadour's neck.

Someone grabbed his gun hand and smashed a fist into his kidneys. Radiating waves of pain spread across his back. As he was twisted around, he saw a grinning Baby Face, trying to wrench the gun from his hand.

Odin held onto it, his only hope as the four toughs closed in on him. Their getting in each other's way, and the bulletproof vest he had worn, kept him from being beaten to death.

He was punched and kicked, handicapped by his weakness, and trying to hang onto the gun. He managed to squeeze the trigger. The bullet flew off into the air. A moment's respite. He swung the gun, catching Baby Face on the side of the head. The young man yowled and fell back.

Bar Fighter kicked him in the gut. Even with the bulletproof vest, the blow nearly knocked the wind from him. Odin squeezed the trigger again. Radio screamed. The bullet missed him, but he was burned by the muzzle blast.

Baby Face bit down on Odin's hand and jerked the gun from him.

Pompadour and Bar Fighter stepped back. Baby Face fired from a few feet away. The bullet caught Odin in the chest, ripping his windbreaker, and baring the bulletproof vest. The blow knocked him back, staggering, rattling his still healing internal organs. He tasted blood in the back of his mouth.

Baby Face realized his error. He lifted the gun and aimed at Odin's face. The ex-cop didn't have the strength to throw himself forward. He had no chance against the four toughs.

He spun and dove into the fetid pool as a shot cracked over his head.

The layer of slimy green on top parted and down he went. The pool was only three feet deep at the shallow end, but the scum on the surface gave him cover.

A shot parted the waters, missing him by two feet. He thought of the laws of refraction in water, information from his days as a SEAL. His chest pounded from the force of the bullet. He couldn't hold his breath very long. He swam underwater to the other side and tried to surface. The bullet proof vest was like lead weights around his torso. He had to put his feet down on the bottom and push up. He gulped air and dove down again.

A bullet skimmed across the surface where he had just been.

How long could he keep this up? How many shots had been fired?

He stayed underwater as long as he could, then surfaced again.

No shot. Had that been a siren? He strained to hear the noise underwater. There was a strange whining noise. But he couldn't decide if it was in his head. He was dizzy. Unable to tell up from down. Watch the bubbles. He blew out air, and tried to follow it up. The vest made him too heavy.

He tried to kick off from the bottom, but he was at the deep end. Eight feet. He flailed his legs, but couldn't get up. His chest felt like it was going to explode. He fought the urge to inhale underwater. Just one breath.

He swallowed a little water. It was slimy, disgusting. He coughed, and swallowed. The pain of his coughs made him even weaker. He let himself sink to the bottom. His feet touched the floor and he kicked off with all his strength. He continued to flutter his legs.

He broke the surface. Air. Too far to reach the side of the pool. Down again. And up.

It had been a siren. The toughs were gone. He touched bottom, and moved over towards the side of the pool. Kicked off again. Reached the side. Dragged himself up and out.

It required every ounce of strength to haul himself out. He gasped for air. The sirens in the distance were getting louder.

Code Three. Shots fired. His brothers in blue.

But they weren't his brothers any more. There would be all sorts of explanations.

He dragged himself, gasping and retching from the fetid water he'd swallowed. He staggered out of the building. He reached his car, but was too weak to drive, too weak to open the door.

Odin crawled through a gap in the wire fence around the park and found a clump of dense laurel sumac bushes. He fell under a bush and threw up. He crawled away from his mess then curled into a fetal position.

The ex-cop lay silent and motionless as the sirens reached a crescendo and two police cars zoomed up from opposite directions. He heard doors slam, a few words exchanged, the squeaking gate.

He breathed in and out, the air hot and dry in his lungs. His mouth felt coated with the pool slime.

A few minutes passed. His breathing returned to almost normal. He heard the cops' voices again. Doors slammed. Black and whites pulled away. Reports of shots fired could mean anything. A backfire. Fireworks. Someone celebrating. No body, no foul. Code Seven, time for lunch.

He got up. The dirt had stuck to his wet clothing. He looked like a scuzzy bum. He dragged himself to his car.

A passing woman with a shopping cart looked at him, disgust clear on her face.

Odin fumbled with the key. He couldn't get it into the lock. "Excuse me, miss, could you . . ."

She hurried away.

He leaned against the car and finally got the lock opened. He fell into the seat, breathed deeply for a few moments. He had to get out of the area. The cops would be giving it more attention.

Odin started the engine and drove home. Twice he had to stop along the way when he got too woozy to focus on the road.

10 After a long hot shower, repeatedly rinsing his mouth with mouthwash and wiping his wounds with antiseptic, Odin stood before the mirror in his bathroom and studied himself. Not a pretty sight. His skin was sallow, his flesh soft, the definition of his muscles gone. There was an ugly mass of scar tissue next to his right eye. The eye itself had a peculiar, unfocused look.

On the cheek under his left eye was a red splotch. He didn't recall being hit there. What if the blow had caught his good eye? The thought made him shiver.

His retirement courtesy badge was gone. So was his gun. So too, if the incident in the hospital was any indication, was his manhood.

He shambled to the bedroom, lay down and stared at the ceiling. Each time he thought he'd sunk as low as he could, he found a new level of depression.

He could give up, take the job Fleming offered. Mokley would disappear, or maybe be caught by police. It wouldn't be Odin's problem. He'd be a security guard somewhere, stopping kids from stealing tee shirts from K Mart. If they'd hire a guard with one eye.

Or he could continue to pursue Mokley. Quite possibly get himself killed. The power of the department was gone. He'd had minimal training as an investigator. Most of his prowess—scaling walls, kicking in doors, sharpshooting—was physical, or at least it had been. Now he was lucky to swim his way out of a shallow pool.

It had been a rotten day for Vic Polanski and Joe Terranova. The two enforcers had been summoned to Nicky Provenzano's office early in the afternoon.

"You are a couple of idiots," Pro had said, enunciating each word. The four other wiseguys in the sumptuous office smirked. The office had been done up by a designer frequently cited in slick magazines. It showed a lot of class and Pro liked to tell people how much it cost.

"Joe, if it wasn't for who your father was, I'd throw you out right now," Pro growled. "The first fucking job I send you two jambonies out on, and you blow it. Jesus fucking H. Christ."

"But Mr. Provenzano—" Joe began.

"Idiots, fuckin' idiots," Pro interrupted. "You go to the garment district and nearly start a riot. Chased out by a bunch of old ladies with sewing machines."

The audience Provenzano had assembled laughed.

"Maybe it's best we don't work together," Polanski suggested.

"Don't flake out on me," Pro said.

"If the Polack hadn't interfered, I coulda handled it," Terranova said.

"By doing what?" Polanski blurted. "Shooting women."

"You wing one, they all back down," Joe said.

Polanski gave his boss a "see-what-I-mean" look but Pro didn't respond.

"You two work together or you won't work at all," Provenzano said. "Understand?"

Vic was smart enough to keep his mouth shut. Joe started to protest again but Provenzano cut him off. "I don't want to hear any excuses. This Mokley deal is an important piece of business. I trusted it to you."

"We'll find him, Mr. Pro," Vic said. "I apologize if we were too enthusiastic."

Pro nodded. "Get going."

In the car, Terranova said, "You sure kissed his ass."

"You ever have a gun that broke?" Polanski asked.

"Sure."

"What did you do with it?"

"I tried getting it fixed. But the guy couldn't do it."

"What did you do with the gun?"

"I threw it out."

"You know what we are to Nicky Pro?"

Terranova thought a minute. "Guns."

They'd stopped at a disco Mokley used to visit, at a bar he favored, and at a friend's address. Despite charm, threats, and offers of money, no one had seen Mokley, or had any idea where he might be.

"He had plenty of friends," the bartender said. "But no one who'd stick their neck out for him. He's kind of, a weasel, you know."

Joe and Vic wound up out in Venice, an unusual community even by Southern California standards. Developed to look like the Italian city it was named after, over the years the neighborhood had deteriorated, and the canals filled with garbage. Discovered by preyuppie yuppies, it had been massively gentrified, with elaborate redwood condos going up next to shambling slums.

Walking on the Speedway, Terranova's eyes were locked on

women in bikinis. He was nearly run over by a musclebound black skater.

"Watch it, nigger," Joe shouted at the skater, who flipped him the finger and zoomed on. Joe started to run after the skater but Vic stopped him.

"Fuckin' nigger," Joe muttered, loud enough for a half dozen gang kids to hear. Vic let his jacket gap open, just wide enough for the kids to see the .45 in his belt.

"Pigs," one of the gang kids said.

Polanski nodded and grabbed Joe's elbow. "Just what we need, to get in a fight while we're supposed to be finding this Mokley," Vic said.

"Why didn't that guy watch where he was going?"

"Why don't you concentrate on the job," Polanski said. "Look, there's the building."

A swinging wooden sign had a picture of *The Scream* by Edvard Munch and the words "I Scream For Ice Cream." A dozen or so sun bronzed and scantily clad bodies were lined up at the window. The enforcers walked around back and up a rickety wooden stairway that led to the second floor.

Polanski knocked on the door. "Police. Open up."

A scrawny man, barefoot, in torn jeans and paint-stained shirt, opened the door. "We already told you, we don't know anything."

Vic pushed past him. Joe gave him an unnecessary shove, nearly knocking the scrawny man down.

"Who is it, Jon-a-than?" a woman shouted from the back. She dragged out the three syllable name with a long whine.

"The police."

She came out of the back, fresh out of the shower, hair wet, wrapped in a towel. Her pleasant features were distorted into a scowl.

"I told you already, I hope to never see that bum again," she said. "Now get out."

Terranova reached out, grabbed the towel, and pulled it

away. She had a very nice body, a trifle on the meaty side. She gasped and tried to cover herself.

"Whoosh," Terranova said, then smacked his lips.

"Hey, you can't do that," Jonathan said. Joe backhanded him. The scrawny man stumbled back, crashing into a canvas on an easel. He and the painting fell to the ground.

"I'll report you," the former Mrs. Mokley said. "I want your names and badge numbers."

"We don't need no stinking badges," Vic said.

"Jon-a-than, did you get their badge numbers?" she asked.

"I, I didn't see any badges," Jonathan said, not daring to get up off the floor.

"Lemme take her in the bedroom and question her," Terranova, smacking his lips some more.

She grabbed a heavy brass lamp and held it like a club.

"I like a little spunk," Joe said, moving towards her.

"Be cool," Polanski said. "Lady, where's Mokley?"

"Like I said before, I don't know," she said. Terranova took another step towards her. The arm holding the lamp tensed. Her lip quivered.

"Please, leave us alone," Jonathan whined.

Polanski walked over to the man on the ground and jerked him up by his hair. He bent his arm behind his back and began pulling it up.

"Where is he?" Vic demanded.

"I don't know, I don't know," Jonathan said.

Virginia Mokley kept an eye on Joe, and was only half interested in the torture of her boyfriend. There was a cracking sound and Jonathan screamed. Vic dropped him to the floor.

The woman did nothing to comfort her boyfriend, who lay on the floor moaning. Joe stared at her, moving closer.

"Let's go," Vic said.

Joe reached out and bobbled one of Virginia's breasts. "I'll be back, sweet meat."

She slapped his hand away.

Terranova and Polanski backed out of the apartment and hurried down the stairs.

"I didn't think the little peckerhead would be so brittle," Polanski said.

"Did you see those tits?" Joe asked.

"I figure they'll be too scared to file a report with the cops," Vic said.

"I bet she's got a box smooth as silk."

"What do we tell Nicky Pro?"

"She was hot for me. Could you tell?"

Vic looked over at his partner. He was about to say something, but sighed and started the car.

The first time Odin called Jan Golden, she was making her rounds and couldn't come to the phone. The second time, she answered the phone at the nurses' station, but had to get off right away because of some crisis. The third time, he actually got to talk with her.

"I owe you dinner," he said.

"That's okay."

"I feel crummy about leaving without saying good-bye. The assistant chief had a whole dog and pony show arranged."

"I saw it."

"So how about dinner?"

"I'm working late."

"A late dinner."

"I've been thinking, it probably is best if we don't," Golden said.

"I've been thinking too. I'm really looking forward to seeing you. I—I'd like to talk to you."

"About what?"

"You'll have to meet me for dinner to find out."

There was silence on the line. "I work until eleven-thirty."

"A midnight snack then. I'll pick you up from the hospital."

"I'm usually late getting out. There's inevitably paper-work."

"I'll wait in the parking lot. You remember what I look like. The Hathaway Shirt man?"

"I do."

"See you later."

She hung up the phone.

"What are you smiling about?" asked Kathy, who was finishing a patient's chart.

"Was I smiling?" Golden asked, trying to wipe the grin away and not succeeding.

"Like we just got a raise."

"Involuntary motor response," Golden said. "I'd like to get out of here on time for once tonight."

"What's his name?" Kathy asked.

"Huh?"

"You're always the one to stay late, work weekends, do double shifts. All of a sudden a smile, an interest in the world outside the hospital walls. Is he cute?"

Golden frowned. "No. I mean, there's no one. I mean, it's just someone who needs help."

Kathy nodded. "Suit yourself."

A call light went on from a patient's room and Golden was glad to get away. But later, when she passed by a mirror, she noticed that she was indeed grinning.

11 Odin had had trouble coming up with a place that wasn't a cop hangout. The places he knew were either greasy spoons where he'd grab a quick bite, or joints where the bar was of more interest than the food served. And he didn't want to meet any of his former colleagues. Then he remem-

bered La Famille, a swank French eatery near Restaurant Row on the border of Beverly Hills.

The valet had a polished sneer as Odin pulled his 1973 Ford Mustang, with a half dozen dents and dings, into the lot.

"I thought we were just going out for a midnight snack," Golden said.

Odin smiled.

The maître d' also sneered. Although the restaurant was half empty, he said he couldn't seat Odin without a reservation. Then the owner saw them and bustled over. He gave Odin a peck on both cheeks, brushed the maître d' aside, and personally escorted them to a table.

"I—I expect to pay for half of this," Golden said. "And not happily."

"Half of nothing is nothing," Odin said, as a bottle of Chateau Lafite Rothschild 1957 was brought over. The sommelier showed the label, opened it, and offered Odin the cork to sniff. The cop, who had never drunk wine that cost more than three dollars a bottle, sniffed it, and nodded. The sommelier poured a half glass. Odin tasted it.

"Good stuff," he pronounced and the sommelier filled their glasses.

Odin lifted his glass. "Cheers."

She clinked glasses with him. "Are you a regular here?"

"LA cops aren't corrupt enough to afford this on a regular basis."

"Would you mind telling me why the red-carpet welcome then?"

"About a year ago, an ex-busboy came in with a sawed-off shotgun. Took hostages, including the owner. My squad was the one that resolved it."

"Killed him?"

"Talked him out. I was lead negotiator. The guy had had a hard life. His kid had just been run over by a car. Somehow he blamed his former boss for it."

"What happened to him?"

"He pled to a reduced charge. Assault or something. Wound up with a year in jail and counseling."

"That's nice. I mean, that you were able to resolve it without violence."

"Most of the time, we do. I mean, we did. I mean, they do."

Odin sipped his wine. She studied him, tenderness in her expression.

"What did you want to talk about?" she asked.

"I wanted to get the name of that martial arts place."

She took out a pencil and paper and wrote it down. "I could've given you this over the phone."

"I guess so."

More silence. The appetizer came.

"I wanted someone to talk to," he admitted.

"What about your police friends?"

"There's two kinds of people in the world. Cops. And civilians. I mean, don't get me wrong, Huey Nichols would cut off his arm for me. I'd do the same for him. But he wouldn't understand."

"Understand what?"

"I don't know. I don't understand it myself."

"Do you have a family?"

"No. You?"

"A sister who lives in Chicago. We kind of lost touch."

The salad came. They ate, occasionally smiling at each other for no particular reason.

"Food's good," he said.

"Yes. I wonder if this could be considered corruption?"

"Only if I promise him special treatment. Besides, I'm not a cop anymore. All I could do is call nine-one-one for him." The hard edge to his tone made her wince.

"What happened to your cheek?" Golden asked.

"Oh, this," Stark said, brushing his fingers across the sore spot under his good eye. I banged into something."

"Or someone."

"What makes you say that?"

"Being a nurse as long as I have, you can tell when someone's been in a car accident, or fallen down drunk, or been in a fight."

"Detective nurse," he said, and instantly regretted it. It sounded snide.

"I don't like being lied to," she said. "If you don't want to tell me how it happened, just say so."

"I went looking for Mokley."

"You shouldn't do that. You could get hurt."

"Thanks for the medical advice," he said.

She pursed her lip.

"Sorry for the sarcasm," he said.

"It was a dumb thing for me to say," she responded. "I sounded like someone's mother."

"That's not so bad."

They played with their food, and Golden commented how good it was. "Though I do feel a bit uncomfortable here."

"Why?"

"I'm not really dressed for it." She wore pale beige slacks and a blue pastel blouse.

"You look wonderful," he said.

"Thank you." Her face relaxed. Her big eyes were gentle, tender.

"I really hope you leave Mokley to the police," she said. "It's not your problem anymore."

He fingered the edge of the eyepatch. "An eye for an eye."

"You wouldn't gouge out one of his eyes, would you?" she asked.

"I was reading about the code of Hammurabi once. People think it's primitive revenge. Actually, it was quite liberal for the time. What it's saying is that if someone takes an eye, you don't kill them. You just take an eye."

"But two officers died because of Mokley."

"Can't kill a man twice."

"You would kill him?"

Odin finished his wine. The sommelier came with another bottle. Golden said nothing while they went through the opening ritual again. Odin sipped from a refilled glass.

"What would it take for you to kill someone?" Odin asked.

"I couldn't."

"If they were attacking you?"

"Maybe. If I knew it was my only way out."

"What if they were attacking a loved one of yours?"

"I'd like to change the subject. This really isn't very pleasant dinnertime conversation."

"You're right. How'd you first get into medicine?"

"My mother was a nurse. It always seemed like what I was going to do. And you?"

"I never planned on being a nurse."

After she laughed, he said, "I went into the Navy to get out of trouble. When I got out, the police department seemed the best place to go."

"What did you do in the Navy?"

"I was a SEAL."

"Huh?"

"That's like the Navy's Green Berets. Sea-Air-Land equals SEAL. Infiltration, neutralize the enemy, exfiltration. Lots of work with explosives. It's kind of ironic, after what happened to me."

"I feel funny being with you. Most of the men I've known were conscientious objectors. It sounds like you were really on the front line. Did you enjoy it?"

He finished the glass of wine, and refilled both of their glasses.

"I suppose I should say no. War is hell and all that. It wouldn't be true. There were times, when I was in the field with my squad and things were going just right, and, well, you couldn't understand it if you never felt it."

"Maybe I have."

He looked at her skeptically.

"Sometimes, when I work in OR or ER, when the team is functioning perfectly and we save a life, I feel a part of something bigger than myself."

"That's probably close to it. The difference is, your own life isn't in jeopardy. There's something about trusting your life to someone."

"There's another big difference. We aren't out there to kill people."

They ate and drank in silence. The more he looked at her, the more he wanted her. He wanted to take her and blot out the rest of the world, forget everything and everyone.

They started talking about their childhoods. She had grown up in a suburb of Chicago, her mother a nurse, her father the owner of a shoe store. It had been an uneventful childhood in a tightly repressed family. She couldn't recall her mother ever showing affection. Her father had died when she was young. Her mother never remarried. Golden grew up taking care of her younger sister.

Odin had been reared near Binghamton, New York. His father had been a carpenter, his mother a housewife. Odin had been a wild kid and his father had tried beating discipline into him. It hadn't worked. Arrested after a bar fight, the judge had offered him the chance to go to the military, or to jail. Odin's father was an Army man. Odin chose the Navy.

"Now you're a cop," she said. "Another irony."

"I guess. I think about all the fights I ever got into, it was always with bullies. You know, that's the first time I ever thought of that. I always figured it was my fault. But I never threw the first punch."

"You put yourself in a position though where a fight is inevitable, don't you?"

Dessert came, and he avoided answering.

"I shouldn't," she said, as the waiter put a strawberry short-cake in front of her. As she took a bite she got a drop of whipped cream on her nose. He reached over and wiped it away. The touch was electric.

Then he thought about what had happened in the hospital with Bobbin' Robin. He'd failed, even under her experienced touch. Could it happen again? The air went out of him like a slashed tire. What would Golden do, offer him pity? Maybe that's why she was with him now. How could he tell what that expression in her eyes really meant?

He dropped her off, dismissing her with a passionless good-bye kiss.

What did I do wrong? she wondered as she turned on the lights to her one-story wood-and-stucco house, located on the fringes of a bad area in West Los Angeles. One bedroom, with bars on the windows. A similar house two doors down had been sold for $250,000.

Her place was comfortable, well kept, but nothing glamorous. No chic art deco frills or deluxe video consoles. She had a small black-and-white TV, which she rarely watched anyway. When she wanted to relax, she'd read medical texts or magazines.

She kicked off her shoes, stripped off her clothes, and sprawled on the floor. She did stretching exercises. The meal felt heavy in her belly. She wasn't used to the rich food. Everything seemed to come in a butter sauce.

Where had the evening gone wrong? Not that she would have had him in. But he got cold, distant, somewhere around the dessert. It had been so long since she dated. Did she say or do something that put him off?

He needed her. He needed something to give him a new support system. She would do it for any patient, she told herself. Would she really, if he was a dumpy old man? She recalled the study that showed that attractive people got better medical care. It was disgraceful.

She wondered how he would be in bed, then pushed the thought from her mind. She took the latest copy of *Nursing Today* magazine, read until she was sleepy, and then shut the lights.

For the first time in a long time, she was aware of how big and empty her queen-size bed was.

12 Bagels hadn't gotten a decent night's sleep since the bomb went off in Mokley's place. He held himself responsible for the death of Finch and Daggett, and Odin's blinding. The narcotics sergeant's wife had tried warm milk, massages, and sex, but still the cop couldn't sleep.

Bagels full name was Robert Begelman. He'd gotten a lot of grief over his name during the David Begelman scandal. It wasn't easy being a Jew in the LAPD. Not like New York, where he'd come from, where the Shomrim Society, the Jewish fraternal police group, had a fair amount of clout. But Bagels had been put off by the accepted corruption in the NYPD, and moved to the land of blond surfers and relatively corruption-free police. He'd been happy with his job, until Mokley.

He'd been convinced that the small-fry dope dealer could be the first link in a major conspiracy case. Mokley had unusually high-quality dope when other dealers were dry, informants had said. Bagels had figured Mokley somehow was close to the mouth of the pipeline.

He'd pushed for the warrant, knowing that Mokley had skipped out and disappeared for two years before getting stopped by a traffic cop in Kansas City.

Begelman prided himself on being well prepared, knowing the suspect. And he couldn't figure out why there'd been a bomb on Mokley's door.

One sleepless night, staring out the window at his well-trimmed lawn, he'd decided the department wasn't putting enough pressure on the lowlifes. The best way to get the underworld to vomit up Mokley was to administer a few emetics.

The next day, he called Tatanya James into his office. She was new to narcotics, but previously she'd worked Seventy-seventh Division, one of the roughest station houses in the city.

James was barely five feet, four inches, a dark skinned black with a knockout body and a pleasant face. She had put up with the goosing and pats from her fellow officers when she first got to Seventy-seventh. One day a suspect had grabbed her buttocks. She had broken his hand in three places with her nightstick. After that, she was accepted as one of the boys and the uninvited fondling had stopped.

James hated dopers. She'd been the terror of Sherm Alley, the street where dealers vended PCP-laced cigarettes without fear. She spoke softly, and carried a big stick. Suspects who gave her trouble inevitably had "resisting arrest" added to their charges, as well as a free trip to Martin Luther King Hospital.

She came by her hatred of dopers honestly. One brother, two cousins, and a childhood boyfriend had all died from overdoses.

When Bagels called her in and outlined what he had in mind he knew what her answer would be.

"You understand what could happen," he said. "Not only in the bar, but we'll be violating all sorts of department rules."

"When do we do it?" she asked.

The Stardust had, for a while, been the hottest club in town. A warehouse turned disco, located in unchic Silver Lake, it was identifiable from blocks away by the limos and luxury autos outside. Private security guards patrolled the area or Blaupunkts would have disappeared faster than cocaine at a Hollywood party.

Mere mortals could dance in the huge outer room and hope

that a rock star or famous actor would choose to mingle. For the elite there was The Back Room, a luxurious private club that had floor-to-ceiling mirrors, a bar stocked with every exotic liquor imaginable, and furnishings designed by an interior decorator to the stars. Prostitutes, both male and female, and a wide variety of drugs were also available in the private club. Gary Mokley had been a frequent visitor to The Back Room.

The Stardust was owned by Kassim, a squat Syrian with untraceable access to cash, an ingratiating smile, and a waxed mustache. His last name was unknown, as was his history. He was rumored to be an ex-gun smuggler, a relative of a sheik, a former hashish dealer. He did nothing to debunk the myths.

After reports of widespread drug taking and drinking by minors, there had been harassment by the Alcoholic Beverage Control Commission, Health Department, Fire Department, Building Department, Police Department. Kassim had made corrections, and made peace. His sizable donations to the mayor and local politicians had changed their opinion of him.

It was a crowded Saturday night and, looking out through the peephole in his office, Kassim was very pleased. He snorted a spoonful of coke. With ten pounds sitting in his office safe, no one would notice the few grams he had taken out for personal use. He spotted a young man out on the dance floor in the main room. He was a sixteen-year-old runaway, a male hooker on Santa Monica Boulevard.

Kassim hit the buzzer. One of the bouncers—none were less than six feet, four inches—came in. Kassim had him look through the peephole at the boy.

"I want him," Kassim said.

The bouncer nodded and went out.

Tatanya James saw the bouncer lumbering towards her, his head a few inches above the crowd. She casually kept her hand on her bag. She wasn't carrying a gun, but she did have her handcuffs—half the crowd on Santa Monica Boulevard carried them.

The bouncer walked past, tapped a young man on the shoulder, whispered a few words, and nodded towards a door at the back of the room.

The young man and the bouncer moved off.

"What are you looking at?" asked the man who had quickly picked her up after one drink at the bar.

"Nothing," she said, yelling to be heard over the music. "Where's the action here?"

"How about back at my place," he said with a grin that exposed a gold star in a front tooth.

"I heard this place was the place for . . ." and she made a snorting gesture.

He pointed to an area by the side of the bar.

She bobbed her way over to the area, her "date" right behind her.

Doper heaven. Pills were being swapped. A young man took a snort from an amyl nitrite vial and sagged against the bar. Vials of coke were as common as salt shakers at a restaurant. All right under the bartender's eyes.

She tilted her head down and whispered, "Bingo. I just witnessed two hand-to-hand transactions."

"Hey, what are you doing?" her "date" asked. He reached for her and she playfully slapped his hand away.

"Look, but don't touch," she said.

"I'm gonna get a drink," the man said, and moved away.

"I see another one. Looks brown. Maybe smack. I'm going in closer," she whispered into the tiny mike under her lapel.

She didn't realize a bouncer had been watching her in the mirror until she felt a hand on her shoulder. He spun her around.

"What's this?" the bartender demanded, grabbing her neck with one huge hand, and the mike with another.

"Get your paws offa me," she said.

"C'mon with me, bitch."

＊　　＊　　＊

"She's in trouble," Bagels said. "Let's go!"

He had six cops, volunteers from narcotics. Huey Nichols, Fleming Jr., and four from SWAT had also joined in.

They rushed the door. The security staff tried to slow them. The gun butts of the shotguns the cops carried put the bouncers on the floor.

It took several moments for the crowd to realize what was happening. Then there were shouts and screams and a mass exodus. Alarms went off as fire doors were shoved open.

Roger Sullivan had just split up with his girlfriend. To make up for the loss he had filled his head with crack and gone to the Stardust. He had more crack—there was nothing better for picking up chicks—and a .25 automatic taped to his thigh. He was carrying lots of cash and figured chicks went for guys with guns.

"Fucking pigs," he yelled, trying to impress those around them. He took out his gun, not thinking about the consequences.

"Drop it!" Huey yelled.

The crowd around Sullivan evaporated, people climbing over each other to get away.

Sullivan leveled the gun. No one was giving him any orders.

Boom! The blast opened a hole in his chest. Several people around him were struck by pellets. More screams. Another man, drunk, wasn't sure what was going on. Screams and gunfire. He drew his gun.

"Drop it!" a narco cop ordered.

The drunk turned, gun still in his hand.

Boom! Another shotgun blast.

Bagels had been battling through the crowd, which was flowing against him, looking for Tatanya.

He found her. She had a clump of hair missing and a small cut above her eye. She was holding a man bent over the bar, his arm twisted behind his back.

At her feet was a bouncer, getting stepped on, trying to clutch his broken jaw and his groin simultaneously. She had used her handcuffs as impromptu brass knuckles and the bouncer's face still bore their imprint. She was trying to get her cuffs on the struggling man bent over the bar.

"I saw an underage being led into the office there," she said. "I'm sorry it didn't go smoothly, sir."

Bagels helped her with the handcuffing and patted her on the back. "You did good."

The disco was nearly empty. The music seemed louder, bouncing off hard walls without the cushioning of so many bodies. The DJ had cut out, grabbing his favorite albums, at the first sign of trouble. The floor was littered with packets of dope. Pills, grass, coke, smack, Sherms, a few syringes.

Bagels led the men towards the door Tatanya had indicated.

"Huey, you want to do the honors?" Bagels asked.

It was a massive steel door, set in a steel frame. Huey got out a long pry bar. Another SWAT cop carried a sledge.

Nichols looked at the door and shook his head. Then he moved over a few feet and dug the pry bar into the wall.

"Sheetrock," he said happily.

The cop with the sledge came over and drew back to swing.

Kassim had a pair of Koss headphones on and was listening to Beethoven's Ninth. He hated disco. He was leaning back in a leather recliner. His pants were down around his ankles.

The runaway had heard the noise from outside. But he had taken a few Quaaludes and some LSD and it didn't seem that important. He was in a hurry to finish blowing Kassim so he could get back outside and pick up a couple of tricks.

When the runaway saw the sledgehammer head crash through the wall, his first thought was, "What a trip."

Kassim, whose eyes were closed, noticed a change in the young man's rhythm. He opened his eyes and was about to reprimand him when the wall crashed in.

Kassim jumped up and fell over his pants. The runaway stayed on his knees, staring in wonderment.

While two of the narcotics cops handcuffed Kassim and the runaway, the rest of the team went through the door at the back of the office, down the short hall, to the door to the Back Room.

"Party's over!" Nichols bellowed, as they threw open the door.

The phone awoke Odin at eight A.M. Sunday morning.

"Hey, you still asleep?" Huey Nichols asked.

"What time is it?"

"Time for some good news. I bet you ain't listened to the radio yet."

"Uhhh. What's going on?"

"We hit the Stardust last night."

Odin was wide awake. "Was Mokley there?"

"No luck. But I whispered his best wishes in Kassim's ear. That'll spread the message. We caught that fucker with his pants down."

Nichols filled him in on the details of the raid. Two dead, a few bystanders with minor injuries. Nichols rattled off a list of celebrities they had surprised in the back room.

"You shoulda seen that place. Before, and after. We had to do a thorough search. We made that joint look like Lebanon after a bombing."

"No dice on Mokley?"

"No."

"Well, I'm glad no one on the job was hurt," a subdued Odin said.

Nichols tried another tack to cheer his buddy. "There's this ballsy fox from narco. I got a date with her next week. You wanna double?"

"Nah."

"Hey, I nearly forgot. Bagels said he had information from an informant about dope in Kassim's safe. We opened it and got ten pounds of nose candy."

"That's nice."

Nichols tried for a few more minutes to get an enthusiastic reaction from Odin, and failed. He said good-bye.

Odin hung up and lay back in bed. He had mixed feelings. He wished the cops had nailed Mokley. But deep down, he was glad they didn't. He wanted the doper for himself.

13 As Assistant Chief Fleming prepared to go into church for Sunday morning services, a gray-suited man sidled up.

"I'm Mr. Provenzano's attorney," he said. "He would like to speak to you on a matter of utmost urgency."

"I know. I just heard about it," Fleming said. "I'll meet him after services."

"He'd prefer to talk with you now."

Fleming brushed past him. "Tell him the usual spot. In an hour."

Fleming's driver parked his car in the lot at the southern end of Griffith Park.

"You want me to come with you?" his driver asked. He was a burly young cop, eager to look good in front of his boss.

"That won't be necessary," Fleming said, walking off toward the bridle path.

Provenzano rode up on a beautiful white stallion. The horse was full of spirit, snorting, and kicking up dust. Provenzano, wearing a western outfit by Ralph Lauren, looked very much the overdressed dude. But he handled the horse with confidence and dismounted gracefully.

He held the reins and led the animal to where Fleming waited.

"The raid went down without notice," Fleming said before Pro could speak. "Apparently some cowboy sergeant in narcotics used his own initiative. If they hadn't come up with all that coke, I could've slapped him down. As it stands, the chief wants to give him a commendation."

"You know, this horse is a good horse," Provenzano said. "But he's got too much spirit. That's the problem with stallions. You gotta cut their balls off or they're a pain in the ass." Pro patted the horse's neck. Its nostrils flared and it sniffed at his hand.

"Kassim will be able to get back in business soon," Fleming said. "Your lawyers will knock out the warrant. I'll take care of the sergeant when the dust settles."

"See the way this horse sniffs the hand," Pro said. "He's used to getting fed by that hand." Pro took a sugar cube out of his pocket and smiled at the horse and then Fleming. "He's gonna be a gelding by the end of the week. And if he breaks a leg . . ." Pro made a classic gun gesture with his finger and pretended to blow the horse's brains out.

"If you're making veiled threats, don't waste your time," Fleming said. "I don't scare easy. I was a street cop for thirteen years."

"I know how brave you are," Pro said. "I also know that we have an agreement. It works well for both of us. I'm out ten pounds of coke and my club was destroyed. How are we going to solve this problem?"

"It can't be that bad."

"That bad? Every piece of glass, every mirror, every lamp, was smashed. They cut up couch cushions. Looking for dope, they said. They embarrassed people who are not to be embarrassed. They killed two people and wounded a dozen others."

"That'll make the crowds bigger. You shouldn't have kept all that dope in the safe."

"I thought we had an agreement. That you were an honorable man."

"I am. It's this Mokley thing. This Jew bastard sergeant was on the raid."

"If I had Mokley, I'd personally hand you his balls. In a glass jar."

"I can hardly tell my people that."

The horse pulled back. Pro jerked the reins.

"We have a problem," Pro said. "What are *we* going to do about it?"

The dojo was located in a loft building downtown. The hand lettered sign by the door said SCALIA. Odin tried the door and found it open.

He stepped into a twenty-by-thirty-foot, high-ceilinged workout room. A canvas mat covered most of the floor, a few heavy sandbags hanging in one corner, a speed bag in another. Brick walls had been blasted clear of paint, giving the place a primitive charm. Bare sprinkler pipes and exposed steel beams made it clear that the building had been built for business. There was the smell of sweat in the air.

About ten people were working out on the mat under the eyes of an assistant instructor. Most of the students, ranging in age from early teens to late sixties, had some form of handicap. A boy in a wheelchair struggled to fend off gentle blows from a pugil stick being swung by a girl with a deformed right arm.

A man on crutches practiced swinging one and striking a sandbag, while keeping his balance. A blind woman swung at the other sandbag. A student with no arms stood behind the bag, bracing it for her. There were a few more blind people practicing Push Hands, the t'ai chi technique that developed balance. A couple of Seeing Eye dogs were at the edge of the mat, watching their masters like protective nannies.

Odin felt a wave of revulsion sweep over him. He had felt that way before at the VA Hospital when he'd visited a buddy from Nam who'd lost both legs to a Bouncing Betty. Odin had been surrounded by young men missing various parts of their anatomy. He'd fought down his sense of horror and had left as soon as it seemed decent.

Now he was with a bunch of cripples again. Only this time he was one of them.

"Hello," the man said softly.

Odin turned. He had come up on Odin's blind side and with the noise in the dojo, the ex-cop hadn't realized he was there.

"I'm Frank Scalia. You must be Bob Odin." He extended his hand. Odin did the same. Slowly, so he would make sure to make contact with Scalia's. It was the kind of small reminder of his disability that harassed Odin several times a day.

Odin sized Scalia up. He was about five-feet-ten-inches tall, broad across the shoulders, conveying a muscular confidence even with the loosefitting judo *gi* he wore. A bushy black beard encircled his Mona Lisa smile. Under his dark-tinted glasses, his eyes had a glassy faraway look. Odin had seen similar expressions on spaced-out religious cultists. He wondered what he'd gotten into.

Scalia moved slowly, as if each gesture required consideration. They shook hands. Scalia's handshake gave a feeling of controlled power.

"Let's talk in my office," Scalia said. "Jan has told me so much about you."

"She didn't tell me much about you," Odin said, annoyed and wondering what she'd told Scalia.

The office had a few statues but no degrees or pictures on the wall.

"What style do you teach?" Odin asked.

"My own."

"Is it mainly tae kwon do. Or jujitsu? Or Shotokan karate? Or kung fu?"

"A little from all of those. Some street fighting, some tricks I picked up in Special Forces."

"You in Nam?"

"Yeah."

"Where?"

"Chu Lai."

"Hmm." For the first time, Odin felt a positive feeling towards Scalia. Chu Lai had been a hot spot. Scalia must be doing something right if he survived untouched.

Odin realized why he'd felt such hostility towards Scalia right from the beginning. The man was whole. Who was he to teach anyone who was handicapped? He couldn't understand.

A pretty, chunky blonde came in. Her Rubenesque figure looked particularly sexy in the *gi* she wore. She was in her late twenties, with pale skin, and a glow in her cheeks. She sized Odin up but hid her opinion. When her look turned to Scalia, it was near reverence.

"Frank, will you start the class the usual time?"

"Take 'em through the stretching exercises, and I'll join you. I want to talk with Bob for a couple of minutes. Bob, this is Connie. My assistant instructor. And my wife."

She gave Odin a toothy smile and a firm handshake.

"Don't forget to have him sign an insurance waiver," she said to her husband.

"She's also my business partner," Scalia said. Turning to his wife, he asked, "You planning on hurting him?"

"Only if he misbehaves." She headed out to the mat.

"Helluva lady," Scalia said. "Now, what do you want to get out of the classes?"

"First, I'd like to hear what Jan told you about me?"

"She didn't describe you as a real life Dirty Harry, but that's the impression I got. She said you took the injury hard and could use physical regimen to get back on your feet. Psychologically, as much as physically."

"That's nice of her," Odin said sarcastically.

"The only reason she told me that much is I turned her down at first. I'm not a money-making franchise of a Hollywood chop-socky star. If I can't devote enough attention to my students, it's not worth their time, or mine."

"Yeah."

"Bob, I don't want to waste your time. It's going to mean pretty heavy reorienting. Your attitude as a cop was very confrontational. Here, I teach how to go with the flow, use what you've got, and not force the issue. Let the problem come to you, and then gently defeat it. With a minimum of effort."

"Like judo."

"Like the philosophy behind judo. As Jigaro Kano taught it initially. Bamboo bending under the weight of snow, then snapping back. The gentle way. In recent years, it's become a sport. Lots of bull strength, push-pull. A big Dutchman came along and whipped all the Japanese stars, showing that size and strength were still important."

"A good big man will always whip a good little man," Odin said.

"True. Of course, your chance of being attacked by a fourth-degree black belt are rather slim," Scalia said. "Here, I teach how to turn weakness into strength, and use your strength against your adversary's weakness. If I had to cite anything as the prime influence of what goes on here, it's taoism. Are you familiar with it?"

"Some sort of Chinese philosophy."

"True. Yin and yang, striving for the medium, avoiding excess. But as Lao Tzu said, 'those who know, do not say, those who say, do not know.'"

"Then how do you get the message across?"

"The way to do is to be."

Odin grunted.

"There's a few other sayings I like. 'He who knows others is wise, he who knows himself is enlightened.' And 'if you do not get it from yourself, where will you go for it.'"

Odin grunted again.

"Of course to you, they just sound like words," Scalia said. "Still interested?"

"I'll try it," Odin said, not really sure why. "Do I have to sign a contract, for six months or anything?"

"No contract. Pay by the lesson. Five bucks a class. Come as many times a week as you like."

Scalia got up and rooted through the file cabinet behind the desk. Odin noticed that the file folders didn't have any writing on them.

Scalia set a paper down in front of him. As Odin read it, Scalia said, "This isn't a macho gym. And not the place to come to work out your frustrations. People here have different levels of skills. Of course you don't seem the type to get his jollies out of beating up a blind man."

Odin said, "Uh-huh" and signed the paper. He'd try one class. If nothing else, he could tell Jan that she'd wasted his time. He could work out on the sandbag. And, he wanted to see just what this Scalia could do.

"Maybe we can take that chip off your shoulder," Scalia said. "It's a helluva weight to carry."

"Don't count on it."

"You want to carry it with you the rest of your life?"

"Listen, I don't mind the two-bit Eastern philosophy. But how can someone like you tell me about what to do, how to live with one eye?"

"I can't tell you how to live with one eye."

"Damn straight."

"Or two eyes. Or no eyes."

"You going to get philosophical again?"

Scalia laughed. Odin got more annoyed.

"Screw you," the ex-cop said. His fists were balled up at his sides.

"Calm down," Scalia said soothingly. "Look at you, getting all worked up into a lather. What have I said that you find so offensive?" His voice was different, soothing.

"It's just, you're whole. You can't understand."

"I agree with you that I'm whole," Scalia said. "Now, meet me out on the mat."

Odin joined the group in stretches and twists. The group was spread out, so each person could receive individual attention, almost a private lesson.

As he sat on the mat, trying to force his hands to his toes, Connie came over to him. "You're doing ballistic stretching, all that bouncing up and down. You're scarring your muscles. Watch me."

She stretched forward, back flat, touching hands to toes, but with no bobbing. "Take it easy. Slow. Do it at your own pace."

She stood behind him as he bent, and leaned against his shoulders. Pushing him down, gently but firmly. He could feel each muscle fiber stretching.

"Ballistic stuff is verboten now. So are conventional sit-ups, deep-knee bends, lots of goodies your high school gym teacher forced you to do."

She let up the pressure and he slowly rose.

Scalia was sitting in front of him. In a wheelchair. He had no legs.

He heard Odin's shocked intake of air. "They do wonders with prosthetics," Scalia said with a grin. "Of course, I save lots of time on the leg stretching exercises."

Several students laughed, though Odin had the feeling it was a joke they'd heard before.

"I'm, I'm sorry," Odin said.

"Nothing to be sorry about," Scalia said. "You were so

wrapped up in your own problems, you didn't have time for other people's." Scalia slid the glasses off. Odin saw for the first time that it wasn't glassy-eyed spiritualism that gave Scalia a faraway look. Scalia's eyes were useless.

"I feel like a real jerk," Odin said.

"Why?" Scalia asked. He was a few feet away, stretching his arms and torso.

"I was thinking, well, I wanted to whip your ass," Odin said. "See how well you could handle yourself."

"You'll get your chance. Most students start out wanting to toss the *sensei* around."

"But, you're . . ."

"Don't forget why you're here," Scalia said. "And why I'm here."

Connie's posture had changed. She was in a modified T stance, arms low but ready to strike. Odin sensed that if he ever hurt Scalia, she'd do everything she could to kill him.

"All right, let's get the pulse rates up," Scalia said, and everyone began jogging in place, to the best of their ability.

After a few minutes Scalia rolled to the side, and Connie led the group through karate *katas*, ballet-like kicks, blocks, and punches. Odin, who had had plenty of hand-to-hand combat training, felt clumsy going through the movements. As he watched those around him, he saw that it was the level of skill, more than the handicap, that determined how good people looked.

A blind man wearing a black belt was beautiful to watch, each movement flowing, rippling fluid power. The student with one arm, who wore a yellow belt, looked clumsy, off balance. A brown-belted woman, whom Odin had seen using sign language to another student, moved with surprising power and confidence.

Odin tried to keep up, but as the movements got faster, he felt winded and had to take a break.

"I'll work with you one-on-one these first few times," Connie said.

"That woman really knows her stuff," Odin said, indicating the brown belt.

"Yeah. She's going to take the test for black belt soon," Scalia said.

"Then I can really push people around," she said.

Odin could barely understand her words. She made her wisecrack simultaneously in sign language and another deaf student chuckled before any of those who could hear did.

"We'll see," Scalia said with a smile. Then he got serious. "You all should remember belts don't mean anything. They're just a symbol. What matters is what's in here." He tapped his head. "And here." He tapped his heart.

Scalia led them through deep-breathing exercises. He concluded the session by telling a long anecdote about three men whose boat capsized in a river. One tried to fight the current, and drowned. Another just bobbed along, and got dashed against the rocks. The third saw which way the current went and swam with it to safety.

"Anyone want to take a crack at a moral?" Scalia asked.

"How about, wear your life jacket when you go boating," Odin quipped.

Laughter all around. None heartier than Scalia's. "Not a bad moral. Class dismissed. Bob, can you please stay?"

Odin nodded. There was a great feeling in the class, a camaraderie, a sense of community. It was not like the karate studios Odin had visited, where macho competition was as dense as the sweat in the air.

Scalia was like the father, with the students sitting around listening to his words of wisdom. But Odin wasn't quite ready to accept him as *sensei*. Scalia was a couple of years younger than the ex-cop. He was glib with the Oriental wisdom, but Odin wondered just how sharp he was.

"Disappointed you didn't get a chance to try me out?" Scalia asked.

"It's not necessary."

"I think it is," Scalia said. "Why don't you attack?"

"Nah."

"You don't need to prove anything to anyone," Connie said to her husband. "I can demonstrate."

"I think it is important for Bob to test me," Scalia said.

"And what about you?" Connie asked.

"It's important for me too," Scalia said.

Odin decided to oblige half-heartedly.

Scalia blocked Odin's slow-moving sissy slaps, caught Odin's hand, and pressed hard on the nerve on the back of his hand. Odin jerked back from the pain.

"Don't ever be condescending," Scalia said. "Either play it real or get out of my dojo."

Odin put a bit more ooomph into his slaps. Still Scalia looked disgusted.

"Is this what they teach you in the LAPD?" Scalia asked. "C'mon, hit me with your best shot."

Odin began circling the wheelchair. Scalia got a beatific smile on his face. Odin lunged, and Scalia ducked. Odin lunged again and again Scalia was gone.

"Do you think you know how to fall properly?" Scalia asked.

"Sure," Odin said. He feinted another slap and came around quick with his other hand. Scalia caught it and brushed it away.

"Better," Scalia said.

Odin thought he sounded patronizing. The ex-cop felt his pulse pounding as he moved quicker, trying to slip in on Scalia. Now Scalia was slapping away his blows, gently, but Odin could feel the sting in his hands.

It was amazing. How could the blind man anticipate where the blow was coming from?

Then Odin tried a straightforward punch. It wouldn't have hurt Scalia if it landed. Scalia blocked the blow and grabbed his arm at the wrist and elbow. He twisted from the hips and Odin was sent flying.

"Enough!" Connie said, stepping between the two men.

"How'd you do that?" Odin asked Scalia.

"I waited until the class had cleared out so it was quiet."

"And I thought you just didn't want the others to see me clean your clock."

Scalia laughed. "I needed to hear you. The rustle of your sleeve, the gulp of air before you strike."

"Incredible."

"Not really. When you were in the hospital, didn't you hear better, use your other senses more?"

"Yes, but not to that degree." Odin, heaving, sat next to Scalia's wheelchair.

"I've had more practice. You can learn to use your other senses, make up for the loss. The human organism is remarkably adaptable."

Connie stood, hands on hips, glaring at both men.

"Like now, I can tell Connie is mad at us," Scalia said. "I can almost hear her nostrils flaring."

"You could've hurt him," she said, unclear which man she was talking to.

"Boys will be boys," Scalia said to her. "It's your turn to make lunch." To Odin, he said, "Connie and I take turns, trying to top each other with culinary delights. Will you join us?"

Bob looked at Connie, who gave a grudging nod.

"Love to," Odin said.

While Connie worked in the kitchen, Scalia and Odin went back into the office. Scalia put on his tinted glasses. As he strapped on his artificial legs, he gave Odin a speech about nutrition, singing the praises of bean sprouts, tofu, and raw egg malteds.

"I'm a steak-and-potatoes man," Odin responded.

"Your body could handle that before. You have to give it a better diet now. At least for a while." He leaned over confidentially. "Every now and then, I sneak out for a hot dog and a few beers. Connie's tough. That's the problem with falling in love with a woman who can split an inch-thick piece of pine with one shot."

"She does that?"

Scalia nodded and led him to the kitchen. Connie was working at the stove. "I told Bob if he didn't clean his plate, you'd break his collarbone," Scalia said. He squeezed his wife, then helped set the table.

"You move like you could see," Odin said.

"I've memorized the apartment and the dojo," Scalia said. "A few embarrassing collisions can be remarkably effective aversive therapy."

"Tell me about it," Odin agreed.

"It requires work. For instance, a door left half open can be a real hazard. A thick piece of molding can be an insurmountable barrier."

"Nothing's insurmountable for you," Connie said. "Soup's on."

Lunch was lots of vegetables with a tangy sauce, but Odin didn't find it very filling.

"Can you really split an inch-thick piece of pine?" Odin asked.

"I used to," she said. "Hate can be a remarkable thing."

"When we met, she was like a bomb waiting to go off," Scalia said, reaching over and patting his wife's thigh under the table. "She was teaching self defense at a rape center. I had volunteered my services and I think she would've killed me if she could've. My approach was too gentle. She favored eye gouging, groin bashing, throat ripping."

"There is a time when that's necessary," she said defensively.

"Definitely. But Connie would call in nuclear attacks if a man so much as looked at her funny."

"What changed you?" Odin asked.

"Time. And Frank."

"She's still got it in her," Scalia said seriously. "I'm afraid what would happen to anyone who assaulted her."

They were silent for a few moments, eating.

"Food's great," Odin said.

"Don't worry, she's never attacked a guest," Scalia said.

Connie grinned weakly.

"It probably tastes like grass to you," Scalia said. "You get used to it, and you'll feel much better."

Dessert was yogurt that was supposed to taste like ice cream. It was fairly filling and Odin was grateful. The meal didn't seem to be sticking to his bones.

"I saw in the paper the other day, they haven't caught the guy who set the bomb that hurt you," Connie said bluntly. "How do you feel towards him?"

Odin didn't answer, but the tightening in his face made his emotions clear.

"You're holding your breath," Scalia said. "And I heard you shift position, to the edge of your chair, ready to pounce."

Odin forced himself to release his breath and lean back.

"You want to know how I lost these?" Scalia pointed towards his legs. "And these." He pointed to his eyes.

Odin nodded, then realized Scalia couldn't see the gesture. "Yes."

Connie began clearing the table. She had heard the story before, and it pained her to hear it again.

"Out on patrol. Infiltrate, slit a few throats, exfiltrate. The guy in front of me stepped on a mine. I was lucky, not that badly wounded. Maybe lucky isn't quite right. Charlie was waiting nearby. I got taken prisoner. You know how wonderful the jungle is for wounds. The POW camp was hardly the Mayo Clinic. They had to amputate both legs before the gangrene set in.

"They figured I was crippled and I got more slack than the other prisoners. After all, how far could I go, right? I made crutches out of bamboo. Hid them near the perimeter, and one night, I made a break for it. They caught me about two miles away. Beat the shit out of me. No special treatment from then on.

"I had trouble seeing after a few days as camp whipping boy. VC thought I was faking it and thumped me harder. Turns out I had a nasty combination of ruptured blood vessels and an infection. Germs went to town behind my eyeballs."

"Frank!" Connie said.

"Sorry, you're right." Scalia smiled. "See, sometimes I start to feel sorry for myself. I need a good kick in the rump as much as the next guy. Anyway, I got released eventually, sent home, dumped out. I hit bottom somewhere around that time. Came close to killing myself. I was pretty messed up."

"What turned you around?"

"Lots of things. Personal things that wouldn't mean much to you or anyone else. I heard a Vietnamese teenager on the radio one day. He had lost an arm, suffered third degree burns on most of his body. Now he was living in America, surrounded by the people who had done it to him. The commentator asked him how he felt. The kid said he was sorry there was so much hate in the world. I just broke down and cried. I thought about what I had done, as well as what had been done to me. You can live on hate, but it's not a nice diet."

Odin nodded. "I guess."

"You'll see," Scalia said. "I know you will. Coming back tomorrow?"

"Sure."

14   "You're looking well," Mary Finch said sourly.
A once pretty woman, she had taken her husband's death badly. She had racoonish rings under her eyes and a bitter tension around her mouth.

"I've been trying to get back in shape. It's been a while," Odin said. He had been out of the hospital for two weeks. "I'm sorry I couldn't get to the funeral.

She shrugged. "You've seen what they're like. The chief

makes a speech, everyone wears their dress uniform, the TV cameras roll." She toyed with her coffee cup.

They were seated in the kitchen of Finch's house in Simi Valley, a community just west of the westernmost part of the San Fernando Valley. It was at the expanding edge of the megapolis. Finch's house was a tract home, similar to the three dozen other houses in the five-year-old Rolling Acres development.

"I met with Gina yesterday," Odin said. Gina was Daggett's widow.

"You're making the rounds," Mary said.

"I just want you both to know how bad I feel, that I'd give anything to have them both back."

"So would I." Mary set the coffee cup down. It clinked on the saucer. She had a slight tremor. "I'm pregnant."

Odin didn't know what to say.

"I'm going to have an abortion," she said.

"Think it over. Don't do anything sudden."

"We've got three kids." She sniffled. "I mean, I've got three kids. I don't want any more responsibility. Not without him."

"It's hardest in the beginning," he said. "Maybe you and Gina ought to get together. She's got a big family. A cop family. They can help. They'd be happy to."

"Happy?" she said, seizing on the word. "Happy! Oh right. Part of the camaraderie. The macho bullshit that Wally told me about. I begged him to get another job. I begged. Even another assignment. But he wouldn't. Wouldn't leave Pete Daggett. Or you. And what did it get him? What did it get him?" Her voice was shrill, harshly echoing off the walls. She burst out in tears and raced away from the table.

Odin sat, not sure what to do. He could hear her sobbing in the other room. He gazed around the kitchen. So typical. Cuisinart on the formica counter. Microwave. Kids' drawings held up on the refrigerator with magnets shaped like hot dogs, watermelon slices.

He walked to her. Her body looked frail, wracked by sobs. "I'm sorry I said that," she said.

He took her in his arms and held her. They were cheek to cheek. He had forgotten how tall she was. She pressed against him, her full body. He could feel her warmth at his groin. Her sobbing subsided, but her pressing continued. Her breathing changed.

He had seen it before. A morgue worker once told him, "I get more pussy than most rock stars." Grieving widows' emotions took erratic swings as they sought to recover from tragedy.

Odin stepped back.

She stared at him, as if rifling through her bag of emotions, not sure which one she'd pull out.

"How come they haven't caught who did it?" she asked.

"They will."

"How can you be so sure?"

"You can bet that every cop in Southern California is thinking about what happened. Everyone would love to get their hands on Mokley."

"It's been more than a month since it happened. Wally always said the colder the trail got, the harder it was to find the bad guy."

"We'll find him."

She sighed.

"Mary, anything I can do," Odin volunteered. "If you need money or just someone to talk to. Whatever."

"Thanks."

"I mean it."

She stepped up to him, a wild gleam in her eye. He took a half step back.

"There is one thing," she said.

"Yes?"

"Find who did it and kill him. Kill him."

*   *   *

YOU CAN FUCK WITH SAINT PETER, YOU CAN FUCK WITH
SAINT PAUL, BUT IF YOU FUCK WITH ONE COP, YOU FUCK
WITH US ALL, read the sign above the bar at Casey's.

It was located on the fringe of downtown, a traditional water-
ing hole for LAPD cops since it was opened by an ex-cop nineteen years before.

Some said that the antics in the bar had provided Joseph
Wambaugh with half his anecdotes. A general level of insanity
prevailed. The sign saying PLEASE CHECK YOUR GUNS AT THE
DOOR was for real. Casey had begun providing lockers after his
ceiling was pocked by a dozen rounds, and a woman walking by
outside was nearly killed by a stray shot.

There was sawdust on the worn linoleum floor, a long
wooden bar, and dark booths. Targets labeled with the names of
various police enemies—defense attorneys, liberal politicians,
pushy reporters—bedecked the wainscotted walls. It was coming
up on five P.M. and about fifteen regulars were enjoying the
Happy Hour.

Odin was seated at the back of the bar, sipping a beer. Casey
had made a big fuss when he came in, but Odin had asked to be
tucked away in a corner. He could have gone to any bar in the
city, but somehow Casey's seemed the right place to unwind.
Besides, he had business to take care of.

"Hey, I didn't think they let civilians in here," a voice
boomed. It was Werner Greene, the obnoxious motorcycle cop.

"Integration," Odin said.

"How you doing?" Greene asked.

"Not bad."

"That's not what I hear," Greene said, loud enough for everyone to hear. "Bobbin' Robin says you ain't a stand-up guy."
Greene brayed.

Among cop buddies, cracks about impotence, homosexuality,
and adultery were accepted banter. But Greene's revelation
clearly was no friendly zinger. Odin sipped his beer.

"Thanks for telling me," Odin said.

"Huh?"

"Now that I know you've been with her, I can warn people away. We wouldn't want your clap going through the department."

The regulars snickered.

"Get up!" Greene ordered.

Odin continued to sip his beer.

"You got no balls, as well as a limp willy?"

All of a sudden, Greene was yelping and being lifted in the air. Eustas Nichols had reached in between his legs from behind and squeezed his testicles, simultaneously lifting the burly motorcycle cop. He carried him to the door and threw him out.

The regulars applauded.

Nichols strode back to where Odin was sitting. Fleming Junior was already seated opposite Odin. Nichols sat down next to Fleming.

"Thanks," Odin said. "Though I could've handled it."

"You white folks is used to niggers handling your garbage," Nichols said. "How you been?"

"Getting better," Odin said.

A cocktail waitress brought beers for the newcomers and a refill for Odin.

"On the house," she said to the cops. "Casey's been waiting for someone to get rid of Greene."

Nichols took his stein and lifted it in Casey's direction.

"I'm sorry about what happened," Fleming Junior said to Odin.

"Hey, that's all you've said to me since it happened," Odin said. "It's done. It wasn't your fault."

Junior just looked down into his beer.

"What's this peach fuzz?" Nichols said, rubbing Odin's cheek, which was getting stubbly.

"I'm going to grow a beard. First time since I was a kid that I can legally have one."

"You're gonna be just another hairbag," Nichols said. "I know this chick, better than Bobbin' Robin. She's real patient, got a mouth like a Hoover."

"Don't sweat it."

"That cunt Robin," Junior said. "Telling Greene that. She ought to keep things confidential. Like a priest or a doctor."

"I'm gonna freeze her out," Nichols said. "Spread the word about her big mouth."

"Everyone knows about her mouth," Odin said.

The three men laughed.

"What's been going on with the Mokley case?" Odin asked.

"Hasn't been much action," Nichols said. "Half the snitches in town claim to have info on him. He's been reported everywhere from Baja to British Columbia. Major Crimes is supposed to be working the case hard."

"Supposed to be?"

"I hear tell they been told to treat it like just another murder. No special treatment."

"That's what they always say."

"Supposedly it's true. Orders from the top. The honchos were pissed at the little raid we staged on Kassim. They say any gung ho stuff will blow the case against Mokley. They're afraid of outraging the community."

"Bullshit," Odin said.

Both men looked over at Junior.

"I don't talk about it with my father," he said.

"Brass Balls knows how important it is to get cop-killers," Odin said.

"Nowadways he don't know whether his loyalty is to the department or the com-mun-it-ty," Huey said, dragging out the last word in a derisive tone.

"How's Mokley been able to slip away?" Odin asked.

"I got a buddy in Major Crimes," Junior said. "Seems that Mokley used to be a radical. Apparently has contacts in that sixties revolutionary crowd. They haven't been under surveillance for years. And it's not like the usual dirtbags, where we can count on informants all over the place."

"That would explain the bomb too," Odin mused. "The Weathermen and their buddies loved toys that went bang."

"Commie bastards," Nichols said.

He heard wolf whistles and looked up as Tatanya James entered the bar. "Excuse me, gentlemen, I see a damsel in distress."

Nichols hustled over to the bar as several cops circled James. She was clearly holding her own. He put his arm across her shoulder and whispered in her ear.

Odin leaned across the table towards Fleming Junior. He gripped Fleming Junior's forearm.

"I need a favor," Odin said.

"Name it."

"I want everything on Mokley. Reports from Major Crimes, Bomb Squad, Narco, everyone."

Fleming Junior sat back. "That's some request."

"Get whatever you can."

"Why, why do you want it?"

"I don't want to find out about Mokley just by reading the newspapers."

"I'll see what I can do."

Odin slapped his arm. "I know I can count on you."

Nichols guided James over to their table. "Gentlemen, let me introduce the only narcotics cop I've ever loved. Tatanya James, this is Bad Bobby and Junior."

The two men got up. When she shook hands with Odin, because of the dim light, he had a little trouble aligning with her hand.

"Uh, sorry," she said, when they finally made contact.

"My fault," he said.

She sat next to him and said, "I've heard a lot about you."

"Don't believe anything Huey told you."

"Hey, tell them what happened," Nichols said.

"They suspended Bagels," James said.

"Why'd they do that?" Odin asked.

"They been looking to get him since we raided the Stardust," she said. "Shooflies came in and went over every report he's ever written. They got him on a chickenshit failure to properly supervise."

"How's he taking it?" Mac asked.

"Gulping Maalox. He's talking about pulling the pin. He's got twenty-three years."

"This department is getting more and more wussy," Nichols said.

15 Odin finished the warm-up kicks and prepared for the workout. He was at Scalia's dojo, and by now its routine was as comfortable to him as a favorite chair. A half hour of stretching, fifteen minutes of kicks, fifteen minutes of punches and chops, and then an hour of various throwing techniques. Those without legs doubled up on the punches; those without arms doubled up on the kicks.

Scalia was a tough taskmaster who seemed to know everyone's limit.

"Today we have a new student," Scalia said. "Leon, c'mon out."

A dark-haired boy peered out of Scalia's office.

"Leon, c'mon. We're all friends here," Scalia said.

The boy didn't move.

"Okay, Connie, can you lead the class through rising right block, knee kick, and ear clap?"

She nodded.

"Bob, come here please."

Odin ambled over.

"I think we got a barricaded suspect situation here," Scalia said. "Can you handle it?"

The boy had disappeared into the office.

"I was kinda looking forward to working out."

"This is another kind of working out," Scalia said. "Working on your gentle side. The yin. Lao Tzu said that was more important than the hard side. When you're a baby, you're soft. When you're dead, you're stiff, solid. So softness is life."

"Yeah, yeah."

"You've done very well in the past few weeks. But you're still much better on hard techniques than soft. You have to balance yourself."

"Okay, I'll get the kid out of there. Is it okay to use tear gas?"

Scalia smiled. "No. But it is okay to use a sense of humor."

"What's the kid's problem?"

"His father beat him up. Regularly. With a wire hanger. Also burned him with cigarettes and did all kinds of wonderful crap when he was drunk. Which was just about every night."

"Death's too good for some people."

"He's getting counseling now. The court's even given him visiting rights. But Leon's having trouble adjusting. His psychologist thought martial arts training might help."

Odin nodded and walked to the office. As soon as he stepped in, Leon cowered in the corner. Odin tried talking softly, urging the boy to come out and join the group. Leon wouldn't budge.

Odin returned to where Scalia was leading the class. "No dice."

"Keep trying," Scalia said.

"I'm not a social worker," Odin said.

"I don't have the time to devote to the boy. If you can't get him out of there, I'll have to tell the shrink we can't help him."

"Maybe Connie can."

"She's busy too."

Muttering, Odin walked back to the office. The boy could sense his annoyance and cowered even further into the corner.

Odin stepped out of the room. He tapped his foot on the mat. Maybe if he didn't tower over the boy. Odin got down on all fours. He stuck his head around the corner of the door. The boy stared at him. Odin shook his head, letting his lips flap and make a silly noise.

Then Odin ducked back, out of view of the boy.

He repeated the act. Leon remained in the corner but he was no longer wide-eyed with terror. He had a curious expression, unsure what it was all about.

Odin did a roll and came up on the other side of the doorway. He made a few faces and then rolled back. He repeated the act a few times.

Leon smiled.

"My name's Bob. What's yours?"

"Leon," the boy said, so quietly Odin wouldn't have known what it was unless he knew the name.

"Well, Leon. Pleased to meet you. Would you shake my hand?"

The boy hesitated, but at last came forward very reluctantly. He shook Odin's hand.

"You want to come out and join us?" Odin asked.

The boy shook his head.

"C'mon. You'll have fun."

The boy shook his head.

"Why not?"

"I don't want to."

"Well, no one's gonna force you."

Odin sat on the floor next to Leon. "I'll keep you company."

Odin kept a friendly smile, hiding his emotions, even when he saw the ugly scars on the boys neck. The two sat on the floor listening to the thump and *kiai* shouts in the dojo.

"You know, that sounds pretty scary," Odin said. "How about we go to the doorway and see what's going on?"

The boy reluctantly agreed.

They sat in the office doorway, watching the class.

Periodically, Odin would say, "Watch that over there" or, "Isn't that neat?"

"Wow, look," Leon said, after a girl not much bigger than he was threw a lanky teenager.

"Nice throw," Odin said. "You know it's not that hard to do."

"Really?"

"Scout's honor," Odin said. "Wanna try?"

Leon nodded.

Odin and the boy stepped out on the mat and the ex-cop began showing the boy basic moves.

They had fifteen minutes' practice before class ended. The boy didn't want it to stop.

"You promise you'll show me more tomorrow?" the boy asked.

"Deal."

Leon raced away.

Scalia came over with a big grin on his face. "Nice job."

"The kid's looking for a normal father figure. It wasn't hard."

"Sure. I bet you liked tumbling back and forth like that," Scalia said. He mimicked the lip flapping face Odin had made.

"I thought you were too busy to pay attention."

"I lied."

"You couldn't have seen me."

"My spies are everywhere."

"Nice. You woulda made a good cop. You can piss in someone's pocket and convince them it's raining."

Scalia chuckled and rolled into his office. Connie came up behind Odin.

"You've got him fooled," she said.

"What?"

"He thinks you're working the hate out of your system."

"And you don't?"

"It takes one to know one," she said. "You're just watching and waiting,, getting stronger."

"Really?"

"Really." She spoke softly, so her husband couldn't here. "I don't give a damn what you do to the bomber when you find him. But it's going to hurt Frank. For that I'll never forgive you."

He called Jan Golden and made a date to go to the beach the next day. Back at his apartment, he rooted through his closet until he came up with the Louisville slugger baseball bat he had used during police department softball games.

Late afternoon, he wandered over to the nearby park, and tried hitting fungoes into the field. He kept missing. After fifteen minutes, he only had a couple of foul tips. He ran around the field, feet pounding the ground until his breath came in gasps.

Back at his apartment, he let the anger and frustration in him grow. It was getting dark. Nearly time.

He took a shower, and then dressed in dark clothing. Carefully, he wound heavy gray duct tape around the base of the bat.

Thinking about it rationally, what he had planned was stupid. Foolhardy.

He removed a 150-foot coil of rope from the trunk of his car. The SWAT cops bought their own equipment. This was 800 pound safe working load, five-eight-inch-thick black nylon. He cut off six feet and made a sling for the bat. Using a slip knot on the top and a half hitch on the bottom, he tied the bat so it hung off his back.

He took the rope and slung the eight-pound coil over his shoulder. He packed a small knapsack with additional gear he thought he might need.

He peered out the window. Dark enough.

Odin drove over to North Hollywood, one block from where Mokley's friends hung out. One block from the punks who had taken his gun, pushed him around, and nearly drowned him in the pool.

As he strolled down the street, he passed a woman walking her Doberman pinscher. No reaction from her. Typical big-city indifference, coupled with Southern California acceptance of weirdos. Just your basic one-eyed man, dressed in black, with a heavy rope coil and a baseball bat sauntering down the street.

He turned into the building behind the one where the punks hung out. He walked to the back, hopped a six-foot cinderblock fence. He came to a second fence, a cyclone fence, and dug out wire cutters. A few snips and he had his own private entrance.

He slunk along the ground, moving smoothly through the cluster of untended Yucca trees. A half dozen cars were parked on the dirt, with nearly as many abandoned or cannibalized vehicles. There were beer cans and broken bottles, a few discarded appliances.

The faint strains of rock and roll in the background reminded him of Nam. Some GI was always playing his radio. Elvis Presley, Jimi Hendrix, Janis Joplin. All of them wound up dead. So did dummies who played their radios too loud and allowed the VC to pinpoint their position.

He reached the house and could peer into the courtyard from the back.

There were four men there. Radio. Baby Face. The Bar Fighter. Pompadour. Thank goodness for consistency.

Odin slipped into a cluster of Monterey cypresses planted next to the house. He used shoe polish to blacken his hands and put war paint streaks on his cheeks.

He tied the rope to the base of the tree. When he was sure the four men were too absorbed to notice, he darted across the rear archway to the other side and tied the rope, ankle high, around a matching tree.

He walked to the front of the house. Breathe in, breathe out.

Composing himself to lose control. It was crazy. So was not reporting his gun stolen. Or going out and buying a new one. But he had to get it back. Himself.

He was at the front. The men were passing around a joint. He unslung the bat and stepped into the courtyard.

With a blood-curdling yell, swinging the bat wildly, he charged the four stunned men. The ex-cop hit the radio with a Babe Ruth swing. It sailed through the air, landing in the pool where it gave a final electronic sputter.

Baby Face took off running. Radio and Pompadour were still frozen. Bar Fighter got into a boxing stance.

Odin rapped him in the shins with the bat. He yelped and hopped around like a crippled flamingo. Odin gave him a mild swat, and sent him into the scummy pool.

Radio took off running.

Pompadour drew a gun. The Asp. Odin caught him in the solar plexus with the tip of the bat. Pompadour gasped. A light bunt sent him to the floor.

Baby Face had hit the trip rope at full speed. He was sprawled on the ground, dazed. Radio had seen the rope, after Baby Face's fall, and hopped over it. He was already nearly out of sight.

Odin bent and picked up his gun. He heard a wet slap-slapping sound and spun just in time to avoid a blow from the soggy Bar Fighter.

Bar Fighter's momentum caused them to both topple. Bar Fighter growled and tried to choke him. Odin prevented him from getting a firm grip on his neck but Bar Fighter got his hand on the gun.

Odin let go of the weapon.

Bar Fighter, not believing his luck, fumbled to aim the gun. With all his attention on the weapon, Odin was able to hit him with textbook perfect blows in the throat and groin. Bar Fighter dropped the gun and yowled.

Again Odin stood and grabbed the gun.

Pompadour and Baby Face were gone. Odin hefted the baseball bat. Bar Fighter looked up.

"Ready for the second inning, scrote?"

Bar Fighter sagged backwards. Odin put the Louisville slugger across his throat and stood, foot lightly pressing on the bat. Any pressure, and Bar Fighter would choke.

"I'm going to ask once, just once. Do you know where Gary Mokley is?"

"No. No, honest."

Beaten at being a tough guy, Bar Fighter's inner core had collapsed. Odin believed he was telling the truth. He didn't have the nerve left to lie.

"Okay, second question. Where's he hang out?"

"Mainly at the Stardust."

"Where else?"

"A bar. Downtown."

"The name?"

"Uh, uh."

Odin put the slighest pressure on the bat.

"The Rocket Inn. That's it. On Figueroa."

Odin picked up the bat. "Remember me, scumbum. 'Cause I'll be remembering you."

Back at his apartment, Odin scrubbed off the paint, showered, and plopped down onto the couch. He field stripped his weapon, cleaned each crevice, and tucked it back into the custom leather holster.

He glanced at the clock. It was nearly eleven, the time Jan Golden would be getting off duty. He called her at the hospital.

"Hi, I was wondering if you'd feel like going out for a drink," he said.

"Uhh. I'm too bushed. We had a Code Blue and a patient go into anaphylactic shock. The paperwork alone will keep me here another hour."

"I can wait. I'll pick you up."

"I really better pass. You sound awfully cheery. Anything special?"

"Nah. Just feeling chipper," he said. "Well, I'm looking forward to seeing you tomorrow."

"Me too."

They broke the connection. He was disappointed, but still felt like singing and dancing. His body had performed as he wanted it to. But it was more than that. The thrill of the hunter at felling his prey. Connie had been right about him.

Yet he could've been rougher with the punks. He could've gone after them, or not checked his swing quite so much. As it was, he guessed they wouldn't have anything much worse than a few bruises tomorrow.

What would Scalia think? Who cared. It was Odin's business. Screw Scalia. Screw the department. Mokley is mine.

16   Odin lay on the beach, the warm rays of the sun massaging him as he dozed. Jan Golden was nearby, under a brightly colored umbrella.

"You don't want to burn," she cautioned.

"Feels good," he said.

"Skin cancer doesn't."

"Live fast, die young, and make a beautiful corpse," he said.

"Is that really your philosophy?"

He sat up. "I don't have a philosophy."

"Everyone does. You might never have stated it."

"What's yours?"

"I try to follow the golden rule."

"No pun intended."

"Yes it was. But it's a good rule. What about you?"

"Well, some of the taoist stuff Scalia talks about sounds good. But sometimes he sounds like that old 'Kung Fu' TV series." Odin put on a mock high-pitched Oriental voice. "Grasshopper, a wise man doesn't order rare hamburgers in a roadside diner named Mom's."

She smiled. "I know what you mean."

"How'd you first meet him?"

"Complications from his leg injury brought him in for treatment. Then I heard about his school, and referred someone there. We got friendly."

Odin heard something in her tone he didn't like. "How friendly?"

"We dated a few times."

"Oh." Odin knew he had no right to be jealous, but still. "You never told me that."

"It didn't seem relevant."

"I see."

He lay back down in the sun.

After a few minutes, she rubbed suntan lotion on him. He purred with pleasure. She did his face, chest, and thighs with no inhibition.

"Is it true what they say about nurses?" he asked.

"What's that?"

"After looking at sick bodies all day, they like nothing better than a romp with a healthy one."

"After looking at sick bodies all day, I like nothing better than a hot bath. I enjoy the challenge, but being a floater is hell."

"A floater?" he asked.

"Yes. That means I work all different assignments."

"A floater in police slang means a badly decomposed body. Usually one that's been in the water."

"That's how I feel sometimes."

He pulled her to him and they kissed. Slow and deep. When they separated, she had suntan lotion all over her.

"Now look at me." He got up and nuzzled her. "That smell

reminds me of coming to the beach when I was a teenager. Looking at the girls in bathing suits until I was too weak to walk." He nuzzled her some more.

"I don't know if that qualifies as romantic," she said.

"It was for me."

She sat back, tucking her legs against her chest. He leaned on his elbow and lay next to her.

"You seem different," she commented.

"It's the full moon."

"There's no full moon."

"Then it's the full sun."

"You're much more relaxed. Have you come to terms with things?"

"Yeah, I guess you could say that."

"I'm glad."

"I'm glad too."

She stretched out and he lay his head down on her stomach.

"You sure you have to go into work today?" he asked.

"At three P.M. the hospital falls apart without me."

They listened to the sounds of radios, children yelling, and waves crashing that were a unique beach symphony. Odin had found he enjoyed listening much more than he did before the accident.

"Have you gone scuba diving much since you were in the SEALs?" she asked.

"Not in a while."

"That's a pity. I always wanted to learn."

"With a pupil like you, I could regain my interest very quickly."

"My last vacation, about six years ago, I went to the Caribbean. I took a quickie scuba class. It was fantastic underwater. Like being on another planet. Weightless. You move differently, can't breathe the atmosphere. Light refracts strangely. And the wild life was so exotic."

"The wild life was pretty exotic in the SEALs. Especially

Pepe's Bar in Tiajuana. That's where we'd go for R and R," he said. He ran his fingertips along the soft skin inside her thigh. "We didn't have much time enjoying the undersea scenery. It was more like how to rip off someone's mouthpiece if you're attacked underwater."

"Don't you ever get tired of all the violence, Bob?" she asked, stopping his hand on its upward climb.

"Violence means never having to say you're sorry."

"You have a strange sense of humor."

"C'mon. Most of the nurses I know have just as sick a sense of humor as cops. It lets off the tension."

"It's too easily misunderstood."

"Do you know what an incurable romantic is?"

"What?"

"Someone with herpes, AIDS, and cancer."

"That's sick."

"What about, do you know what Gracie Allen had that Natalie Wood didn't?"

"I really don't like those sort of jokes."

"Okay."

"I guess we better head back."

After a few more protests from him, they did. They held hands as they walked to the car.

During the ride, Bob persisted, "Why don't you call in sick?"

"I can't do that."

"Why not?"

"I just can't."

"C'mon. When was the last time you played hookey?"

"I did a few times in high school."

"You're past due."

"I really can't. They need me."

"They'll get someone else."

"We're always stretched so thin, if one nurse doesn't show, the rest of the team has to work much harder. I couldn't do that to them. You wouldn't have let your squad members down, would you?"

"I did."

"No, you didn't," she said, squeezing his hand. "Don't even think that. You did your best."

"Hmmmmn."

They were at her house.

"Last chance," he said. "We could spend the afternoon soaring on the wings of eagles."

"I'm sorry." They kissed long and slow.

He got out, opened the door for her, and followed her up the steps to her place.

"I've just got time to get dressed and run off to work," Jan said, glancing at her watch.

"I could come in and help."

"Do what?"

"Soap you down when you shower," he suggested.

"It's probably best we say good-bye here," she said, with a businesslike tone, but a smile.

They kissed again. She pulled away.

"Ouch. That stubble hurts."

He rubbed his hand over his face, making a scratchy noise. "Sorry. How do you think I'd look with a beard?"

She studied him for a moment. "Nice. But you look nice without it too. It's been fun." She dug the key out of her purse and put it in the lock.

"It has. Jan?"

She turned.

"Don't be afraid of having fun," he said.

"I'm not." She folded her arms across her chest.

"Classic defensive posture," he said.

She let her arms down. "Okay. I'm a spoilsport. Can you accept me the way I am?"

"Sure. What about you? Can you accept me the way I am?"

She nodded.

He gave her a peck on her lips, and breezed away.

Riding back in his car, he switched the radio on and blasted sixties rock and roll. While disappointed he didn't have a chance to go further with Jan, he was on another level, quite glad. He hadn't had to perform. He kept thinking back on the episode with Bobbin' Robin.

He'd go for an afternoon workout at the dojo. He had a special kind of date planned for that night.

"Connie told me about your stubble," Scalia said. "Let me feel."

Odin leaned forward and Scalia brushed his fingers across Odin's face.

"You trying to look like me?" Scalia kidded. They were sitting in Scalia's office, a few minutes before class.

"I'd have to get hit by a truck first," Odin said. Then he realized it could be taken to be a reference to Scalia's legs. "I mean, to rearrange my face like that."

"No sweat. I knew you weren't talking about my legs. Part of the problem of being accepted as quote normal unquote is you forget I'm blind and legless. I'm sure people have said all sorts of things about eyes to you, and then gulped."

"For the first week or so, I kept noticing it," Odin said. "A sight for sore eyes. Keep an eye out. Knock your eyes out. I got my eye on you. Feast your eyes on that one. Since then, I haven't much noticed."

"Can't let it bother you," Scalia said. "You're making great progress. Physically, and mentally. Have you thought about working towards a black belt? Maybe become an instructor?"

"Nah. It's not my cup of tea."

"Do you know what you're going to do?"

He shrugged. "Not yet. I can almost live on the disability check. For now I'm just getting reacclimated to society."

"Keep it in mind. What you've done with Leon has been wonderful."

Class began, with Connie leading them through tough stretching exercises. Using Odin as his model attacker, Scalia demonstrated defense against a knife. He cautioned his students that nothing you carry in your wallet was worth getting killed for.

The younger students had begun to gravitate around Odin. Leon, at first jealous over the intrusion, had become Odin's "assistant." He gave fierce little yells and kicks, and was a stern instructor.

Odin frequently had to stifle a grin as he watched the kids work out with grim seriousness. He didn't know how effective a kick from a scrawny eight-year-old could be, but he had seen the tremendous change in attitude.

Class was winding down, with Scalia sitting in front, sharing anecdotes and snippets of Oriental philosophy. Odin wondered how much went over the kids' heads. But they listened dutifully to Scalia's soft tones as he quoted from the *Tao Te Ching*.

"Clay is molded into jugs, and because of the space where nothing exists we are able to use them to hold things," Scalia said. "Doors and windows are cut into the walls of houses, and because of the emptiness, we can use them.

"On one hand we have the benefit of existence, on the other we use nonexistence," Scalia said. "Only from the interaction of opposites do we get the tao. Okay. Class dismissed."

Students scurried to the dressing rooms to get back into street clothes.

A man stood by the doorway. He looked vaguely familiar. Odin watched him out of the corner of his eye. Whenever the sight of someone tickled his subconscious, he immediately assumed he had once arrested the person.

Scalia was asking a question, something about when would Odin next be at the dojo. Leon came out of the dressing room and walked hesitantly towards the waiting man.

Then Odin realized. The man looked a lot like Leon grown up. His father. The bastard who abused the boy.

Scalia went to get the ringing telephone. Odin watched the boy go to his father. The man grabbed Leon's hand and tugged.

"We're late," the man said.

His big steps were too much for the boy to keep up with and Leon stumbled as they headed towards the door.

A blinding rage swept over Odin. He ran at the man, who raised his arms to protect his face. The ex-cop got in two shots before he was knocked to the floor. Someone had smashed him between the shoulder blades.

He turned. Connie had launched a flying side kick and kicked him to the ground. The man was staring at Odin in horror. Leon was crying. Connie got up, warily watching Odin, in a combat stance, ready to defend herself.

"After what you did to the kid, I oughta kill you," Odin hissed at the man.

"What did I do? What did I do?" the man asked.

"Bastard."

Connie had edged so she was between Odin and the man. "Take it easy. Cool out."

"I come here to pick up my nephew, and this guy goes crazy on me," the man complained.

"Nephew?" Odin asked. "Oh shit."

"Well, you're one lucky sonofabitch," Scalia said, rolling into the office where Odin was waiting. "He's not going to press charges. I explained about your background, and he knows what his brother did to the kid. He says he can understand what you felt."

"He shouldn't'a pulled on the kid so hard," Odin said.

"Maybe. But most parents have given their kid a yank at one time or another. It's wrong but it doesn't mean you should knock his spleen out. You messed up good. I'm just glad you didn't have your gun with you."

"I wouldn't have shot him."

"I wish I could be sure of that." Scalia sighed. "Connie warned me about the hatred in you. It's one of those times when I wish I could see, see your face."

"It won't happen again."

"What do you think you taught Leon today? Swing first, and ask questions later. Great values. A great role model."

"I said it won't happen again."

"Not here it won't. You've got to take some time by yourself. Work it out. I don't want someone studying with me whose got so much negative energy in him."

"You're throwing me out?"

"Come back when you have it under control. You'll be welcome then."

Odin left without saying good-bye. Connie watched him go with the same wary look she'd had when she'd stopped his attack on Leon's uncle.

The dojo had served its purpose, Odin rationalized. He was back in shape, ready to nail Mokley.

Mokley. Once he got that little dirtbag, he could get on with his life. In a couple of hours, he'd take the next big step.

He went to the range and Palermo let him fire until his hand ached. The bullets punched out fist-sized holes in the targets' hearts.

17 The Rocket Inn was located in downtown Los Angeles, on a block with a tattoo parlor, two pawnshops, a porno movie house, a liquor store, and two boarded-up businesses. Just the way Casey's or the Stardust had a very specific clientele, the Rocket Inn had its own special patrons—the people who would be unwelcome in any other bar.

Bikers, bums, pimps, hookers, muggers, scamsters, and dope dealers bellied up to the bar. Drinks were expensive since the owner was constantly fighting to preserve his liquor license. The Alcoholic Beverage Commission made periodic raids, as did the LAPD. Still the bar kept reopening.

The neon sign in front was broken, and flashed ROC INN. The window was the smallest size mandated by the ABC and was so grimy no one could peer in or out anyway. The front was mainly sprayed stucco, caked with filth. The door was a sheet of steel.

It was nearing midnight when the man with dark gradient sunglasses pushed his way through the door. Several patrons wore dark glasses, so he didn't stand out.

There was a hint of a moment's silence as he came in. Two enormous bouncers, like lions guarding a temple gate, stood on either side of the door. One gave the newcomer a rough, thorough frisk, then grunted. They waved him through. The frisk would've picked up a wire recorder or transmitter as well as most weapons.

It was impossible to see the newcomer's eyes beneath the sunglasses. But a grisly patch of burned skin next to his right eye was visible. He had the scuzzy beginnings of a beard and a slight sneer.

Odin breathed slowly in and out, his nose suffering the stench of spilled beer, marijuana, poppers, and urine. Music blasted from the jukebox, heavy metal, black rap, new wave. The noise made anything but shouted conversation impossible. And cut down on Odin's confidence. He had come to rely heavily on his sense of sound to fill in for his limited range of vision.

There were a dozen small round wooden tables on one side of the room and a densely packed bar on the other. All around him, Odin saw deals being made. Packets of white powder, baggies of leafy green material, pills—being swapped for money. At one table a man was trying desperately to interest another in a small TV. At another, a teenager was hawking a few watches.

Odin made his way to the bar and ordered a drink. He had gulped down half the bottle of Pepto Bismol shortly before entering. The coating would reduce the effects of the booze he would be consuming.

After an hour of drinking, he had been offered a hot Rolex watch, marijuana, Quaaludes, heroin, PCP, cocaine in several forms, a Blaupunkt radio with wires hanging from it, and three unnatural acts, two from women and one from a man.

He had given gruff "no's" to all of them. Those who had persisted, he'd told he was looking for someone who owed him money. Gary Mokley.

"He's too hot, man," one of the dope dealers had said. "You won't see him around."

"The cops already iced Gary," another said. "They're hushing it up. His body's chopped up in the desert."

One of the prostitutes who offered her services said, "I heard from a girlfriend he's in Mexico. Got a friend in the government down there. Living on a villa."

After another hour of drinking, Odin went to the john and drained off some of the four beers he'd consumed. Hidden in a stall, he took another swig of Pepto Bismol. Coming out, he was propositioned by another gay hustler.

His place at the bar had been taken.

"You again," one of the hookers said when she bumped into him. She was a chubby woman, who looked as though she was coming hard on forty. Her massive breasts were pushed up and half bared, like a fleshy counter under her chin. She had a dopey, happy smile and awkward movements. Either she was under the influence of some drug or brain-damaged. "Change your mind?" she asked.

"Not tonight," Odin said.

"Watch out Cookie don't lift your wallet," a man next to Odin warned.

"Pig!" Cookie spit out at the interloper. She looped her arm through Odin's. "He's an old friend."

"Hey, Cookie, get your chi-chis over here," a male voice bellowed from the other side of the room. She scurried away.

"Not even twenty years old and she's rutted with half the barbarians in this room," the man next to Odin said. He took a sip of his beer and shook his head. "She's got the IQ of a gerbil."

Odin turned to face him. The man was in his late thirties, small, skinny, and pale. He looked nearly as bad as Odin had in the hospital.

"I haven't seen you around here," the man said.

Odin shrugged. "I been around."

"How long have you known Cookie?"

"What's it your business?" Odin asked. Friendliness was mistaken for weakness in a place like the Rocket Inn.

"I'm the social director for this place."

"I'm looking for someone."

"I've been coming here three years. I'm not proud of it, but it's got a great ambiance. My name's Ben." He extended his hand.

"Bob." They shook hands.

"Who are you looking for?" the man asked.

"Gary Mokley."

"You a cop?"

"Do I look like a cop?"

"They make cops in all shapes and sizes."

"Okay. I'm a cop. Piss off." Odin returned to his beer.

The gambit worked. "You can't be too careful. The heat's been on because of Mokley. The Broken Noses have even been looking for him."

"Who?"

Ben pushed his nose to the side and put on a raspy tone, "The guys dat talk like dis and break bones for a livin'."

"Why?"

"I don't ask them questions. Probably because the cops get conscientious when one of their own gets blown away. They put heat on the big boys, who beat the bushes for them."

Odin nodded. "You don't know Mokley?"

"I didn't say that."

Odin unconsciously stepped closer to hear better. The Doors's "The End" was blasting from the jukebox.

Ben's mug was empty. He looked mournfully into the glass. "I talk better with a moist larynx."

Odin signaled for the bartender to refill Ben's glass.

"Not that pisswater," Ben said. "Remy Martin, please."

The bartender got a bottle down off a high shelf, and poured. Ben took a sip.

"Mokley, like myself, doesn't really belong in this world," Ben said, gesturing to the rest of the denizens of the bar. "I sense you too have evolved above the primordial slime that most of these animals inhabit."

"Heroin's the great equalizer," Odin said.

"You can tell?"

"Aside from your swaying back and forth, it's not too bad," Odin said. "You don't fit in with the surroundings."

"I knew you were a kindred spirit. May I ask what is your interest in Mokley?"

"He owes some people money. I collect."

"Ahh. And you feigned ignorance of Broken Noses. You duped me."

The Remy Martin was half gone.

"You gonna tell me about Mokley or just jerk my chain?" Odin snapped, getting the questioning back on track.

"Of course. Mokley and I shared the same connection."

"Who is he?"

"That will cost more than a drink."

"How much?"

"Fifty."

"After I talk to him."

"Before."

"Twenty before, thirty after."

Ben nodded. "Do you have the money on you?"

"Yes."

"I'll take twenty now. I'll give him a call." He pointed to a pay phone at the back of the bar.

Odin nodded, passed him the twenty, and got up.

"Wait here. I don't want you to see his phone number."

Behind the phone was the bathroom. The rear exit was off to one side, and there was no way Ben could slip out. Odin agreed. Ben made his way across the crowded room to the phone, picked it up and dialed a number. He began talking intently into the mouthpiece.

The crowd shifted. Odin's view was blocked for a fraction of a second.

Ben was gone. Odin forced his way through the thick crowd, earning quite a few angry pushes back. Odin made it to the bathroom. A couple of junkies were nodding out.

"He went that-a-way," one of them said, giggling and pointing to an open window. Through it, Odin saw Ben hightailing down the street. The window was too small for Odin to crawl through. By the time Odin pushed through the crowd to the exit, Ben would be blocks away.

Odin kicked the stall door, denting the metal. The door flew open, exposing a copulating couple. Odin ignored them and stormed out.

"Gimme a straight scotch," he said. The bartender passed it over. Odin had to dig out another ten. The money he'd left on the bar had been stolen as soon as he'd turned his back.

He chugged back the scotch, enraged at Ben and angry at himself. As a patrol and SWAT cop, he was not used to the subtleties of dealing with informants. Especially from a non-threatening, undercover position. Fifteen minutes passed and he was ready to leave. He'd come back the next night, and the next, until he caught up with Ben.

"Ben rip you off?" It was Cookie again. There was a few drops of dried semen caking in her greasy black hair.

"Get away," Odin snarled.

"I know where he went," she said.

Odin turned on her. "Where?"

"It'll cost you twenty bucks."

"I already played that game."

"I'll go with you. Gimme the money once you get him."

"Let's go."

They walked six blocks to a rundown strip of Spring Street on the edge of Chinatown. The smell of garbage from the many restaurants was heavy in the air. A rat jumped out of one can and Cookie yelped.

"He lives up there," she said, pointing to an apartment above a knickknack store with Vietnamese writing on the front.

She pulled up her dress, baring an enormous hairy mound. "For another twenty bucks, you can do me." She reached for his crotch. He pushed her hand away.

"We have our deal," he said.

"How about up the ass? You want to do me up the ass?" She turned, offering him a view of huge buttocks.

A driver passing by honked his horn.

"Cookie, put your skirt down," Odin said.

"I need the money. Ten bucks. Any way you want to."

Odin looked at the buzzer. BEN WATERS 2B it read.

Next to it, someone had written "or not 2B."

He gave Cookie a twenty-dollar bill. "Go."

"I'll wait. You steal anything good, I know the fences. I'll get us a great price."

"Cookie, I'm going to kill him. A sweet young thing like you don't want to get involved in murder, do you?"

She shook her head.

"Good."

She lifted her dress again and stepped into the doorway. "Five bucks?"

"Go back to the bar."

She flounced away. Odin walked quietly up the stairs. He reached 2B and pressed his ear against the door.

A door down the hall opened and a heavyset woman stepped out.

"Whatchyou doin' over there?"

"Get back in your apartment," Odin growled.

"Fuck you," she said.

He took a step towards her. She returned to her apartment and slammed the door.

Odin hurried to 2B and tried the door. Locked. He stepped back and kicked it in, the flimsy wood shattering easily.

Ben was sitting on the stained, torn sofa, about to shoot up. Seeing Odin he panicked, and pushed the plunger although it wasn't in his arm. The heroin spewed on his scrawny forearm. He cried out and licked his arm, oblivious even as Odin closed in on him and lifted him in the air.

Ben was crying and shaking. "My fix, my fix."

"You ripped me off, shithead."

"My fix, my fix."

Odin threw him back on the sofa, the only piece of real furniture in the one room apartment. There was a sheet and army surplus blanket on the floor. Plastic milk crates served as chair and table. On one of the crates were a few dirty plates and empty soda cans. Another had papers and a black book.

The walls were stained and the paint peeling. The linoleum had buckled in parts. In an inset in the wall was a stove and refrigerator. The only reason Waters hadn't sold them off for dope was they were too old to be marketable, not quite old enough to be antiques.

Waters was curled up in a ball, crying.

"You were lying to me, weren't you?"

Waters nodded.

"Do you know anything about Mokley?"

"I met him a few times. We know some of the same people."

Odin walked over to the papers, clippings from a UCLA Extension catalogue. Ben Waters was listed, teaching interior design. The papers were yellowed with age.

"Leave that alone," Waters said, though he didn't move from his position.

Odin picked up the black book. It was filled with names and

addresses. Gary Mokley's number was in there. Odin turned to the Ws.

"Who is Constance Waters? Or Janie Waters."

"Leave them out of it."

"How much do you need to get another fix?"

The change that came over Waters was miraculous. He sat up, no longer self-pitying. He wiped the tears from his face. "Twenty."

"Who is Constance Waters?"

"My mother."

"And Janie?"

"Sister."

"And this one, scratched out. What is Pam?"

"My ex-wife. Will you give me the twenty? Please. It's a sickness. You wouldn't let a sick man suffer?"

Odin took the black book. "You're going to help me find Mokley. I'm from the Cleveland Mob. Your mother, your sister, your ex-wife, everyone in here, their lives are in your hands. Understand?"

"Are you gonna give me the money?" Mokley asked.

"Are you listening?"

"Yes, yes."

"I want Mokley. Can you find him?"

"Yes, yes."

Odin held out the twenty. Waters grabbed it and hurried towards the door.

"One last question, what did the cops ask you about Mokley?"

"They never questioned me," Waters said, hurrying to the door.

Odin wrote his home telephone number on a piece of paper and left it on the table. "You give me Mokley and there's five hundred bucks in it for you," he added.

As he left Ben's apartment, the woman down the hall glared.

Odin stood under the steaming shower for as long as he could stand it. He felt like the filth he'd been in had permeated the deepest parts of his body. The liquor he'd imbibed just made him feel worse.

He'd go to the dojo tomorrow and work it off. Then he remembered he was no longer welcome at the gym. Cursing, he slammed his fist into the wall.

It wasn't right. It wasn't fair. What had he done to deserve this? Nearly killing an innocent man, fraternizing with vermin, being propositioned by the lowest whores, threatening scrawny junkies.

He got out of the shower and went to the mirror. He wiped the steam away. His face was a horror. Three quarters of it normal, and then that patch that looked like a Hollywood make-up artist's worst visions.

He was due to go back to the hospital to have his good eye checked. There was talk about a plastic surgeon. But he'd have to wait months before the tissue was healed enough for them to begin reconstructive work.

For the while, it was just another reminder of Mokley.

The phone rang and he dripped his way to it.

"This is Ben," the voice said. It was calm, confident, a little sluggish. "I believe you have something of mine. My address book, specifically."

"You've got a week until I start visiting the people in there," Odin said.

"They, they don't know what happened to me," Waters said. "They think I'm overseas."

"That's not my problem. I want Mokley."

Odin hung up. What would he do after a week? Mail the book back. It was a bluff, but still he felt disgusted with himself. He'd given Waters money to shoot up. He knew narco cops aided their informants in scoring. Some even held back dope on seizures and paid directly with it. But the thought made Odin feel sick. The whole night had been disgusting. His whole life was disgusting. Ruined. He wasn't a cop.

He rushed to the sink and threw up.

He held onto the sides of the sink and stared into the mirror. His face seemed blurry. He squinted his good eye. Better, but still blurry.

The second wave of nausea hit him, and again he bent and retched.

18 Over the next three days, Odin hit low-life night spots where Mokley had been known to hang out. Twice he was involved in minor scuffles. He met various creepy characters and garnered several promising leads. All of them washed out. His clothes stank from cigarettes, his breath from beer, and he felt like he could never wash the filth off.

By the fifth morning, he didn't want to get out of bed. How could anyone be an undercover cop? It was bad enough dealing with the scum as a patrol officer. To wallow in the slime with them, befriend them, get to know their twisted hopes, dreams, and then bust them, was beyond Odin's comprehension. And guys did it for weeks, for months.

This morning, he had to wonder whether he had enough spirit left to get up and get coffee. What he dreaded was that he knew he'd have to go back to the underworld until he got Mokley.

He'd avoided seeing Jan, afraid somehow she would see the dirt on his spirit. She had sent him a book about people who had overcome the handicap of having one eye. Aviator Wiley Post, Admiral Horatio Nelson, Israeli leader Moshe Dayan, entertainer Sammy Davis, Jr., French artist Degas, inventor Gugliemo Marconi, President Theodore Roosevelt.

There was a gentle knocking at the door. Odin rolled out of bed, grabbing the Asp from the night table. He moved towards the door from the side, out of the line of fire. His moping was forgotten.

"Yeah?"

"It's Junior."

Odin opened the door. Fleming Junior was nervously looking over his shoulder. He hurried into the apartment.

"What's the matter?" Odin asked.

"I got those papers you wanted," Junior said. "I hope they weren't watching me."

"Great. Don't sweat it, kid. No one wants to tangle with an assistant's son."

"Oh, yeah? My father's got as many enemies as friends. Maybe more. The chief doesn't like him. He'd love to see my dad go down in flames. Same goes for the other two assistant chiefs. If I got caught, it would kill my father."

"Don't worry, he'll be the next chief," Odin said, reaching for the manila envelope Junior slid from inside his shirt. It was damp with sweat.

Odin set his gun down and opened the envelope. Junior went to the window and peered out.

"They might be watching your place," Junior said.

"They who?"

"Internal Affairs." While Assistant Chief Fleming, as head of Operations, controlled the largest number of officers, units like Internal Affairs and Administrative Vice were under the Assistant Chief in charge of Special Services. The third assistant chief, who generally had the least clout, was in charge of administration.

"Why would they waste their time on me?" Odin asked.

"You never know," Junior said, turning to Odin. "I overheard my father on the phone. He's gotten a few calls on you. Something about you beating some guys up with a baseball bat."

"Hmmm," Odin said as he shuffled through the papers.

About fifty photocopied pages. There were detective reports, intelligence division reports, patrol officers' reports, a DEA report, IRS report, and FBI report. There were a few magazine articles with Mokley's byline on them.

"What happened?" Fleming asked, breaking in on his thoughts.

"A minor disagreement. Why didn't you call? I could've picked it up from you if that would make you feel better."

"They might be listening in on your phone," Junior said. "I just hope they haven't bugged your apartment."

Odin threw a fatherly arm over Junior. "Take it easy. You're getting paranoid."

"You don't know what it's like. I've seen it because of my father. I better go." Fleming's head darted from side to side, as if checking the apartment out for opposition.

Odin picked up his gun. "Want me to cover you?" he asked with a wink.

"Be careful," Junior said humorlessly. "You're not on the job anymore. You're not used to dealing with the department from the outside. Having those papers alone is a misdemeanor."

"Thanks for them, Junior. Don't worry. I won't let them catch me jaywalking."

Fleming reached for the door. "I'm sorry about what happened. I . . ."

"It wasn't your fault. Thanks again."

Fleming was about to say something, thought better of it, and slipped out.

Odin made himself coffee and a peanut-butter-and-jelly sandwich, and sat at his small kitchen table with the papers.

When he next looked at the clock, he had finished the papers, his eye was sore, and it was past lunchtime.

Gary Mokley had been a drug culture pioneer, a teen during the early sixties, on the fringes of Timothy Leary's group, the intelligence division report said. He'd run errands for Owsley, taken part in the Free Speech movement at Berkeley, been arrested at People's Park.

After the demonstration at the Democratic convention in Chicago, where he'd been arrested again, he'd dropped out of sight. An informant said he'd joined the Weathermen.

He wasn't seen much over the next few years, but according to the FBI report, he was suspected of harboring fugitives. Patty Hearst and her SLA captors reportedly stayed a couple of nights at Mokley's place on the edge of Oakland. None of the reports could be verified.

In 1969, Mokley had his first article published, "Confession of a Burned Out Radical." *Rolling Stone* had run it as a cover story. The piece was heavy on anecdotes about Mokley's experiences with rock groups like Big Brother and the Holding Company, Jefferson Airplane, and the Grateful Dead.

He subsequently had articles published in *High Times*, *Esquire*, *Penthouse*, the *Village Voice*. He specialized on celebrity interviews and commentary on coming of age in the sixties. One of his pieces inspired a film. Mokley moved to Malibu. Got married. Divorced.

He had always used drugs for recreational purposes, but by 1978, he had a five-hundred-dollar-a-day cocaine habit. He had gotten a paunch on his five-foot-nine-inch frame but he lost it. Plus forty pounds more. As well as his house in Malibu and all his nondoper friends.

He checked himself into a drug rehab clinic. Six months after graduating, he was back to a five-hundred-dollar-a-day habit. By 1981, Mokley was a heavyweight cocaine dealer. He used his role as a free-lance journalist to gain access to various celebrities. He freelanced for *People*, *US*, and the *Star*. During the interviews, he let it be known about his sideline.

He had a dozen leading film and TV stars as his clients. Mere mortals wanted to let it be known that their dealer was the one who provided dope for so-and-so.

He moved to Laguna Beach and bought a house on the water. He had legendary parties. Surveillance reports listed the in crowd who enjoyed his orgies. Agents from William Morris, ICM, and Creative Artists begged to be allowed to attend, to approach the stars when their guards, as well as their pants, were down. Mokley became a Hollywood power broker.

In 1984 the feds busted him. DEA and IRS. And IRS assessment of his finances showed that most of his assets came from drug trafficking and the hard-nosed federal judge ordered everything seized.

Mokley was pressured to testify against his clients, and suppliers. He refused. He skipped out on a million dollars bail. When he was caught four months later, the judge declared him a flight risk and ordered him held without bail.

Convicted at trial, Mokley received the maximum sentence, twenty years. Since he had skipped out previously, the judge remanded him to custody immediately. After a year in prison his case reached the 9th Circuit Court of Appeals. A key notebook was ruled inadmissable. Mokley was freed, retried, and found innocent.

His customers had found new dealers, or given up drugs. It was no longer chic to have cocaine bowls out next to the dip at parties. Mokley made a living selling free-lance pieces and dealing grams and an occasional ounce. There were rumors he was working on a tell-all book.

Surveillance reports listed him visiting a half dozen low-life sites, including the Stardust and the Rocket Inn. One included his boast to an informant that they would never take him alive. The informant confirmed that Mokley was now carrying a gun.

There was one LAPD Intelligence Division report that set Odin's hackles up. It noted that Mokley had been suspected of involvement in several Weathermen bombing incidents.

Why the hell hadn't Odin been told before they'd raided his apartment? The narcotics cop, "Bagels" Begelman, had briefed them before the raid. The briefing had been concise, leaving out most of Mokley's rise and fall, highlighting just the possible dangers. But certainly his connection with bombings was something Odin should have been told.

Odin got up and kicked the chair. Maybe he would have

been more careful. Then Finch and Daggett would be alive, and I wouldn't be a cripple, the ex-cop fumed. If Bagels had been around, he would have hit him.

Again that overwhelming rage swept over him. Mokley. He had to get Mokley.

He rubbed his good eye. It was burning. Everything was blurry. All that reading. He threw cold water on his face. He did a half hour of exercises, stretching, push-ups, sit-ups, chin-ups, then kicks, punches, and blocks. Dripping sweat, he threw himself in the shower.

Mrs. Peckman was dying. No sooner would the doctors control her diabetes, than her heart would act up. They'd get that under control, ship her back to the nursing home, and two days later, she'd be rushed back by ambulance with kidney failure.

Jan Golden had seen Peckman a half dozen times, for various ailments. She liked the old woman, who hoped to live to reach her ninety-second birthday.

"Did I ever tell you I was a singer?" Peckman asked, commencing her story without waiting for an answer. Golden had heard it at least twice. How Peckman had sung back-up for Benny Goodman and been besieged by suitors, including the King of Swing himself.

Golden nodded along, helping Peckman up, guiding her in a walk around the room, then settling her down. If there was the time, which was too seldom, Golden would brush Peckman's hair, and put makeup on her. It was the highlight of Peckman's day and Jan felt guilty that she only got to do it once or twice a week.

Golden glanced at her watch. By cutting lunch down to a quick bite, she could groom Mrs. Peckman.

"Sweetie, you're wonderful, but I know you don't have time," Peckman said.

"For my favorite patient, there's always time," Jan responded.

It was their usual patter. Golden got the hairbrush from the drawer and began stroking while Mrs. Peckman cooed.

"You married?" Mrs. Peckman asked.

"No."

"My son got married again last year. To a spoiled *shiksa* witch. That's why he doesn't come. She won't let him. She's too busy with her tennis and social groups. He takes care of her kids from her first husband. He's an angel to her."

Peckman launched into a tirade against her son's current wife. Golden had heard it before. She knew what the ending would be. She didn't put any makeup around Peckman's eyes and had the box of tissues handy.

"He hasn't come to see me in months," she said, and the tears began to roll. "If my husband were alive, it would kill him."

After a few minutes of consoling, Golden eased her back into bed. She checked on the seven nurses she was supervising—as well as four patients she was responsible for—and raced to the cafeteria for a fifteen-minute lunch break. There was too long a line for her to get a meal.

Mary Tallero was sitting at a table and waved her over.

"I don't have time," Golden said.

Tallero pointed to a piece of cake on her tray. "Go ahead. Eat mine. High calories. Give you energy."

Golden dug into the food. She picked french fries from Tallero's plate and gulped down water.

"In exchange for stealing food from out of my mouth, do you have any good gossip?"

"Nothing exciting," Golden said.

"How about rumors that a pretty brunette currently working on the sixth floor is involved with a former police officer?"

"Who told you that?"

"No names. Enquiring minds want to know."

"We've gone out a few times."

"What's he like?"

"Troubled. But nice."

"I mean in bed."

"Mary!"

"C'mon. This is the eighties."

"I hardly know him."

Tallero bit into her pastrami sandwich and chewed slowly.

"I haven't heard from him in a few days." Golden sighed. "I've always told nurses not to get involved with cops. Half of them are nuts. The other half are married and screwing around."

"I suppose nurses are all well-balanced and monogamous."

"That's exactly it. We're too similar. We both see people at their worst. Keep screwy hours. Have unpredictable days. Deal with death and suffering. We'd never work as a couple."

"From the general to the specific."

"Okay. I'm attracted to him. Why hasn't he called?"

"Call him."

"I can't."

"Like I said, this is the eighties. Women call men. Women enjoy sex. Men get to cook and cry at movies. It's a fair trade-off."

"Maybe I will."

"Maybe you won't. Scaredy cat."

Golden glanced at her watch. "If I make it a quick call . . ."

"You can use the phone in my office."

"No way. I want my privacy."

"Going to make lovebird talk?"

"Sometimes you can be really obnoxious."

"Shut up and finish my cake before I do."

"I'm glad you called," Odin said when he picked up the phone and heard Jan's voice.

She was equally glad that he was at home. She'd envisioned him with another woman. "I hope I'm not interrupting anything."

"No, I was just looking through old papers." The reports on Mokley were spread out in front of him.

"What sort of papers?"

"Unimportant stuff."

"I—I was wondering if you wanted to see that Woody Allen movie I was telling you about."

"*Annie Hall*. Yeah, I'd like to see one of his movies. You keep raving about him. But only if I can take you to dinner."

"You drive a hard bargain. I get off at three-thirty. How about you pick me up at five for an early bite? The movie starts at six-thirty at the Nuart. It's playing with *Manhattan*."

"See you at five."

Bob hung up, feeling good. He thought about going to the dojo, then remembered how he had screwed up. Who gave Scalia the right to throw him out? Had Scalia slept with Jan Golden? He didn't need the bearded creep anyway. The anger welled up directed at Scalia. Odin recognized it was misplaced. Mokley was the one.

Seeing Jan meant he wouldn't get to go out barhopping. He was glad for the excuse to stay out of the slime. He glanced around his apartment. Speaking of slime, it needed a cleaning. Bad.

Humming, "I'm in the Mood for Love," he began tidying up. The first thing he did was hide the papers Junior had brought him.

19 Assistant Chief Fred Fleming finished a hundred push-ups. He lay on the shag-carpeted floor. His wood-paneled office had a sweeping view of downtown Los Angeles. On the walls were plaques and medals from his police career, including the Medal of Valor, the highest honor. There were several photos of Fleming with U.S. presidents.

In a small glass display case were two brass balls, with a small plaque saying "In case you need a spare." It had been given to him by the officers in his last field command, after he had been transferred to headquarters.

Fleming rolled over, preparing to do a hundred sit-ups, when there was a light rap on the door.

"Yes?"

His aide—an attractive redheaded policewoman with pale skin and an hourglass shape—came in. "Your son's on the phone."

He glanced at his watch. "Come here," he said, crooking his finger. She shut the door. He pulled her to the floor.

Fifteen minutes later, while she brushed her hair and adjusted her clothing, Fleming picked up the blinking phone.

"I'm sorry to bother you, sir," his son said. "I know how busy you are."

"Very," the assistant chief said, zipping up his fly. "What is it?"

"I heard that you're having Huey, the captain, and some other guys in to see you. Is it about Bob?"

Fleming gestured for his aide to leave. She gave him an annoyed look, but obeyed.

"I presume you're referring to former sergeant Odin. The answer is yes. Your friend hasn't even cleaned out his locker yet and already he's creating problems." Fleming thumbed reports on his desk. "Four punks in North Hollywood claim he assaulted them. Informants have placed him at a couple of the downtown bars, where he got involved in an incident with a junkie."

"I'm sorry."

"That's wonderful," the assistant chief said snidely.

"What did you want Huey and the others for?"

"Is it any of your business?"

"Well, I thought, maybe . . ."

"It's not. Simple enough. But I'll tell you. I hope that one of them might speak to him, get him to back off. Hero cop arrested in downtown bar brawl won't do him or the department any good."

"That's nice of you."

"Is that all?"

"Yes, sir."

Fleming senior broke the connection.

As he was hanging up, his private telephone line rang. Only the president of the United States, the heads of the major studios, and a dozen other corporate heavyweights had the number. Even his family did not have it. He straightened, unconsciously adjusting his tie, before answering. "Yes?"

"Know who this is?" Nicky Provenzano asked.

"How did you get this number?"

"It was written on the bathroom wall in one of my bars."

"What do you want?" Fleming felt like Provenzano had broken into his house. There was a constant power play between the two, and Pro seemed to be winning.

"It's not what I want, it's what you want."

"Don't give me that cryptic dago bullshit," Fleming snarled.

"Hey, let's not get personal. You don't want to know where Mokley is, I'll hang up."

"Okay, okay, where is he?"

"Not even an I'm sorry?"

"I'm sorry."

"Good. I've got a couple of my boys watching him right now. You want them to take care of him?"

"No. Where is he?"

"You still owe me."

"Of course, of course. We'll talk about payment later. Not over the phone."

"Okay. He's in Oceanside. Room twenty-six at the Seashore Motel."

"Room twenty-six. The Seashore Motel. Oceanside."

"I can make him disappear," Provenzano said cheerfully. "Nice and easy."

"No. That would only complicate things."

"He could turn up dead in his room."

"Too many questions would be asked. I'll handle it. Thanks," Fleming said begrudgingly.

"What's a little favor among friends."

As Provenzano was about to hang up, Fleming said, "Wait a minute. You have people down there?"

"That's right."

"I've got an idea."

A cold wind whipped off the ocean and Jan hugged Odin for warmth as they walked out on the Santa Monica Pier.

"I'm glad you enjoyed the movies," she said.

"La de dah, la de dah," Bob said, grinning and mimicking Diane Keaton. "I liked the last line in *Manhattan*. 'Everyone is corrupted.'"

"The voice of cynicism."

"The voice of experience."

Their banter was vaguely teasing, vaguely challenging. It had persisted through their meal at the seafood restaurant at the foot of the pier, and continued as they walked. It felt comfortable, easy.

"They're showing *Hannah and her Sisters* and *Stardust Memories* next week," she said. "If you're interested."

"Only if I can find a date to take. Otherwise, I'd prefer a Clint Eastwood film festival."

"I thought of you as a Stallone fan."

"I never enjoyed watching boxing. Fighting was something I did because I had to. As far as the *Rambo* crap, making combat look like fun doesn't jibe with my memories."

She gave him a peck on the cheek. "Just when I think I've got you pegged, you surprise me."

"But Dirty Harry is a character I can enjoy. A cop who kills people, what can be bad?"

She gave him a gentle punch in the ribs.

"Assaulting an officer." He paused. "An ex-officer. I'll have to take you into custody."

He pulled her roughly to him and they locked in a deep kiss. In the distance, the calliope of the carousel sang.

She sat on the sofa, somewhat primly, sipping a cup of coffee. He sat next to her, arm across her shoulder, leaning back. There was a tension in the air, a promise of passion to be fulfilled.

"What sort of papers were you looking through today?" she asked.

"Why do you ask?"

"If you don't want to tell me, it's okay."

He went to the coffee machine and poured himself a cup.

"I asked because it's normal to go through a period of re-evaluation after a tragedy," she explained. "People root through photo albums, letters from old girlfriends, souvenirs of high school. Trying to find out where you've been, what you've done, if it's been worth it. Sometimes it's part of a depressive funk. Sometimes it's a positive sign."

"You're trying to diagnose me?" he asked, annoyed.

"No. Just if you dredged up anything interesting, I'd like to see it."

"Part of my therapy?"

"Stop being defensive. Part of my interest in you."

"La de dah, la de dah," he said. "Okay, want to see my photo album?"

"Great."

He fetched an album from the bedroom. They sat close and went through it. There was a picture of a man who looked like Odin, with twenty pounds of weight and as many years added. He had a wooden toy boat in his hand. In back of him was a sophisticated wood shop.

"My father," Bob said. "He was a carpenter."

"What was he like?"

"Didn't talk much. But when he did, it was usually worth listening to. Lots of what he taught me about wood is as philosophical as the Lao Tzu stuff Scalia preaches."

"Like what?"

"Before you make a cut, get to know the wood. You can cut with the grain, or against it. A workman is only as good as his tools. A poor workman blames his tools. There's a quick way, and the right way. The stuff sounds like clichés when I say it, but when he did, it came out important. Maybe it's because he only spoke about three times a day."

"You loved him?"

"Of course." A long silence. "Another one of his maxims was spare the rod and spoil the child. He broke my leg once when I stole something."

Jan looked horrified.

"He didn't mean to do it. He'd had a few belts of Wild Turkey. Didn't realize how strong he was. He used a piece of wood to paddle us. Just hit me the wrong way, I guess."

"If you had a kid, would you beat him?" she asked.

"Not beat him. Maybe give him a whack if he acted up. I don't know."

"Corporal punishment is bad."

"You're right. I wouldn't hit him. Maybe a cattle prod would be better. Doesn't leave marks."

"Some things I don't joke about," she said. "I've seen too many child abuse cases."

"So have I," Bob said. "You want to swap horror stories?"

"No."

He flipped through the pages of the album, pointing out members of his family. Odin had been, by his own admission, a troublesome youth and had wound up in the SEALs.

"There's only a couple of pictures of me and the guys," Bob explained as they came to a page with crew-cut young men forming a human pyramid. "They kept a hush-hush atmosphere. My letters to my folks were censored, even when we were still in training in San Diego."

"Are you still in touch with any of them?"

Bob pointed to a figure at the bottom of the pyramid. "I heard from him a few months ago. He's got a car dealership in Portland." He pointed to two men in the next layer. "Dead." He pointed to another two. "They became career soldiers. Last I heard, one was in South Carolina, the other in Germany. A few of the others fell through the cracks. Never really adjusted to civilian life. They take months training you for combat and not even minutes to help you readjust."

"What was your most exciting time?" she asked.

He thought for a moment. "We had been dropped by parachute way up the Mekong. About midnight, and the temperature was still in the eighties. High humidity. No moon. Cicadas chirping. Smell of water buffalo crap in the air. Dark, so dark." Odin leaned back and closed his eye, immersing himself in the memory.

"We came out of a bamboo grove and encountered a patrol. They outnumbered us two to one. We had surprise, but they knew the turf. In the firefight, one of our guys bought it. We lost more than half of our explosives.

"We made it to the target area and infiltrated a VC compound. We neutralized about twenty of them. There was this bridge that had to be taken out. But we didn't have enough explosives to handle it.

"Here we are, forty klicks into VC territory, the bridge just standing there, and we can't do anything about it. Then I got an idea. You know what tamping is?"

She shook her head.

"An explosion goes boom in all directions. If you can focus it in one direction, it makes it much stronger."

"Like Mount Saint Helens blowing out the side of the mountain," she said.

"Right. We used the VC bodies to tamp the charge on the bridge. Blew that sucker into a million pieces. Slowed down their supply trail for a week."

He had grown animated as he told the story. She just stared at him.

"Uh, we got out of there safely without any more casualties. I got a DSC for it. Distinguished Service Cross."

"That's nice."

"You sorry you asked?"

"Maybe."

"It's war. And I was good at it." He stared off into space for a moment and she asked what was the matter.

"Ironic, isn't it? I mean, the charge being tamped at Mokley's is why I'm like this." He tapped the eyepatch.

She turned the page in the album. There were photos of Odin as a student at the police academy. "You went right into the academy?"

"No. I kicked around for about a year. Worked as a shoe salesman. After some broad—I mean woman—had tried on twenty-five pairs and then walked out without buying, I wanted to strangle her. The only thing that kept me going was the women who came in in short skirts with no panties."

"Charming."

"Every job has its perks. Then I worked in a warehouse, on a loading dock, handling major appliances from forklift to truck. The highlight of my day was sitting in the bar, swapping war stories with other bored vets. I went with them to take the civil service test. I did well. Top five percent. Which must mean the test was geared for morons."

"Don't knock yourself."

"I know my limitations. The academy was great. I slipped right back into the military lifestyle. Short hair. Tough instructors. Hard work. The biggest problem was the differences between what we learned in the classroom, and in our workouts. In class we had guys teaching us the laws, the proper way to make arrests, the sociological differences with minority groups. Yatter, yatter, yatter. In the gym, the instructors told us 'kick 'em in the nuts, and then ask questions.' The old timers we met said the same thing."

"I had the identical feelings in nursing school."

"They told you to kick patients in the balls?"

"Only cops who gave us a hard time," she said. "Seriously. We had two days of classroom, where they taught us the right way to do things. You know, take fifteen minutes to give a patient a back rub or a bed bath. Then we'd have two days working in the hospital, where you were lucky if you had fifteen seconds for a procedure. It used to make me crazy. It seemed like everyone was taking shortcuts that were improper and dangerous."

"Cops too. You start out wanting to do everything by the book. After a few months on the job, you realize no way, José. If you don't take shortcuts on the paperwork, you'll spend your life writing up reports on one misdemeanor."

"So similar," she said.

He gazed at her. "I'm glad I met you."

"I'm glad I met you too." She broke the intense looks that were passing between them. "What's this?" she asked, pointing to a picture of a lieutenant in uniform dripping water.

"That's this dorky lieutenant we had at the first division I worked at," Odin said. "We booby-trapped his locker once a week. He finally transferred. You know what I'd like?"

"What?"

"One of those fifteen-minute back rubs."

"I'm off duty."

"Nurses are like cops. You're on duty all the time."

"What's in it for me?"

"I'll drop all charges against you."

"What charges?"

"Assaulting an officer. Resisting arrest. Interfering with an officer in the performance of his duties. Loitering. Disorderly conduct. And I noticed the tail light on your car wasn't working."

"Lie down on the couch."

He peeled off his shirt and she began softly massaging his lower back. She moved up to his trapezius, then increased the pressure as she moved downward.

"Mmmmmmn," he purred. "Ever think of opening a massage parlor?"

"Only if I could find someone to act as a bouncer for unruly customers," she said.

He sat up when she had finished and took her in his arms.

"Shit!" Odin bellowed and got up out of bed. He was naked. Golden pulled the covers up to hide her own unclothed body.

"Take it easy," she said.

"Now you can go and tell all your nurse friends I can't get it up," he said.

"You really think I'd do something like that?"

He didn't answer.

"Come back to bed. Let's just snuggle," she said.

"Yeah. Like little kids," he said with a sneer. He was standing by the window, glaring out at the street, fighting his blinding rage.

She came up behind him and put her arm around him. He shuddered. It was hard to keep control. He could see himself shoving her away, hard enough to knock her down, crash into the wall. Is that what he wanted?

"You know it's not uncommon after an eye injury for a male to suffer sexual dysfunction," she said.

"Oh yeah? You go to bed with a lot of blind guys?"

"I can show you the article in one of my nursing magazines," she said, ignoring his belligerence. "One theory is that there's some sort of shock to the pituitary gland. Another thinks the pineal gland may be affected." She could tell he wasn't really listening to her words, but her soft tone was soothing. "The pineal is a vestigal organ at the back of the head. Some scientists think it might have been a third eye. It's amazing how little they know about the human body, isn't it?"

"It's really normal to be impotent after what I went through?"

She nodded. "It is. Come to bed. I just want to feel your body next to mine." She took his penis and pulled at it like it was a dog's leash.

Grumbling, he let her lead him. They got under the covers and held each other.

"How about a deluxe back rub?" she asked.

"Okay," he said, without much enthusiasm.

As her hands did their work, he couldn't help but relax. She praised his muscle tone.

"This isn't the first time it happened," Bob said, ignoring her compliments. "The guys brought me a visitor in the hospital."

"I know. Your nurse wrote up a report."

"There's no privacy, is there?"

"She was annoyed. Deservedly so. You could've ripped a suture."

"Yeah, well, nothing happened then anyway. And the bitch blabbed about it."

Jan shook her head. "Was she a girlfriend of yours?"

"Nah. A police groupie. I never bothered with her or the other blue belles when I was healthy."

"And you wonder why you didn't respond to her?"

"It never interfered with me before."

As they talked, her hands continued to roam. They kneaded his thighs.

"You've slept with many women you don't care about?" she asked.

"Some."

"That's sad."

He shrugged. Without his realizing it, her hands had moved to his groin. Her manipulations had brought the blood flowing. He rolled over, excited, and pulled her down to him.

But as he parted her, his mind drifted to the Rocket Inn, to grotesque visions of Cookie and the creatures of the night. Again he lost it.

"Shit!" he yelled.

"Take it easy," she said. "It happens."

"How do you know? Do all your boyfriend's have limp dicks? Does Scalia? Huh, does he?"

"Just calm down," she said firmly. "Who are you really angry at? Me? Did I do something that offends you?"

"Stop being so damn calm and rational."

"How dare you talk that way to me?" she said in a falsetto angry tone. "Who do you think you are? What am I doing here? My mother warned me against men like you. You're no good. You're all no good! I'm leaving." She returned to her normal voice. "Would you like that better?"

"No."

"Then relax, okay? I enjoyed being with you when we weren't in the sack. Just enjoy the massage. The only rule is, no matter what, we won't go all the way tonight."

"Kind of like on a first date?"

"Right. Deal?"

"Deal."

She resumed her ministrations. She told him about her day, about Mrs. Peckman, and the heartache of growing old alone. She told him about her friend, Mary, and about politics at the hospital.

Twice he grew hard, and tried to instigate sex. She refused, and let him get soft before snuggling up with him.

"You're a real little cocktease," he told her.

"I bet you say that to all the girls."

The third time he felt ready. She didn't resist.

The phone rang.

Bob debated whether he should answer it. Jan regarded him quizzically, thinking it was another woman.

Bob picked it up. "Yeah?"

"Odin?" a strange voice asked.

"Who is this? Ben?"

"You want to know where Mokley is?"

Odin sat bolt upright. "Yes."

"The Seashore Motel. In Oceanside. Room twenty-six."

The line went dead.

Odin jumped up.

"What's going on?" Jan asked.

Odin dressed quickly.

"Where are you going?"

"You better go home," Odin said.

"What's going on?" she repeated, not sure whether to be scared or angry. Odin was suddenly a cold, malevolent presence.

"I've got business." He took his gun out, checked it was loaded, and got an extra clip out of the night table.

"Bob, what's going on?"

He was already out the door.

20 Oceanside is a town of eighty thousand a half hour north of San Diego. Its major industry, aside from deep sea fishing, is providing services for the 125,000 acre Camp Pendleton Marine Corps base located on the edge of town. While bookstores are scarce, pool halls, rowdy bars and tattoo parlors thrive. There are lots of out-of-state cars on the streets, driven by young men who've escaped the Midwest winter to be browbeaten by Di's in sunny California.

The town has two kinds of motels. Those that cater to visiting friends and relatives of servicemen and those that cater to servicemen and ladies of brief acquaintance. The Seashore Motel, which was much closer to the freeway than to the Pacific, was in the latter category.

Vic Polanski and Joe Terranova sat in the Friendly Café, across Hill Street from the Seashore Motel. The twenty-four-hour eatery was neither friendly, nor a café. It had a perpetual smell of cigarette smoke and old grease. The stainless steel fixtures were stained. The counterman's apron had a rainbow of splotches. He chatted with the bored waitress. The only other customers were two long-distance truckers who were testing the durability of their stomachs with Friendly Café House Special Burgers.

"Why the fuck we got to stay in this piece of shit town?" Terranova complained.

"Because Mr. P wants us to."

"Why?"

"I told you why," Polanski said, biting off each word.

Polanski sipped his coffee and watched the motel. Terranova drummed his fingers on the counter. Four young Marines, heads shaved and jostling each other with boyish energy, passed outside.

"Town's full of jarheads. Lookit them," Terranova said. He had been in the Marines for six weeks, before receiving a dishonorable discharge. "If Nicky wants this guy dusted, we can do it as good as anyone," Terranova said.

"Just drink your coffee."

Terranova toyed with the minature jukebox on the table. "Look at this collection. Shit-kicker music. Not even one damn Sinatra song. What kind of dump is this anyway?" he asked loudly.

The stocky, overly made up waitress came over. "You want something else?" she asked hostilely.

"Yeah, I wanna know when the Health Department last came here? Or are they scared of the rats?"

"Moron," she muttered.

Before Terranova could respond, Polanski said, "How about a Danish?" She tossed Joe a contemptuous look and went to get a pastry from under a glass bell on the counter.

"Cunt," Terranova muttered.

Vic just shook his head and glanced at his watch.

On the ride down to Oceanside, Odin rarely did less than seventy-five miles an hour. Driving with one eye was still a strain. He had to compensate for reduced depth perception. Sometimes he'd change lanes and find himself inches from another car's bumper. Other times he'd brake, thinking he was about to bump the car in front of him, when there'd be a car-length's cushion.

On his lap he kept a two-year-old mug shot of Mokley. A ferrety face, trying to be cool. Mustache. Brown hair, thinning, blow dried. Looked older than his thirty-eight years.

Odin mentally played with the face, imagining various configurations. Mokley weighing ten pounds more, hint of a jowl, rounding the cheeks. The hair cut short or allowed to grow long. Or without the mustache. Odin had seen suspects make every change imaginable. A bearded murderer with an Afro had changed himself into a clean-shaven skinhead, even shaving off his eyebrows. The victims had been unable to identify him. Details of his ploy went around the prison faster than a new load of contraband grass.

Then he was in the north end of Oceanside. He stopped at a phone booth and learned the address of the Seashore Motel. It took him a few minutes to find the street and then the motel.

He sat in the car, pulse throbbing, staring at the building. It was a ramshackle two-story structure with peeling white paint on wood clapboard. A large, chipped pink plaster shell clung to the wall. The grass on the tiny strip of dirt in front was parched and barely clinging to life. The neon vacancy light was on.

Odin took out his gun, worked the action, and checked that there was a round in the chamber. He tucked the gun into his belt, adjusted his jacket, and got out.

Across the street, in the Friendly Café, Polanski set down his coffee. "He got here quick."

"Fucking hero cop don't have to worry about a ticket."

"Let's go," Vic said. He dropped a few bucks on the table and the two men hurried out.

"Is Gary Mokley in?"

The woman behind the counter had hair curlers on her head and a sour look on her face. "You woke me to ask that?" She had come out from behind the torn curtain. Through the doorway, Odin heard a TV playing.

"Is he?"

"I don't know anyone by that name."

He dropped the mugshot on the counter. "Him?" he asked.

Odin saw the flicker of recognition in her eyes.

"He in Room twenty-six?" Odin asked.

She pointed to a sign on the wall. "No visitors after ten P.M. No exceptions." She crossed her arms in front of her ample chest. "Come back in the morning."

Odin fought the urge to smack her. If he was a cop he'd be able to threaten her with building, health, and fire code violations. Instead he took out his wallet and dropped a ten-dollar bill on the peeling linoleum counter. It matched the peeling linoleum floor. "It's important I see him right away."

The ten disappeared. "That's for waking me. The information will cost you another ten."

He dropped another bill. It too vanished.

"You gonna make trouble?" she asked.

"No."

"I don't want no trouble. I run a clean place."

"No trouble."

"You sure?"

"I'm sure," Odin said.

"If you're gonna make trouble, take him somewhere else. Like down by the beach. You understand?"

Odin nodded.

"He's a weird one," she said, now seeming to want to chat.

"Stays in his room all the time. Just goes out to grab junk food and make phone calls."

Odin started up the stairs.

"No trouble," she called out.

He unbuttoned his jacket and moved silently up the stairs. He drew his gun as he walked down the hall.

"He got past the battle-ax at the desk," Terranova said.

"He's upstairs?"

"Yup. You ready?"

"Give him another minute."

Odin reached room twenty-six. It was at the back of the motel. He studied the door for wires, any indications of a booby trap. Nothing. He listened at the door. Silence.

There was a window next to the door. He tried peering through it, but curtains blocked his view. Odin walked down to the pool area and picked up one of the wrought iron lounge chairs. He hurried back upstairs.

"Hey, what're you doing over there?" It was the curlered night manager, waddling out of the front office waving her arms. She was several dozen yards away, moving slowly but determinedly towards him.

"No trouble," he said. He tossed the heavy chair through the window and leaped in after it.

Mokley screamed.

Odin confirmed it was him. Skinny. Pale. But Mokley. The object of all his hatred.

Odin's finger tightened on the trigger.

"Hear that?" Terranova asked.

"Sure did," Polanski said. He got out of the car and hurried towards the phone booth. He put a cloth over the mouthpiece and dialed 911.

Odin held his finger on the trigger.

"Who are you? Who are you?" Mokley repeated in a quavering voice.

Seconds passed. Odin savored each moment. Mokley trembled like he was having a seizure. Then he recognized the one-eyed Odin. "The cop who was injured. I didn't do it. Honest, I didn't do it."

There was nothing else in Odin's existence, his attention screwed down tightly on a point on Mokley's forehead, the point where the bullet would enter, bore its way through the skull, and pass into his brain.

"I ran away," Mokley continued. "I never planted that bomb. Who would put a bomb in my place? I didn't do it."

The words spilled from Mokley like blood from a wound. Odin aimed, gun in police combat stance, a few ounces of pressure away from silencing him.

"Honest, please," Mokley whined. "I deal dope. But I'm not a killer. I'm not. Ask anyone. Don't hurt me. I don't want to die. I didn't put the bomb there. Please." He got up on the bed and had his hands clasped in front of him. "Don't, please don't."

Odin was at the point of no return. He only had to give the barest hint of a squeeze, as much force as it required to brush an eyelash, and the Supervel hollow point would leave the barrel at thirteen hundred feet per second.

Mokley stopped trembling. He knew he was going to die. Traffic noise drifted in through the smashed window.

"Get dressed," Odin growled in a barely audible voice.

"What? What?"

"Get dressed, scumbag. You're under arrest." Odin couldn't believe he was saying it. He felt separated from his body, an onlooker. A part of him yearned to pull the trigger. Yet he heard his voice repeating the Miranda litany.

Mokley pulled on pants and a shirt. Odin desperately wished the dealer would whip out a gun, give him an immediate reason to pull the trigger.

Odin ripped a lamp cord out of the wall and used it to bind Mokley's wrists behind him. He led him out the door.

As they stepped out onto the balcony, the spotlight hit them. "Police! Freeze!"

Odin heard the chunk-ca-chuck of pump-action shotguns being worked.

He felt the Asp in his hand, and an irrational desire to blaze it out.

"Drop the gun!" the faceless voice commanded. "Now!"

PART THREE

21 The sun was coming up as Odin reached his apartment. Though he hadn't slept, he wasn't the least bit tired. He made himself a pot of coffee and sat and stared at a wall.

He called Finch's widow, waking her and telling her of Mokley's capture. She took it quietly and thanked him as if he'd just opened a car door for her.

Daggett's widow had already heard through the police grapevine. She congratulated Odin and wanted details, but he didn't feel like talking and slipped off after a few minutes.

He couldn't sort out his feelings. He regretted not pulling the trigger and wondered why he hadn't. It was as if his body let him down again. Had he lost his edge?

No. Deep down he had a vague uncertainty. What was making him question whether Mokley did it?

Things just didn't add up. Like how come the Oceanside cops got there so quick? The motel manager must've called. But it was almost as if they were waiting, setting him up. If he'd wasted Mokley, he would have been nailed.

The phone began to ring with calls from reporters. No sooner would he hang up on one than he'd get another. He took the phone off the hook.

The bed was messy, with the clear indentations of two bodies. Jan. It seemed so long ago.

He put the phone back on the hook. It rang immediately. He lifted it.

"Hey. This is David Colker from the *Herald*. I'd like to . . ."

Odin hung up and dialed Jan's place. She answered after two rings.

"Hi," he said cheerfully. "Hope I didn't wake you."

"No. I've been up."

"I'm sorry about running out like that. You know what happened . . ."

"I heard on the radio."

"What did they say?"

"You arrested the suspect who planted that bomb," she said.

"Right. Want to hear what happened?"

"I've got to get ready for work."

"Why the cold shoulder? Do you realize I didn't kill the bastard? I could've. Easily. But I didn't. I'd think you'd be real proud of me for that."

"When you left, you didn't care about me, about anyone. All you wanted was blood."

"But I held back."

"I've got to go now."

He slammed the phone down and kicked the small table. The phone fell to the floor. He picked it up and replaced the handset. It rang immediately.

Hoping it was Jan, he picked it up.

"Hello. This is Patty Klein from the *Times* and . . ."

"Leave me alone!" Odin yelled and slammed the phone down. He ripped it from the wall.

A few moments later there was a knock at the door. Expecting it to be a complaining neighbor, he yanked it open.

A TV camera crew was on the steps. He slammed the door in

their faces before they could say anything. He heard noise in front of his building. Another TV crew had arrived. Neighbors were sticking their heads out of windows. A few print reporters had gathered.

Odin climbed out the back window. A half hour later, he was knocking at the door of Eustas Nichols's apartment in El Segundo.

"What is it?" a voice bellowed from the other side of the door.

"It's Bob."

Nichols, wearing a silk robe with a dragon embroidered on the back and holding a .38 in his hand, threw the door open. "What's happening?"

"The press has been all over me. I got Mokley."

"No shit."

Nichols and Odin went to the kitchen. Huey put up a pot of coffee and turned on the all-news station.

"The suspect in the bombing that killed two police officers and seriously injured a third was arrested early this morning in Oceanside by the officer he injured.

"Gary Mokley was arrested without incident by former SWAT cop Robert Odin. The hero cop was also taken into custody by Oceanside police, after he had charged into a motel room and grabbed Mokley at gunpoint.

"We asked Assistant Chief Fred Fleming why it was that one man acting alone could find someone his entire department couldn't.

"'You're looking at it wrong,' Fleming said defensively. 'It's actually a reflection of the high standards of training we impose that Mr. Odin, even without department cooperation, was able to track down and arrest the suspect. We're very proud of Robert. As you know, my son was nearly killed in that bombing, so I take a personal joy in hearing of the suspect's capture.'"

"You made old Brass Balls happy," Nichols said.

Odin listened intently, but the commentator was already

moving on to traffic reports. Odin spun the dial, looking for more news segments.

"A hero," Nichols said. He put on an adoring voice. "Can I have your autograph? I mean, I've never met someone who made Brass Balls happy before."

"Lighten up. I need peace and quiet."

"Of course. You're a genuine hero. When they make the movie, I want Lou Gossett to play me."

"I wish those damn reporters would just disappear."

"Then why you spinning the dial like that trying to hear more news?"

Odin stopped and let the dial rest on a rock music station.

"Grab a cup of coffee, white boy, and follow me."

Nichols's living room was done up like a *Playboy* magazine fantasy of a bachelor pad. Heavy, wooden furniture. Pseudobrick walls and a built-in gas fireplace. Romantic, colored lighting. A stereo system that made even the worst music sound symphonic. Erotic oriental art on the wall. Thick white wall-to-wall carpet, with a bearskin rug.

"You should be used to attention," Nichols said, plopping down in a soft bag chair. His robe gaped, exposing a powerful hairless chest.

"It's not that. It's just, I guess I was building myself up towards killing Mokley. Then I didn't."

"Kinda like a big date, and you don't get laid."

"I guess I believed once I killed him, it would all be better. Now I'll never know."

"I don't understand why you didn't waste that fucker. You coulda said he made a move on you. No one in that motel room but you and him. You think any cop's gonna make a case against you? Or they gonna pin a medal on your chest?"

"I can't say why I did it. Or didn't do it."

"How'd you know where he was?"

"A phone call. I've been beating the bushes for the past few weeks."

·Odin told Nichols what he had been up to and the lieutenant nodded along.

"It's tough to kill an unarmed suspect in cold blood," Nichols said. "I don't honestly know what I woulda done. I mean, that fucker coulda killed me too. I think about him, I say I could drop the hammer. But I don't know if I really could. How many you eased into the afterlife?"

"Counting Nam?"

"No."

Odin leaned back. "Three."

"I got two scalps. I still dream about them. Even though one was aiming at me, the other had a knife to a woman's throat."

Odin nodded.

"Some guys just shrug it off," Nichols continued. "Some wind up psychoing out. That reminds, me you know Greene left the department. Combination psycho and physical disability."

There was a thump outside. Odin was up with a start, reaching for his gun.

"Take it easy," Nichols said. "That's just the daily rag."

Odin hurried to the door and retrieved the newspaper.

"You're better than a well-trained dog," Nichols said. "Fetch my slippers and pipe?"

Odin was too busy reading to acknowledge his joke. The short newspaper article on page three, squeezed in just under deadline, didn't have anything much beyond the radio interview.

"Hey, what's with your eyes?" Nichols asked.

Odin was holding the paper a couple of inches from his face. He quickly set it down.

"My eyes, my eye, is just tired. Can I sack out here?"

"Anytime."

Odin shook his head and headed to the bedroom. More Casanova chic. Mirror on the ceiling and headboard. Little pools of red light.

"I got to get dressed," Nichols said. "I'll try not to disturb you."

But Odin was already asleep.

Assistant Chief Fred Fleming gritted his teeth and pulled down as hard as he could on the metal bar. He was damp with sweat, from the cloth band around his forehead, to the tips of his Reeboks.

The health club was one of the most expensive in the city, an exclusive facility where the locker rooms smelled like a pine forest, and the sweats were created by a top designer. It was a place to build muscle and network with the power brokers of Southern California. With few exceptions, film people and other nouveau richers were excluded. Two individuals who had been accepted into the Jonathan Club were turned down by the exclusive gym.

Fleming strained at the lat machine until the weights grudgingly rose.

"Need a hand?" The voice belonged to Nick Provenzano.

Fleming lowered the weights. "What are you doing here?"

"Is that any way to talk to a new club member?"

"How'd you join?"

"Time's are changing. I hear they're gonna be letting in Jews next. You want me to see what I can do?"

Fleming returned his attention to the lat machine. He struggled against the weight, but succeeded in doing four more.

Provenzano climbed on a LifeCycle, set the computer for an easy ride, and pedaled. One of his bruiser bodyguards stood nearby, contemptuously eyeing the exercise machines.

"Seen the papers?" Provenzano asked as Fleming changed to a biceps developing machine.

"I'm quoted in the frigging articles," Fleming said.

"That don't mean you have to read them. My uncle Tony was always in the papers, but he never read 'em. Said reporters know as much about the truth as nuns do about fucking."

Fleming grunted as he curled seventy-five pounds.

A potbellied banker climbed on a machine next to Provenzano and began pedaling. The banker called over to Fleming, "Fred, good job that they caught that bomber down in Oceanside."

"That's the way we feel," Fleming responded.

"Surprised he wasn't shot while trying to escape," the banker said with a chuckle.

"You know how it is nowadays, Bart," Fleming said. "His relatives would crawl out from under their rocks saying we violated his civil rights. The city would have to defend itself in another nuisance suit."

"What about the civil rights of the two cops who were killed?" the banker asked.

"Absolutely," Provenzano piped up.

Bart the banker tossed him a who-are-you-and-I-don't-care-anyway look.

"How's that little security problem you were having at the Westwood branch?" Fleming asked the banker.

"Resolved nicely, thanks to you," the banker said. "We caught the thief. I'd like to buy you lunch sometime."

"It would be a pleasure."

The two men made small talk for a few more minutes, vowing to get together the next week. Fleming finished his circuit training, working out on all fourteen machines in the room and headed to the jacuzzi. Provenzano followed.

Fleming waved away the masseur who offered to do his shoulders while he sat in the swirling water. The whirlpool was empty. Fleming eased himself down into the hot water.

He was furious about what had happened in Oceanside. Fleming had been the one who'd given Odin the late-night tip-off. He couldn't understand why Odin hadn't killed Mokley.

"You look like you got constipation?" Provenzano said, sliding into the water opposite Fleming. The mafioso was wearing an electric-blue bikini that came close to the limits of decency.

Fleming hoped other club members didn't think he and Pro were friends.

"Who was that fart Bart?"

"Another member."

"Jeez, I never would've figured that out. I mean, where does he work?"

"Why do you ask?"

"I'm a curious kinda guy."

"Curiosity killed the cat."

"Satisfaction got it back. We gonna recite nursery rhymes to each other?"

Fleming lowered himself into the tub until the water bubbled right under his nose. Provenzano wiggled until a jet was blasting right against his back. He groaned with pleasure at the pounding.

Fleming sat up. "I need another job done."

"What are friends for."

Fleming glanced back and forth. They were alone.

"My watchdog's playing in the weight room," Pro said. "Think I could get him a membership?"

"I want Mokley killed."

Provenzano shifted, and groaned again with pleasure. "The massages here any good?"

"Did you hear what I said?"

"I don't have water in my ears," Pro answered.

"Well?"

"Why didn't you let my boys do it in the motel? It would've been a lot easier."

"I had my reasons."

"Lemme guess. You expected that one-eyed wahoo to dust Mokley. But he didn't. Mokley got something on you?"

"Can you do it or not?"

"You know, I used to use Mokley. He'd give me little tips, tidbits that he coudn't get into an article or that I'd pay more for."

"What did he tell you about?"

Pro put on a coy expression and changed the subject. "My old man, he used to always meet with guys at Turkish baths. He figured there was no way they could bug 'em. I hear nowadays the feds got waterproof mikes just for that."

Fleming stood impatiently and took one step out of the jacuzzi.

"Take it easy," Provenzano said. "I'm happy to help a buddy."

Fleming settled back down into the water. "How soon can you have it taken care of?"

"There's paperwork got to be shuffled," Provenzano said. "Mokley's probably got keeplock status. Got to find out who in the jail who can do a piece of work and get Mokley somewhere where we can put them together."

"How long?"

"With your help, a day or so."

"What do you mean, with my help?"

"You'll have to play lucy goosey with the bureaucracy. Maybe get him shifted to a holding cell for a lineup that doesn't happen."

"The jail is run by the sheriff's department. We have no say over what goes on."

"Then it might take weeks. Or months."

"I can't be connected with this at all."

"I'll protect you. I take care of my friends."

Fleming was silent as another member passed by on the way to the pool. The assistant chief exchanged pleasantries with him.

"Okay," Fleming said when he and Pro were alone.

"Good." Provenzano got up and dripped his way over to where their towels hung. "I'll be in touch."

22 Odin pulled the trigger and Mokley's head exploded in a burst of gore. The blood stuck to Odin and burned his flesh.

The ex-cop woke up clawing at his skin. He wasn't sure where he was and rooted for his gun under the pillow. It wasn't there.

It took several frightening moments of consciousness before he recognized Nichols's bedroom. His shoes had been taken off and his gun lay on the night table. There was a note by the weapon:

> Grab whatever you want out of the fridge.
> You're welcome here as long as you want. P.S.
> You're about the ugliest thing I ever had in my
> bed, but you got a nice Asp.

It took him nearly an hour to get to the county jail, on Bauchet Street, just outside of the downtown area. Like most urban jails it was grossly overcrowded. Long lines of friends and relatives, mainly female, waited with crying babies in their arms. There were junk food wrappers all over the floor, gang graffiti on the hard chairs.

Odin filled out the paperwork and waited, watching the scene. There was a cow-like hopelessness on so many of the faces—visiting the jail was just part of the routine. The men would be in and out of jail, the women would collect welfare, eat too much, have babies, and visit. Kids would be born into the cycle, and doomed to follow it.

A deputy sheriff with a shaved head and gleaming black skin came over to Odin.

"You're Bob Odin?" He had a mellifluous voice.

"That's right. I recognize you. Sheriff's SWAT. We trained together during the Olympics."

"Right. C'mon with me."

As they walked down the hall, the deputy, who was now a sergeant, said he got transferred back to the jail—all sheriff's deputies begin their training with eighteen months in the jail—when he made his promotion.

"Can't wait to get back to the streets," the deputy said. "I got to take three showers when I leave here, trying to get the smell of these lowlifes offa me."

"I can understand that. Where you taking me?"

"The Attorney Room. You get more privacy."

They reached the door and the sergeant signaled another deputy behind a thick glass window. Odin thanked the sergeant, stepped into a solid metal revolving door. A long horseshoe-shaped counter, with attorneys on the outside and inmates on the inside, dominated the room. The inmates wore color-coded jumpsuits indicating their floor and status—trustees, escape risks, known snitches, and homosexuals (who required special protection). A few inmates were shackled to the metal stools set in the counter.

A deputy at a raised bench watched from the far side of the room. Before anyone could pass anything across the counter, he had to signal for the deputy's approval.

In ten minutes, Mokley was led in. He had been classified "keeplock"—the same as snitches and gays. Suspects in high-publicity cases often got such status since another inmate might attack them for the glory.

Mokley's shoulders were hunched over, his skin made sallow by the hard fluorescent light.

"My lawyer said I shouldn't talk to anyone," Mokley said as he was shackled opposite Odin.

"You owe me at least a few words."

"For what?"

"For not blowing your head off."

Mokley chewed his lip. "Got a cigarette?"

"No."

"I don't have to worry about it being bad for my health, do I?" Mokley said sardonically. "I mean, they can fry me for this."

"They don't fry in California. They use gas."

"That makes me feel much better."

"I came to hear your side of the story."

"You don't think I did it?" Mokley asked expectantly.

"Let's say I'm willing to listen."

"How do I know you're not trying to trick me? Find out my case and then tell the DA?"

"I could've iced you and I didn't. I don't exactly know why myself. I give you my word if I find anything that clears you, I'll do my best to see that all charges are dropped. If I find evidence that makes you guilty, I'll stand in line to drop the pill into that bucket of cyanide."

Mokley gulped.

"Where were you on the morning we raided?"

Mokley bit his lip. His eyes shifted around the room. "With my girlfriend."

"You're lying."

"No, I'm not."

"Then why the reckless eyeballs?"

"She's married."

"They don't prosecute for adultery. And they sure as hell don't give the death penalty for it."

"She won't come forward. She's the wife of a studio exec. He'd ruin her."

"Sounds like a great lover. What's her name?"

"The cops already spoke to her. She denied even knowing me."

"Her name?"

Mokley's fingers drummed on the counter. He twitched his shoulders, then his eyes. "Ella Singleton."

"How's someone like you shack up with someone like her?"

Mokley looked offended, but couldn't keep up the expression. "She's a cokehead. She'd hump a warthog for an ounce of seventy-five pure."

"You tell the cops that?"

"No. They'd just pile dope charges on me."

"Did you put the bomb on the door?"

"No! My stepson was due to come visit me that day. I'd never do anything that would jeopardize him. He's a great kid." Mokley suddenly began to cry.

"Where were you?"

"I told you. With Ella."

"Where exactly? At her place?"

"She's got a condo just this side of Palm Springs. We go there for overnight parties."

"Who's at these parties?"

"Just us."

"Anyone who can place you out there? A gas station attendant? A neighbor?"

"No."

"Who would want to blow you up?"

"I've made a few enemies in my time," Mokley said, almost proudly. "I used to be a pretty good reporter. Stepped on lots of toes."

"You screwing anyone else's wife?"

"No. You think Lew Singleton did it?"

"Who was the last person you wrote about?"

"All my work recently has been puff pieces. You know, like authorized biography stuff. The only thing controversial is do you use the star's real birthdate or the one on the press release." He sniffled. "Actually, I haven't had anything published in close to a year."

"How'd you support yourself?"

Mokley avoided his eyes.

"Dealing?" Odin asked.

Mokley nodded.

"Who are your enemies who would have the balls and the resources to put a bomb in your door?"

Mokley chewed ferociously at his lip. A droplet of blood appeared. "The Mafia."

"What?"

Mokley looked back and forth. "I did work for the Mafia."

Odin smirked.

"I did, I did," Mokley insisted.

"What? Leg-breaking? Contract killing?"

Mokley bent closer and whispered. "I gathered info."

"Lean back over there!" the deputy bellowed from where he was watching.

Mokley obeyed.

"What sort of info?" Odin asked.

"Nick Provenzano wanted anything juicy. At first it was stuff I couldn't get into the articles. Rumors, hearsay, you know, like I heard Rock Hudson had AIDS about two months before it went public," Mokley boasted. "I know who was hooked on coke, who embezzled from the studio, who liked kinky stuff with hookers. Provenzano wanted it all. He paid for it too."

"What did he do with the information?"

Mokley shrugged.

"Did you have a falling out with Provenzano?"

"No. He was always very happy with my material."

"Burn anyone on a dope deal?"

Again Mokley's offended look. "Never. My word is my bond."

"What about people from your radical days?"

"Hell, most of them are about as radical nowadays as Nancy Reagan."

"Old grudges?"

"Forgotten."

"Who were the bombers you were with?"

"I never was with any bombers."

"During your radical days?"

"I'm telling you, I didn't hang out with bombers. I was for peace."

"So was the SDS. Who were your associates?"

"The people I hung out with were interested in pissing off their parents, smoking dope, and getting laid. Not wasting people."

Odin got up. "You think about it."

"It's true," Mokley whined.

Odin walked away.

"Come back soon," Mokley shouted, earning annoyed glances from the attorneys and other inmates. "And bring cigarettes."

A deputy unshackled Mokley from the wall, connected the handcuffs, and led him away.

Odin was pissed. He had begun to believe Mokley, then caught him lying about the bombing connections. Who knows what else the dirtbag was lying about?

Odin returned home. The press had moved on to their next cause, tragedy, drama. Maybe he shouldn't have blown the media off. Publicity might help him get a job. While pondering his options, Odin found Ben's address book. He realized he didn't have the address to mail it to and he owed Ben for the information.

The ex-cop drove downtown, glad to be able to put the future on hold. Ben Waters wasn't in but Odin found him slumped on a park bench a couple of blocks away.

"Wake up," Odin said, shaking the junkie.

Waters opened his eyes and smiled. He was far into the nod, above pain.

"How's it going, my man?" Waters asked.

"I brought back your book. And the money."

"The root of wisdom, and the root of all evil."

Odin tucked the check for five hundred dollars in Waters's

pocket and dropped the book on his lap. "Good-bye," Odin said.

"What's this for?"

"I nailed Mokley."

"I wish I could've helped."

"You did. Your friend called me."

"Friend?"

"He called and told me where Mokley was."

"I didn't tell anyone about Mokley."

"No one?"

"Not a soul."

"How about when you're under the influence?"

"I still know who I'm talking to and what I'm talking about. Like now." Waters rocked slowly back and forth. "My sensory motor skills are impaired, but my conversational abilities are par excellence." The junkie's words were a trifle slurred. "Excuse me, time for nappie." Waters seemed to melt as his body dissolved onto the bench. He snored loudly.

Odin debated going back to his apartment, but the thought was depressing. What was he going to do with the rest of his life?

He stopped at a florist, bought a twenty-dollar bouquet, and drove to Queen of Mercy Hospital.

He found out where Jan Golden was working from the information desk, and headed up to her floor. Twice he was stopped by hospital staff, who told him visiting hours didn't start until later. He was allowed to pass when he explained he was there to give them to a nurse.

Golden was at the nurse's station, conferring with another nurse about an unclear notation on a chart.

"Can you read this?" the other nurse was asking. "Is it q.d. or q.i.d.?"

"You'd need a code expert to read that," Golden said. "Call the doctor."

"I'll check the PDR."

"No. Call the doctor," Jan ordered.

The other nurse noticed Odin waiting, recognized him from floor gossip as "Golden's boyfriend," and bustled away.

"Can I help you?" Golden asked him.

He awkwardly offered her the flowers. "I'd like to kiss and make up."

"That's not so easy," she said.

"Why? I thought we were going to accept each other just the way we were."

"You scared me. It was like I was with a cuddly Saint Bernard and the next minute he bared his fangs."

"I wasn't baring them at you."

"I have to think about it." She still hadn't taken the flowers.

"How about we think about it over dinner tonight?"

"Not tonight. I'm busy."

"Another boyfriend so soon?"

"I'm meeting with a few other nurses. If it's any of your business. Which it is not."

"Will you take the damn flowers?"

"When you put it so sweetly, what woman could resist? You keep them."

Odin stormed away. Golden returned to reviewing a form.

Odin looked for a trash basket to slam the flowers into. He saw none. As he waited by the elevator, he heard moaning. He glanced into the nearest room. An elderly lady lay in bed. Her soft moaning wasn't even a complaint. It was as though the sound she was creating was her sole companion.

She saw him in the doorway. "Are those for me?"

He nodded.

"I knew my son hadn't forgotten me," she said. "He's a good boy."

"He's sorry he couldn't come," Odin said.

"Such beautiful flowers he sent. He must have spent a fortune."

"They were only . . ." Odin stopped. "They're only a small token of his love for you."

"Bring them here," she said. When Odin did, she sniffed them. "So sweet. So sweet."

She wouldn't let him put them in a vase. She insisted that he let her hold them in her hands. She cuddled them as if they were a baby.

Odin was watching the six o'clock news when the phone rang.

"Yeah?" he answered.

"It's Jan."

"What is it?"

"Mrs. Peckman died."

"Lucky lady."

"But she was happier today than she'd been in a long time. Those flowers you gave her really made her day."

"I'm glad."

"Anyone who can be so nice to an old lady can't be all bad. How about a late dinner?"

Odin looked over at the microwave, which was heating up a TV dinner. "Just name the place."

The cramps hit Gary Mokley an hour after mealtime. He cried out, bent double by the agonizing waves. His first thought was that he had been poisoned.

The guards, after initial skepticism, took him to the infirmary. He was given a painkiller and had his stomach pumped. He was one of a half dozen inmates to have gotten food poisoning from the meatloaf.

There was less supervision in the infirmary, which was pretty much run by trusties. Most of the precautions were designed to keep the inmates from getting their hands on drugs. In general, due to the unsympathetic nature of in-house medical care, patients were so sick they couldn't even get out of bed.

A half hour after lights out, however, an inmate—who also supposedly suffered food poisoning—silently got out of bed and made his way to where Mokley lay.

Odin finished reciting what had happened. He and Jan were in a restaurant on Melrose, a trendy place that had been done up to look like an untrendy place. The prices were high, the food more than edible.

"How can you be sure Mokley was lying about his radical connections?"

"I saw it in the report."

"And you'll believe what a cop says over what a civilian says any day of the week?"

"Not any civilian. A dirtbag. An admitted dope dealer."

"Hospital staff is like that. A patient will say 'I'm a diabetic' but if it's not on their chart, no one believes them. People don't believe people. They prefer to believe paper. Especially paper generated by their own bureaucracy."

"So you think I should keep looking into it?"

"If you believe he's innocent, I think it's your responsibility."

"It's funny, I never wanted to be a detective on the job. Lots of guys would've killed for it. Me, I liked being in the street, kicking ass and taking names. And here I am, playing Joe Friday." Bob sighed. "Nothing much better to do with my life."

23 As Odin walked up the wooden stairs to Virginia Mokley's apartment, he heard sobbing inside. He knocked anyway. A man with one arm taped to his side nervously opened the door as wide as the chain lock would reach. "Yes?"

"My name's Robert Odin. I'd like to speak to Virginia Mokley about her ex-husband."

"Now is a bad time."

"It's important."

"Wait here," the man said.

Through the door, Odin could see him solicitously whispering to a woman sitting on the lumpy orange sofa. The woman's makeup had run, giving her a ghoulish, clownish face. As Odin leaned against the door the chain lock parted from the rotting door jamb.

The woman looked up from the sofa and screamed. A classic horror-movie scream. Before Odin could say anything, she reached under the couch and took out a double-barreled shotgun. He dove for the floor as she let loose with a barrel, peppering one wall with shot.

"Bastards! Murderers," was all Odin could understand from her yelling. He was more concerned about avoiding the load in the second barrel.

Odin was behind a rickety bookcase. He removed a spy novel by Scott Ellis and tossed the book to the far side of the room, near the sofa.

She let loose with the second barrel. Stuffing from the sofa exploded like an artificial storm of yellow snow clumps.

Odin vaulted over a chair and grabbed the shotgun. She tried to bludgeon him with it. When he got it away, she battered him with her hands. She was not a small woman and the blows hurt.

He slapped her. She collapsed on the mortally wounded couch. Odin let her cry. The man emerged from the closet he'd crawled into. He brought her a box of Kleenex, sat by her side, and tried to calm her.

Odin put the shotgun high up in a kitchen cupboard. He took a hard-backed wooden chair from the kitchen and set it down facing the woman. He reintroduced himself and found out the man's name was Jonathan and the woman was indeed Virginia Mokley.

"The cops just left. They told her Gary was murdered," the man said, patting Virginia's cheek as he held her head against his shoulder.

"When? How?"

"In jail. Smothered with a pillow in the infirmary."

"Who did it?"

"They didn't catch anyone."

Odin blurted out a string of curses.

Virginia looked up. "You're the one who put him there."

"His bomb nearly killed me. Killed two cops. He's lucky I didn't blow him away when I had him in my sights."

"Gary wouldn't have anything to do with bombs," Virginia said.

She sniffled, wiped her eyes, and composed herself. Her crying was through. She was back in her tough mode.

Jonathan's posture visibly softened. Being the brave one was a role he had held briefly, unwillingly. He could go back to being number two in the pack.

"What about in his radical days?"

"Gary? He didn't have the guts to paint a peace sign on a building at night. It was hard enough getting him to sign a petition. He was afraid the FBI would start a file on him."

"Planting bombs is a coward's crime."

"He was no good around anything mechanical. One time he tried to fix the toaster oven. Nearly electrocuted himself. If he was a bomber, his first victim would've been himself." She realized that he was indeed dead, fought for control, and regained it.

"You were quick to start shooting," Odin said.

"You'd be too, after what happened," she said.

Jonathan shuddered.

"What happened?"

"Two goons, said they were cops. Came in here and pushed us around. Dislocated Jonathan's shoulder."

Jonathan nodded, confirming the diagnosis and pleased with the attention and sympathy.

"What did they look like?"

"One was very big. Much more than six feet tall. The other was normal size. Meaner," she said.

"How old? Hair color?"

"Late thirties, maybe early forties," she said. "The big one had dirty blond hair, almost brown. The shorter one had greasy black hair. Almost an Elvis hair cut."

"I'd know their faces anywhere," Jonathan said. He didn't see her 'be quiet' look. "I'm an artist," Jonathan continued proudly. "I have a knack for remembering faces."

"Would you be willing to come downtown with me, look through mug books?"

"Yes," Jonathan said.

"No," Virginia said.

"You two thrash it out," Odin said. "I have to make a phone call."

He went to the phone and dialed the Organized Crime Intelligence Division. Ben Waters had said the "broken noses" were snooping around on the Mokley case and Mokley himself had claimed to work for the Mafia. Maybe there was something to it.

Odin got Sergeant Greg Braxton on the phone. He had been on a police softball team with Braxton, and over the years, they'd shared a few beers. OCID was located in the same building as SWAT—the Central Division, about a half mile down Los Angeles's skid row from headquarters. Braxton agreed to let Jonathan come in and view the books.

But when Odin returned to the couch, he found that Virginia had made up her mind for the couple. Neither would cooperate.

"Do you want to live the rest of your life in fear?" Odin asked. "With a shotgun under the sofa, flinching every time there's a knock?"

"Life is tough," she said. Jonathan sulked on the seat next to her. Odin sensed there was no point in appealing to him to be independent. The ex-cop had to win the widow over.

"Gary's gone," she said. "They won't bother us anymore."

"Maybe. Maybe not. Maybe they think you know something. Maybe they know I came here."

"I can take care of myself."

"What about revenge for Gary's murder?"

"Who knows that they did it? He made his own bed. Let him lie in it."

Jonathan gave her a shocked look.

"What about revenge for what they did to you and Jonathan?" Odin asked.

"I was a legal secretary," she said. "I know how the courts work. They don't give justice. And it takes too long."

"I'm not taking this through the courts."

She stared into Odin's scarred face and understood what he meant. "What will you do when you find them?" she asked, leaning forward eagerly.

"Will you help me or not?" he asked.

Virginia turned to Jonathan. "It's up to you."

"Let's go," Jonathan said.

Central Division was a squat three-story fort located a block from the Greyhound Bus Terminal. The general rule that the bus terminal is located in the scummiest part of the city held true. Winos, junkies, and assorted transient losers drifted around the streets and into the bars. The Rocket Inn was right nearby, as well as a dozen or so other bars barely a notch above it.

The sooty gray-and-yellow police building was part of the Central Services Facility, a block-long city edifice built in 1977. To try and make the entrance to the police fort less threatening, a somewhat surreal tile mural, bearing the LAPD slogan "To Protect and Serve" had been put on the front. The mural was done in a primitive style, but depicted what was supposed to be the police in Los Angeles of the future, with computers and a monorail. The consensus of the building's inhabitants was that the artist should've been busted for fraud.

Inside the building, officers at the front desk limited the entry of vermin to the front hallway and office. To get further into the building, visitors had to be buzzed past a heavy metal door.

The watch commander recognized Odin, made a few moments small talk asking about the ex-cop's health, and buzzed him and Jonathan in. The watch commander had assumed Odin was heading to the third floor, where SWAT was based.

But Odin and Jonathan rode the elevator to the second floor and the OCID office. Braxton, a middle-aged cop with a dour expression and an Afro at maximum police department length, gave Odin a quick nod and signaled him to go to an interrogation room at the side of the office.

"No point in calling attention to yourself," Braxton said as he entered, carrying two massive photo albums.

Odin had always found intelligence cops to be vaguely paranoid, blaming conspiracies for everything from bad weather to the Dodgers losing. But in this case he appreciated Braxton's caution.

As Braxton thumped the books down on the metal table, Jonathan—who had been gazing around the closet-sized, cinder-block room—jumped. He didn't know whether to be scared or excited.

"These two books are the leading strongarms," Braxton said. "You see any familiar faces, let me know. You gonna tell me what this is about?" he asked Odin.

"Later, Greg. I owe you."

Braxton nodded.

"Maybe we can speed it up," Odin said. "It's a Mutt and Jeff team. The big guy's got dirty blond hair, the little one black hair, à la Elvis."

Braxton, pointed out photos, but Jonathan didn't recognize any of them. Braxton left them alone.

Jonathan thumbed through the books. He stared in fascination at the scowling faces. A couple of times he stopped, but when Odin asked him if he recognized anyone, he said no.

He was two thirds of the way through the second book when he stopped and slammed his finger down on the page.

"This one. Definitely."

Victor Polanski.

"This is the bigger one," Jonathan said.

Odin signaled for Braxton, who came in, looked at the picture and grumbled.

"He's never worked with a partner before," Braxton said. "He's a bonecrusher for Nicholas Provenzano."

Odin remembered the name from Mokley, but didn't say anything. Jonathan flinched at the word "bonecrusher." Braxton walked out, and returned with a file card.

"Victor Polanski. Male white. Born nineteen-fifty-one in Chicago. Currently a union rep. Boxed Golden Gloves, heavyweight finalist. A five-page rap sheet, with charges of assault predominating. Three convictions, including one for extortion. Less than two years total incarceration time," Braxton recited. "Most of the time, witnesses change their testimony."

Jonathan continued to flip through the mug book. Braxton signaled for Odin to step outside the room with him.

"Polanski has never worked with anyone," Braxton said. "He's big and he's good at what he does. I can't see him being paired up with a punk. It could happen, but I think your witness won't stand up in court. He looks like a flake."

Odin nodded.

"You're planning on making a case, aren't you?" Braxton asked.

Odin shrugged.

"I don't want to know about it," Braxton said. "Maybe you better go. I've only got one more year before I can put in for my pension. If I was any part of a conspiracy . . ." He let his words trail off.

"Tell me about Nicky Pro," Odin said.

"The teamster boss?"

"One and the same."

Braxton looked around, and saw no one was watching them. "Some say Nicky really runs the rackets here and lets the usual cast of losers get arrested and get their names in the papers. We never been able to make a case against Nicky." Braxton was even more sourpussed. "The feds tried. And they can use wiretaps. We can't. Gutless creeps in the legislature—"

"What about Nicky?" Odin asked, knowing that Braxton could launch into a fifteen-minute tirade over the lack of a wiretapping law.

"Nicky's untouchable. Mr. Clean. At the best functions, gets his picture taken with the Mayor. He's got bucks and labor clout. When the electricians's union was going to shut down Columbia's blockbuster for labor violations, Nicky negotiated a settlement. When a church on the east side was ripped off right before Christmas, Nicky donated money to refurbish it. The thief was found with his eyeballs poked out." Braxton looked at the one-eyed Odin. "Sorry."

Odin waved his hand in dismissal. "If I want to talk to him, where do I go?"

"Don't even think about it."

"I'll find him one way or the other. You can help me be better prepared. You don't have to. I appreciate all you've done."

Braxon looked out at the squad room, then back at Odin.

"This isn't like kicking in the door on a PCP psycho," Braxton said. "This sucker is organized. People like Pro are slicker than the cowboys back east."

"Where can I find him?"

Braxton threw his hands up in disgust. "He's got an office in Westwood. On the top floor of the Western Bank building. Also a house off Mandeville Canyon in Brentwood. His office and his house are well protected. We've never been able to do a surveillance without getting burned."

"I need addresses."

"Nicky's not even in town. There's a Teamster bash in Las Vegas."

"Do you know where he's staying?"

"You'd go to Las Vegas and put the arm on a Teamster hood? That's like going to hell and shaking down the devil."

"When I was on the job, I didn't put up with crap from anybody."

"You ain't on the job any more."

Heavy silence.

"I'm sorry," Braxton said.

"I can take it. What's Pro's address here?"

"You think you're so cool, don't you?" Braxton exploded. "You couldn't even handle a scumbum at the Rocket Inn."

"What do you know about that?"

"Word travels fast."

"Pro's address?"

"You're a doorkicker. A damn good doorkicker, but still a doorkicker. Leave the investigation to the Department."

"What's the department done so far?"

Braxton shook his head.

"Do you know anything about Buchanan?"

"Is he handling it?"

"Yes."

"He's respected."

"Yeah?"

"A Major Crimes Squad prima donna. Sharp, impressed with himself." Braxton paused.

"You're holding something back."

Braxton muttered an obscenity. When he spoke, his voice was barely audible, and he was nervously looking to make sure no one from his squad was listening. The nearest officer was ten yards away.

"Buchanan is one of the insiders. When they want a case handled with kid gloves, he's the one."

"That doesn't sound so bad."

"Remember that comedian that OD'd in the hotel?"

"Sure."

"There was evidence there that would've embarrassed some people. People who don't get embarrassed in this town. Buchanan was the one who cleaned that up. That's just a rumor. I'd deny ever mentioning it."

"Cops can be a gossipy bunch of old women. You know how quickly bullshit spreads. Like that story that the Chief caught the clap from his girlfriend."

Braxton grinned. "I did *my* best to spread it."

"How solid is it about Buchanan?"

"Exhibit B. You know that state senator, the one who likes the young girls?"

Odin nodded.

"One of his girls killed herself. Supposedly. She had written a diary, had names and places of the state senator playing bouncy bouncy with ten-, twelve-year-olds. This kid had turned fourteen, and was too old. So she hung herself. Buchanan took care of it. The diary was vouchered. When the DA went to look at it, the book was missing a half dozen key pages."

"Who does he cover for?"

"Maybe the Chief. Maybe the Mayor. It sure as hell ain't for me."

"This is the guy handling my case?"

"He's a top notch investigator. Clears a lot of cases. But he knows the party line."

"I'm gonna pay him a visit."

"You are one dumb bastard."

"You gonna give me his address?"

"Buchanan. He's at Parker Center."

"Not Buchanan. Pro's home."

"No."

"Thanks anyway."

Braxton grabbed Odin's shoulder. "Five guys from the building' have died in the past year. The Bobbsey Twins. Two from heart attacks. One was shot by a doper."

"I know. Last time I saw you was at his funeral."

"You know what I'm saying?"

"You don't feel like going to any more funerals?"

"Not for a long, long time."

As Odin turned, Braxton recited Provenzano's address. "He's got alarms on the windows, a couple of closed-circuit TV cameras sweeping the grounds, and nasty dogs. Always has a few gumbahs roaming around. Don't do it, man."

"You're a pal, Greg."

Jonathan called them into the interrogation room.

"This is the other one. Though it's an old picture."

Joseph Terranova.

"He's got connections to Pro," Braxton said. "But that's not his line of work."

"What does he do?"

Braxton made the motion of someone pulling a trigger.

Jonathan paled.

"He also usually flies solo," Braxton said softly, so Jonathan couldn't hear. "Mainly because no one wants to work with him. He just got out of being a guest of the government. No doubt he's rehabilitated." Braxton went out of the room to get Terranova's file.

"Maybe, maybe it isn't him," Jonathan said.

"Yes or no?"

"I'm not going to have to identify him in court you said?"

"That's right."

"It's him."

Jonathan got up and was at the door when Braxton returned.

"I've got to go," Jonathan said.

Braxton got a cop to escort him downstairs.

"You know how much trouble I could get in if this ever comes out?" Braxton asked rhetorically.

"I appreciate what you're doing."

Braxton opened Joe Terranova's file. "Eight-page rap sheet. Assaults, attempted murder, murder, rape, forcible sodomy. A fine human being. Nothing about any association with Polanski. I'd have thought Polanski had better taste. Nicky Pro too. They're bedbugs, but a better class of bedbug."

"Can I take a look at the files?"

Braxton shook his head. "I meant what I said before. You better be going."

"I really do appreciate what you've given me."

Braxton shrugged. "It's a one shot deal. Lose my number, please. Now go. I've got to belt back a gallon of Maalox after this."

Both Odin and Braxton knew that the interrogation room had a hidden microphone. But neither realized that one of the officers in the squad had turned the mike on as soon as he'd seen them go in.

While the officer pretended to listen to a tape on headphones, he had actually been eavesdropping. He took an early lunch and went to a pay phone in the Greyhound Bus Terminal.

"Nicky, do you know who this is?" the officer asked when he was put through to Provenzano's suite.

"Sure," Provenzano said.

"You said it's worth a grand every time your name comes up. I got something worth twice that."

"I'll be the judge."

"We got a deal?"

"I play, I pay."

"That cop that got injured, Odin, he was just by. A couple of your boys roughed up Gary Mokley's ex-wife. Polanski and Terranova. Their mugs got picked out. Your name came up too."

"*Bava fangool*," Provenzano muttered.

"Odin's looking at you for what happened to him. He's going to see Buchanan."

"The pigeon that made the ID, he pressing charges?"

"No."

"Anything else?"

"That's it."

"Two gees. Deposited the usual way?"

"It's a pleasure doing business with you, Mr. P."

24 Chuck Gilbert was a burly fireman with an undiagnosed disease. He'd been in and out of the hospital four times over a six-month period. Initially, he had been quite a charmer, flirting with the nurses, bantering with the orderlies. But as his condition worsened and the doctors were unable to help, he grew more and more irritable.

"I'm sick and tired of being stuck and having my blood taken," he snapped at Jan Golden. "You people must be selling it or dumping it down the toilet."

"C'mon, Chuck, you know better than that." Golden had gotten friendly with him, and was less formal than with most patients.

"Why the hell can't they tell me what's wrong?"

"You know they're trying."

"Trying? You know how much they've billed so far? Still I feel like I got the flu. I ache all over, get headaches that knock me down."

"Any change in the symptoms?"

"They're worse. My knee feels like someone's grinding an ice pick into it. Sometimes the whole leg goes numb."

She listened carefully. A patient's description of a symptom could give a vital clue, like whether the pain was stabbing, achey, or came in waves.

Gilbert's doctor was Marshall Urhammer, a leading internist, an old timer, on the board of the hospital. He was highly regarded, though a bit of an aloof aristocrat.

"I know what everyone thinks," Gilbert said. "That it's all in my head. Psychosomatic, right?"

"That's the name for it. But the cause is still unknown."

"You think I enjoy this? That I'm malingering, that I like being here."

"Chuck, believe me, we're doing the best we can. It's very frustrating to doctors to have this sort of thing happen. They want a cure almost as much as you do."

Gilbert's mood shifted. "You know, I used to be an active guy. Me and my girlfriend would take off, go camping up near Mendocino. It's beautiful up there. You ever been there?"

"I haven't traveled much."

"What do you do on your vacations?"

Golden shrugged. "Read. Maybe see a movie."

"You party animal," Gilbert said with a smile.

She smiled back.

"Thanks for listening to me spout off," Gilbert said. "If it wasn't for you sometimes, I'd go crazy."

"That Odin's been good for you," Mary Tallero said as she and Jan grabbed a quick lunch in the cafeteria.

"Why do you say that?"

"You're letting your hair down. Figuratively and literally. It looks nice."

Golden unconsciously patted her hair.

"You're wearing makeup now too."

"Just a little. It's such a nuisance putting on."

"You get used to it. War paint. You seem distracted?"

"No."

"Don't tell me no." Tallero covered Golden's plate with her hand. "Quick, what are you eating?"

Golden thought for a moment, then had to look down. It was

the cafeteria's Chinese food special, nicknamed "chicken toe main."

"Okay," Jan acknowledged.

"Thinking about Robert?"

"A little. More about Chuck Gilbert."

"You little devil, you," Tallero said. "What's he like?"

"He's a patient. Undiagnosed. A fireman."

"You're becoming a civil service slut."

"Stop it. I'm trying to figure out what's wrong with him. Something's tickling me."

Tallero looked under the table. "Don't see anyone."

"You know what I mean. Urhammer's tested him for virtually every infectious disease. Glandular disorders. Damage from toxic waste exposure at work. M.S. Heart disease. Got a battery of psychological tests. No clues."

"You're on lunch. Take a break."

While Golden nibbled, Tallero told about her hot date for that weekend, an intern with a winter home in Palm Springs. "I can't wait to get away for a few days with him," Tallero said.

Get away. Vacation. Camping. Mendocino.

"That's it," Golden said suddenly.

"Did I miss something?"

"I've got to go to the library."

Golden ran from the table, leaving her meal unfinished.

Dr. Marshall Urhammer didn't like seeing Chuck Gilbert. There weren't many patients Urhammer couldn't diagnose. Rather than deal with a frustrating "etiology unknown," he dismissed the ailment as psychosomatic.

Urhammer, a tall, patrician man with white hair and a fifteen-hundred-dollar suit, was talking to the resident in the hall when a nurse approached. He read her name off her nameplate and gave her a polite greeting.

"Doctor, may I speak with you privately for a moment?" she asked.

Urhammer granted her an audience as the resident returned to his duties.

"It's about Chuck Gilbert."

"What is it?" Urhammer asked impatiently.

She took out an article she had photocopied in the library. "Could you read this please?"

Urhammer went to tuck it into his pocket.

"Please, doctor, now."

He harrumphed, took out tortoiseshell reading glasses and read.

An hour later, Gilbert began receiving intravenous antibiotics. Urhammer took credit for the correct diagnosis but Mary Tallero, through her gossip grapevine, spread the word on what really happened.

Golden had recalled an article on tick-borne Lyme disease. The *borrelia burgdorferi* bacteria had first been identified in 1979, four years after an outbreak of what was originally diagnosed as juvenile rheumatoid arthritis near Old Lyme, Connecticut.

"So did you let Chuck Gilbert know how you saved him from a life of misery?" Tallero said, over lunch the following day.

"No. Let Urhammer take the credit."

"I've heard firemen got great hoses."

"Mary!"

"Hey, it's the Hathaway shirt man," someone yelled when Odin walked into the Metro squad room.

"No, looks more like Long John Silver," another wit shouted. "Ho, ho, ho, me hearties."

There was lots of backslapping and shoulder punching from

the dozen or so men in the room. SWAT cops made up one quarter of Metro, an elite two-hundred-officer citywide anti-crime task force that would be rotated among the divisions with the highest crime rates. The SWAT officers would handle regular Metro functions until there was a call-up, when they'd rush to the latest hostage taking or dignitary protection assignment. SWAT was made up of six ten-man squads divided into two five-man teams.

A combination of factors—including the Watts Riot of 1965 and the 1974 shootout with Patty Hearst's captors, the Symbionese Liberation Army—led to the development of SWAT. Originally a group of gung ho military combat volunteers who brought their own guns to incidents, by the time Odin had joined the unit had evolved into one of the most professional, and mimicked, law enforcement teams in the world.

Fleming Junior gave Odin a hug and practically had to be pulled off him. "It's great to see you. Ooops. I mean—"

"Don't sweat it, Junior," Odin responded. "I know, I'm a sight for sore eyes."

"What're you doing down here anyway?" a clerk asked Odin.

"Just lurking around. I wanted to check out old hangouts. See what I was missing."

After a few minutes of frequently obscene banter with various cops and staffers, he edged Junior off to one side.

"I haven't seen any more reports since that first batch?" Odin asked, keeping a casual smile on his face and talking too softly for anyone else to hear.

"I—I didn't know you were still interested."

"What?"

"I mean, I hoped maybe you'd drop it, after seeing that the department was working on it. Besides, Mokley's dead."

"I heard. How'd it happen?"

"Guys get killed in jail all the time," Junior said. "Over a pack of cigarettes, a nasty look, a tight ass. You know that. Good riddance to bad rubbish."

"Can you get me the report on Mokley's death?"

"I don't think so. That's Sheriff's department."

"Who gave you the reports on Mokley before?"

"I shouldn't say."

"Freddy."

"I don't want to get him in trouble."

"Was it Buchanan?"

Junior gulped. "No." He was a lousy liar.

Once a cop worked out of Parker Center, the eight story blue glass building named after legendary police chief "Big Bill" Parker, he was at the center of police power in Southern California. Or so most ambitious cops believed.

Odin walked into the third floor office of the Major Crimes Squad. They included some of the LAPD's best and brightest and often led in investigating the serial killers who terrorized Los Angeles. No other metropolitan area spawned quite as many serial killers: The Hillside-Trash-Bag-Skid-Row-Freeway-Night-Stalker-Slasher-Killer-Slasher. Experts blamed the mayhem on disturbed dreamers migrating to the land of fruits and nuts to seek their fortunes, on the multiple law enforcement jurisdictions, on sexual permissiveness, on the Santa Ana winds.

When the fifteen-man squad wasn't tracking a serial killer, they would tackle cases that had thwarted local homicide units. Any high-publicity case, for example, the mugging-murder of a senator's niece, could lead to their assignment.

Odin stood in the office doorway. It was not much different than any other squad room. Clipboards holding mug cards, notices of retirement, crime reports; favorable articles tacked up on apple green walls; bulletin boards with bits of paper. Cluttered desks with evidence sealed in plastic bags, reams of reports, overfilled ashtrays and stained coffee cups with "Support Your Local Police" and pig motifs.

"Odin, right?" a cop asked, standing up and extending a thick hand. "I'm Rodriquez. Can I help you?" Rodriguez had the build and manner of a friendly bear.

"I'm looking for Buchanan."

"He just stepped out. You want to talk to him about Mokley?"

"That's right."

"He's been busting his chops on it. You can imagine how we feel. I went to the Academy with Finch. He was a good man."

"Yeah. When will Buchanan be back?"

Rodriguez held up a hand, indicating for Odin to wait. The homicide cop chatted with another cop and returned with bad news—Buchanan was gone for the day. The other cop regarded Odin sympathetically.

Odin tried to get information from Rodriguez. The bearish detective was friendly but didn't know, or wouldn't say, anything of value.

Back in his apartment for barely five minutes and the phone rang.

"Turkey! Why didn't you have them radio me when you stopped by the office?" Lieutenant Eustas Nichols asked. "We're working Rampart. I could've been over in a second."

"I figured you were sick of my face. Thanks for tucking me in."

"I had a bedtime story all picked out. How's it going?"

"Pretty fair."

"You gonna crash at my place tonight? I shoulda left a key."

"Nah. I'm no longer a news item."

"I met Braxton in the elevator. He told me you stopped by."

"Oh."

"You told the guys you were just visiting. He told me something else."

"He should know not to talk."

"He knows I'm your buddy. Leave it lie, buddy. You heard Mokley's dead?"

"Maybe I will."

"Bullshit. I know you better than that."

"Then why bother telling me?"

"'Cause I like pissing into the wind."

"Singleton residence," the voice said. It was what a servant's voice should be—perfect pronunciation, vaguely British, arrogant, but ready to turn properly obsequious at the mention of the right name.

But Odin's wasn't the right name. The servant refused to put him through to Ella Singleton.

"Tell her I'm a friend of Gary Mokley," Odin insisted.

"She's in the sauna right now."

"Get her out."

"One moment."

The servant returned in a few minutes. "She says she doesn't know anyone by that name. Good day."

"Tell her I'm in the snow cone business. For her next party."

"Send us the information."

"Tell her."

An impatient woman's voice came on the line after five minutes. "Who is this?"

"My name's Bobby Blow. I'm taking over for Gary."

"I don't know what you're talking about."

"Snow. Pure white snow. Like the kind that falls in the Andes."

"Yes?"

"Gary's out of the picture."

"Should I care?"

"Would you like to see my product? I provide free samples to build customer goodwill."

After a moment's hesitation she said, "Be here at seven P.M."

25 Odin drove to Ben Waters's apartment. It was locked. He forced the door open without much effort. The place had been cleaned out of the little that had been there.

Odin hit a few of Waters's usual hangouts. In return for ten dollars, Cookie told him, "Didn't believe it but I heard he checked into VA drug rehab program. Told me he was gonna do it but he's been saying that for a long time. Wanna do it for another ten?"

The drug rehabilitation section is located at the northern end of the six-hundred-acre Veterans Administration spread in Westwood. Nearly one hundred fifty buildings are on the grounds, dominated by the six-story concrete Wadsworth Hospital. For those who can't be helped, the cemetery is just on the other side of the San Diego Freeway.

Odin asked one of the dozens of handicapped men limping, rolling, tapping, their way around the grounds and found the substance abuse unit. The first person he met going through the doors offered to sell him an ounce of grass.

Waters was living in one of the small, barrackslike dorms behind the main hospital building. He was thrilled to see Odin. The two men strolled on the large field behind the barracks. From the nearby duck pond there were squawks, as well as a scattering of feathers and duck droppings. A couple romped in the grass. Odin and Waters found a graffitied, whittled, charred but comfortable wooden bench and they sat looking at the clump of trees.

"I owe this to you," Waters said, gesturing to the grounds.

"What happened?"

"Your giving me the money. It was an honorable gesture. I had forgotten there was such a thing." Waters reached into his pocket and took out the five-hundred-dollar check. "Whenever I feel myself backsliding, I take it out and it gives me strength."

"I'm glad."

"It's not difficult kicking the habit. More like a bad case of the flu than what they show in those antidope films. The test comes after you've graduated the program. When the world starts pressing in. You know with one shot, you can blot it out." Waters offered the check to Odin.

"Keep it. I found Mokley, thanks to your friend's call."

"But I told you, I never told anyone."

"No one?"

"Positive." Waters extended the money again.

"Keep it. For moral support. Or when you get out of here, if you need something to get you started."

"That's decent of you."

"But I need a favor."

"Just ask."

"I need to get a hold of quality cocaine."

The junkie looked at Odin horrified. "Don't start, please."

"It's not for me."

Waters gave him a I've-heard-that-line-before look.

"I need it to help me question a witness. She won't talk without it."

It took fifteen minutes of persuasion but finally Waters gave him a name and the address of a rock house at the north end of Watts.

Odin was the only white face in the area as day turned to night and he drove around the rock house. Los Angeles ghettos aren't like those in less temperate climates. There were pleasant little houses, gardens, lawns. But the crime that plagued low-income areas didn't go away just because of the sunshine. Crips or Bloods had claimed most walls with gang graffiti. Abandoned houses were stripped of anything worth selling and vandalized. Rock houses were islands of prosperity in a sea of economic bleakness.

It was a typical Hollywood bungalow, with big porch and overhanging roof, wooden clapboard sides. The present owners had added heavy bars over the windows and a steel door with a small slot in it.

Rock houses had become popular to thwart police raids or stick ups from predators who targeted dope dealers. They were minifortresses where the dope could be safely destroyed before the police could gain entry. Cops had responded with an armored car converted to a battering ram but that plan had faltered after several embarrassing raids on the wrong homes.

As Odin passed the first time, a kid barely out of his teens was inserting money into the slot in the heavy steel door. Out popped a tiny envelope and the youth hustled off. The next time around the block and a woman in her late teens was making a buy.

Odin sauntered up to the door, drawing stares from two men leaving and tugging open their packets.

The Judas hole in the door slid open. "Yeah?"

"Tell Vince that Benny sent me. A few grams of your best coke."

The man on the other side laughed and repeated Odin's words to the people on the inside. There was rude laughter. "Get outta here, white bread." The Judas Hole shut.

Odin rapped on the door.

"You hear what I said?" the man on the other side growled when Odin kept up the pounding. "Vince got busted yesterday."

Odin held up his money. "Five hundred."

"You scaring away our customers," the door guardian said. "Git!"

Odin turned. A few young dudes were watching, eyeing the

money in his hand like dogs looking at a piece of fresh roast beef.

"I want to make a deal," Odin said.

The door flew open. The doorway was filled by the bulk of a huge man, a mixture of fat and muscle that was less than six feet but weighed in at four hundred pounds. He had a short-barreled shotgun that he gripped easily.

"Gimme the money."

Odin handed it over.

The man stepped back inside and slammed the door.

"What about the coke?" Odin shouted.

The man's guffaw could be heard through the heavy metal door. The ex-cop put his hand to the Judas Hole and measured. The hole seemed wide enough.

Odin returned to his car. He dug two police-issue tear gas grenades and his rope from the trunk.

A couple of people in the street stared as he moved in a half crouch towards the building. He tiptoed onto the porch, tied the stout rope around the door knob, and then looped it around one of the pillars that held up the porch.

He walked around the building. As he suspected, it was sealed tight. He climbed up on the porch railing and pulled himself to the sloping roof. He walked quietly to the painted brick chimney, pulled the pin on the tear gas grenade, and dropped it down.

Thunk, and then shouting, coughing, gagging.

He swung off the roof onto the porch. The coughing and wretching grew louder. The metal door he'd tied in place shook in its frame as though a demon from hell was on the other side.

"Hello," Odin shouted pleasantly.

The Judas Hole slid open and the guardian launched a string of expletives, punctuated by deep coughs.

Odin responded by dropping the second tear gas grenade in through the slot.

The guardian shoved his shotgun out the hole and tried to

aim but he was coughing too hard. Odin wrested the weapon from his hands without much difficulty.

The ex-cop looked out into the street. Nearly twenty people had gathered, young and old, male and female, all black. There was ominous murmuring as they watched.

Odin kept turning his head, keeping his eye on them, as he addressed the guardian.

"I want the coke," Odin said.

A package was shoved out of the slot.

Odin tucked it into a pocket.

A stocky black woman had stepped forward. Odin held the guardian's shotgun casually but ready to swing up at a moment's notice.

"We thought you was going to clean the place up," the stocky woman said. "But you just another ripoff artist."

"You want the place cleaned up?"

"Damn straight," she said, and was echoed by the others in the crowd.

"Step back."

The crowd moved into the street. Odin untied the rope. The door exploded open. Guardian was the first out, rubbing his hands in his eyes and nearly bent double from his coughs. Odin gave him a boot in the rear and he fell down the four stairs onto the lawn. A skinny man followed him out and received the same treatment. A woman came after that. Odin let her run off down the street.

Odin took a few deep breaths, then went inside. He checked that there was no one else in the building. He came back out, breathed in and out again, and returned to the interior. He found a six-inch-high pile of cocaine on a folding table in the kitchen, along with paraphernalia to dilute and package the drug. Regular cocaine, crack, and freebase, in neatly marked envelopes. Against a cracked plaster wall were stacked chemicals for refining the cocaine into its more powerful cousins. The five gallon cans marked "Ether-Danger-Flammable" caught Odin's eye.

Once again he stepped out and caught his breath. The crowd had deduced what he was up to. They chanted "Go! Go! Go! Go!"

He returned to the kitchen, blew out the pilot lights, and turned on the gas oven and all four burners. He found a pile of dirty rags on a counter and poured ether over them.

He piled the rags strategically, gradually backing towards the door. A few feet from the doorway, he lit a match, tossed it, and hurried out.

The Guardian was waiting at the doorway. He threw his massive bulk at Odin just as the flame hit the first rag.

The Guardian's bulk knocked Odin back into the house.

There was an explosion in the kitchen and an orange glow. The temperature soared.

The fat man was sitting atop Odin. He tried to wrench the sawed-off shotgun out of Odin's grip.

Odin got his thumb on the fat man's bicep and hit the pressure point on the muscle's crest, numbing the arm. The Guardian refused to give up and continued to use his weight and good arm.

Suddenly someone was tugging at the Guardian's hair, ears, and shoulders. A few of the neighbors were pulling him off of Odin. Another looped an arm under the ex-cop and helped him out.

One of them held the shotgun, aimed at the Guardian. Another was binding the big man's hands behind his back with wire.

"Better let me go," the Guardian said. "I got connections. I know my rights."

A late-middle-aged man with bad teeth kicked him in the shin. "You gots the right to get out of our neighborhood," the man said. "You ain't gonna be selling dope to our kids no more."

"You tell him!" several voices echoed.

"You okay?" the heavyset woman asked Odin.
Odin felt at his ribs. "Seem to be in one piece. Thanks."
The building exploded.
"Thank *you*," she said.

26 The reception was part of the benefit for the Museum of Contemporary Art. It was a black-tie function, held in the museum's largest room. Music by John Cage. Premier California and French wines. Catered by Spago. The rich and famous meet the powerful and savvy. The Mayor was talking earnestly with the head of the ICM talent agency. Studio chief Lew Singleton was absorbed in conversation with an attorney from the influential O'Melveny and Myers law firm. An actress with three facelifts to her credit was talking to a performance artist in a velveteen tux.

Assistant Chief Fred Fleming was trapped in the corner by a Republican power broker. Raymond Tully was the scion of a four-generation California family that had made its money exploiting the land and publishing bad newspapers. Tully had inherited millions, as well as an affinity for alcohol.

"Freddie, have you thought about politics?" The bigwig had a large nose mapped with broken blood vessels. His deep-set eyes also were redlined.

"Not really. Police work is a demanding mistress."

"Mayor Bradley was a former policeman. State Senator Davis too. You've got a built in law-and-order magnetism. I've been watching. You've got charisma, know your way around."

"I'm flattered."

"I'm not just saying that because of the nuisance you cleared up for me."

Tully had hit a pregnant woman who was crossing the street.

His blood-alcohol level had been twice the legal limit. The victim was a poor illegal alien who had no idea what had happened. The bigwig had provided a few thousand dollars and she'd been hustled back across the border.

"I hear the state police chief is retiring?" Tully said. "Interested?"

The California State Police department was a relatively small police agency, responsible mainly for guarding state buildings and state officials.

"Los Angeles has always been my love. I'd hate to have to go to Sacramento."

"Think about it. The pay's not bad. I hear the chief down here's going to be sticking around for a few more years. You know he's not going to let you go anywhere."

"We have great mutual respect for each other."

Tully smirked. "Yeah, and the Pope's a Jew."

Fleming noticed that a man nearby seemed to be paying great attention to the conversation. The man's back looked familiar. Nicholas Provenzano.

After a few final pleasantries, Tully drifted off to get a fresh drink.

"You gonna take the job?" Provenzano asked.

"How did you get in here?"

"I donated a few grand, like everyone else," Provenzano said. "Except you. Cops always get in on the arm, don't they?"

"The people know me."

"Your boss ain't here."

"He doesn't like these sort of affairs."

Provenzano shook his head, and pointed to a sculpture that was a mass of wire hangers welded to a trash can. "They call this art? I used to do better junk in reform school."

Fleming turned to walk away.

"You oughta take that job," Provenzano said.

"I don't need career advice."

"You know how much dirt you'd get on the politicos?"

Fleming spun to face Provenzano. He was about to blurt out his anger when Pro held up a placating hand.

"Now, now, now. You owe me, *compadre*. I got names and papers on the Mokley transfer. You think the people you used would hold up under pressure?"

Fleming gritted his teeth.

"You see, one of my heroes has always been J. Edgar Hoover. Files. The old Mustache Petes, they thought you could get what you want by busting heads. That's outdated. Information is the best club. Let's see, you know the guy over there in the gray three piece with the hankie in the pocket? He's got his own company, a big subcontractor to Lockheed."

"I know him by sight."

"Well, he's a degenerate gambler. Bets about thirty grand a week. You know where he gets that money?"

"No."

"Neither do I. But I got an accountant going over his books on the QT. I'll see if he's skimming, and then offer to help him with money management. Pretty smart, huh?"

"Your mother must be proud."

"You know U.S. District Judge Wilcox over there? The old conservative fart. Well, when he was a kid in college, you'll never guess what he did. Go ahead, guess?"

"I have no idea," Fleming said coldly.

"He joined the Communist party. What do you think his Republican cronies would say about that?"

"Didn't he issue a ruling on a big labor case last year?"

"Right. Favorable to my union. A surprising change of opinion for Wilcox, the legal eagles said." Provenzano winked. "See, I'm telling you this because I want us to be friends. Good friends."

"Two more things, buddy," Provenzano said, putting his hand on Fleming's shoulder as the assistant chief turned away. Fleming looked at it like it was a loathesome insect but Provenzano kept it there.

"You never asked what I wanted from you for helping you out. Quid pro quo."

"I knew you'd ask sometime."

"Files. The Public Disorder Intelligence Division files and the unexpurgated Marilyn Monroe file."

"The PDID files were destroyed. The Monroe file was released."

A slim young man in a snazzy tuxedo came over and shook hands enthusiastically with Fleming.

"My house was burglarized last week," the man said with a vaguely French accent. "Your officers arrived within minutes. A couple of days ago, they arrested the *cochon* who did it. I wish to commend you for a job well done."

Fleming took the praise, made a few minutes chitchat, and the man moved on.

"Hey, that was rude, not introducing me," Provenzano said.

Fleming took a drink off a tray held by a passing waitress.

"Your Frenchy friend and I have mutual acquaintances. I know the dealer who keeps him in dope."

Fleming tried not to look surprised.

"Sure. He's different than most of the Hollywood bozos. He likes heroin, not coke. I call him the French Connection. You know how much smack he shoots?"

"No."

"I do. Anyway, you were just bullshitting me about those files. I know for a fact dupes of the PDID files were kept. I'll call you tomorrow with the numbers. I'm particularly interested in the one with the surveillance report on the prosecutor who was selling scripts under a pseudonym to a studio he was investigating. He's working OC now. That union leader who made the sweetheart deal and later got an interest-free loan also. It's important I know who's doing what among my peers, right?"

"Why the Marilyn file?"

"I hear two brothers from a certain well known family were banging Monroe. One got there shortly after she OD'd. Had a private ambulance take her to the hospital. She was DOA. So they drove her back and did a nice cover-up."

"Even if that was true, why would you care? Both of them are dead."

"But their family lives on. When the next generation makes their run on the White House, a file like that might be worth something."

"You're scum."

"I wasn't the one who first put all these files together. Ciao."

As the reception ended, and the crowd drifted toward the banquet tables, he found Provenzano at his arm again.

"What is it?" Fleming demanded.

"Your boy Odin. I been keeping tabs on him. He's a loose cannon."

"I'll take care of him."

"You better. Or I'll have to."

Odin pulled up to the wrought iron gate between stone stanchions. The house, like others along the winding street in Trousdale Estates, was set back from the road. All a passerby could see was a high stone fence and thick hedges. Odin tapped the intercom button.

"Yes?"

"This is Mr. Blow. Mokley's friend."

A low hum and the gates slowly swung opened. Odin drove the long circular driveway to the house. The grounds, which must have covered at least two acres, were dotted with exotic flora. The home looked like a miniature White House. Spotlights illuminated the outer walls, making it stand out against the dark.

The ten-foot-high wooden door was opened by a butler out of a British sitcom.

"This way," he said.

The room was all white. There were a few flecks of color in

paintings on the wall. Modern art splotches. The room would be blinding in bright daylight. Subdued recessed lighting gave it an eerie charm.

All the whiteness reminded him of a hospital, and Jan, and he felt a pang of longing for her. What would she think if she saw him now, knew what he was up to?

Ella Singleton read the expression on his face and didn't understand it. She had arranged herself for maximum effect. She was stretched out on the white linen sofa, baring one tanned leg. She wore a white gown that simulated discretion, and yet revealed large parts of her chest, back, and legs. Her blond hair was pulled back from her face in a leonine mane. She held a gin and tonic in one hand, a cigarette in the other.

She got up languidly, her red-painted toes sinking into the inch-thick white shag. She walked over to where Odin stood. She studied him from inches away. He didn't move.

"I know your face," she said. "You're the cop who was injured. Are you trying to frame me?" Her voice was husky, sensual, her tone unthreatened, if anything bemused.

It was strangely familiar hearing that voice, since Odin had seen her in three or four films. She usually played the sensuous, treacherous woman.

Singleton had strikingly fine features, a smooth, determined jaw line, pert nose, tempting lips. She conveyed the feeling that she was bored with everything, challenging a man to show her something different. Yet in her eyes there was a ferocious hunger, a frightening desperation.

Odin didn't know what to say. He took out the cocaine. She seemed to calm down, to turn off the thousands of watts of personality.

"What's your story?" Singleton asked, pulling him down on the couch next to her.

"I've got to find a way to make a living," he said.

"You fascinate me," she said. "Getting to know you could be fun. For both of us."

He recalled her using a similar line, maybe those exact words, in one of her films. How many of her real life moves, her manners, her words, had been dreamt up by a screenwriter?

She dropped her hand to his knee. Odin glanced around.

"Where's your husband?"

"At some reception. It's just you and me. Got any ideas what we can do?"

He smiled.

"What are you smiling about?" she asked, sounding threatened.

"You used that line in 'The Chasers.'"

"Did I? I don't recall it."

"In the scene where you first meet the hero. After the fight on the bridge."

"Hmmm." Her finger traced a pattern on his thigh. She leaned against him, heavy with perfume.

"I can see why Mokley spent so much time out here," Odin said.

"Hmmmmm," she purred, her hand moving up higher.

"He told me he was out here when the bomb blew up," Odin said.

Her hand brushed across his fly and felt the bulge. She sat up, assured that her gambit was working. "How about a little toot?"

"Was he here?"

"Who?"

"Mokley."

"Hmmmmm."

She removed the cocaine from Odin's pocket, opened the bag, and took out a pinch. She vacuumed it up like a mountain man getting a fresh pouch of snuff.

"Hmmmmm," she said, then repeated the snort on the other nostril.

She lay back, head in Odin's lap. "Nice." She rolled her head around. Odin struggled to keep his mind on business.

"Tell me about Mokley," he persisted.

"What about him?"

"Why'd he set that bomb?"

She shrugged. "Why do people act the way they do?"

"Did he ever talk about it?"

She did another two hits of coke.

"Don't try and bullshit a bullshitter," she said. "I can tell why you're out here."

"Why?"

"You want to find out about Mokley. Check out his alibi. Right?"

"Right."

She was sitting up, prim and proper, the strident sexuality turned off. "I don't think he did it. He was a complete dork when it came to anything mechanical. He tried to do a burn test on some coke once. Wound up ruining the whole thing. I don't think he could work a balance beam scale without screwing up."

Odin tucked the coke into a pocket. "Who would've tried to blow him up?"

She reached over and took the coke from him. As she did, her gown gapped open. She wasn't wearing a bra. She saw him looking and moved back very slowly.

"He had plenty of enemies. But none of them thought of him as very significant. He's like the paparazzi. A fly. Not even worth brushing away."

"How about your husband?"

She bent over, baring her cleavage again, and took two more lines. This time Odin didn't bother to look. She sat up and flicked her tongue out, catching a few crystals that remained on the tip of her nose.

"This is primo stuff. Where'd you get it?"

"It's a long story."

She glanced at a thin gold Patek Philippe on her wrist. "We've got a couple of hours at least."

"I'd rather talk about Mokley."

"He's boring."

"Not to me."

"Most men would've been all over me by now," she said.
"What about Mokley?"

"He was all over me right from the beginning. He wasn't a
very good lover, but he tried."

"What about the bomb?"

"I don't understand it," she said, toying with Odin's fly. "He
couldn't have planted it, and if someone was after him, I
would've known it."

"How?"

"He was a scaredy cat. I could've felt it. He was always ter-
rified my husband would walk in on us." She tugged at the
zipper, taking it down a quarter inch. "I bet you're not scared of
anything."

"Someone could've been after Mokley and he didn't know
it."

She pulled his zipper down. He pulled it back up. She
pressed her lips against his. He tried to concentrate on questioning her. The throbbing at his groin was too insistent. When she
tugged his zipper again, he didn't resist. She made a peculiar
animal hissing noise as she guided him into her.

He was singing Rolling Stones tunes in his car on the ride
home. He was completely drained. Singleton was incredibly
passionate. He felt like the coolest stud in town. He hadn't even
thought about his "problem" until lying on the sofa afterwards.
And by then his "problem" was clearly gone. He'd helped her
hit the high notes a second time before heading out.

Ella Singleton. He wasn't the kind to gossip. Maybe he'd just
tell Huey. Nichols would appreciate it. Quality, not quantity.
The lieutenant wouldn't believe him. But hell, Singleton had

told him to come back any time. Of course he couldn't tell Huey what he'd used to get in.

Then it hit him. He patted his jacket pocket. The cocaine was gone. His joy turned to rage. He felt like turning back, forcing his way in, and taking the coke. What was left of it. Singleton probably had snorted it up by now. Odin felt like a putz.

When had she lifted it? When they were sprawled on the couch, or bouncing on the floor, or bent over the coffee table? Odin, super stud. Yeah, right.

As he parked his car near his apartment, he heard Jan's voice. "I guess you forgot about us."

Jan Golden, arms folded, was leaning against her car.

"Oh no," he said.

"I've only been here an hour," she said dryly. She held a nursing magazine in her hand. "A good issue. I've been meaning to catch up on my reading."

"I've been, I've been working on something," he said, walking to her. He felt guilty and it was hard to be convincing. "I'm sorry."

She sniffed, and caught Singleton's expensive scent.

"Did it go well?" she asked cynically.

"I learned more about Mokley."

"Bully for you. Well, good night."

"Wait. Why don't you come in? Or we can go out to have a bite somewhere?"

"I've lost my appetite." Golden was speaking through clenched teeth. "The only reason I stayed was because I was worried about you. I didn't like the feeling. I know we don't owe each other anything, but the least you can do is keep an appointment once you've made it. Good night."

He hurried after her. "Jan, I said I'm sorry. It was business, honest."

"I can imagine the kind of business it was, Mr. Odin."

"Calm down, okay. Let's talk like adults." He took her arm.

"Keep your hands to yourself." She pulled away and climbed into her car.

"Will you get off your high horse for a second and listen to me?"

She started the engine and drove off.

27 It took a long time for Odin to get to sleep. Several times he tried calling Jan Golden but her line was busy. Out of service, the operator said. Off the hook, he figured.

When the alarm sounded the next morning, he felt like lying in bed all day, brooding. He considered swinging by her house, making a shot at reconciliation. He showered and dressed. He grabbed a couple of chocolate doughnuts and a cup of coffee at the Winchell's Donuts.

During his weeks at the dojo, Odin had forsaken the junk food he'd lived on for so long. He had felt better, but who could say whether it was the food, or the exercise, or the hope.

He realized how much he missed Scalia's dojo. It had given him a group to belong to at a crucial point. Maybe Scalia would act as a go-between with Golden.

Odin watched the class through the doorway. About ten students, Scalia and Connie. She was the first to notice him. Somehow she communicated that to Scalia, though Odin couldn't tell just how.

The *sensei* rolled over to him.

"Welcome back," Scalia said as if nothing had happened. "You feel like a workout?"

"I'd love it."

"Class is just starting. Do some stretches, then join in."

Odin removed his shoes and bowed slightly as he stepped onto the mat. Bowing in as a sign of respect to the school, the teacher, and the fellow students was one of the few Oriental rituals Scalia insisted on.

It was a great class. Odin enjoyed two hours of punching, kicking, blocking, grabbing, twisting, throwing. Midway through the class, he admitted to himself how much he had missed the workouts. Leon was coming along nicely. And seeing the disabled students working around their handicaps gave him a thrill. They were no longer grotesque. They had a courage that he admired.

Odin was breathing hard as the class wound down and they sat on their knees—except for the two students in wheelchairs—facing Scalia.

"A young monk and an old monk were traveling through ancient China," Scalia recounted. "They came to a fast-running river. A beautiful woman in an expensive silk dress was standing at the side of the river, crying. The older monk asked, 'What's the trouble, little sister?'

"'I must get to my father's house without ruining my dress, and there's no boatman,' she told him.

"'Hop on my back,' he told her.

"She climbed up and they made it across the river. She thanked him and hurried off. Now the younger monk was outraged. There were strict religious laws against a monk having any contact with a woman. Especially a beautiful woman. Just like I demand from my students."

Benny, a young man paralyzed on his left side, chuckled.

"All right, Benny, twenty-five pushups for thinking evil thoughts," Scalia said, and then everyone laughed. "Now, where was I, oh, so monks weren't supposed to have any contact with women.

"These two monks had gone another fifteen miles. The young monk didn't say anything, but he was steaming. Finally, the older monk asked, 'Is something troubling you?'

"'That woman, how could you touch her?'

"'I set her down miles ago. It's you who are still carrying her.'"

There was silence in the dojo, and then a few heads bobbed in understanding.

"We carry burdens in life," Scalia said. "Sometimes, we can get rid of the burden by changing the outside world. Like if you have a neighbor who's a real pain in the butt, you can move. Or set fire to his house."

He paused until the laughter died down.

"Maybe you can't move. And you can't get him to move. Then you have to change yourself. How upset are you going to be that his garbage cans are uncovered, or that he plays disco until two A.M. most nights? Does it hurt him if you toss and turn and eat yourself up? Who are you hurting?"

Heads bobbed.

"All right, class dismissed. See you Thursday." Scalia rolled to where Odin stood.

"You have time for a cup of tea?" Scalia asked.

"I'd love it."

"The kids missed you," Scalia said.

"I missed them too."

"It was wrong of an old Taoist like me to try and change a leopard's spots. You know, they have a saying like that in Chinese. It's not just an American cliché," Scalia said. "Have you ever thought about working with kids? I mean professionally. You've got a knack, you know. Too many adults, especially men, get awkward around kids."

"What should I become, a damn nanny?" Odin said.

"Feeling sorry for yourself?"

"Yeah, I'm feeling sorry for myself. What did I do wrong? I served my country, got a shitload of medals. I come back here, work as a cop. Save a few lives, take out a few bad guys. More fucking medals. I played by the rules. What does it get me?"

"You've got a lot of damn nerve," Scalia said in a level tone.

"What?"

"You're feeling sorry for yourself. Wimping out."

An angry Odin stood up to leave.

"You think it's fair that Benny was in a car accident and one side is paralyzed? You think it's fair that Jim's mother took PCP while she was pregnant, so he's blind and brain damaged? Or maybe it's fair that Pat's father beat her so much as a kid that she still shivers if you raise a hand? Or that Eileen lost a leg to diabetes?"

Odin hesitated in the doorway.

"Or maybe what happened to me was fair?" Scalia said.

Odin cleared his throat, but didn't say anything. He returned to his seat.

"I can sympathize and help with any disability," Scalia said. "But I won't put up with self-pity. From no one. Not you. Not Connie. Not myself."

"So what's the answer?" Odin challenged.

"If I knew, I'd be a guru with lots of rich followers giving me money," Scalia said after a long pause. "Instead I'm a cripple with a loft teaching other cripples how to get by in a rotten world. It is a rotten place lots of times, but it's the only one we got."

They sat together in silence. Scalia reached over and squeezed Odin's arm.

"So you think I should open a day care center?" Odin asked.

"What I think doesn't matter. But if you keep running around playing cops and robbers, you can't bitch if you scrape your knee. At least you got a knee to scrape," Scalia said, patting the stump of his own leg.

More silence. Connie came in with a fresh kettle of tea, refilled their cups, and walked out without saying a word.

"She still hate me?" Odin asked.

"Not much," Scalia said. "What are you going to do?"

"Find the guy that planted the bomb."

"The guy that got killed in jail didn't do it?"

"He just doesn't feel right for the part."

"You've got to trust your instincts," Scalia said. "Do you have anyone in mind?"

"No. It's just, well, this sounds paranoid, but I feel like there's something going on I'm not seeing. Like with these mob hoods bouncing around the edges. I get so overwhelmed sometimes I want to chuck it all. Give up."

"Why don't you?"

"Why don't I? Because I'm walking around with this," Odin pointed to his ruined eye, "and some scumbag is going around just fine."

"Think you'll feel better after you find them?"

"Maybe. But I know they'll feel a whole lot worse."

Scalia sighed. "If the guy in jail didn't set the booby trap, either he was the target, or you were."

"Me?"

"Not you specifically. Maybe your SWAT team."

"But how could they have . . ." Odin hesitated.

"What're you thinking?"

"About the number of people who would've known we were going to hit the place. There's the deputy DA who prepared the warrant, his boss, their secretaries, the judge, his staff, the squad, our boss."

"A couple dozen people?"

"Give or take."

"Can you vouch for all of them?"

Odin shook his head.

"Don't forget, us blind boys can't see a head shake."

"I'm sorry. No."

"After a while, you can tell the difference between a shake and a nod. More fabric rustling with a shake," Scalia said. "What are you going to do now?"

Odin shrugged.

"That was a shrug, I take it?" Scalia said.

"Sorry. Yeah, it was."

They sipped tea.

"I was thinking, you know, what you said when we were doing those circling blocks earlier. About the power of the circle, going back to the beginning."

"You'll start the investigation all over?"

"Can't dance."

He was so absorbed with catching the bomber that he had forgotten about Jan.

28 The bomb squad office had the usual cop shop clutter of battered file cabinets and desks. There were a half dozen chairs well worn from supporting beefy butts and the grime that somehow tinges law enforcement offices.

There was no mistaking the special interest of the twelve officers who worked out of the first-floor office. Deactivated hand grenades were used as paperweights. A brass shell casing served as an ash tray. On the wall were blow-ups of cross sections of various explosive devices ranging in sophistication from a pipe bomb to a nuclear weapon. Bookcases held titles like *DuPont Explosive Materials* and *Terrorist Bombing Patterns*.

If ever the LAPD had to defuse an atom bomb, it would probably be Beth Lerner who'd get the assignment. She was tall, thin, with long tapering fingers. She had a knack for being able to develop a profile of a bomber by careful examination of an explosive device and its surroundings.

Was the bomb placed where it would do the most damage? Was it antipersonnel or antiproperty? Had it been neatly packaged or was it makeshift? Was it low to the ground or high up? Stolen military ordnance or homemade?

She occasionally taught her methods at seminars open to a

variety of law enforcement agencies but she couldn't teach the instincts developed over eleven years on the job.

Odin had met her a couple of times on assignments. After he called, she agreed to meet him at Miriwa restaurant in Chinatown.

"Why did you call?" she asked after terse greetings. She didn't offer to shake hands but Odin knew she was always that way. Lerner was wary that no galumph of a cop would crush her sensitive digits. She wore the slight scent of machine oil the way most women wore perfume. On her, it was not unattractive.

Odin ordered an assortment of Chinese *dim sum*. He asked about her husband and kids and how things were in the bomb squad. She asked him how he was feeling, what he planned for the future.

She had a vaguely prissy, school-teacherish manner. In fact, she had been a teacher for four years before taking the test for the LAPD. When asked if she was scared working on the bomb squad, she would quip that it wasn't as dangerous as teaching a classroom full of ten-year-olds. She didn't joke very often.

They were halfway through the meat buns when Odin asked, "Would you be willing to go over your impressions with me?"

She delicately wiped a bit of sweet pork sauce from her lips and took a piece of paper out of the pocket of her blue blazer. "I was waiting for you to ask." She put on no nonsense black framed glasses and read her notes.

"The device was made out of gunpowder with a relatively simple clothespin trip mechanism."

"I know."

"How do you know?"

"I saw your report."

"That's a confidential police document. How did you get it?"

"Don't worry. I'm not a scumbag defense attorney. Uh, sorry about the French."

"I've heard worse. But it's dangerous for any documents leaving the department."

"The person who got it for me knew it would go no further."

"There's limited distribution. Who gave it to you?"

"I can't say."

She folded up the paper she'd been reading, and returned to her lunch.

"Beth?"

"If you don't share with me, I won't share with you."

"It's not like that."

"It is to me."

She finished the pork bun and *shao mai*, wiped her mouth again, and reached into her purse. "I'll split the check with you. Obviously, you didn't get what you wanted."

He paid the bill in full, despite her protests, and they walked out.

"Beth, this means a lot to me. But it doesn't mean so much that I'd be willing to burn a source. Someone on the job trusted me with the information. I'm not going to give up who they are. I wouldn't even do it in court. You've got to understand that I wouldn't give you up either."

They walked a couple of blocks without her responding. She turned to face him, like a lover about to give a last kiss. Odin sensed she was making a decision, and his best bet was to keep quiet.

They were by Olvera Street, the bustling block of Mexican souvenir shops and restaurants at the oldest part of Los Angeles. A dozen Mexican pioneer families had first established El Pueblo de Nuestra Senora La Reina de Los Angeles, de Porciuncula in 1781. On any given day, there were more people shopping in the stores than had lived in "El Pueblo" for the first fifty years.

Brightly colored tourist geegaws, ponchos, and leather purses, postcards and piñatas, all tried to catch the eye simultaneously. Instamatics clicked and children demanded toys.

Lerner and Odin waded through the crowd and made it to one of the park benches that faced the gazebo.

"Why do you want to know about the bomb?" she asked like a teacher quizzing a student.

"Something doesn't quite add up."

It was the right answer. "I feel the same way."

"What is it?"

"I don't know," she said, removing her notes again.

"Will you think out loud for me?" he asked.

"The bomber was most likely a male, operating alone. That's just a statistical thing and I haven't felt any vibes to make me feel he was atypical. I'd also throw in probably older than twenty and younger than sixty. Not Latino. Rarely do Hispanics go for bombs. Probably white, but could be black or Oriental. Statistically, Arabs and Armenians make for good suspects.

"Gunpowder was used," she continued. "From samples put under the gas chromotagraph, I determined they were from Winchester Super X shotgun shells."

"Any way of pinning down where they were bought?"

"It's a common brand, sold everywhere. It does show that our bomber doesn't fancy himself a chemist. It's among the more easily made explosives. Not a very powerful one, though."

"It killed Finch and Daggett."

"You know why? It was tamped. You know what that is?"

"I was in the SEALs."

"I had forgotten." She took out a pen, and made a quick sketch on the back of her note paper. "Look at the foyer and the hall."

The confined space of the tiny foyer had directed the blast from the door out into the hall. If there hadn't been a foyer, most of the force would've been dissipated into the room. Lots of bang, but little blast.

"Then there were the chemicals Mokley was storing in the closet. Methamphetamine precursors. All flammable and explosive. What was attached to the door was not much worse than a heavy-duty firecracker. But those other factors multiplied the effect."

"Clever bastard."

"That's what I don't know. It seems kind of silly to arrange it like that. It would've been easier to just plant a stronger device. I almost think it was an accident."

"Why the bomb on the door in the first place?"

"If I knew, I'd tell you. It's got me stumped."

"What else can you tell me?"

"It was a relatively simple device," she said. "I even show how to make a version of it at some of my lectures," she said. "I make a similar model and use it to explain basic principles. Then I conclude with a bang, which really is the most effective part of the discussion. It scares the bejesus out of the students. I don't want any hero cops trying to defuse a bomb."

Odin didn't hear her last few words. He was wondering if someone who had sat in on one of her lectures could've gotten the idea.

"Did you hear what I said?" she asked him abruptly.

"What? Oh, sure."

"Repeat it then."

"You don't want any amateurs getting cocky and trying to defuse a bomb."

"After that?"

"I missed it."

"I was talking about the simplicity of the device. How it only had one means of detonation. A string attached to the door which pulled out an insulator from the clothespin when the door was open. What are other possible activators?"

He thought back to his SEAL days. "There could be a timing device or a motion sensitive activator. Like a mercury switch. Or it could be spring loaded."

"Correct. A more professional bomber has a couple of different activators." She studied her notes. "The bomb was planted about chest level. Which makes for a more deadly explósion. Yet it wasn't an antipersonnel device. No nails or glass shards to maximize flesh wounds. The height would make the bomb more easily discovered. And deactivated. Which is why I thought the occupant of the apartment had planted it. But that doesn't jibe with the way it was secured. It's not like a permanent mount, a perverse sort of burglar alarm. It's a real puzzle."

"Any wild hunches?"

"No." She stood up. Class dismissed.

"Thank you."

"Why do you want to know? Really."

"I want to find out who did it."

"Then? No, don't answer." She took off her glasses and nibbled an end. "You know, when I was a teacher, I was very liberal. I thought education was the answer. Help people up by their bootstraps. No such thing as a bad boy and all of that. Now when I hear a pipe bomber blew his hands off because he didn't realize there was explosive in the threads as he screwed down the cap, I have to watch that I don't applaud."

"I hear what you're saying."

"I don't like it in me, or in other people."

"I can understand that."

She shivered. "I hate bombers."

He nodded.

"I better be heading back. Perhaps it's best if we're not seen together."

He reached for her hand, took it, and pressed it gently to his lips. "Thanks again."

He rented a car and drove to Finch's home in Simi Valley. A couple of preschool kids were playing on the sidewalk in front of the neighbor's house. Otherwise, it was a typical lifeless suburban street: identical houses; cars in garages; lawns neatly trimmed; sprinklers hissing.

"Yes?" a woman's voice answered nervously when he rapped at the door.

"It's Bob."

Finch's widow opened the door a crack. "I don't want your company." She wore a house robe, her hair unwashed, no makeup. She looked like she hadn't slept in a week.

"I'd like to talk."

"I wouldn't."

"Please. A few minutes. I drove all the way out here." Like a tenacious salesman, he'd slipped his foot into the door. He gently pushed forward. She let him in.

There were dirty dishes on tables, the TV was blasting, clothes lay on the floor. It reminded Odin of his own place at its worst moments of bachelor sloppiness.

"How are you, Mary?" he asked.

She shrugged.

He shut off the TV. She didn't react. He gathered the clothing and brought it to the hamper. He collected the dishes and carried them into the kitchen. The cleanup took four trips.

"Where are the kids?"

She thought for a moment. "Oh, they're staying at my sisters' for a few days I guess."

He loaded up the dishwasher and tried to turn it on.

"It doesn't work," she said. "Nothing works."

"I'll wash, you dry," Odin said, tossing her a dish towel. She missed it, picked it up, then stood like a robot waiting to be turned on.

He washed for a few minutes without saying anything. She dried, the mechanical repetition somehow soothing, a simple task to focus on.

"I miss him too," Odin said, trying to get her talking.

"I just keep thinking about how much I miss him. Little things remind me of him. I'll find something he dropped, a note he left, a grease stain on a chair, and . . ." She sniffled. "I can't cry anymore."

"Have you spoken with anyone about it?"

"Like who?"

"A priest. A psychologist. Your family. Ginger Daggett. There are support groups for police widows."

"I don't feel comfortable going out."

"There's times when we all need someone to talk to."

She concentrated on her drying and didn't answer.

On seeing Odin barge in, the children next door had run into the house.

"Mommy, a bad man just went in to Mr. Finch's house," said the older child, a girl with a ponytail.

"How do you know he was a bad man?" her mother asked, amused as she continued to stir a Betty Crocker cake mix.

"He looked like a bad man," the girl said.

"Yes. Like on TV. He had a beard, and an eye patch and a scar," her younger brother piped up.

"That doesn't mean he's a bad man," the mother said, half doubting her children's account.

"He pushed his way in," the girl said.

The woman didn't know Mary Finch very well, but she knew Finch's husband was a police officer who had been killed not that long ago. The neighbor set down the big spoon and walked to the wall nearest the Finch home. She opened the window a crack and listened. She strained for any sound of a struggle or cries for help.

"Is there anything about the birdman you'd like to talk about?" Odin asked.

"Do you really want to hear about times we went walking in the night, squeezing each other like teenagers? How cute he looked coming out from under the four-by-four covered with grease? How that rotten job took him away for hours and hours.

229

And then forever." She sniffled again. "Is that what you want to hear?"

"Anything you want to talk about."

"What are you looking for?" she asked coldly.

"Did he ever talk about problems at work?"

"Almost never. He said he didn't want to bring it home with him. He'd talk more about his four-wheel drive than work. Except to say how great you guys were." Bitterness welled up in her words.

"Did he ever talk at all about threats? Someone he'd locked up threatening him?"

"One time we had to change our phone number, but he never said why. That was years ago. He insisted I learn how to shoot, but that was years ago too."

"Did you ever get the feeling he was caught up in anything?"

"Like what?"

"I don't know." Odin found it awkward to say. "Sometimes, cops get caught up in things. Good cops."

She stared at him. "Corruption?"

He nodded.

"How dare you!" she said.

"It can happen to anyone."

"Get out! Get out!" She was screaming now. "He gave his life for your miserable department and you come here and smear his name. You ugly cripple! I hope you rot in hell."

She ran from the room, up the stairs. He heard the bathroom door slam.

The next door neighbor had been ready to dismiss her children's account when she heard Mary screaming "Get out!" The neighbor ran to the phone and called 911.

"A man just forced his way into my neighbor's house. She's a policeman's wife. Widow." She told the operator the address and added, "Please hurry."

Odin debated whether he should leave. Visions of Mary swallowing a bottle of pills or slashing her wrists, convinced him to go upstairs and rap on the door.

"Mary, I'm sorry if I upset you."

"Get out of my house," she said.

"I'll go as soon as I see you're all right."

"Get out."

"C'mon. Let's talk."

"Get out!"

"Please come out."

Silence.

"Mary?"

Still silence.

He hesitated a moment, stepped back, and kicked the door. The wood near the lock shattered.

She was sitting on the hamper, staring straight ahead.

"Let me put you to bed," Odin said.

"Don't touch me."

"Mary, I loved Finch too. Maybe you can't understand that right now, but you've got to believe me."

"Just leave me alone."

She didn't fight as he put his arm around her and guided her to the bedroom. By the time they reached the bed, she was sobbing. He lay her down and tucked her in.

Odin picked up the phone and dialed Daggett's house.

"Ginger, this is Bob Odin."

"How are you, Bobby?"

"Pretty fair. I'm over at Finch's. Mary's pretty busted up. I wonder if you could come over and give her a little of your strength."

"I'm keeping it together, but I don't know how well."

"Does that mean no?"

"I suppose I've got a little to spare. I'll be by but I have to drop the kids off with a neighbor. It'll be about twenty minutes."

"Thanks. You're a lifesaver."

Odin turned. Mary was fast asleep, snoring slightly. She looked like hell. He remembered her as such a pretty woman, frisky, full of energy. He sighed.

He had a dirty job to do. He began rooting through their drawers, searching for anything incriminating. In the night table he found a box of condoms, right near Finch's off duty 9-mm Beretta. He felt embarassed as he discovered frilly Frederick's of Hollywood panties and a bra with nipple cutouts in the six-foot-high oak chest of drawers.

The shoe box was in the bottom drawer. He dreaded opening it. Would it be filled with cash? What would he do then?

He jerked the lid off, realizing simultaneously that it could be a bomb. But it wasn't. The box held a collection of love letters from Finch to his wife, from when Finch was in the service. Odin nearly cried. His head was throbbing. He squeezed his head with his hands.

He had to continue his search. The ex-cop hurried downstairs to the den.

29 There were a couple of baseball trophies on a shelf and books on military history on a shelf, as well as an eight-point buck's head on the wall. Odin went through Finch's desk, keeping both ears open for any sound from upstairs. Mary's committing suicide while he invaded their privacy was a nightmare, but he needed to clear Finch's name in his own mind.

He found their checkbook. A few hundred dollars, no unusual transactions. He dug out their bankbook. Three thousand dollars, and no unusual deposits or withdrawals. He realized he was holding the passbook inches from his face. He was having trouble reading the print.

"Freeze, motherfucker!"

For a millisecond, Odin thought he was back on a raid. A part of his brain was convinced he was in SWAT, making an entry into a dope dealer's pad. Then he realized that the two young cops were pointing their guns at him, and he was the suspect.

"Hands in the air!" said one of the cops, who had a nearly see-through blond mustache. Barely into his twenties, he had the build of a weight lifter, and his head looked too small for his body. The silent cop, who appeared even younger, was a few feet away, and looked scared.

"Take it easy," Odin said. "I used to be on the job."

"Don't move!" Weightlifter shouted. "Hands up."

Odin knew how little pressure it took on the trigger. He froze and studied the men. Simi Valley Police. The department had been wracked by numerous scandals, including officers raping female suspects in the jail, corruption, and excessive force charges. The Los Angeles suburb had boomed but the caliber of the police officers had not developed as quickly as the streets had been laid out. Yet there had been several reform campaigns in the department, and the young men facing him were making all the right moves. They were in the classic combat crouch, a few feet apart, out of each other's line of fire.

"I'm Finch's former sergeant," Odin said as coolly as possible. "I'm looking for some paperwork."

"On the floor, legs spread, fingers intertwined behind your head," Weightlifter said.

Odin knew that if the Simi Valley cops followed the textbook, they'd have to move to certain spots. They were young, green, and probably still stuck exactly to the rules. But their lack of seasoning could make them more dangerous, more subject to overreacting.

"Okay," Odin said. "I'm not going to give you a hard time. But we're on the same side."

"Shut your mouth and get on the floor," Weightlifter ordered. He was just out of reach, advancing slowly. One hand held his gun, the other was detaching handcuffs from his belt.

There were footfalls at the top of the stairs and Mary Finch came into view. She stared at the scene.

"Murderer!" she screamed, looking straight at Odin.

Weightlifter lifted his gun, as if to fire. Odin planted a whirling snap kick in Weightlifter's belly, knocking him back and directly into his partner's line of fire as the gun went off. The bullet hit the ceiling, making Mary Finch scream harder.

Odin closed in quickly, his only chance. He grabbed Weightlifter's arm and twisted it up, holding the wrist. The muscular cop yelled. His grip on his gun loosened and Odin seized the weapon.

Mary Finch swayed at the top of the stairs, her screams interrupted only by her intakes of air.

Silent Cop stood stock still, his gun wavering, unable to get a shot without hitting his partner.

"Frrrrreeze! Don't move. Drop it!" the no longer silent cop yelled.

Odin, using the muscular cop as a shield, aimed the confiscated gun at the once silent cop, who was now shouting a stream of contradictory orders.

"Drop your weapon and I won't have to hurt you or your partner," Odin said. He held Weightlifter's thick arm in a hammerlock. He gave a little jerk and the muscular cop flinched.

Mrs. Finch continued to yowl. The widow's screams added to the tension and made it difficult to tell if there were any sirens in the distances. Odin guessed he had barely a couple of minutes before backup units arrived.

Silent Cop finally dropped his gun.

"All right. I won't hurt you. I was really on the job," Odin said softly. "Lay down on the ground. Assume the position."

Silent Cop reluctantly obeyed. Odin felt Weightlifter's muscles tense as he prepared to make a move. Odin switched grips and stuck the gun into the cop's side.

"Don't make me hurt you," Odin said. "Handcuff yourself to your partner. Now!" Odin stepped back out of arm and leg's reach.

Scowling, the muscular cop obeyed.

"Now, cuff your right leg to his left."

But the muscular cop's ankle was too thick for the handcuffs. Odin had Weightlifter put his leg in between the other cop's hands, and then cuffed the hands together. Odin squeezed the handcuffs down, and heard the reassuring click, click, click.

He took the cuff keys away from the cops. "I'll drop these by the curb. I know how much grief you'll get for losing gear."

The cops just glared at him.

Mary Finch was at last quiet. She was sitting on the top step, head between her hands.

There was a knock at the door. Odin leaned against the wall, gun raised. Another knock, and then the door was pushed open.

"Anybody home?" Ginger Daggett came in. "I saw the cruiser outside and . . ." She froze when she saw the cops on the floor.

"It's okay, Ginger," Odin said before she could panic. "Just a misunderstanding."

"What's going on?"

"I don't have time to explain." Odin went to the phone and ripped it out of the wall. He gestured for her to follow him into the kitchen, where he ripped the handset off another phone. "I'm sure there's extensions. I'll ask you not to call nine-one-one for a few minutes but you might have to or they'll bring you in as an accessory. Trust me."

"My husband would have, but I don't know."

"Take care of Mary," Odin said.

"I'll delay making the call as much as I can," she said.

"Thanks. It'll all make sense someday. I hope."

He double-timed out to the living room. The two handcuffed cops looked like they were performing an unnatural act. They had wriggled so they'd be nearer the door.

"Let's not make trouble, guys."

"You'll never get away with this," Weightlifter said.

Mike Williams sauntered into the men's bathroom on the first floor of police headquarters. He closed and locked the door to the bathroom stall. He removed a small glass vial with a tiny spoon from the chest pocket of his dark gray suit. He spooned up two nostrils full of 85 percent pure coke.

Press conferences were getting harder and harder to do. The same stupid questions, the same stupid answers. Shouting and raising your hand, like a kid who wanted permission to go potty.

He was three years past forty. A difficult time for local newsmen. Eager young Turks or wise old pundits were both acceptable to the viewing public. No one wanted to see a middle-aged man just going about his business. He was bored with his job, but unwilling to give up the $135,000 a year.

Williams had begun to take foolish risks. Like shoplifting. Drunk driving. Snorting coke under the cops' noses. He'd been caught once. Assistant Chief Fleming had covered up for him. Now, Fleming used him to leak out info, usually derogatory, about the chief. It was a symbiotic relationship, with Williams's star rising as he garnered confidential information from "a highly placed source."

Williams exited the stall and studied himself in the mirror. The nights of dissipation were beginning to show. He wouldn't make it more than a few more years. He tugged back at his cheeks, trying to reduce the bags under his eyes. He did a few facial stretching exercises.

A fat cop came in, looked at him, and went into a stall.

Williams wet his index finger and moistened his eyebrows. He ran his tongue along his lips. The newsman used a dab of skin-colored makeup base to smooth over irregularities in his cheeks, then headed to the press conference. He had a debt to pay back.

The crew had set up. They winked at Williams. His sound man was his best connection for coke.

The room was bright with TV lights on stands at either side of the podium. The thousand-watt quartz bulbs, coupled with the two dozen bodies filling the metal folding chairs, made it hot and stuffy.

Assistant Chief Fleming was behind the podium, the American flag on one side, the California flag on the other. A dozen microphones, with prominently displayed call letters reached up for his words. He studied his notes, removed his steel-rimmed reading glasses, and smiled out at the group.

"It's always nice to see so many friendly faces," he said with a hint of amiable sarcasm. He rustled his notes. "For those about to die, we salute you," he said. It was a joke he often used, repeating the salutation given gladiators before they entered the Coliseum. "Let the festivities begin."

"I understand that Robert Odin is currently wanted for questioning in connection with an assault on two Simi Valley police officers?" a beefy reporter from a local TV station shouted.

"It's true," Fleming said. "You'll have to get any additional information from them, Tim."

"Will you arrest Odin if he turns up?" asked a brunette reporter from the *Herald Examiner.*

"We always cooperate with other law enforcement agencies," Fleming said. "As you know, Robert Odin was injured during a bombing incident two months ago. He has not been a member of the Los Angeles Police Department since then. You know what an outstanding officer Odin was. His actions since then are still subject to investigation. I urge you not to convict him before he is tried."

"Is it possible he suffered brain damage?" asked an AP reporter.

"Anything's possible, Linda," Fleming said. He gave his professional smile. "I know he suffered extensive injuries in the bombing. Physical injuries. Perhaps mental or emotional ones too. As you know, that incident killed two officers, nearly claimed my son's life as well."

"What about Gary Mokley?" asked a TV reporter with curly blond hair.

"The late Mr. Mokley remains our primary suspect, but we haven't closed the investigation yet."

"Anything new on Mokley's death?" another reporter asked.

"You'll have to talk to the sheriff's department. Of course we're cooperating with them fully, but it's their baby."

"So you're saying that Mokley might not have planted the bomb?" the *Herald* reporter asked.

"We're continuing to pursue several possible leads," Fleming responded.

Fleming's eyes roamed the crowd. He signaled Williams to speak even before the newsman had raised his hand.

"Is it true that former LAPD sergeant Robert Odin is now himself a suspect in that bombing?"

The room was suddenly silent. All attention was on Fleming. He held it, milking it, looking thoughtful, puzzling over an answer.

"Let me emphasize that everyone involved in the bombing is being investigated," Fleming said.

"You didn't really answer my question," Williams said.

The cameraman recorded it all. Great footage. Reporter getting tough with the Assistant Chief. Definitely the top story for the six o'clock news.

"Robert Odin is being investigated in connection with the bombing at the residence of the late Gary Mokley," Fleming snapped. "No further comment."

The Assistant Chief barreled from behind the podium as other reporters fired questions at his back.

As soon as the Assistant Chief was gone, the reporters swarmed Mike Williams, demanding to know what else he knew.

"You kids are just going to have to watch the news. You know what station gets it first, and gets it best, don't you?"

30 "How could he say that about you?" Jan Golden demanded as she angrily clicked off the television set.

Odin sat unmoving in a chair, staring at the now blank screen. He felt weak, nauseous, more alone than he had ever been. He had showed up at Jan's apartment after an hour of wandering. She had taken him in without question.

"Finch's widow might press charges for trespassing, assault. The cops certainly will go for assault and battery, resisting arrest. Now this," Odin said, pointing at the blank TV screen.

"You have to get a lawyer," Golden said. "Prove you're innocent."

"No," Bob whispered so softly she didn't hear it. He held his head between his hands and pressed. "Do you have aspirin?"

She got two tablets from the bathroom and he gulped them down. "Thanks."

"You owe me at least an explanation as to what's happened," she said, folding her arms across her chest. She still had mixed feelings. The night of his impotence, she had suppressed feelings that it was her fault. Then, when he had come to her stinking of another woman's scent, she had been ready to dump him. But seeing him helpless again had brought back her old feelings.

"The cop was going to shoot," he said. "I had to take action."

"I can understand that. But why not turn yourself in and we'll get it cleared up?"

"I can't."

"Why?"

His voice was soft as he struggled to keep himself under control. "I know the way the system works," Bob said. "If they want to railroad me, they can railroad me. Once I lose control, they can do whatever they want."

"Who's they?"

"I don't know. I do know that what happened to Mokley could easily happen to me."

"They'd put you in protective custody."

"Like Mokley? Mistakes get made."

"We'd have a lawyer get you out on bail right away anyway."

"You don't understand. When the police department turns on you, it's like a marriage gone sour. When you're accepted as a cop, you can do no wrong. If you're presumed to be a dirtbag, you can't do anything right. Half the guys on the job are already saying 'Yeah, that Odin, I was always suspicious of him.'"

"You sound paranoid."

He didn't answer. He ground his knuckles into his temples. "These damn headaches."

"How long have you had them?" she asked, shifting into a professional mode.

"A few days."

"Any other symptoms?"

"Sometimes lights look kind of funny."

"How?"

"They have a bluish halo around them."

"Any loss of peripheral vision or night vision?"

He thought he had noticed a slight loss of peripheral vision but hadn't been sure if it was only his imagination. "I don't know," he told her.

"Have you called Doctor Keene?"

"I don't have time."

"Bob, it sounds to me like glaucoma."

"Only old people get that."

"Anyone can get it. Behind your cornea is a fluid-filled cavity. There's a porous structure and a canal to allow pressure to equalize into the scleral veins. If there's a blockage the pressure on the blood vessels supplying the retina and optic nerve builds. The cells don't get nourishment and are permanently damaged."

"I'll get it checked right after I catch the bomber."

"Your optic cells could be dying even as we speak."

"I can't go to a doctor. He's liable to turn me in."

"Just about any optometrist can make the diagnosis. They put a device called a tonometer on your cornea and see what the pressure is."

"Later."

"You can aggravate it further by physical exertion. Anything that might increase the pressure. Bob, you've got to get it checked."

"What do they do for it?"

"Prescribe drugs usually. Sometimes surgery."

"If I have this surgery, how long will I be laid up?"

"A few weeks. Not painful, but you'll have to take it easy to let the surgery heal."

"I don't have that sort of time."

"We're talking about blindness here."

"Let's not get melodramatic," Odin said. "My uncle had glaucoma for years."

"That's chronic and it's bad enough to neglect. You have an acute condition. The pressure builds more rapidly. You can go blind within days. Even hours."

"I can't stop."

She grabbed his shoulders and searched for the words to convince him. "You're going to be literally blinded by hate. No vision. Blackness. Do you understand me?"

"Just leave me alone."

"You came here."

"Maybe that was a mistake."

"Maybe it was," she snapped in frustration.

He stood. "If that's the way you feel . . ." He took a few steps toward the door and turned to apologize.

A tear ran down Jan's cheek. When he wiped it away, she shivered.

"Are you scared?" he asked.

"Yes."

"Of what?"

"Of what will happen to you. And of you."

He stepped back. "Me?"

There was a knock at the door.

Bob dove to the floor, shoving Jan in the opposite direction. As he hit the floor he rolled, coming up with his gun in his hand, off to one side, out of the line of fire.

Golden lay on the floor, stunned. Odin didn't look at her. All his attention was focused on the door, waiting for it to crash open.

She watched him, a wild animal, as beautiful and as frightening as a stalking lion. Odin advanced slowly to a position next to the door, gun raised, muscles in a state of relaxed tension, ready to propel him to another position instantly.

He looked back to her and put a finger to his lips to indicate silence. She sat wide-eyed, watching the drama. She didn't believe it was really happening.

"Bobby, it's Huey," a voice said through the door. "I'm here alone. I wanna talk."

Odin signaled to Jan to respond.

"He's not here," Golden said.

"Don't make the little lady lie for you," Huey said. "I heard your voice. Open this door before I have to huff and puff and kick it down."

Odin shook his head.

"He's not here," Golden repeated, her voice quivery.

"Let me in and cut this jive," Huey said. He tried the door, rattling the knob. "I'm just gonna go and stiff in a call to nine-one-one if you don't open up in a second."

Silence.

Bob signaled for Jan to open the door. She slowly walked to the door and opened it halfway. Odin remained in position. Huey didn't enter. He stayed in the doorway.

"That's some boyfriend you got," Huey said to her.

Jan said nothing.

"Bobby, you gonna jump out and shove a gun in my face? I know where you're hiding, buddy. Let your gal pat me down, then put your gun down. I don't like nobody sticking guns in my face. Least of all friends."

"Check him," Odin said to Golden.

She gave him a superficial frisk. "Nothing."

"Again. Pay special attention to the armpits, small of the back, ankles, and groin."

"Only if you love me," Nichols said, trying to keep a light tone.

She did it again. "He's clean."

"C'mon in," Odin ordered. "Shut the door."

Odin lowered the gun to his side.

Huey stared at him. "Boy, you are fucked."

"Is that what you came here to tell me?"

"I came here to find out what's going on."

"You don't know?"

"I hear Fleming blowing smoke and I want to know what's going on. You punched out some Simi Valley cops?"

"I had to."

"So that's true?"

Odin nodded.

"What about the bomb?"

"What about it?"

"You have anything to do with it?"

Odin said nothing.

"Yes or no?" Huey demanded.

"Do you think I did?"

"No."

"Then why ask?"

"I want to hear you say it?"

"I had nothing to do with the bomb. Other than nearly losing my face to it."

"Okay."

Huey took a step to the side, and Odin raised the gun.

"You gonna shoot me?" Huey asked.

"Only if I have to."

Huey moved to the couch, despite Odin's weapon. "You shoot me, you're really up the fucking creek." He turned to Golden. "Honey, would you mind making us a pot of coffee?"

Golden nodded and went to the kitchen.

"They're setting you up, Bobby," Nichols said. "You had the bombing background in the SEALs. You ain't been Mister Stability since the incident."

"Who would be?" Odin growled.

"That ain't important. I want to help."

"Yeah. You're here from the government and you're here to help me."

"A bunch of the guys in Metro want to do what they can. I know Junior would cut off his right nut if he thought it would help you."

"I don't need anyone."

"You think I couldn't'ta taken you out?"

Odin didn't answer.

"You think I had to come here alone? I coulda come with a dozen guys. You're tough but you ain't that tough. And I'm not the only one who knows about you and nursie. Where you gonna go? What you gonna do?"

"I'll take care of myself."

"I'm offering you a hand. You gonna spit on it."

"How can I know I can trust you?"

Huey slammed a hand down on the table, making a bang nearly as loud as a gunshot. "Jesus Fucking H. Christ. You're the one on the run. You gonna get yourself killed. What about your girlfriend?"

"She's not my girlfriend."

"Okay. She's an innocent bystander. You're gonna get her killed too."

"Fuck you."

Nichols reached to Odin but the ex-cop shoved his hand

away. "You got your head so far up your ass you can't see the light."

"Leave me alone," Odin snapped as he walked to the door.

"Where you going?" Huey shouted. But Odin didn't answer as he stormed out of the apartment.

Golden came into the living room with the coffee.

"What happened?" she asked.

"He's hell bent on killing himself."

Huey and Jan walked to the window and watched as Odin plunged into his car and screeched away from the curb.

Down the block, as Odin passed, another car pulled out and began following him.

Nichols muttered a string of obscenities and raced into the street. By the time he got to his car, both Odin and his tail were long gone.

Golden, seeing his concern, had followed him down. "Who's following him? Police?"

"Yeah, must be," Nichols said, though he didn't believe it. The second car was too big and flashy. Probably a Caddy. As far as he knew, not even the FBI used Cadillacs on surveillances. Also, the cops probably would've just busted Odin on the spot.

"What are you going to do?"

"I'm going to work."

"I mean what are you going to do about Bob?"

"Nothing. He's a big boy now."

Golden didn't believe Nichols. His words said one thing, his concerned tone another.

He hurried to his car. She watched his tail lights disappear up the block. What was going on? Why did she care so much about Odin?

He had a decency that she believed she could bring out. But maybe it was a fool's dream, like women who got involved with alcoholics, thinking they could reform them.

Maybe if he actually did go blind . . . God, what a terrible thought. She got pangs of guilt. Could she wish another person blind? But he was doing it to himself.

She walked slowly back to her house.

31 "Fucking guy drives like a maniac," Joe Terranova complained into the cellular car phone of the Cadillac.

"Just keep up with him," Nicky Provenzano answered.

"Which way he heading?"

"East on the ten. Goddamn!"

"What happened?" Provenzano asked through the phone.

"We just did a three-lane change and swerved around a semi," Joe said. He covered the mouthpiece and said to Vic Polanski, "Don't get us fucking killed."

Both of Polanski's big hands were clamped on the wheel. Beads of sweat glistened on his brow despite the car's fan blowing on his face. The speedometer went from seventy to a hundred miles an hour as they swerved in and out of traffic.

A truck's horn bellowed in their ear.

"Fuck you!" Terranova shouted.

"What's going on?" Provenzano demanded.

"Look out, look out," Joe yelled.

Vic hit the brakes and they skidded onto the shoulder, narrowly avoiding a pickup that had changed lanes without looking.

Polanski hit the accelerator, smashing a few piles of debris along the shoulder. They bounced and bumped and then were back in the fast lane.

"Keep me posted," Provenzano said, breaking the connection.

"Keep me posted," Joe mimicked. "Fucking guy's sitting in some Vegas hotel room getting head from a half dozen show girls, we're out busting our *cojones*, and he wants us to keep him posted."

"You sure he can't hear you?" Polanski asked. "They got phones you can hear through even when its disconnected."

Terranova stared nervously at the phone. He lifted it from the receiver, listened to the tone, and put it back. He glanced up and suddenly screamed, "Look out!"

"Look out!" Terranova screamed.

A van in front of them slowed and Polanski had to switch lanes, inches from the van's rear bumper.

"I'm gonna kill that guy," Terranova said.

Huey Nichols slammed down the phone.

"What's the matter?" Fleming Junior asked.

"Just stay out of my face, Junior," Nichols said.

Fleming nodded. "We going on patrol soon?"

Nichols stormed out with Junior in his wake.

They had been cruising Rampart Division for a half hour before Nichols said, "I called and tried to run a make on a Caddy through a friend in OC Intelligence. He's been transferred. Effective immediately. Damn good cop and they put him in personnel. Make a file clerk out of a guy who knows more about the mob than just about anyone. This department is getting more and more bullshit every day. I got half a mind to pull the pin."

"You can't. We need you," Junior said.

Nichols grunted.

"The SWAT pups say they've learned more from you than anyone else," Junior continued. There were three new cops in Nichols's unit, replacements for Finch, Daggett, and Odin.

"I'm tired of wet-nursing babies," Nichols said. The "babies" were veteran cops who had to have a minimum of four years police experience, with an exemplary record, and at least six months in Metro. To even apply, a cop had to have served in one of the rough-and-tumble divisions where their experience under pressure could be assessed.

Nichols used the radio to check on his "babies." They all were cruising. One thought he had spotted a drug deal in a parking lot. Nichols arranged for a couple of units to back them up.

"Do you miss Bob?" Junior asked.

"Of course I miss him," Huey snapped. "After I teach the sonofabitch so he knows the way I like things, he nearly gets his head blown off."

"No, I mean, miss him like as a person?"

Nichols grunted. He would never reveal how much he missed Odin.

"I feel terrible about what happened," Junior said.

"Yeah."

"What's Bob doing? Do you know?"

"He's trying to find out who did it. I got a coupla ideas myself. I was thinking about what your Dad said. About Bob planting the bomb. Got me to wondering about a few things."

Traffic began to thin and Odin was able to floor the car, getting it up to a solid ninety miles an hour.

He opened the sun roof. The nightime sky got clearer as he reached the edge of the megapolis. Bitter cold night air rushed in, making him more alert. He put on the heater to warm him from below and let the air tear at his face. The wind whipped across the scar tissue, a peculiar calloused feeling. He wished it could blast away the damaged skin, somehow bring back his ruined eye. Or at least keep him from losing his remaining one.

He turned on the radio. The Rolling Stones were praising a "Street Fighting Man." The first time he'd heard the Stones had been in Vietnam, blasting from a black GI's radio. A war with a soundtrack.

The music made him glad to be alive. On a mission.

He was so absorbed in his thoughts he had no idea he was being followed.

*   *   *

"I bet the fucker is going to Las Vegas," Terranova said as they passed by a billboard that pictured a giant show girl, each of her breasts bigger than a Volkswagen.

"Call Mr. Pro and tell him what's going on," Vic said. "Tell him traffic's thinned out. We can catch up with him, if that's what Mr. P wants."

Joe dialed Provenzano. "Mr. P, we're getting nearer to you."

"He's coming to Vegas?"

"Looks that way."

"I don't want him making trouble here," Provenzano said. "You got Feebies and reporters up the wazoo. That's all those creeps need to make a mess of this convention."

"Take him out?" Joe asked.

"Do what you gotta do," Pro said, clicking off.

"Party time," Terranova said, taking a short-barreled shotgun out from under his seat. "Nicky said I should do him before he gets to Vegas. Can you bring us up next to him?"

Polanski nodded.

"I got deer slugs in here," Terranova said, patting the weapon and checking that it was ready. "There won't be nothing left."

Odin hadn't noticed the Cadillac keeping pace with him for several hundred miles. Not that Polanski was a bad tail. Wherever possible, the Mafia gunman had hung behind trucks or stayed in another lane, to make himself a little less noticeable.

Up ahead was an overpass. A perfect spot for a motorcycle cop to lie in wait, Odin thought, letting the needle drop below eighty. Then he remembered that there was an arrest warrant for him floating around. He let the speed drop to seventy.

"The fucker's slowing," Terranova said. "Pull up. Pull up."

"I don't like it," Polanski said.

"There's no one around. Let's do it."

Odin was through the underpass. Because of his bad eye, he couldn't see if there was a cop waiting. He glanced in his rear view mirror, and saw the Cadillac coming up fast.

A red light blinked on by the side of the road. Score one for me, Odin thought. A CHP motorcycle cop came racing up just as the Cadillac was about to pass Odin. Odin slowed, and the Caddy and the cycle cop zoomed by.

Inside the Caddy, Terranova wondered, "Should I kill the fucking cop?"

"Hide the shotgun," Vic snapped. "Even if you kill the cop, Odin will be on to us. Let Nicky take care of him when he gets to Las Vegas."

Polanski put on his blinkers and signaled that he was pulling over to the side of the road.

Odin drove by at a modest sixty-five miles an hour. The driver looked familiar. Who was it? It was five miles up the road before Odin realized that it had been Vic Polanski.

In his office at the back of the Eights and Aces Casino—a small, moderately shabby joint located in mid-Strip—Nick Provenzano snapped shut his attaché case. "I've got a flight to catch."

Petey, his mustachioed majordomo, folded his arms across his barrel chest. "What do you want me to do about this Odin?"

"If he's dumb enough to show up, smack him around and send him back to LA."

"You want him sent back in a box?" Petey was a second-generation Las Vegan. At fifty, he had worked at jobs from keno runner to pit boss. He was stocky, often arrogant, and distrustful of everyone. His graying hair, thinning and greased back on his head, exaggerated his sharp features.

"No. His own people in LA are supposed to take care of that. We don't need any extra dirty work. Just teach him respect."

"What's he look like?"

Provenzano provided a description. "Be careful. He's a hard case."

"In Las Vegas even the Cub Scouts are hard cases."

"Don't underestimate him," Provenzano cautioned. "Now get me to the airport before I miss my flight."

Before going to the Eights and Aces, Odin stopped at a Radio Shack and an auto supply store. He spent a half hour preparing a package, then headed to the casino.

It was a two-story building, four storefronts wide, that would have fit in better in downtown Las Vegas than on the Strip. Provenzano had been given the joint outright as a settlement in a dispute with Kansas City mobsters. That, plus his skim from two of the major casinos, provided about one-third of his million-dollar-a-year cash income.

Eights and Aces catered to the working class, drawing in hordes of polyester-clad yokels with discount coupons and promises of the best blackjack deals in town. Petey also had arranged to kickback to a half dozen tour bus operators and inevitably the lot was filled with buses.

Carrying a toaster-sized box, Odin strolled around the casino. A mock Old West motif, with Styrofoam beams made to look like weathered wood. Fake "Wanted" posters and toy six-guns on the wall. Lots of noise, levers being pulled, gears clunking, coins dumping into the mouths of slot machines, sirens, shouts. Almost pretty cocktail waitresses in Wild West outfits circulated, offering jiggling flesh and cheap drinks. Lights on video poker and blackjack machines blinked. An eye-burning cloud of cigarette smoke. More shouts. The smells of beer, popcorn, tobacco, and sweat.

The security people were dressed like cowboys, big bruisers, heads swiveling, shoulders bobbing. Not as smooth as the well-dressed thugs in the classy casinos but just as effective. They'd limit customers to light grabbing of the cocktail waitresses, and more important, keep them from smashing the machines when they failed to pay out.

As a cocktail waitress passed, Odin leaned over and asked, "Excuse me, where's Nicky Pro?"

"Who?" she asked with a flat Midwestern twang.

He dropped a five on her tray. "I got a delivery for him."

She jerked her thumb towards a panel of mock weathered wood off to one side. Odin drifted towards it. Had the security cameras panning back and forth on the ceiling picked him out yet?

A bruiser lumbered up. "What's in the box?" he demanded, reaching for the package.

"Something for Mr. Pro."

"I'll take it."

"No you won't. I got orders to give it to him personally."

Odin continued walking. The bruiser clamped a hand on his shoulder. "I'm talking to you."

Odin grabbed the guard's pinkie and bent it, forcing the man to release his grip. Odin walked quickly towards the door.

The bruiser caught up with him right by the door. The two men were concealed behind the panel shielding the door to the back room.

He grabbed Odin's lapel. Odin stomped his instep. The guard swung a right hook. Odin blocked it, spun and slammed an elbow to his solar plexus. He backfisted the bruiser's face, and swung down, using the same fist on the bruiser's groin. As the dazed guard swayed, Odin clapped both hands on the man's ears. Open palmed, so he didn't kill him.

The guard sagged to the floor. Odin lifted him, and stepped up to the door to the back room. There was a peephole in the middle of the steel door. Odin rapped.

"Yeah?"

"It's me," Odin mumbled, holding the guard's head up close to the eyehole. He balanced the package under his arm while supporting the bulky bruiser.

"What is it?" a voice grumbled through the door.

"I gotta talk to Nicky," Odin said, again playing the ventriloquist.

A bolt slid open. Odin entered the room.

Petey was leaning against his desk, smiling. There were two men on either side of the room. All four held guns leveled at Odin.

32

"Let him go," Petey ordered.

The Bruiser made a dull thump as he hit the floor.

"Where's Pro?" Odin asked.

"You missed him by about fifteen minutes," Petey said, an amiable smile crinkling his features.

"Where'd he go?"

"Los Angeles."

Odin took a step backwards but one of the gunmen slipped between him and the door and kicked it shut.

"Not so fast," Petey said. "You've got time for some Las Vegas hospitality."

Two of the gunmen holstered their weapons, loosened their jackets and stepped forward. Petey slipped on a pair of brass knuckles.

"How nice," Odin said, unwrapping his package. "I've got a token of my appreciation."

It was the size of a shoe box, with a pressure sensitive switch and a keypad on the top, as well as a couple of red and green light-emitting diodes.

"I brought this for Nicky," Odin said, depressing the switch. The four other men in the room stared at the blinking red LEDs.

"What's that?" one of the gunmen asked.

Odin lifted the lid on the box, revealing four sticks of dynamite nestled in a tangle of wires and electrical hardware.

The gunmen stepped back.

"If I let up on this switch, we all get wings and harps. Understand?" Odin said calmly.

Petey nodded. The gunmen bobbed their heads like toy puppies in a car's rear window.

"Good. You stay with me," Odin said, pointing to Petey. "Tell your goon squad to go have a drink. Make a bet. Don't call the cops, and don't panic the customers. You answer a few questions, I leave without rumpling your suit. You make trouble, this place gets an instant remodeling job. With us in it."

Petey nodded and the four gunmen hurried away.

There were a couple of monitors on Petey's desk and Odin could watch the action in the main room. He walked over where he could eye the monitors and Petey. The casino boss's smile had been replaced by a tight frown and sweat beaded on his dark eyebrows.

"Where is Nicky Pro?" Odin asked.

"On his way to LA."

"If I find out different, I'll be very annoyed," Odin said. He spoke in a melodious voice, precisely pronouncing his words, mimicking a lunatic he had negotiated with during a hostage crisis. He hoped his demeanor was as disquieting to Petey as the hostage taker's had been to him.

"Just deactivate that bomb."

"Bomb? Right. It was a bomb that did this." Odin popped his eyepatch, baring the scarred tissue.

Petey winced.

"Did Nicky tell you he did this to me?" Odin asked.

"No. No. He didn't."

"How'd you know to wait for me?"

"He said you were coming."

"What were you supposed to do?"

"Just teach you manners."

"What's that mean?"

"Slap you around a little and send you on your way."

"To where?"

"LA." Petey's eyes were focused on the blinking red light. He was almost hypnotized, imagining the boom and splatter of an explosion.

Odin kept his patch up and Petey tried to avoid looking at the ugly scar tissue. But Odin moved so his face was barely a foot away. "That's it?"

"We were only supposed to push you around. Mr. Pro said your own people would take care of you."

"What?"

Petey hesitated, regretting having blurted out the words.

"He said your people would take care of you."

"What does that mean?"

Petey shrugged. "I dunno."

"What does that mean?" Odin shouted.

"I don't know. Really."

"It means kill me, doesn't it?"

Petey shrugged.

"Doesn't it?" Odin screamed.

"No."

Odin shifted his gaze to the security camera. The casino was nearly cleared out. A few diehards were still working the slots.

Odin tapped out a pattern on the bomb's keypad and the green light began flashing. "How do I get out of here?"

"What did you do?" Petey asked.

"I activated it. We've got five minutes."

"Back door, there's a back door."

"Sit down."

Petey sat in the chair behind the desk. Odin put the bomb on Petey's lap. The lights were flashing.

"In five minutes, if you don't move, the lights will stop. Hit the button once and the bomb is harmless. If you so much as burp before then, boom. Understand?"

Petey began to nod, then froze. "Yes," he said, trying to move his lips as little as possible.

Odin hurried out the door. He jumped in his car and raced to McCarran Airport.

Petey was bathed in sweat by the time the five minutes was up. Every muscle in his body was cramped. His bladder felt like it was going to burst.

The light went off. Was Odin lying? The ex-cop was clearly a psycho, barging into his place like that. But Petey didn't have a choice but to trust him. He pressed the button.

Nothing happened. Slowly, stiffly, Petey got up and set the box on his desk. He ran from the office.

The casino was eerily quiet. Three people, oblivious to the world, maintained their positions at the slots. Petey raced out into the street as the first police car was screeching up.

"Bomb!" Petey said. "In the back office."

Odin parked his car in the long term lot, then prowled down the rows feeling the car hoods. He broke into a Trans Am with a warm hood. The owner must just have left—he wouldn't notice its disappearance for a while.

Odin couldn't take a chance on renting another car. They could have put an alert on his charge cards. He swiftly hot-wired the car.

The driver had left his parking stub on the dashboard.

"You just got here," the clerk at the gate said, looking at the time-stamped ticket.

"I forgot some papers at home," Odin said. "I can race back and get them in time for my flight."

"Good luck. No charge," the clerk said.

"Thanks," Odin said, and he accelerated off.

"Assistant Chief Fleming's office," the female voice answered.

"This is Lieutenant Eustas Nichols. Metro Division. I need to talk to the assistant chief."

"He's busy right now," the woman said.

"I need him immediately."

"Is this something that can be handled through the chain of command. You can file a . . ."

"Get Fleming on the phone or I'll come over and rip your heart out."

"Well, I never," the woman said. She was used to screening out pushy administrators who wanted to curry favor with her boss, but this aggressiveness was unbelievable. "Just hold on."

She marched into Fleming's office. He was reviewing a report on the budget for the CRASH (Community Resources Against Street Hoodlums) program.

"There's a very rude lieutenant on line three," she said. "He threatened me."

Fleming nodded and picked up the phone. "Who is this?" he demanded.

"Lieutenant Nichols. Metro," Nichols said.

"I hope you've got a good explanation for yourself, lieutenant."

Fleming's female assistant was standing, listening, eager to hear her boss put the lieutenant in his place.

"I know who planted the bomb that killed Finch and Daggett, and injured Bob Odin."

Fleming felt like all the air had been sucked out of the room. He waved his aide out.

"What have you heard?"

The Las Vegas bomb squad cop cut open the box on the side using a plastic scalpel. Working with a flashlight, probe, and mirror, he gazed at the sticks of dynamite.

"Road flares," he muttered.

Still, he opened the box cautiously. It was no more dangerous than a brick.

When the cops came out to question Petey, he refused to tell them anything. That was standing orders from Nicky Provenzano. An aggressive young sergeant threatened to take Petey into protective custody. Petey made a phone call to someone, the sergeant got a call, and Petey was released.

The casino began to refill as the cops pulled away.

Petey had a waitress bring him a tumbler of scotch. He locked the door to the back office and put as many men as he could muster on the lookout for Odin. They covered McCarran, the bus terminals, the train station. He alerted a couple of people in Barstow, and at gas stations along the way. The wiseguys had a network to catch escaping deadbeats.

Petey had made it a rule never to take business personally. But Odin had crossed that line. Whatever Nicky Pro wanted to do didn't matter. Petey wanted Odin dead.

After two full glasses of scotch, Petey was ready to put a call in to Nicky Provenzano.

"This Odin is a wild man," Provenzano said. "Either you take him out of the picture right now, or I will."

Assistant Chief Fleming muttered a long, low, sincere string of obscenities.

"How do you think I feel?" Pro asked. "He's costing me time and money. Disrupting business. Hurting my rep. I can't let him get away with that. Even if he was the fucking Pope, I couldn't let him."

"I'll take care of it."

"Damn right you will."

"There's another problem," Fleming murmured.

"Oh yeah? What?"

"A lieutenant. Huey Nichols."

Elysian Park, named for the mythological final resting place of downed Norse heroes, is the third largest park in Los Angeles. The 585 acre preserve, located a few minutes from downtown, was heavily used—evidenced by the discarded cans and bottles every few feet. Two reservoirs, Dodger Stadium, and the Police Academy are located in the huge park.

After a few words on the phone from Nichols, Fleming had cut him off and insisted they meet, secretly.

Nichols parked his car by the grove of Indian palms that lined the main road. He set off running down Solano Canyon Drive. After ten minutes, his pale blue sweat suit was soaked at the armpits and groin. Nichols was breathing hard. He wasn't pleased. Too many beers, too many nights dancing in the sheets. Too many excuses not to go to the gym. But the exertion felt good. What he had to say to the assistant chief already had his pulse pounding.

Huey had met old Brass Balls many times over the years. At one point, Huey had even served under Fleming. But this was different.

He heard the footfalls and turned. Brass Balls, immaculate in a maroon sweat suit, was coming up fast. Not a hair was mussed. The light sheen of sweat looked like a make-up man had put it in place.

"Have you heard from Odin?" Fleming asked as he caught up and kept pace with Huey.

"I saw him last night at his girlfriend's place," Nichols said.

"His girlfriend?"

"He's gotten chummy with that nurse Jan Golden."

"Where is he now?"

"I don't know," Nichols said. "We had words. He got pissed and marched out."

"Any idea where he went?" Fleming asked. He turned down a woodsy path, cut over to Park Road, and then headed towards the reservoir at the eastern edge of the park.

Fleming had once been a physical education instructor at the Academy, Nichols recalled. How many times had he gone up and down the hills? The assistant chief was in great shape, barely breathing hard. Nichols wanted to stop, but he wouldn't give up.

"He was getting kind of paranoid," Nichols said. "Starting to talk about conspiracies. I just laughed it off, but there was a car tailing him when he split."

"I see."

"It wasn't one of ours either. A flashy looking Caddy."

They were near the junction of the Pasadena and the Golden State Freeways. The traffic noise blew through the groves of trees, making it sound like there was a giant river swooshing nearby.

"You tell anyone what you told me on the phone earlier?" Fleming asked.

"No sir. I want to do what's best for the department."

"Good. I'll take care of it. But it's important you keep it under your hat. For now." Fleming slowed to a walk and patted Nichols's shoulder. "Good man," he said.

"Sir, I need to know what you plan to do?"

"I will take care of it," Fleming repeated.

There were two guys up ahead, leaning against a red pickup, drinking beer. Open container violation.

Nichols glanced over at the Assistant Chief. Would he want to enforce the law? The two men were in an out-of-the-way place, no one else around. It seemed harmless enough. But Fleming was known as a stickler.

Nichols decided they would probably let it slide. If an incident occurred, others would wonder what the Assistant Chief and a SWAT lieutenant were doing running in the park together. If questions were asked, it would uncover the very secret they were trying to handle, the information Nichols had unwittingly uncovered.

As soon as Fleming and Nichols had come into sight, Joe Terranova had rested his hand on the gun hidden in the brown paper bag with the beer. Terranova was wearing a surgical rubber glove over his shooting hand.

The joggers came closer. A couple dozen yards away.

Vic Polanski had a shotgun hidden in the back of the pickup. But it was important that they see the .45 automatic in the brown paper bag. It was Odin's on duty weapon. The Assistant Chief had removed it from the SWAT cop's locker right before Odin's medical retirement was finalized. Fleming had then short-circuited the "lost weapon" paperwork.

"That nigger is big," Terranova hissed.

"Shut up." Polanski was nervous.

Terranova looked like a kid the night before Christmas, loaded with happy expectations.

A dozen yards.

"He better go down right away," Terranova said. "Or move in and fill him with buckshot."

"Just shut up."

"Got the jitters?"

Polanski didn't answer.

Five yards.

Nichols had his eye on the two men. Then Fleming gave a casual wave, as if he knew them. Nichols relaxed.

The shorter man was reaching into his bag, as if to get them a beer. It was dark and Nichols couldn't see what he came up with. But he knew it wasn't a beer. Not by the way he was holding it. He was only a few feet away. No chance to run. Had to charge them. He couldn't let them assassinate the assistant chief of police.

Terranova's first round missed.

Huey charged.

The second round caught him in the right shoulder. It felt like someone had hit him with a baseball bat. It was the first time that he'd ever been hit. So that's what it feels like, he thought calmly as he reached for the gunman.

The man pulled the trigger again.

His chest felt crushed. He had the taste of blood in his mouth. He glanced over to see if Fleming had also been shot. The Assistant Chief was standing, watching, frozen.

The second hit man had a shotgun and was trying to swing it into play. Nichols grabbed the shotgun and struggled with the big man. But the lieutenant was weak, so weak. He felt like a baby could overcome him.

The man jerked the gun and Huey fell.

The other gunman stepped up, put the gun to Nichols's head, and pulled the trigger.

33 Vic Polanski tucked his shaking hands into his pocket so Terranova wouldn't see.

"Stop playing with yourself and gimme a hand," Terranova ordered as he spread the tarp in the bed of the pickup.

He and Polanski struggled to lift Nichols but the dead cop weighed too much.

Terranova turned to the assistant chief. "Don't just stand there, make yourself useful."

Fleming, in a daze, obeyed. The three men lifted Nichols's corpse and dumped it in the back. Terranova spread a second tarp over the body. Blood had spattered the side of the vehicle and Terranova wiped it clean with a rag. He and Polanski hopped in the pickup and drove off.

Fleming watched the truck disappear. Other than the palm-size patch of blood on the dirt, there was no sign of what had happened. Fleming kicked dirt over the bloodstain, and smeared whatever footprints he could find. He didn't really have to worry about the crime scene. The murder would never be traced to that spot. He moved briskly, looking for anything that might be incriminating.

He resumed his jog. A few hundred feet along the main path, he noticed droplets of blood on his cuff. The nausea hit him. He leaned against a tree, fighting to keep his stomach down.

A couple of jogging cops saw him.

"You okay sir?" one of them asked solicitously.

"Fine. Leave me alone," Fleming growled.

Fleming heard their rude laughter when they were nearly out of earshot. Brass Balls staggering like a wobbly drunk.

He dragged himself over to a picnic bench and sat, trying to keep a dignified appearance. He didn't succeed.

Odin took his time driving back. Not that he drove slowly. Driving fast was a joy. And Nevada was the state to do it in.

He traveled a circuitous route, wary of bumping into any of Provenzano's people along Interstate 15, the traditional Las Vegas–Los Angeles route. He drove northwest, on 95, with the Desert National Wildlife Area passing to his right and the Amargosa Desert off to his left. At Beaty, with Bullfrog Hills coming up, he turned left onto Nevada Route 58. After ten miles, he was in California, on the same road, now called 190.

Off to his left were the Funeral Mountains. And Death Valley Buttes to his right. He passed Stove Pipe Wells and Emigrant Junction.

He recalled camping out there with his wife. She had hated camping, but that was back when she was still making an effort to keep their marriage together. She had probably hated it as much as he hated opera. He'd gone to several performances, she'd gone on several camping trips. It hadn't brought them closer together.

It was dusk, failing light. A beautiful sunset over the southernmost tip of the Sierras. He blinked and squinted. His night vision had definitely deteriorated, as well as his peripheral vision.

"Your optic cells are dying even as we speak," Jan had said. The phrase haunted him. But he couldn't let anything stop his momentum. If there was something wrong, he didn't want to know.

Switching onto 395 south, he was doing eighty-five miles an hour when he came up on a slow-moving farm truck. With his faulty depth perception, he nearly hit the truck. He swerved off the road, bouncing off the shoulder, across a low ditch, and into the sands.

The truck backed up. "You okay?" the driver yelled.

Odin sat in the car, catching his breath. "Fine!"

"Need a hand?"

Odin pulled back onto the road with a minimum of wheel spinning. He gave the truck driver a thumbs-up. The trucker rode off.

Maybe I'll die in a car wreck, Odin thought. That would be a fucking joke. It was better than living life blind, he thought. He got a twinge of regret, a desire to race in to the doctor, beg him to immediately do whatever was necessary to save the remaining eye. No. No distraction, no diversion. He was too close, he had gone too far to stop. What if the doctor blew the operation? What if Pro got to him while he was laid up in the hospital?

He had kept the speedometer at sixty-five, but by the time he passed the China Lake Naval Weapons Center, he was back at ninety miles per hour.

"Have you heard from your cop boyfriend?" Mary Tallero asked as she and Jan Golden walked to McDonald's.

Golden shrugged.

"Tell me about it. I promise to only gossip to my ten closest friends."

Jan gave the administrator a questioning look.

"Just kidding. My lips are sealed." Tallero made a zipping motion over her mouth.

They walked another block without saying anything. Then the words exploded from Golden:

"He's a macho buffoon. He's willing to risk his vision to keep after whoever planted the bomb. In a way, I think he's really crazy. Too much hate."

"Don't believe what they tell you," Tallero said. "Hate is stronger than love. My ex-husband is a case in point."

"But there's so much humanity in him," Golden continued without hearing what Tallero said. "I don't understand him. I'd like to change him. Yet I know that's foolish."

"Would you really want to change him?"

"What do you mean?"

"He's a tough guy. Isn't what he is what's attracting you to him? Would you really be happy if he became a sensitive quiche-eater type?"

"Not a quiche eater. Just not violent."

"Primal man," Tallero said, and gave a mock growl. "Grab you by the hair and ravish you."

"It's not like that."

"How disappointing."

"He can be very tender. But there's this violence there. You should have seen him when he thought there was an attacker at my apartment. He went from teddy bear to grizzly bear in a millisecond."

"Sounds real sexy to me."

"What do you mean?"

"Women are the nurturers, men are the hunter-killers."

"Those roles are obsolete."

"So is your appendix. You know many people born without one?"

It had been a rotten day at work for Golden. She kept having dire premonitions about Robert Odin. Twice she called his apartment and got no answer.

A seventy-nine-year-old woman recuperating from a diabetic coma had died in her ward. A suspected nosocomial infection, the kind of microbe only found in hospitals. The Infection Control investigators had cleared Jan and her staff, but still Golden was shaken. A relative learned that the death might have been due to hospital neglect and loudly berated them. Golden kept up a professional front but as the relative was escorted out by security, she hurried to the nurse's lounge and composed herself.

Golden called Odin's house several times when she got home after her seven-to-three shift. No answer.

When the doorbell rang, she ran to it. If Odin had been there, she would have thrown herself in his arms and everything would have been all right.

There were two men with grim expressions standing on her doorstep.

"Miss Jan Golden?"

"Yes. What is it?"

"I'm Detective Brown. This is my partner, Detective Cutler." Detective Brown held up a leather badge case with his silver and brass LAPD detective's shield in it.

"Yes?"

"We're here about Robert Odin."

"What is it?"

"He's been in a traffic accident. He's been slipping in and out of consciousness, asking for you."

"I'll get my coat."

The two cops waited inside her foyer as she grabbed her coat and purse. Her mind flashed back to the hundreds of car accident victims she'd seen. Their injuries ranged from a few broken bones and bruises to devastating head wounds.

"How is he?" she asked as they pulled away from the curb.

"We don't really know, ma'am," the talkative cop said. The silent cop was sitting in the back seat, next to her. His attentive expression made her uncomfortable.

"Where was he hurt?"

"On the freeway," the driver said.

"No. I mean, what part of his body?"

The silent cop had a lewd smirk. "Not where it counts," he said.

"I think his chest," the driver said.

She picked at her nails anxiously as they drove for several minutes. "What hospital are we going to?"

"Uh, UCLA Medical Center."

That was reassuring. It was one of the better facilities in Southern California. A teaching hospital where they kept up on the latest techniques. She tried to think of people she might know on the staff there. She would arrange for Odin to get VIP service. Maybe she could take a short leave, work as a temp there. She'd pull whatever strings she could. He needed her.

Why was she so anxious? Odin was seriously injured. No. It was a different kind of anxiety. Something didn't feel right. It wasn't just the expression of the cop next to her. She glanced around the car. Nothing special, a large-size sedan. Well kept. A smooth ride. Quiet. That was it. Quiet. No police radio.

"Excuse me, I've got to get out and make a quick call," she said.

"You can do it from the hospital," the driver said.

"I need to make it right away," she said.

"We've got to hurry," the driver insisted.

As they stopped for a light, she yanked her door handle. The knob was disconnected and came off in her hands.

The quiet cop grabbed her and pushed her down. No passerby could see what was going on as he slipped out a Baggie and took a chloroform soaked pad from it. She struggled but he was too strong and she was pinned in an awkward position.

The pad pressed over her nose. She held her breath and sagged. She thought she had the quiet cop fooled but then he punched her in the stomach. She gasped for air, inhaling deeply. Then it was dark.

"She okay?" the driver asked.

Joe Terranova took her wrist in his hand and felt her pulse. "She's fine. Sure put up a fight." He stared at her unconscious body. Her blouse had torn in the struggle, and her dress was hiked up. Terranova lifted it further.

"What're you doing?" Polanski demanded angrily.

"Seeing if she's wearing underwear." He squeezed the flesh of her inner thigh. "Mmmmmm."

"Prop her up and leave her alone."

Terranova adjusted her, resting her head on his shoulder so she looked like she was sleeping. "No skin off Nicky's nose if I play hide the salami with her. He's gonna kill her anyway."

"You know they can tell all about you from your come nowadays. Is a piece of ass worth a murder rap?"

"I'll wear a rubber," Terranova said. "I still don't understand why we got to snatch the snatch anyway."

"Mr. P wants to see what Odin told her. Then he's gonna do her up, make it look like Odin did it."

"Why not just kill Odin?"

"'Cause if he gave any evidence to anyone, this will discredit him. Make him look like a psycho perv."

"Nicky sure plays all the angles. What do you think he's gonna do to her?" he asked eagerly.

Polanski didn't answer. They were at Provenzano's Westwood office building. As they drove into the underground garage, Terranova took Golden's head and kissed her. The parking attendant couldn't see her face. He gave Vic a wink.

When there was no one around, they carried her to the private elevator to Provenzano's penthouse offices.

As the elevator rose, Terranova propped Jan against the wall and admired her. Polanski smoothed her clothing.

"I liked it better the other way," Terranova said.

"Don't be an animal, okay?"

Terranova shrugged. "What do you think Nicky's gonna do to her?" he asked again.

34 As Odin reached the north end of the Los Angeles sprawl, the phrase that had been repeating softly in his head grew to deafening volume. "His own people will take care of him."

Cops. They were his people. His family. The men in his squad were closer to him than anyone had ever been. Even his parents, his ex-wife, his girlfriends. Only with the crew in Nam had it been nearly as powerful. But there, death was too common. A guy could die of an incoming round at any second. The closer the buddy who got hit, the closer you felt to death.

Cops. Could they have betrayed him? But who? And why?

Why hadn't his SWAT team been properly briefed about Mokley's radical past? Who had phoned him with the name of the motel Mokley was at? Who had notified the Oceanside cops? How did the Mob get involved? Too many questions. No. He'd have to tackle them one at a time.

He thought back to right before the incident. Any clues that something was amiss? He visualized the premission briefing, the intelligence reports, the word from Narco, going over the layout with Junior, getting prepped, Junior stumbling over the homeless vet in the hills, the Bobbsey Twins their usual competent selves. The door opening. The blast.

Bagels. The cop who had retired. Maybe there was a reason for his getting out. He should have let them know about

Mokley's radical past. The more Odin thought about Bagels, the more he was convinced he knew something. Odin worked himself into a murderous fury. Though his conscious mind would never admit it, he could see subtle changes in his vision. It was tougher to see in low light conditions and his peripheral vision had narrowed. His time, and his sight, were limited. He headed to Bagels's house.

The ex-Narco sergeant lived in a well-kept, ivy-covered building on the border between Hancock Park and Hollywood. Hancock Park was a neighborhood of magnificent old houses, minimansions dating back to when Los Angeles was still a frontier town. Hollywood was chock-a-block with Hollywood bungalows, one-story houses with big porches, sloping roofs, and rumors of previous exotic tenants.

Bagels's house was of Hancock Park grandeur but located on the Hollywood side. Odin had once been to a gathering there. The majority of cop parties ended with drunken officers passed out on the lawn. The most dramatic incident at Bagels's place had been when a cop and a public defender got in a polite argument over liberal former Supreme Court Justice Rose Bird.

Odin sat in his car, parked at the curb outside the house. The ground floor of the Spanish style home was obscured by high hedges. Odin could see movement at a second-story window. A teenage girl on the phone.

He had been ready to tear Bagels apart. Seeing the house, realizing he had a family, remembering Bagels's chubby wife's hospitality, and thinking about the incident in Scalia's gym, made Odin relax and take a dozen deep breaths.

Odin rapped on the door. He knocked for quite a while before it was answered by the teenage girl he'd seen at the window. She was about fifteen, pretty, and very aware of it. She cocked a hip forward, nibbled her pouty lips, and studied Odin flirtatiously. Bagels had himself a handful.

"Yes?" she said, dragging out the word.

"Is Bagels around?"

"Who are you?"

"My name's Odin. I'm a friend of his from the department."

"He's in the den," she said, turning from Odin and hurrying upstairs.

For a cop's daughter, she wasn't very cautious. Odin entered the house. There was an unhealthy quietness about it, like a place where someone had died and no one dared raise their voice. Odin felt a heavy wave of depression and half expected to find Bagels with his head blown off.

"Bagels?" Odin shouted, after his knocks on the door to the den produced no answer. He pushed the door open. The top of a balding head was visible in a high-backed chair. Bagels was wearing headphones.

"Bagels!"

The chair swung around. At first Odin didn't recognize the figure in it. It looked like Bagels's older brother. Then he realized it was Bagels, his face sagged, his muscles seemed barely able to support his head. He had large rings under his eyes. His thinning hair was uncombed and had much more gray.

"Bob!" Bagels said, pulling off the headphones and getting up. "How are you?" He gave Odin a hug. "Don't answer. You look great."

"You do too," Odin lied.

Bagels shrugged. "I just have no energy." He lowered his voice. "I'm trying to adjust. I never thought the job meant that much to me. But I'm like an old fire horse. I keep waking up in the morning and getting dressed to go into work. Each time I realize I've got no place to go, ah, who cares about that, what are you doing here?"

Odin hesitated. He couldn't very well give his real reason.

"It's not a social call," Bagels said. "But I'll turn it into one. C'mon in the kitchen. I'll put up a pot of coffee and get some bagels."

As they walked to the kitchen, Bagels continued his manic talking. "You know, my psychologist says I shouldn't answer to the name Bagels. He said that would help me readjust. My wife never called me Bagels. She doesn't like the nickname anyway."

"What does your daughter call you?"

"Lucinda calls me Daddy. That's when she wants to borrow something. When I marry her off, it'll be cruel and unusual punishment on some young fella," Bagels continued. "See. My therapist warned me to watch out for that. Law enforcement jokes. He doesn't even want me watching cop shows. Wasn't being on the job just like *T.J. Hooker?*"

"I don't know. I never watched it."

"It's hilarious," Bagels said as he got the coffee pot brewing. "You ought to catch it sometime. The only thing that's realistic is the color of the uniform. And they never show a skid row scrote tossing his cookies all over it. Something wrong with your good eye?"

"What do you mean?"

"You look like you're straining, squinty."

Odin blinked a few times and forced his eye wide open. "I'm fine."

"Well, so, what can I do for you?"

"I want to know about Mokley."

"I figured as much. You saw he got killed in jail?"

"Yes."

"The whole thing stinks from beginning to end. You can't imagine how many times I've replayed the incident, trying to make sense out of it. I shouldn't say that. I bet you can imagine. It's worse for you than for me, isn't it?"

"It's bad."

"I know you probably feel responsible for Finch and Daggett. Thing is, I feel responsible for all of you. It doesn't make sense. Mokley wasn't that heavy duty a dealer. Calling you guys in was pro forma. I practically went there myself and grabbed him." He paused, pouring coffee. "I wish I had. How many times I wish I had." Bagels let out a long, slow sigh. His hand pouring the coffee shook, spilling a few drops.

"No point in kicking yourself for what happened." Odin hesitated about asking the questions he'd come to ask. Bagels was on the edge. A few unkind words could put him over.

"Mokley was a scummy little dirtbag," Bagels said. "He crawled around the fringes. He didn't have the guts to rig a bomb and no one cared enough about him to plant one on him."

"What about his old radical friends?"

"What do you mean?"

"The SDS types. They liked playing with bombs."

"He never hung out with SDS types. He was strictly with the limp-dick liberals who liked the glamour of radical chic. The kind who'd throw fundraisers for the Black Panthers, and piss and moan when half the furniture got ripped off by their honored guests."

Odin got annoyed. "Don't jerk my chain, Bagels. I saw the report."

"What report?"

"The intelligence report on Mokley. All about his bomber connections."

Odin had raised his voice. Bagels responded in kind.

"He didn't have any bomber connections."

"Don't lie to me."

"I'm not lying."

The ex-cops glared at each other.

"You think I'm covering up something?" Bagels demanded. "You think after what happened I wouldn't tell you the truth? I swear on my wife's head there was no report on any bombing."

"I saw it."

The two men were standing a few feet apart, shouting.

"I get it now. You came here thinking I was a part of a conspiracy, didn't you?"

"I just wanted to ask you some questions."

"Get out of my house," Bagels said, giving Odin a light shove.

"Take it easy," Odin said.

"Don't tell me what to do, you bastard. You think I did something crooked."

"You can't trust anyone."

"I was right!" Bagels pushed him again.

The third time he pushed, Odin caught his hand and twisted his arm into a forceful, but painless, control hold. "Just take it easy."

"You let go!" a quivery voice said from the doorway.

Both men turned. Bagels's daughter stood in the doorway, her father's service revolver held outstretched. It was pointed at Odin, but because of her shaky hand, swung over much of the room.

Odin released Bagels. "No harm done. Just put the gun down."

"My daddy said get out."

"We were just blowing off steam," Bagels said. "It's all right, sweetheart. Put the gun down."

She hesitated, pumped full of adrenaline and not sure what to do.

Odin sidled closer. He grabbed the cylinder on the gun so it couldn't turn. Careful not to catch her finger in the trigger guard, he took the weapon from her.

Bagels hugged his trembling daughter. "Did you see what she did?" Bagels asked Odin. "She would've killed you."

"I can't say I'm as pleased about that as you seem to be," Odin said.

"What made you think I was involved in anything improper?" Bagels asked.

"I didn't really think that."

"Cut the BS" Bagels patted his daughter's hair. "Pardon my language, cupcake."

The sniffling girl composed herself. Her makeup had run. Black lines radiated from her eyes, giving her a frightening appearance. She caught a glimpse of herself in the smoked glass mirror on the wall. She did a double take and hurried from the room without a backward glance.

"Quite a girl," Odin said.

"She would've killed to protect me," Bagels said, beaming.

Odin snapped open the empty gun and handed it over. "I'm glad there weren't any bullets in it."

Bagels chuckled. "My wife hid them when I retired. My women take care of me." The bad feelings that had been building between the men were diminished. "What made you think I was a dirtbag?"

"I never felt that way."

"Okay, okay. What made you decide to pay me a social call?"

"An intelligence report you got before we did the raid. It laid out Mokley's past clearly. Told about his radical days. I saw a copy of it. The report you gave us had been edited."

"Come with me," Bagels ordered. He marched back into the den, with Odin a few paces behind him. Behind a small desk was a half dozen cardboard cartons. "This is it. All my paperwork. I took it home with me since I still got a few cases I'll have to testify on."

Bagels began rooting through the boxes. "Look at this," he said, holding up an FBI poster. "Picked him up on a raid. Damn Feebies took the credit." He pulled out another paper. "Remember this?" It was a rough sketch of a Colombian dope dealer's pad that SWAT had raided and found a record amount of cocaine. The record had held for two weeks, until another raid produced a few kilograms more.

Bagels slowed, caught up reading through various papers. "I was looking for this one. We found the dealer hiding in a cabinet no bigger than, ah, I'm rambling." He resumed his search.

Odin leaned against the doorframe, wondering what Bagels was trying to prove.

"Ah ha," Bagels said, triumphantly holding up a report. "I knew it was here."

He read it over quickly, then passed it to Odin.

It was essentially the same as the report Odin had seen, but the information about Mokley's bomber friends wasn't there.

"You believe me?"

"I don't understand it."

"I had no idea you were coming. There was no way I could've phonied it up. Which means . . ."

"Either the one I saw was phony or you were given a bad one to start out."

"You know what my advice is? Let it drop. Maybe a clerk just made a mistake somewhere."

Odin gave him a cynical look.

"All right, we both know that's bull. Let it go, Bob."

"No way."

"You're going to play avenging angel?"

"I have to." Odin didn't say that another bomb was ticking in his good eye, that he didn't know how long he'd have before his sight was gone. There was no point in discussion. No one could end his vendetta.

Bagels grabbed Odin's shoulder and squeezed. The men hugged.

"If there's anything I can do, let me know," Bagels said.

"Sure." But Odin had no intention of bringing anyone else in. The revenge was a personal matter. And he couldn't trust anyone else anyway.

35 What next, Odin wondered as he drove back towards the city. It was coming up on 4:30 P.M. The freeway going the other way, coming out of the megapolis, was already jammed. Soon it would be bumper to bumper on his side as well. Since Los Angeles was a city with so many centers, people lived and worked in all different directions.

It boiled down to the report on Mokley. A piece of paper had become the center of his existence. He had always been amazed at the power of paper. One wrong word on an Officer Involved Shooting report and a career was shattered. How much of his life as a cop had been spent processing paper? How could you capture an incident on it?

He'd have to talk to Fred Fleming, Jr. But first he'd check in with Buchanan at Major Crimes. Maybe there was new info or maybe a way to dig up the original copy of the Mokley report.

Odin pulled off the freeway in Mission Hills, a few blocks from the San Fernando Mission. On Sepulveda Boulevard, the lengthy north-south thoroughfare that paralleled the 405 freeway, he found a phone booth at the side of a service station.

He dialed Major Crimes.

"Buchanan, this is Odin."

A brief hesitation, as if Buchanan was recalling his name, and then a warm hello.

"I was curious if you've made any progress on Finch and Daggett's murder," Odin said.

"It's moving along."

"Good news?"

"Might be. Would you like to come in and chat?"

"I can't get down to HQ. Tell me about it."

"I prefer not over the phone. What say we meet. Where are you?"

"In Mission Hills."

"Where?"

The question struck a false note. The diffident homicide cop was too eager.

"You know the park right across from the San Fernando Mission?"

"No. But I can find it. Wait there. I'm on my way." Buchanan broke the connection.

Odin's hackles were up. Buchanan had made it clear that

Odin was an outsider. What was Buchanan up to? Trust your instincts, Scalia had kept repeating.

Odin parked in the San Fernando Mission's lot. Built in 1797, it is one of the twenty missions the Spanish established running the length of California. It contains a restored church, monastery, living quarters, and workroom as well as landscaped grounds.

Odin rooted around in the trunk of the stolen Trans Am and found what he'd hoped for—a squeegee. He tucked it into his pants, then flapped the shirt down over its head so it was invisible. He slipped on a pair of large, dark sunglasses.

He paid the entry fee and went inside, accepting a self-guiding tour sheet from a freckled girl with a "Jesus Loves You" button. A few paces from the front entrance he found a fire bucket filled with sand. He took the bucket and produced his squeegee. He looked like a maintenance worker. He walked to a low parapet, scrambled up, and walked along the roof. With his reduced depth perception, he had to move slowly. He reached a point where he could peer over the top of the mission wall.

Twenty police cars had ringed the park across the street. Cops with guns drawn had surrounded the small park house. There were San Fernando cops, L.A. County Sheriff's deputies, California Highway Patrol officers, and four cars from the LAPD. They had raced up without sirens. From the roof position, he could hear their radios crackling.

The Sheriff's SWAT team was deploying. Odin watched with professional interest. They had a different conformation and slightly different tactics from LAPD SWAT. Since they often operated in more rural areas than the LAPD, they included an extra man, a trained paramedic, on their team. The sheriffs followed the so-called eastern concept, which had the crisis negotiator heading the operation, as opposed to the western concept, where the SWAT commander would run the show. With the eastern approach, pioneered by the NYPD, the negotiator had face-to-face contact with the suspect and more authority.

The western approach, pioneered by the LAPD, allowed for better control of the entire scene, but took autonomy away from the cop who might know best when to switch from talk to action.

The cops had established a perimeter and were narrowing down the circle. Civilians had been hustled from the area. A command post was established. Everyone moved slowly but smoothly.

Shit! Odin had been so caught up in watching the game that he'd unwittingly chosen the best high ground position for a SWAT sniper. He saw a long rifleman and his spotter double-timing through the parking lot towards the mission.

As Odin scrambled down off the roof, a priest stepped in front of him.

"What were you doing?" the priest demanded. He was a middle-aged man with rosy cheeks and a smug smile.

"I was just looking out at the street, father," Odin said.

"You know what they say about idle hands," the priest said sternly. "The rear pond needs cleaning. Get to it."

"Yes, father."

Odin turned and began walking off.

"What's your name?" the priest demanded.

"Excuse me?"

Odin saw the SWAT deputies racing up. Did they have a detailed description of him? Odin turned his face so they couldn't see it.

"What's your name?" the priest repeated.

"Uh, Golden. Bob Golden," Odin said.

"Robert, why are you wearing those sunglasses? It's nearly night time. You can injure yourself."

"I have sensitive eyes, father."

The priest snorted. "Why, when I tell you to clean the rear pond do you head in the opposite direction?"

"I was going to get my tools."

"The maintenance shed is the other direction," the priest said, pointing.

He proceeded to lecture Odin on the dangers of shirking and the joys of doing the Lord's work. Odin had trouble concentrating as he watched the SWAT cops work their way to exactly where he had been standing. Had he left any clues?

"I haven't seen you around here," the priest said.

"I just started."

"So you are on probation. Do you appreciate the honor of being allowed to work here?"

The priest seemed indifferent to the SWAT cops' activity, protected by the three-foot-thick walls of the mission and his clerical collar.

"Come with me," the priest ordered.

Odin docilely followed him across the quadrangle to the maintenance shed. He fetched a shovel and a bucket, and the priest led him to the pond. Odin proceeded to clean it up under the priest's stern eye.

"Very good," the priest said after fifteen minutes. "You may go home now. But report to my office tomorrow morning. You need supervision."

"Yes, father," Odin said, wondering what the priest would do when he found out there was no Bob Golden on staff.

Odin stowed the gear and walked cautiously toward the front. The cops were gone from the roof. He strolled through the heavy wooden doors, half expecting to be hit with a police spotlight and ordered to freeze.

Calm had been restored. The only sign of past excitement were a couple of cops in their cars filling out reports.

Odin drove off in the Trans Am. He switched the radio to KFWB, the all-news station. They were giving traffic information. He spun the dial to KNX, the other all-news station. A sports update. He kept jumping back and forth between the two.

Finally they mentioned the big call-up in San Fernando, but they said details were sketchy and police were not releasing word on whom they were searching for.

He drove a few miles south, into North Hollywood, called the TV station where Mike Williams worked.

"I'll see if he's available," the woman in the newsroom said doubtfully. "He goes on the air in fifteen minutes. Who's calling?"

"Bob Odin."

Williams got on the line a few seconds later. He sounded breathless. "Bob, good to talk to you. Would you mind if I taped this call?"

"Why?"

"I tape my calls."

"I do mind."

"It's strictly routine."

"I don't like being taped." Odin had a cops' aversion to tape recorders. They were for capturing a suspect's incriminating words, and more trouble than they were worth. They inevitably broke down when you needed them most.

"You sure?" Williams persisted.

"Positive." Odin was pressing his forehead with his free hand. Maybe it was just a sinus headache, though he'd never gotten them before the bombing.

"Would you like to come in and talk?" The reporter sounded as eager as Buchanan.

"About what?"

"Whatever you want? Being a cop. The Mokley incident. Lieutenant Eustas Nichols."

"What about Huey?"

"Whatever you want to say."

"Why are you interested in Huey?"

"It hasn't been released yet. They found his body in Chavez Ravine."

Odin's knees buckled. He clutched the side of the phone booth for support. Huey was invulnerable.

"How?" he gasped.

"Shot a bunch of times."

Odin swayed back and forth, fighting for air.

"Bob? Bob? They'd like to talk to you about it. Would you care to comment on reports that your gun was used?"

"What?"

"Would you want to turn yourself in on camera? I guarantee you'd be the top story."

Odin hung up. Huey'd been murdered, and he was a suspect. He leaned against the dirty booth wall.

A young man with a spiky haircut and metal-studded black leather wrist bands rapped angrily on the glass. "Hey man, I need to make a call."

Odin stepped out of the booth, pale and wobbly. The young man's expression changed.

"You all right? Want me to call an ambulance?" Odin stumbled to the car and sat in the driver's seat.

Again the young man was rapping on the glass. "You shouldn't be driving, man."

Odin nodded and put the key in the ignition.

"You on drugs?" the young man asked, reaching in and putting his hand over the key.

Odin shook his head, too crushed to even push the hand away. "I'll stay here," Odin said. "Maybe you should call an ambulance."

The young man nodded wisely and returned to the phone.

Odin started the car and screeched off.

Where could he go? Jan Golden. She'd help him. He longed to curl up in her arms, feel her stroking him, her voice assuring him it would be all right.

But it wouldn't be. He had to straighten this out himself. Despite the pain in his head. And the slow countdown to blindness.

Jan Golden awoke in a chair in a dark room. She tried to get up and found she was strapped down. She didn't care. It seemed funny.

Doped. She tried to guess what it was. What were the names of those funny little drugs that made your brain go pitty pat? Morphine. That was one. Ooooh, a bad one. Demerol. Damn it all. Have a ball.

A flashlight snapped on and she flinched.

"You're awake," a man's voice said.

That was silly. Of course she was awake. She tried to recall how she got there.

"It's terrible how nurses steal drugs sometimes, isn't it?" the voice said.

That's right, I'm a nurse, Jan thought.

"Turn off that light please," she said.

The light came closer. Suddenly the right side of her face was stinging.

"You don't give orders," the voice said. "You answer questions. Understand?"

Jan nodded.

Now the left side of her face was stinging.

"Answer me."

"Yes." She nodded her head. "Yes."

The pain actually was good. Literally knocking sense into her. It also meant the drug wasn't a painkiller. What could it be? What were those things called?

"Where am I?"

Crack! Again the person hit her.

"Who are you?"

Crack!

A muscle relaxer, she thought. Or maybe a sedative. Phenobarbitol. She was regaining her wits. She needed time. She visualized her liver, her kidneys, and ordered them to work harder filtering the drugs out of her system.

"We're going to talk about Robert Odin. What did he tell you?"

"I don't know what you're talking about," she said, trying to make her voice even more slurred.

Crack!

She feigned unconsciousness.

Someone shook her roughly. She let her head roll from side to side.

"You hit her too hard," a commanding voice said. "You kill her?"

A hand grabbed her wrist and felt for a pulse. "Nah. This cunt can't take a few love taps."

"Go get cold water," the commanding voice said. "Be careful. You don't want to kill her before I get answers."

"Uh, Vic said maybe I could do her up. I'll wear a rubber."

"Not 'til I find out what I want. You can't control yourself even with your dick in your pants."

The man who'd slapped her grunted. "I heard about this way they used to question VC poontang over in Vietnam. You put a broomstick up their ass and . . ."

"Go get the water," the commanding voice interrupted.

There was a spray of light as the man who hit her went through the door. Golden got a feeling for the layout of the room. The man with the commanding voice was off to her right, in a chair. She hadn't been able to see his face since the light came from behind him. The man who'd walked out was one of the two who'd picked her up. The supposed cops. The one who'd sat next to her.

They were in an office. The door shut. Somehow the darkness was less frightening now. She had a frame of reference. This must be what it was like to be blind, she thought. Then she thought of Bob. Where was he?

Assistant Chief Fred Fleming owned a half-acre estate in Brentwood, one of the more prestigious and pricey areas of the city. He had inherited money, supposedly parlayed it into big bucks. And his wife came from an old California money family.

They lived in a two-story edifice, colonial white with high

columns in the front. Featured once in *Better Homes and Gardens*, it had lots of dignity, with neatly trimmed rose bushes, a well-manicured lawn, a freshly tiled roof. There was a tennis court and a swimming pool. And a guest house.

The guest house was Odin's destination. Fred Fleming Junior lived in the one bedroom cottage. It was white too, but lacked columns or the grandeur of the five-bedroom main house. The cottage could not be seen from the road.

A six-foot-high stone fence with an iron gate ringed the property. Odin checked for alarms and scrambled over. Dusk was falling and he hustled across the grounds quickly, using the few jacaranda trees for cover.

He didn't see Fleming Senior's city car, but Junior's Mazda was parked in the garage. It was the only car there. Both Fleming Senior and his wife must be out.

Odin hurried to the cottage. He peered in a window. Junior was sitting on the couch, watching the news. He was wearing an LAPD tee shirt, blue jean cutoffs, and a sad expression. He looked like a teenager who'd been turned down after asking a girl out to the prom.

Odin rapped on the door. Junior opened it without even asking who was there.

"Bob!"

"Hello, Junior."

"What happened? What's happening?"

"That's what I want to know."

"What do you mean?"

"The report on Mokley."

"Yes?"

"The report you showed me was bogus."

"No."

"I saw the original. Bagels had it."

Junior paled.

Odin seized Junior's shoulders.

"You're gonna tell me about it."

Junior hesitated, chewing his lip. "My father is a good man. He'll be a great chief."

"Mokley," Odin growled.

"I didn't mean for it to happen. I swear on my mother's life." Junior grabbed Odin's arms. "You got to believe me. I didn't mean for it to happen the way it did."

"Tell me about it," Odin said, forcing his voice to remain calm.

"Do you believe me? I didn't mean for it to happen."

"Tell me the whole story," Odin said.

"You know how many medals my dad had by the time he was my age? I'll tell you. Eight. What have I got? Zip. I know guys on the job talk about me behind my back. They say I'm only kept on board because of my father. Maybe they're right. I am no good." Junior bowed his head. "I just wanted to be a hero. It's not my fault, really."

"You planted that bomb?" Odin asked, his voice dropping to a low rumble.

Junior nodded.

"I went to check the place out the day before. My first time on point, I wanted to do extra homework. I saw Mokley's place was empty. Looked like he'd be away awhile. Then I got the idea for the bomb. I could've defused it. Everything would've been all right. I would've been a hero. Like my dad. Huey would've respected me. He never did, you know. Poor Huey."

"You planted the bomb," Odin said, no longer a question.

"I never figured on hurting you or the Bobbsey Twins. You were nicer to me than anyone. I didn't know there were those chemicals there, or that it would be such an explosion. How could I have known?"

"You're a cop in the best department in the world, in one of its best units. And you're not satisfied. How could you do it? How could you do it?"

"After it happened, I didn't know what to do," Junior said,

not hearing Odin. "I told my father. He was enraged. But he took charge. He—"

"Enough!" a voice barked.

Odin spun.

The Assistant Chief glowered from the doorway with a .45 in his hand.

PART FOUR

36 "Dad!"

"You stupid little snitch," Brass Balls said. "At least when you confessed to that nigger lieutenant, you had the brains to keep my name out of it."

Like Bagels, the Assistant Chief seemed to have aged rapidly in a short period of time. He held himself stiffly, his features pinched tight, as brittle as an old man.

"You killed Huey?" a stunned Odin asked.

Fleming Senior didn't answer but his son stared, open mouthed.

There was a long silence. The TV program had changed to a game show. The announcer gave a cheery welcome to the O'Day family from Arlington, Virginia.

"He's got to kill me," Odin said.

"No!" Junior shouted.

Odin was calculating distances, trying to figure out if he could disarm Fleming Senior. It didn't look promising. The Assistant Chief was about ten feet away, with a wooden side chair between them. Maybe if he could kick the chair—

"The bombing was bad enough, but no more than a man-

291

slaughter beef," Odin said to Junior. "But you know what it would have done to Brass Balls's career. Whatever cover-up he arranged, he did for himself." Odin turned to Fleming Sr. "How far did it go? I know there are wiseguys involved in it. Did you call up Nicky Pro and ask for a favor? Is it the first time you two have gone to bed?"

"I've never taken a dime from anyone," Senior said.

"It's my fault," Junior said.

"Stop whining," Senior said.

"I want to turn myself in," Junior said.

"You can't," Senior said.

"It's gone too far," Junior said.

"It goes no further," Senior said. "After Odin's gone, it will die down." While Fleming Senior spoke to his son, his eyes and gun were focused on Odin.

Another long silence. On the TV, a contestant had just guessed how many vertebrae were in a giraffe's neck.

"He's gone bad," Senior said to no one in particular. "After killing his lieutenant, he came here to get me. There was a struggle and I shot him."

"I won't cooperate," Junior said.

"You will."

Junior took a couple of steps towards the phone. "I'm calling the police."

Odin snorted. "We've got an ex-cop, a cop, and one of the department brass, at crossed swords. Calling nine-one-one won't make things better."

Junior froze with his hand on the phone. "What should I do?" he asked Odin.

"My way is the only way," Senior said. He lifted the gun to fire.

"No!" Junior screamed, lunging for his father.

The gun exploded as he tackled Brass Balls. The big bullet ripped through Junior's chest.

Odin had dived for the floor in a forward roll as soon as Junior had moved. He came up a few feet from Brass Balls.

The Assistant Chief was staring at his son, who had toppled back over the chair. Air made a disgusting sucking noise in and out of his chest cavity and then stopped.

Brass Balls had regained his composure quickly. The gun again was aimed at Odin's chest.

"It's too late for me," Fleming said.

"Put the gun down."

"I wish I could," Fleming said. "I wish I had."

"Did you kill Huey?"

"Indirectly. I set him up."

"Nicky Pro did it?"

"A couple of his people."

"You could testify against him. You can afford the best attorneys. Your record will help. You'd get off with less time than you think. Give me the gun."

Odin took a half step forward.

Fleming raised the weapon.

The stench of death was in the air. Cordite, fresh blood, and the effluvium from the young man's colon and bladder.

Odin had his hands up. He was just out of striking range.

"If only you'd killed Mokley," Fleming said. "I wouldn't have had to turn to Provenzano."

"Why couldn't Mokley live?" Odin asked, sidling a half step closer.

"If he had been cleared, there'd be too many questions. My son would've cracked eventually. Ruined everything. Mokley was just drug-dealing scum anyway. No loss to humanity. But look what happened." Fleming seemed to see his dead son for the first time. "It's over now. All that I worked for, all these years." In one smooth motion he put the gun in his mouth and pulled the trigger.

Odin turned away as the Assistant Chief's head exploded, blood-spattering his son's poster of Clint Eastwood as Dirty Harry.

*   *   *

I knew what Brass Balls was going to do after he killed his own kid, Odin thought as he drove away. I could've stopped him.

Odin felt cold inside, colder than he had ever felt before. Numb. Ruthless.

He had been through it before. In combat, during and immediately after a SWAT call-up, he functioned like the professional he was trained to be. No sign of stress. Sometimes it came hours later, sometimes days, where the shakes would set in and he'd think about what he'd seen.

He could just turn his evidence over to the authorities. What evidence? The statement of a dead man, relayed by a prime suspect. They'd wind up charging him with the murder of Fleming Senior and Junior. No, this was a time for street justice.

He saw a Trans Am, similar to the one he was driving, parked on a side street. When he'd fished the squeegee out of the trunk, he'd noticed a tool kit. He parked his Trans Am, went back to the trunk, and took out a pair of pliers. He switched license plates with the parked Trans Am. That would buy him a couple more days. He wouldn't need that much time anyway.

He drove by his house. There was a phone company van parked up the street with a man sitting behind the wheel. It could be a phone company employee on a break. It could also be LAPD using one of their favorite surveillance vehicles.

He drove on.

The answer to the Nicky Pro problem was simple. Again Scalia's words came back to him. The power of the circle. The beginning is the end. A bomb. Provenzano might be surrounded by a half dozen strongarms, but one blast, and all things would be equal.

Demolitions had been a major part of his SEAL training, as important as scuba diving or small arms work. The SEALs were, after all, an outgrowth of the UDTs, Underwater Demolition Teams, formed to do everything from destroy enemy ships to clear obstacles to facilitate beach landings.

What came back first was the safety precautions, since the instructors had drilled those into their heads.

One person should be responsible for preparation, placement, and firing an explosive. The vertical concept, don't divide responsibility. Don't leave explosives unguarded. No smoking or spark-producing metal. Your own caution could override an admiral's orders. Keep detonators and explosives separate. Display the Bravo flag on any ship transporting explosives. And on and on.

He enjoyed the mental review, like he was going through a photo album with pictures of friends and loved ones.

Method of detonation: primacord, safety fuse, blasting caps.

Explosive materials: ammonium nitrate, B-2, C-3, HBX-3, Pentolite, PETN, RDX, Tetrytol, TNT.

Packaging: bangalore torpedo, Claymore mine, fifteen pound, shaped charge, 2.5 pound block, Flexible Linear Demo Charge, MK 135.

The military had the best stuff. He might be able to hook up with a disgruntled grunt in a bar and get high-power explosive. But that was too risky. Take too long.

He passed a construction site. A sign warned NO RADIO TRANSMISSION—DANGER BLASTING. He drove around the block several times, sizing up his target.

There was a construction trailer parked in the street. A night watchman was visible inside, watching a tiny black-and-white TV. Behind the six-foot high wooden fence that formed the perimeter, a small shed was visible with the "Danger—Explosives" sign posted on the outside. The warnings were like dangling a shiny lure in front of a barracuda.

He parked his car a short distance up the block. In the tool box, he found a thick screwdriver and a claw hammer. No pry bar. It would have to do. He tucked them in his belt and strolled to a spot out of view of the guard shed.

Odin clambered over the fence and raced across the open space in a half crouch, taking advantage of the shadows. He paused by a parked tractor to catch his breath and listen. The ex-cop heard the normal sounds of the city, along with his own slightly labored breathing.

He hustled toward the shed. It was on the edge of a man-made twenty-foot precipice, the depression that would be the parking garage under the apartment complex.

Odin squinted. It was hard to see in the darkness. But how much of it was gloom and how much was his own deteriorating vision?

The shed was lit by two spotlights. Their going off was sure to attract the guard's attention. That would be the most effective way of doing things. Draw the guard in, neutralize him, and take time getting the explosive. But Odin wanted to avoid any encounter with the rent-a-cop. He wanted to save his violence for Provenzano, the man who'd murdered Huey.

He reached the shed. There was a hasp and padlock on the wooden door. The hinges were screwed in solid with one-way screws. Locking pins. The door was three-quarter inch plywood. He circled the shed. Solidly built. Probably better than the two-story garden apartment complex that was going up.

Odin shoved the screwdriver between the door and the frame, near the hasp, and pushed.

The screwdriver snapped.

He forced the nail-pulling end of the claw hammer into the crack and pried. The door gapped a bit but remained solidly in place.

In his half crouch, Odin raced to where flatbed trucks had dropped off the construction supplies. Lots of two-by-fours, four-by-eights, roof tile, bags of cement, reinforcing rods.

Odin grabbed a steel rod and hurried back to the shed. He

had to tap it a few times with the hammer to get it in place. He used a piece of his shirt to cushion the top of the rod to reduce the noise.

He paused, listening. No unusual sounds.

He leaned into the rod and the hasp ripped out of the wood with a pained cry.

He listened again. No unusual sounds.

He set the rod and the hammer down outside the shed. The less metal the better. He took off his belt, which had a metal buckle, and went inside.

A little light filtered in. He dared not turn on the single bulb that hung overhead. The shed was ten-by-twelve, packed solid with supplies. Once again the safety markings made it clear where the goodies were. Two wooden crates were marked TNT in red.

He tried to open the wooden lid. No luck. He had to fetch the hammer and pry it up. Carefully. He didn't need to read the stenciled warning on top about the danger from sparks, smoking, or friction.

He pried it open. The TNT looked fresh, no signs of sweating. Old trinitrotoluene gave off an oily liquid that was a low-power, easily ignited explosive. Odin took six sticks. He tucked them into his waistband in the small of his back.

A box on the other side of the room held electric blasting caps. He took a dozen and shoved them in his front pants pocket. If they were to go off—say from a stray radio signal—there wouldn't be much of his lower torso recognizable.

Odin stepped out and tried to make the shed look untampered with. But it was impossible. The opening had done too much damage to the lock.

He took a dozen steps away from the shed when he heard the jingling of the guard's keys. The guard wasn't in a hurry and not concerned about intruders. He was singing to himself. Odin recognized a Temptations tune from the sixties.

The ex-cop crouched down near the same tractor that had

hidden him on his way in. The security guard passed. He was a young Hispanic man wearing a light blue shirt that said PACIFIC COAST SECURITY SERVICE. He wasn't tall, but his muscular arms bulged at the biceps and his tread was soft and sure.

He spotted the tampering with the shed and spun around, muttering curses.

Odin took off running. The guard didn't appear to have a gun, and with his head start, Odin could definitely outrace him.

Suddenly he felt a stabbing pain in his thigh. He looked down. What appeared to be a gear was embedded in the meaty part of his leg. A *shuriken* dart.

The guard running toward him had taken out a pair of nunchaku. Chuka sticks. Two pieces of wood joined by a chain. Modeled on an ancient Oriental threshing tool, they could be a devastating weapon. Most who used them were infatuated by Bruce Lee movies and wasted their energy with razzle-dazzle movements. The guard who was nearly upon him had been professional in tossing the dart. The way he held the sticks indicated he was a lot more than a chop-socky movie buff.

Odin moved as swiftly as he could towards the construction supplies. He jerked the dart out of his leg and threw it back at the guard. It made the man hesitate a millisecond but came nowhere near to hitting him.

Odin reached the supplies and grabbed a steel rod. He held it in front of him.

The nunchaku made a swishing noise as the sticks swirled through the air. The guard had a contented, almost dazed smile on his face, a martial artist getting a chance to paint a masterpiece. Odin poked with the rod, trying to keep the guard at a distance. The man kept backing him up.

Odin felt the dirt crumble under his heel. He was at the edge of a precipice. The twenty-foot drop wouldn't kill him, just cripple him long enough for the cops to come. The blasting caps should be insensitive to impact, but even low-intensity explosives could be temperamental.

Odin swung the bar. The man dodged it.

Suddenly agony on the back of Odin's hand. The chuka stick had caught him. He dropped the bar. The guard charged.

Odin grabbed a two-by-four and swung low, catching the guard's ankle. A cry of pain and the man stumbled. Odin swung again, not a killing blow, but enough to render the man unconscious. If it had connected. It didn't.

The guard blocked with his chuka sticks. Odin jerked and the man lost his grip on the weapon. Odin closed in, holding the two-by-four in front of him like a pugil stick.

The man lashed out with his boot, splitting the two-by-four in half.

"Can we talk?" Odin asked.

The man answered by launching a *shuto* strike at Odin's neck. A classic karate chop.

Odin blocked it with his left, pivoted, and tried to catch the guard with a side kick. The guard blocked and tried to trap Odin's leg but the ex-cop broke free.

The guard's half smile hadn't changed.

They sparred, swapping blows, kicks, and blocks. Odin didn't want to kill his adversary, just incapacitate him. The guard had no such reservations. Odin couldn't convince him that he was a good guy. Not many good guys break into construction sheds and steal explosives.

An attempted gouge of Odin's eyes dislodged his patch. The night air was strange on his dead eye, making him feel naked. The thought of his functioning eye being injured gave Odin a sense of desperation and fear.

Neither Odin nor the guard landed any solid blows. Odin's forearms ached from blocking the guard's powerful attacks.

Don't fight fire with fire, Scalia had warned. If you're facing a boxer, kick. If you're up against a *tae kwan do* man who favors his legs, punch. If your opponent is from a hard school, be soft. Never let your opponent decide how you're going to fight him.

The next time the guard charged, Odin dropped to the floor. Scalia taught numerous defenses from the floor to his handicapped students. Odin gambled that the martial artist attacking him was more used to a face-to-face battle.

The guard studied him, not sure if he had finally succeeded in landing a stunning blow. He advanced. Odin kicked low, hooking one foot behind the guard's shin and kicking his knee cap. The man's knee hyperextended.

The guard yelped and fell. Odin jumped up and closed in. He grabbed the guard in a choke hold and quickly rendered him unconscious. He adjusted the guard's body so his injured knee was laid out properly and would not be further damaged.

Sore and weak, Odin stumbled away. His thigh was bleeding, but not badly. His forearms felt like they'd been run over by a bus. His ribs were sore where the guard had landed a few glancing blows. He wanted to take a hot bath and wrap himself in cotton batting for a week.

He thought of Nicky Pro, and Huey. Once again hate proved an effective mainspring.

37 Odin sagged into the car seat. He knew what he was feeling was just the beginning—it would get worse before it got better.

He stopped at a Rankin drug store. The bright fluorescence hurt his eye. He bought a new patch—the old one had gotten ripped in the fray—two Ace bandages, gauze bandage, antiseptic, and aspirin. A small knapsack caught his eye, and he bought that too.

He checked into a motel off the San Bernardino Freeway. The "Vacancy" sign was missing letters and an exterminator could probably make a career out of what he'd find. The lobby smelled of mildew.

"Is there anything I could get you?" the desk clerk asked with a bored leer.

Odin ignored him and took the key from his outstretched hand.

The room had a bathtub and a queen-size bed. While the tub filled with hot water, Odin gulped a couple of aspirin, and lay the dynamite on the bed. Only one of the sticks appeared to have gotten cracked. He put the blasting caps on the far side of the room, confident that they were far enough off the freeway to avoid CB radio traffic.

He wiped the shallow wound from the *shuriken* dart with antiseptic. He wiped antiseptic over a half dozen other small cuts he picked up during the scuffle.

He eased into the tub, with water as hot as he could take. The trick was to slide in slowly and not move once you were in, a Japanese girlfriend had once taught him. She had a big hot tub on the deck of her condo, and they would spend hours looking out at the Santa Monica Mountains. Those moments of tranquility seemed unbelievable.

Thoughts of her reminded him of Jan. Would it be possible to get together with her? Never.

He might not be able to clear himself of the homicide charges. His best answer was to leave the country. Where?

Maybe Israel. They could always use someone who was good with a gun. And one of their national heroes had one eye. Or somewhere in Africa. A mercenary. But he'd have to have sympathy for the side he was working for. Underdogs usually didn't pay well. But he wouldn't need much money.

Was the French Foreign Legion still in business? What kind of scum were attracted to an organization where they didn't ask any questions about your past?

How much of his thoughts were romanticized bullshit? The noble warrior going off into the sunset. Without even a horse.

He dozed off.

He awoke with the now cool water lapping at his chin. He'd slid down in the worn tub. After all his struggles, to die by drowning in a bathtub seemed ridiculous. It reminded him of the soldier who raised the flag at Iwo Jima, who later died drunk in a mud puddle he'd fallen into face down.

He got out of the tub, stretched, and studied himself in the mirror. The pains had settled down to a dull ache. He wiped the thigh again with the antiseptic, laid the gauze pad across the wound, and pinned it in place with the Ace bandage.

He phoned the desk clerk and asked where the nearest Radio Shack was.

"I've been asked about bars, restaurants, cockfights, whore-houses, and gambling joints," the clerk said. "Never a Radio Shack. Hold on." Odin could hear telephone pages being rustled. The clerk read him out an address.

Odin went to the store where a fresh-faced young man wearing a white shirt and a tie sold him two radio-controlled race cars.

"If you want that gift wrapped, you have—"

"No, thanks." Odin also bought a soldering gun and solder, a coil of wire, and batteries.

He would have liked to go to a gun store, but to get a weapon without a two week wait, he'd have to show law enforcement ID. Too risky.

Back at the motel, he unwrapped the toys and began disassembling them.

There were so many ways to trigger a bomb. It could be rigged to an altimeter and would detonate when a plane reached a given height. Or hooked up to a Timex and go off when the big hand hit the little wire. Or spring loaded, pressure sensitive. Or attached to a door.

But Odin wanted to press the button, to watch as Nicky Pro was reduced to atoms.

It took an hour to wire up the explosives. One set of devices for the Provenzano house. Another for Nicky Pro's office. Each stick of TNT had two blasting caps—a primary and a backup. He taped the broken stick of TNT. He used the boxes from the racing cars to hold the explosive devices. In the old days, this would've taken less than half an hour, he thought. His eye throbbed from doing the fine wiring and his head ached. There's still time for treatment, a chance to save my sight. No. Have to get Pro. Might go blind anyway. Then what? Beat Pro to death with my cane? he thought bitterly.

He had stiffened from tension. He gulped more aspirin, did a few minutes of stretches, and headed to the Provenzano home.

Odin surveyed Provenzano's place from a tree limb in a neighbor's yard. The fence was eight feet high, topped with a pressure sensitive snitch wire. Spotlights lit the grounds around the redwood plank home. Lots of glass, solar panels on the roof. An Olympic-size pool off to the right, a tennis court off to the left.

He also saw a couple of kids' bicycles lying in the driveway.

What if a kid was blown up? Was that something he could live with? Even Pro's wife. Sure she was living off the proceeds of Pro's crime, but did that make her a fair victim?

There was no sign of Nicky Provenzano.

He heard a low growl. Four Rottweilers, so black he could've easily missed them, were watching him. They were trained to attack, not alert anyone with their barking.

Odin decided to catch Pro at his office.

"Fleming's wife says she doesn't know where her husband is," Provenzano complained, slamming down the phone. "The son of a bitch is supposed to deliver the files to me tonight and he plays hide and seek."

"You want me to go out to his place?" Vic asked.

"We could smack his bitch around," Terranova volunteered.

Pro shot Joe a dirty look and steepled his fingers in front of his face.

The questioning of Jan Golden was not going well. Terranova wasn't the only one who was frustrated. As far as they had been able to tell, she didn't know Odin's whereabouts or how much he really knew. But she kept getting incoherent or passing out. It sure looked real, though Provenzano had doubts. He'd never doped a woman before, and she was much smaller than those he'd usually dealt with. He had to keep the drug level down. He didn't want it showing up in her blood. And he had to be careful that Terranova didn't kill her before he wanted her dead.

Jan Golden kept scraping her short cut nails across the rope that bound her to the chair. Fortunately her captors had been frequently distracted and fallen for her doped out appearance. She'd observed enough people under the influence of various drugs to be able to simulate a variety of intoxications.

At last the rope parted. She could hear the men's voices in the next office over.

Stiff and wobbly, she grabbed a chair and slid it against the door. Then she listened. The men were talking about going somewhere, but Nicky Pro vetoed the idea.

"I've just about had it with her," Provenzano was saying. "Vic, you got one last chance at making her talk. Then let Joe have his fun."

She hurried to the window. A dozen stories up. No ledge. It didn't even appear that the window could be opened.

Someone tried the door.

"Hey, it's stuck," Polanski said from the other side.

She pulled one of the other doors. A clothing closet. Then she saw the recessed panel. Barely visible. She broke a finger-nail trying to open it. She ran to the desk and got a letter opener.

A man's bulk hit the door she'd blocked with the chair and the chair was pushed back.

She used the letter opener to pry the recessed door open. A hidden escape. It led to a service corridor.

She ran in, not knowing where it went to, but knowing that she had to be better off.

"We're closed for the night," the overweight security guard said. His belly flopped out of a soiled uniform. He was standing in front of the underground garage entrance.

"Whose cars are those inside?" Odin asked, pointing to a few cars still parked in the garage.

"They work here. Not that it's any of your business. Scram," the guard said. He patted a canister of Mace on the Sam Browne belt he wore.

"I've got a present for Mr. Pro," Odin said, taking one of the racing car boxes from the day pack.

"Either come back in the morning or leave it with me," the guard said.

"What's that kid doing over by the car?" Odin asked.

The guard turned. Odin hit him one chop on the side of the neck and the fat man went down. The ex-cop lugged the guard to a storage closet. He bound the guard's hands with his tie and knotted his shoelaces together. Odin donned the man's jacket, which had an "Always Alert" security patch.

He moved silently into the fire stairs and began climbing. He heard noises coming from the top.

Jan Golden knew she would never make it all the way to the lobby. The men were faster and she was still wobbly. She ran down one floor, and out into the corridor.

Someone, please be here. A night watchman. A maintenance person. A late worker.

She looked back to the fire door. The three men came barreling through it. One had his gun drawn.

"Put that away, idiot," Pro ordered Terranova.

Terranova holstered his gun.

Golden dashed down the hallway. She had lost one shoe

somewhere. She kicked off the other one and ran barefoot on the carpet. At the far end of the hall was another fire stair. She'd have to try running down the eleven flights.

The men were gaining on her.

She reached the doorway. The door was stuck. She gave a frenzied yank. Nothing. Then she realized she had to push. She shoved through.

She was panting as she raced down another flight of stairs and out the door onto the next floor.

Please, why can't there be someone here?

Odin was breathing hard when he reached the top floor. The door was open to Nicky Pro's office. Great luck. He went in cautiously. It was silent. Empty, though it looked like someone had just been there. A coffee cup was steaming on a desk.

Could Pro somehow been alerted that he was coming?

No. The mafioso would've left a trap.

Odin put the bomb in a desk drawer and hurried out.

He broke into the office across from Provenzano's to wait for the mafioso's return. The force of the bomb should be limited to Pro's office.

If I miscalculated, and the blast gets me, so be it, Odin thought. I've lost my eye, my job, my best friend. There's a chance that even if I live through this, I'll be blind. But at least I'll see Nicky Pro get his before I go.

38 Jan Golden bolted down a corridor, trying doors as she ran. She found an open one and ran into the office.

She banged into a desk and stifled a pained grunt. She didn't dare turn on a light. Golden felt her way to the front of the desk and crouched inside the kneehole.

She tried to breathe quietly but wound up heaving. There was a tingly excitement, the thrill of besting the hunters, the fear of being caught.

Out in the hall, she heard men's voices. Confused.

She knew she was going to die. Unfair. There was so much she had to do. She thought about dates she'd skipped to study, vacations she'd passed on to do volunteer work, pleasures she'd denied herself.

The door opened. Light flooded in from the hall. It was the one called Joe.

"Here, pussy, pussy," he cooed. "Come here like a good little girl."

"What ees going on there?" said a new voice, Spanish-accented English.

She heard the leader's voice, Nicky Pro, then the Spanish speaking voice saying, "Excuse me, of course, thank you Mr. Pro." She heard the cleaning cart being wheeled away.

She could scream. But what would happen then? Would the maintenance man persist in investigating when Nicky Pro had either bought off, threatened, or conned him? And how could he help? She'd just get them both killed.

Terranova saw the woman's foot sticking out from the corner of the desk. He was going to call Vic and Nicky Pro, who were checking other offices. Then decided to have fun.

"I guess she ain't here," he muttered, and turned as if to leave. He took a step towards the door. "Ah, heck, better check again."

He sauntered around the room, leisurely looking behind a sofa, pulling open a closet.

"I think I'll just sit down and take a break," he said.

He walked over to the desk.

"Well, well what do we have here?" he asked, looking under the desk at Golden. He smirked.

"I always wanted to play a big businessman," Terranova said, sitting down in the desk chair. He unzipped his fly. "Now, if you're good, maybe I'll let you go."

Golden cringed against the back of the desk, trapped.

"You hear what I said?"

She didn't move.

He reached under and grabbed her hair, then yanked her forward. Her face was inches from his erect penis.

"Go to it, bitch."

He grabbed her throat and she opened her mouth.

He leaned back and thrust forward.

She bit down as hard as she could.

Three floors above them, Odin had dozed off. He awoke with a start by what might have been a man's scream. He stood stiffly. He could barely move. The ex-cop blinked and rubbed his good eye. It was blurry and reduced in scope, sort of like looking through a cardboard tube with a shower curtain over the end. He didn't need to see very far to push a button.

He stretched and gulped a couple of aspirin. The pills stuck to his palate, leaving a vinegary taste.

He listened for any activity. Nothing. Where the hell was Nicky Provenzano?

At the last millisecond, Jan Golden had stopped short of putting all the strength of her jaws into the bite. She shoved Terranova backwards in the rolling office chair and exploded out from under the desk. He tried to get up, still clutching his groin. She hit him in the chin with the heel of her hand and ran past him.

She sprinted into the corridor and toward where she believed the maintenance man had gone.

A figure stepped out of a doorway, grabbing her around the

mouth from behind. She slammed an elbow into his solar plexus. He caught her arm, nearly yanking it out of the socket. She clawed at his face. When she'd taken the self-defense class from Scalia—how she wished she'd taken more—she'd never believe she'd be able to claw someone's eyes. Now, she only wished her nails were longer.

But the man twisted aside, and she barely raked his cheek. She saw the fist coming and tried to turn but he compensated and it caught her on the jaw. Blackness.

Voices. Odin wished he could open the door to be sure who it was. He couldn't risk being discovered by the wrong party.

He pressed his ear to the thick wooden door. He could barely make out the words. A man was moaning, making the conversation difficult to hear.

"I'll just tell everyone Joe got his dick caught in the office shredder," a voice said.

"Fuck you," Joe said in between moans.

"Knock it off," another voice said.

"I'm in pain. What if I can't use it again?" Joe asked. "What if they got to amputate?"

"Vic used to work as a cut man," Pro said. "He'll patch it up. Right?"

"You'll be ready to go three rounds in no time," Vic said. He laughed.

"Cocksucker. I oughta . . ."

They were going into Pro's office.

"Shut up. We got to finish up. I got business to transact. Understand?"

"Yes Mr. Pro," Vic said.

Perfect, Odin thought. Pro and two of his goons. From what he'd heard, he guessed they had gone somewhere to shred papers and one of the goons had gotten hurt.

Odin took the radio remote control device out of the day pack and played with it, savoring the moment.

He was about to commit murder. He hesitated. He thought about Huey, and the good times.

He pushed the button.

Polanski, who was carrying the unconscious Jan Golden across his shoulder, dropped her down roughly onto the sofa in Pro's inner office.

"Cunt!" Terranova said, kicking her in the side.

"Okay, okay, ease up," Pro said. "She's got balls."

"If she'd had a bigger mouth, she'd have Joe's balls as well," Polanski said.

Terranova staggered towards his partner, hands up in a boxing position. "I've about had it with you."

"You lift one finger, I'll give you a kick and get the bleeding started again," Polanski said. "Those tissues I put on there ain't much protection."

Joe hesitated.

"Drop your drawers and I'll put antiseptic on it."

Terranova hesitated. Nicky Pro came out of the bathroom carrying a first aid kit.

"Do it," Pro commanded.

Terranova pulled his pants down. There was a few drops of blood on the wad of tissues. Vic peeled them up.

"Ow. Be careful," Terranova complained.

Polanski dabbed iodine on the cut.

Joe yowled. "Fucking bastard. You're enjoying this."

"You think I like handling your pecker, you got another think coming," Polanski said, putting a sterile gauze pad over the cut. "This is temporary. Better go to a doctor tomorrow. It's easy to get an infection." He taped Terranova's penis, adhering to as many pubic hairs as possible. Getting it off would be quite painful. "I hear that human spit got more germs in it than dog spit."

"You mean I could get rabies or something?"

"Yeah."

Terranova glared at Golden. "Oh, is she gonna die."

Nicky Pro looked around the office. "You hear that?"

"What?"

"Like a buzzing."

All three men were silent. Pro and Vic stalked around the room, listening. Joe pulled up his pants and zipped up.

Provenzano and Polanski neared Pro's desk. Pro opened the drawer and saw the racing car box.

Provenzano opened the box.

"What the fuck . . ."

He and Polanski took a step back.

The electrical blasting caps hummed but refused to detonate the bomb.

Terranova breezed over. "What's going on?" He saw the dynamite in the box. "Holy shit!"

Next door, Odin kept pressing the button, but nothing happened.

He muttered a string of curses. Civilian explosives weren't up to military specs. Maybe from the bouncing they got during his struggle with the ninja security guard. Whatever. What was supposed to boom had apparently fizzled.

He hobbled to the office door and cracked it open. Pro would hear about his overcoming the man in the garage, and be even more on his guard. It didn't matter. Odin knew his limits. He wasn't in shape to do much more than push a button.

He slipped out the door and made his way to the fire stairs. He was about to go through when he noticed something lying on the floor. He bent to pick it up. A shoe. A sensible woman's shoe.

He held it a foot from his face as he examined it. His stomach did flip flops. He recognized whose shoe it was.

*   *   *

Nicky Pro took the bomb into the bathroom and threw it into the toilet.

"That gonna stop it?" Joe asked.

"They always put bombs in a bucket of water," Pro answered.

"Maybe we oughta get outta here," Polanski suggested.

"That bomb wasn't there earlier today," Pro said.

"You sure?" Polanski asked.

"Sure I'm sure," Pro said, reaching into his desk drawer and taking out a pearl-handled .32. "It was put in there while we were out."

Vic and Joe drew their guns.

"It looks like the kind of bomb you set off with a radio," Provenzano said. "A guy in the union in Detroit used to do that sort of thing. Most of those radios don't have much range. Especially in a building with steel beams. He's around here somewhere."

"I'll stay here and guard her while you guys look around," Terranova said. As soon as the other men were out of the room, he would strangle Golden. The hell with Nicky Pro. The bitch had nearly cost him his manhood.

Nicholas Provenzano realized Terranova's intentions. Pro also had no desire to go hunting Odin. Not that he was a coward, he rationalized. It's just that was muscle work. He had outgrown that.

"You and Vic look for him," Pro said. "I'll stay with her. Joey, you got the most experience pulling the trigger."

Terranova fell for the flattery. He nodded and worked the action on his 9 mm.

"Don't worry about her," Pro said, nodding towards Golden. "When you get back, you can do whatever you want."

39

"Hey! Down there," Terranova shouted, and snapped off two quick shots.

The bullets whistled by Odin's head, shattering the window at the end of the hall. Terranova fired twice more. One shot furrowed the carpet at Odin's feet. The other dug into the wall in front of Odin's face.

Odin dashed around the corner and tried the first door. Locked, with a simple snap lock. He crouched and used a credit card to loid it open.

He opened the door and threw himself in. He banged against the wall, stumbled over a vacuum cleaner. It was a maintenance closet. Nowhere to run or hide.

"C'mon," Terranova yelled to his partner and began cautiously advancing down the corridor. Odin hadn't returned fire, but they didn't know whether he was armed or not.

Not even a broom to use as a weapon, Odin thought as he groped around. Cleaning solvents, the vacuum, and boxes of towels and paper goods.

"We got him, we got him," Terranova hissed excitedly.

On the back wall of the closet was a metal box. The main service panel for the floor. Odin yanked it open, exposing the rows of circuit breakers. He couldn't find a master switch. He grabbed a bottle of chlorine and poured it into a gap in the cover.

There was an explosive sparking, as though the box contained a Fourth of July explosion. Then the entire floor was dark.

"What the fuck!" Terranova shouted.

Odin pulled the maintenance closet door shut. The goons would have to try every door in the area before they could get him.

Unless the stench of chlorine gave him away. In the small closet, the smell was dizzying. He fought the urge to cough.

Days passed. He could hear Terranova and Polanski trying doors. They reached the maintenance closet and tried the knob. Odin stood as much to one side as he could, hands ready to lash out.

"Whatta they got, a fucking swimming pool here?" Terranova asked.

"Chlorine," Polanski answered.

Hearing the spoken word "chlorine" jogged Odin's memory.

He'd been a young patrolman. The call was in Encino, a crying child, no answer at the door. He'd kicked it in. They'd found the mother unconscious on the bathroom floor. Choking and gasping, Odin had managed to carry her out. The paramedics had explained to him what had happened.

The two killers moved on, their voices growing fainter. Odin groped around on the shelf. He lifted a bottle, unscrewed the cap. It was some lemony cleaner. He sniffed a second bottle more cautiously. Lysol. The third cap made his eyes water with an acidy smell. Carbolic acid cleanser. He took that bottle down.

He exhaled deeply, then inhaled deeply, then exhaled. Divers used to hyperventilate in the SEALs to get a few seconds extra time underwater. More than three times and the body's feedback system was thrown off. Too much oxygen, too little carbon dioxide, and dangerous unconsciousness.

He poured the bleach into the gallon bottle with the carbolic acid and quickly screwed on the lid. Still, a little of the gas leaked out. It felt like someone had poured scalding water down his throat.

What had nearly killed the housewife was chlorine gas, produced by the inadvertent mixture of toilet-bowl cleaner with chlorine. The toilet-bowl cleaner contained more than five percent hydrochloric acid, which reacted with the bleach to produce chlorine gas. The woman had been revived, but still suffered through a bout of pneumonia and a month-long hospital stay. Any acid mixed with bleach results in the release of chlorine gas.

Odin eased open the closet door. Bullets ripped into the door, smacking it back against him. Carefully cushioning the bottle, he did a quick, low roll. It was too dark in the hall to see the killers but their muzzle flashes made their position clear. He heaved the gas bomb.

It shattered. Coughs, gasps. No more shots.

He waited in the darkness for the killers. They had to flee the toxic cloud.

He heard a figure clomping toward him. Heavy tread. The larger one. Vic.

When the big man was right by him, Odin lunged, smashing him against the wall. Vic didn't go down. With a savage strength, he swung an arm out and caught Odin's shoulder, slamming the ex-cop back. Polanski charged, butting with his head.

They exchanged blows in the darkness, bruising each other, but nothing conclusive. Odin visualized his assailant, a hulking ex-boxer. He'd probably be in a classic boxer's stance. Odin threw out a jab. It was blocked and counterpunched.

Odin threw another jab, pinpointing Polanski's position. The ex-cop launched a roundhouse kick that landed in Vic's groin. The big man let out a pained groan.

Odin knew he'd probably be hunched over. He closed in on Vic, the series of blows almost preprogrammed. Grab the hair in the hands, lift the knee to Polanski's face. Vic fell.

Odin stood, silent. Where was Joe? The agonized coughing had stopped. Wind whistled through the bullet holes in the window at the end of the corridor. Ducts breathed air into the corridor. Odin's gas bomb wouldn't have been debilitating in the airy hall.

Could Joe have gotten past Odin in the darkness?

The hypochlorite smell suddenly got stronger. Then Odin heard a slight swish.

Odin knew a second before Joe was upon him. The smaller man moved silently, swinging a knife in front of him blindly. The blade raked Odin.

The ex-cop leaned back to kick. All his weight was on the leg the guard had hit with the shuriken dart. It gave out. Odin fell.

Joe jumped on him. Odin rolled aside and the knife buried itself deep in the carpet where his neck had been.

The two men stood. Terranova fought ferociously. His blade slashed Odin twice but the ex-cop's dodging limited it to superficial damage.

Odin landed a solid punch in the solar plexus, then attacked Terranova's floating ribs. One blow on either side. Odin grabbed Terranova's chin with one hand, and the back of his head with another. Odin twisted his whole body, taking only Terranova's head with him. *Kubi nage.* A neck throw. There was a snapping sound, like a dried turkey bone being broken.

Odin threw the body to the floor. He picked up Joe's gun, checked that the safety was off, and padded toward Nicky Pro's office. Odin's night vision was all but gone and he had to feel his way along the wall in the dark corridor.

He was on automatic, a leopard with the scent of prey.

Jan Golden awoke again in darkness. Her first thought was that she was back in her bedroom, she had to go to work, and she'd just come out of a crazy dream. Then she realized her arms were bound behind her and the nightmare was still going on.

"Take it easy, sleeping beauty," a man's voice said softly. It was the leader of the trio that had kidnapped and abused her. The one called Nicky Pro. She was half sitting, half lying on a couch. Pro was next to her.

The office overlooked the Los Angeles Basin and the sun was

just beginning to put a glow over the metropolitan sprawl. From the faint orange light it provided, she could see the gleam of metal in his hand.

"My boys versus your boyfriend. I'm not making odds. What do you think?"

She didn't answer.

"You know, I wanted to get away from violence," Pro said. "My people are past that. We leave the bloody work for the wetbacks and niggers. But look what's happened. What a mess, huh?"

"You could stop the violence. Turn yourself in."

"What a great idea. I'd probably only spend the rest of my life in the joint. Surrounded by morons like Joe. Worrying if some hopped up nigger with a head full of prison hooch won't try and make his rep by offing me."

"No more killing. *Please.*"

"Tell your boyfriend that."

"If I convince him, will you let us go?"

"And me?"

"We'll leave, leave you alone."

Pro shrugged. "You can try it but your boyfriend won't go for it."

"You don't know him."

"Believe me, sweetheart, I know him better than you do. I've had guys like him working for me all my life."

40 Odin paused outside the door to Nicky Pro's office. The mobster had decided to play out the battle on his home turf.

A glimmer of the morning sun came in from the window at the end of the corridor. Odin checked the gun he had gotten from Joe's body. With his weakened vision, he had to hold it a few inches from his face. A 9-mm Browning Hi-Power. Ten shots left in the fourteen-shot weapon. Safety off.

He advanced. From inside the inner office, he could hear two voices. Jan and Nicky Pro. He couldn't make out the words.

"Bob! Bob, are you out there?" she shouted.

His hand tensed on the weapon. He couldn't see into the inner office—the door was half closed and it was dark. But from the sound of her voice he guessed she was against a side wall.

"Bob, please listen to me. Mr. Pro says that there's no need for any more killing. He'll let us go if we leave him alone. Can you hear me?"

She probably believes in Santa Claus too, Odin thought.

There were a few low whispers from Pro.

"Bob, he's got his gun against my head," she said. "If you don't respond right away, he says he'll kill me."

What a lady, Odin thought. Although she was pleading, her voice was calm. She had her fear under control.

"I'm here," Odin said. He was pressed flat against a wall in the outer office.

"Bob, did you hear what I said?"

"I heard."

"Will you do it?"

"Kiss and make up?"

"Bob, please, for me."

More whispers from Nicky Pro. Nearly impossible for Odin to place exactly where he was.

"He's going to count to ten and if you don't throw your gun down, he's going to kill me," Golden said.

"That doesn't sound very peaceable to me. How about this, if he throws his gun down, I'll throw mine."

"I don't trust you," Pro said.

The voice was coming from right where Jan was. Did Odin dare to step into the doorway and snap off a fast shot? If only he knew the layout of Pro's office. In the faint light, his vision weakened, not knowing the terrain, with a hostage at stake, he couldn't take a chance.

"I don't trust you either," Odin said. "We've got a standoff."

"No, bright boy. I've got a hostage."

Provenzano grabbed one of Golden's fingers and twisted hard. She cried in pain.

"Leave her alone!" Odin yelled.

"Throw your gun down."

If he threw it down, they would both die. If he didn't, Pro would continue to abuse Golden.

On the couch, arms tied behind her back, Golden stared at Pro in horror. When he'd twisted a finger it had been so dispassionately. He was not sadistic. He didn't see them as human beings.

She stomped Pro's instep and jumped up. He grabbed her hair.

Odin heard the scuffle and charged into the room.

Pro tried to pull her in front of him. She bit his hand and stumbled away. Pro got his gun up to shoot.

Odin aimed. "Don't," he ordered.

"Well, now we really got a standoff," Pro said, sounding almost amused.

"You drop it and I will," Odin said.

Pro looked at him. "You couldn't kill me in cold blood. Not in front of your lady friend. Right?"

Odin nodded.

Pro dropped his gun. It was only a few feet from him on the floor.

"Now you drop yours."

Odin's eyes were taking in the office. Were there any other weapons in sight? A heavy crystal ashtray on a side table would make a good bludgeon. Pro had an old-fashioned news editor's spike on his desk, holding a sheaf of papers. Barring fancy moves—seize a picture off the wall, use the glass, or the picture wire as a garrote—that was about it.

Odin threw the gun out, farther from him than Pro's weapon was.

"Good," Provenzano said. "Now we can talk."

"We have nothing to talk about," Odin said. "You killed Huey, didn't you?"

"Not personally. I just acted as a facilitator for your assistant chief."

Jan Golden leaned against a chair, heaving.

"Maybe you want to untie your girlfriend," Provenzano suggested.

Odin didn't move. Mongoose and cobra stared at each other.

"So we just walk out of here?" Odin asked.

"That's it."

"Aren't you worried I'll call the authorities?" Odin asked.

"They want to lock you up more than they do me," Pro said with a grin. "By the time you straighten things out, I'll be sipping piña coladas in Mexico. I've got contingency plans, my friend."

Odin nodded.

"Please, let's get out of here," Golden said.

Odin half turned to her.

Pro made his move, diving forward for the gun. Odin let him bend before lashing out with a front kick. Due to the injury in his leg, the kick was weaker than it should have been. Pro's head snapped back but he continued his dive for the weapon.

Odin closed in but ignored the gun. He concentrated on getting into position, bending low, twisting so his back was to Pro.

His hands grabbed Pro's arm and shoulder at the same moment that Pro's hand closed on the gun.

Odin locked on Pro, and straightened up, twisting his arms in a perfect *ippon seonage*, a shoulder throw that sent Pro flying through the air.

The mobster landed on his desk. Papers flew.

For a long, silent second, it seemed as though he was feigning injury. Then the blood burbled out of his mouth.

Odin cut Golden's bonds. He was surprised at how quickly she hurried to Pro and checked for a pulse. "I don't understand," she said, finding none. "It was a hard fall, but it shouldn't have been fatal."

She turned Pro on his side. The base of the copy spike protruded from between his shoulder blades. The spike was the perfect length to have punctured his heart.

E P I L O G U E

The first sound he heard when he woke up in blackness was Dr. Keene.

"How are you feeling?"

"I've been better," Odin said. "But I've also been worse." His head was wedged between two special foam pillows, holding him immobile. "When can I move?"

"In about twenty-four hours. I've got good news and bad news."

"Don't hold back."

"The good news was the surgeon was quite pleased with the way the operation went."

"The bad news is my bill?"

"The bad news is you nearly waited too long. There was permanent cell damage."

Odin was silent.

"I'm blind?"

"You'll have vision in your good eye. It may just be motion and shapes, it may mean you have to wear glasses."

"I can live with that."

"Whatever it is, you'll have to learn to live with it," Keene said. "Are you ready for company?"

"Sure."

Keene exited. Odin heard a wheelchair squeaking on linoleum.

"Frank?"

"No. Actually Mr. Scalia asked me to look into your case. My name's Dennis Palumbo. I'm an attorney." Palumbo said. "You're in a heap of trouble."

"Uh-huh."

"I've spoken to the district attorney. Despite the public support for your actions, you're going to go to trial. Unless you want to plea bargain," Palumbo said. "Our discussions were strictly informal since I told him I did not yet represent you."

"What sort of deal?" Odin repeated.

"Consolidate the charges, get a concurrent sentence on most of them, probably no more than six months or maybe even community service."

"Six months!"

"For possession of a bomb, attempted murder, manslaughter, assault, breaking and entering, auto theft et cetera, et cetera. It's not a bad deal. The feds are being hard-nosed about the incendiary device charge and the interstate transport of an auto. It might actually work to our benefit. I can get you six months in minimum security at Lompoc. I'm sure you realize that time there passes a lot quicker than at a state facility."

"Peachy," Odin muttered.

"You're lucky Victor Polanski survived. He's going into the Witness Protection program. He's cleared you of suspicion in the death of your lieutenant. The feds hope to make big cases with him."

"He'll get off with nothing for murdering Huey?"

"He'll do time. He'll probably be in the hospital for another couple of months. Apparently you broke half the bones in his body."

"I should've killed him."

"I didn't hear that," Palumbo said. "As for community service, Frank has volunteered to take you in. If the court is amenable, and I see no reason why they shouldn't be, you can work it off teaching at his dojo. There's also someone named Ben Waters who has offered to take you in. He's assistant director at a drug rehab program and says you're the greatest thing since sliced bread."

Odin grunted. "Is this the best deal you can get?"

"Most likely. Of course, I'll work to get you off with no time."

"You're hired."

"Don't you want to know my fees?"

"I'm sure you're worth whatever you charge," Odin said.

A hand patted his chest. "We'll get along just fine," Palumbo said with a chuckle. He rolled from the room.

Odin heard a familiar tread on the floor.

"Jan, how are you?"

Golden's arm was in a sling. It had been dislocated during her struggle with Vic. The finger Pro had broken was in a small cast. Her minor cuts and bruises were already healing and she told Odin that.

"The nightmares are the worst part," she said. "My therapist says they're a good sign. That I'll work through it."

"When I realized I could've killed you with the bomb . . ."

"I'm glad it didn't work."

"Me too. Come here."

She came and held his hand. But her touch was reserved.

"What's the matter?"

"I don't know," she said. "I don't know about us."

"Why not?"

"What are you going to do when you get out of here?"

"Assuming the judge doesn't jack up the bail, I'll go to my apartment and vacuum. The dust balls are probably as big as tumble weeds."

She squeezed his hand.

"I'm serious. I think Provenzano was right. He said he knows your type."

"He was a lying slimeball." Bob began to sit up.

"Please. Don't move."

Bob slumped back. "Listen, I heard what you did when you were attacked. Biting, gouging, kicking. It sounds pretty violent to me."

"I've thought about that too. But even a deer will kick when it's trapped. You're different. If I'm a herbivore, you're a carnivore. I'm not saying what you do is bad, just that I don't know how I feel about it."

"I'm not going to be doing much of it anymore."

"It's a part of who you are," she said. "I need to think about things. I'm taking a few weeks off. Going away with a friend."

"Oh."

"A female friend. Mary. You'd like her."

"Where you going?"

"Maui. I'm not much good on the ward with a busted wing."

"I'm not going anywhere," Odin said bitterly.

She bent over and kissed his lips. "Maybe I need an animal in my life.

"I appreciate that you didn't shoot Provenzano. You tried to do it nonviolently. That shows he couldn't be completely right. It's just a pity your throw worked out the way it did and he landed on that spike."

Bob went to nod his head but the pillows kept him immobile.

She kissed him again and walked out. He released the muscles he had involuntarily tensed.

He could convince Jan he had changed. After all, she already believed he had tried to settle it without lethal force.

He would never tell her he knew Provenzano would make a dive for the weapon. And his judo throw had been perfect.

Pro had landed exactly where Odin wanted him to.